When I Come Home

Michael Grant

When I Come Home

DEDICATION

To my mother and father, Anne and James, on whose lives
this book is based. They left this world far too soon.

Other novels by Michael Grant

CHAPTER ONE

October 1940
New York City

I'll never smile again... until I smile at you...

Nancy Cavanaugh absentmindedly stirred the big iron pot as she sang along with Frank Sinatra on the radio. She had a clear, sweet voice with just a hint of an Irish brogue. Her voice was hardly professional quality, but it had been good enough to win an amateur contest in Coney Island the summer she'd turned eighteen, almost ten years earlier. For a long time after that heady experience, she would cuddle with the great stuffed teddy bear she'd won as a prize and fantasize about becoming a famous singer like Kate Smith or Doris Day. Then she'd be rich and be in the movies and live in a mansion in Hollywood where she would rub shoulders with the likes of Clark Gable and Tyrone Power.

It had been a wonderful dream, but, like all good dreams, it had to come to an end. It just couldn't compete with the reality of her life as a domestic servant for a wealthy family in Stamford, Connecticut, which meant, among other things, getting up at four every morning to start her chores. For a while, the dream had taken her mind off the grinding drudgery of her wretched life, but in the fullness of time Nancy came to realize that eighteen-year-old domestics from Ireland didn't become famous singers and live in Hollywood with the likes of Clark Gable and Tyrone Power.

A sharp pain brought her back to reality and she put the wooden spoon down. She patted her bulging stomach and automatically looked at the wall calendar, which had large Xs crossing out the spent days. "Just two more months, little baby," she whispered to her stomach. "Don't be so impatient."

She tasted the stew, decided it was done to her satisfaction, and called out, "Come and get it."

No sooner were the words out of her mouth when there was the sound of stampeding feet racing through the railroad apartment. Five-year-old Fiona and Patrick, a year younger, were at the stage where they took great delight in tormenting each other and being first at the table was an excellent opportunity to humiliate the loser.

Patrick slid into his seat a second before Fiona "I beat you," he said with a self-satisfied smile.

Fiona pushed a mass of baloney curls away from her face. "You cheated. Mommy, he tripped me."

Patrick stuck his tongue out in rebuttal.

"Put that tongue back in your face," Nancy said, ladling out the stew, "or it will freeze like that. Where's Maureen?"

"I'm coming."

Maureen came into the kitchen with a quiet dignity that Nancy always found astonishing. How, she wondered, could a six-year-old be that mature? In Ireland they called children like that "auld souls".

Patrick looked down at his plate. "Stew again. Yuk. I hate stew."

"You hate everything, Patrick," Fiona announced.

"I hate you."

"Stop." Nancy's tone froze both of them in mid-insult. "Patrick, say grace."

"I did it last. Make Maureen—" He saw the expression on his mother's face and bowed his head. "Blessed oh Lord for these thine gifts..." Fiona started to giggle. Patrick made a face at her and hurried through the prayer. "...which we are about to receive from thine bounty through Christ Our Lord, Amen. What's so funny, Fiona?"

"It's "thy" gifts."

"Is she right, Mommy?"

"Yes, but it's nothing that requires correction, Fiona."

"Where's Daddy?" Maureen asked.

"Working." Maureen didn't notice the flash of anger that crossed her mother's face.

"But it's Saturday."

"Don't I know that. He's off working his second job. Now eat your stew and stop asking so many questions."

After dinner, Fiona and Patrick rushed off to listen to that new Superman program on the radio. Maureen stayed behind and sat at the kitchen table watching her mother iron. "When is the baby coming?"

"He's due December twentieth."

"Why do you say he?"

"You were all he. You, Fiona, and Patrick. He's the only one I was right about."

"If the baby's born on Christmas day he'll get gypped out of birthday presents."

"Santa will make sure he gets all that's coming to him."

"I can't wait. I want to hold him and bathe him and take care of him."

Nancy stopped ironing and smiled at her daughter. "You will, Maureen. Mommy's going to need help with the new baby."

And she would, too. Of her two girls, Maureen looked the most like her. Fiona, with her mass of black curls, was her father's spittin' image and that was a fact. Nancy was eternally grateful that she had Maureen. The child was wise beyond her age and she would indeed need her help. The first three years of marriage had produced Maureen, Fiona, and Patrick in quick succession. They were active kids, all in diapers at the same time, and they had worn Nancy out. Shortly after Patrick was born, she'd announced to her husband that she would have no more kids and the Pope be damned. Connor had put his arms around her and whispered in her ear, "Sure I don't give a shite about the Pope, but what about me?"

"You'll manage."

And they did. With a combination of a great deal of luck, a little abstinence, and an indeterminate number of mortal sins, they managed to remain childless for the next three years. It was Nancy who changed her mind. To her surprise, God help her, she discovered she missed having a baby in the house. But now that the baby was almost here, she was having second thoughts. Maureen was no bother, but Fiona and Patrick were still a handful. Oh well, she thought, using her favorite phrase, we'll manage.

***

It was after eight by the time the children were in bed, the ironing finished, and the dishes done. She set the stew pot on a low flame and went into the living room to watch for Connor.

Their railroad apartment was on the third floor of a five-story walk-up. The view from the kitchen wasn't much to look at—just a weed-covered backyard obscured by a crisscrossing network of clotheslines. But the view from the living room overlooking busy Amsterdam Avenue was much better. There was always something happening on the busy street, especially at the firehouse directly across the street.

Nancy, always appreciative of a moment of blessed, peaceful respite from her hectic day, sat down by the window with a cup of tea to watch the world of the Upper West Side pass by.

Suddenly, there was the clang of bells and the firehouse came alive. Red lights flashed and fireman scurried about, tugging on their boots, slipping into their great coats. Then they were gone in a swirl of red lights and wailing sirens.

The firehouse was a great source of entertainment for Patrick who spent endless hours watching the firemen, especially on Saturday mornings when they pulled the trucks out of the bays and washed them and polished the bright brass and chrome fittings. One day, the firemen rolled the hook and ladder truck out onto Amsterdam Avenue and cranked up the ladder to the rooftop of the building across the street. Patrick watched open-mouthed as the fireman scurried up the ladder and onto the roof. Casting aside his dream of becoming a policeman, Patrick announced that night at dinner that when he grew up he was going to be a fireman.

Two young women passed under Nancy's window with their hair done up and wearing their best dresses, no doubt on their way to a Saturday night dance somewhere downtown. The sight of the laughing girls, electric with anticipation, gave her a momentary pang of regret for her lost youth. She was only twenty-seven, but with three children and one on the way, she was—if not exactly old—certainly no longer youthful. Not that she minded. Still, when she saw young girls out for a night, she did miss the fun of a Saturday night with highballs and dancing.

As she watched the girls skip across the street and yell something sassy to a passing cabbie, she recalled the first night she'd met Connor. She wasn't even going to go to the dance at St. Bridget's, but her friend Nora insisted. Nancy loved to dance, but the men seldom did and she was tired of dancing with other girls. Connor was standing in the corner with three friends and she thought he was the most beautiful thing she'd ever laid eyes on. He was tall with curly hair, pale blue eyes, and a smile that would melt ice itself. When he asked her to dance, she was lost all together. He danced like an angel and he told her she had a laugh like a silver bell. They were married three months later.

A taxi's insistent horn brought her out of her reverie and when she saw the reason for the horn blowing, her hand shot up to her mouth. "Jesus, Mary, and Joseph!" A taxi was bearing down on Connor, who was crossing Amsterdam Avenue like he was taking a bloody stroll in the park. The taxi screeched to a stop as Connor spun away with the grace of a Matador. Then he looked up at her and waved. She shook her head in exasperation and went into the kitchen to turn up the heat under the stew.

A minute later the door opened and he breezed in with the energy and compactness of a man who worked physically hard for a living. Connor, who'd just turned thirty-two, had an angular face that made him almost handsome. His best feature was his eyes, big and blue and reflecting sincerity and mischievousness all at the same time.

"Will you never learn to look where you're going?" Nancy asked.

He came up behind her and kissed the back of her neck. "Sure I'm used to cows in the road, not bloody automobiles. And how is my Irish colleen?"

"Your Irish colleen's back is killing her."

He held up the bag of ice cream he'd been hiding behind his back. "You're in luck. I have just the thing for backaches."

In spite of herself, Nancy had to smile. It was hard to stay mad at a man who brought home your favorite dessert.

"I'm not supposed to be eating that. I'm getting fat as a house. What kind is it?"

"Chocolate. What else? If you don't want it, I suppose I could wake the kids. They'd—"

"You wake those kids and I'll brain you."

She snatched the bag from him and gave him a kiss. "Sit down and have your dinner. Maybe I'll have just a mouthful of this."

While she spooned the ice cream right out of the container, she watched him eat. She knew what would be coming next, and it turned her stomach upside down, but she promised herself she wouldn't start up about the part-time job. Sure enough, like clockwork, as soon as he finished eating, he jumped up and hurried into the bedroom. A moment later he was back carrying a black and white writing tablet. The sight of the bloody thing set her teeth on edge. She pushed herself away from the table and busied herself clearing dishes. While she furiously scrubbed a pot, she watched his weekly ritual out of the corner of her eye with mounting anger.

He opened the writing tablet to a page with neat columns and rows of numbers and, with the exaggerated meticulousness of one who had had limited education and exposure to numbers, carefully entered the amount he'd earned this week from the part-time job. When he'd finished, he sat back and looked at the numbers proudly. To him, each entry meant he was getting closer to paying off the farm debt. But to Nancy, the page after page of entries represented the countless hours, days, months, years... Years? My God, she realized with a start, it had been almost two years since he'd started paying off the farm debts. She resented all that time away from her and the children. She was rubbing the pot so hard it slipped from her hand and crashed to the floor.

Connor was up like a cat. "Are you all right?"

She pulled away from him. "No, I'm not all right. Do you see the time? It's almost nine o'clock on a Saturday night and you're just coming home."

Conner fell into a chair. "I'm sorry, Nancy. I had to work overtime. They had cement that needed to be unloaded."

"An entire Saturday goes by and the kids don't so much as catch a glimpse of their father. It isn't right."

Connor ran his hands through his curly hair, something he did when he was frustrated. "I know you hate the part-time job, Nancy, but why can't you understand this is something I have to do. It's almost paid off."

"I've been hearing that for almost two years. That damn farm is three thousand miles away. You don't have to do this."

"But, Nancy, I do. It was I who worked those fields."

Nancy slammed her dishrag down on the table in frustration. "Of course you worked those fields, Connor. Didn't your drunk of a father run off leaving your mother, you and your sister to fend for yourselves?"

Connor turned away. "Aye, but he did come back," he said softly.

"Yes, he did. And promptly ran you off the farm and put it in debt before he drank himself to death. I just don't understand any of it. It's not your responsibility, Connor."

"Whose is it then? He's dead. My mother's dead."

"What about your sister, Eunice?"

"Ach, it's not her farm," he said with a sweep of an arm. "Nancy. It's mine. As the eldest son, it's me who inherited the farm and it's me who has the duty to pay off the bills."

"You inherited nothing but crushing debt." She turned her back on him and finished drying the dishes.

By the time she put them away, her anger had dissipated and she was feeling ashamed of herself. She wasn't being fair. It wasn't as though he spent his day sitting in a bar drinking or gambling.

He worked hard, even if it was for a damn fool reason. The truth was, she had much to be grateful for. In spite of the depression, he had steady work on the docks, the kids were healthy, and they had clothes on their backs – even if most of them were hand-me-downs. It was true they had never seen a Broadway play and seldom went to the movies. But they did have good friends they could invite over to share a pail of beer with and sing songs. In short, she had a reasonably good life and had nothing to complain about.

"Well, at least you'll be home tomorrow," she said, trying to make peace. "It's supposed to be a lovely fall day. We'll take the kids to the park."

He looked up from the Daily News sheepishly. "Ah, no. I'll be working tomorrow."

Nancy took her apron off, balled it up, and threw it on the stove. "It's Sunday, Connor. For God's sake, the kids never see you."

"It won't be for long." He closed the tablet and patted it with a callused hand. "I'm almost all paid up."

Without a word, she turned and stalked off into the bedroom.

Connor took a sip of his tea, but it was cold and he pushed it away. At times like this, even he wondered why he broke his back working two jobs—in times when most men could barely find one—to pay off debts on a farm he hadn't seen in fifteen years.

But he had his reasons. Pride being one of them. He was a Cavanaugh and as long as he had two hands to work, by God, no Cavanaugh farm would be sold off to pay debts. But there was another, even more important, reason. He knew he was a poor man and that he would always be nothing more than a common laborer. The farm, such as it was, was probably the only thing he would ever own in his life. And then, there was that dream that maybe, someday… He shook the dream away. There was no time to think about that now.

He patted the tablet again. "Sure it's almost paid up," he said to the empty kitchen.

.

CHAPTER TWO

Monday morning a steady rain fell, soaking a knot of longshoremen huddled around the pier gate. As they did every morning of every working day, these men assembled for the ritual "shapeup", a demeaning process by which the day's work crews were chosen. Even though these men belonged to the longshoreman's union and paid their dues religiously, few of them could be sure that they would work on any given day. In this time of high unemployment, there were always more men than there were jobs to fill and it fell to the hiring boss to pick who would work.

Inside a heated shack, Terry Boyle, the pot-bellied hiring boss, sat drinking coffee and peering out the window at the men shivering in the cold. He liked to think his job was one of great responsibility. After all, wasn't he the one to decide who would work and who would go home? But truth be told, there wasn't much to decide. The decision process entailed an entrenched and rigid set of time-tested protocols, which, if he valued his job, he would follow to the letter.

The first to get work would be "family" – deadbeat friends and relatives of the union bosses and others in high places. Next would come the "payers" – the men who had the good sense to seek him out on payday and slip him a few dollars to show their appreciation. Then he'd fill in the rest of the slots with the "workers" – the ones he could count on not to hide in a ship's hold and drink themselves into oblivion or take all day to unload a pallet of bananas. In short, the "workers" were the ones who would do most of the real work.

Standing in the rain-soaked crowd, Connor Cavanaugh was in the latter category. He had no friends in high places and he refused to pay for the privilege of breaking his back while the hiring boss sat on his fat ass in his heated shack drinking coffee laced with whisky. Connor relied on his reputation as a tireless man who did the work of two men.

As Boyle came out of his shack and began to call out names, a man with a cap pulled down over his eyes slipped up alongside of Connor. He was about Connor's height, but with a thicker neck and broader shoulders. He had a broken nose – the result of an errant kick from a horse back on the farm in Ireland – but it served to make him good looking in a Jimmy Braddock kind of way.

Neil Cullen was Connor's best friend. They'd met at the longshoremen's hiring hall on their first day and they'd been friends ever since. It has been said that opposites attract and that certainly seemed to be true for these two men. Connor favored a drink, Neil was an abstainer. Where Connor was exuberant, Neil was serious and quiet.

"Jasus," Neil said, glancing at his friend, "you look like death warmed over."

Connor grinned. "I worked twenty-six hours over the weekend. I'm on me arse."

"The farm debt is it? Are you trying to kill yourself all together?"

"It's got to be done." He pulled his collar up against a sudden gust of wet wind. "But God knows I'm not looking forward to working all day in this cold rain."

"You'd best get the sleep out of your eyes or old Boyle won't give you work."

Connor grunted. "He's no choice. Look at the first six men he picked. Sure the lot of them couldn't do an honest day's work between them. He needs me."

"He may need you, true enough, but he doesn't like you. Why are you always on him?"

"Because he's a pompous old arse who needs his balloon pricked once in a while."

"I'm telling you—"

"Cullen." Boyle pointed at Neil and jerked his thumb toward the gate. "Go in."

Like Connor, Neil refused to pay for work, but he was a skilled forklift driver and they were always in demand. Unlike so many other forklift drivers, he could be counted on not to drive his forklift off the pier, crush a union official's car with a stack of pallets, or pierce the hull of a ship with the forks.

A few more names were called and now the crowd was thinning out. All that was left were a handful of young men who were neither "family," "payers," nor "workers." Then there were the old drunks who prayed that there would be no work so they could withdraw to a warm, dry saloon and complain about the unfairness of the system.

And then there was Connor.

Boyle ambled over to Connor and gave him a humorless grin. Having no choice but to play the hiring boss's dim-witted game, Connor smiled back. He knew Boyle liked to call him last so he could watch him squirm and let him wonder if he was going to get picked at all. In spite of what he'd just said to Neil, Connor knew there was no guarantee that Boyle would pick him. Just a few months ago, during a heated argument, Connor had called Boyle a drunken old blatherskite in front of everyone. At the next morning's shapeup, the furious hiring boss, just to spite Connor, picked a notorious drunk and sent Connor home. But Boyle's nastiness backfired. In his blind desire for revenge, he'd forgotten that the docks were a dangerous place and certainly no place for a witless drunk. Just before the lunch whistle sounded, the drunk managed to stumble in front of a forklift and was seriously injured. Worse, production had to be halted until the ambulance could get the old man off the pier. There was a great deal of time and money lost. If Boyle hadn't been the brother-in-law of a top union official, he'd have lost his job that day.

Still, Boyle was a malevolent grudge-holder and Connor could never be sure if the ignorant man might once again cut off his nose to spite his face. To Connor, there was nothing worse than the prospect of no work. It meant having to go home and face Nancy and tell her that there would be no money that day. The thought of not working twisted his stomach, but he refused to give Boyle the satisfaction of seeing his distress.

"You're looking a bit sleepy," Boyle said. "Maybe you shouldn't work today."

"Ach, I'm okay, Terry."

"I don't know about that. I've been watching you. Your eyes are all droopy. A weary man doesn't do a good job."

Connor tried a smile. "Boyle, don't do this. You know I'll do the job."

Boyle looked around to see who was left in the crowd. Connor had been counting and knew there couldn't be many jobs left. Would Boyle pick someone else? He felt his stomach tighten. He whispered, "Terry... I want to work... I need the work."

Boyle's smile revealed a mouthful of uneven yellowed teeth. "Speak up, bucko. I didn't hear you."

Connor knew how to stop the cat and mouse game, and at times like this he wondered why he didn't. All he had to do was catch up to Boyle in Darcy's next Friday. Buy him a drink, slip a few dollars into his hand, and all this would stop. But Connor couldn't do it. He'd die before he'd take the money away from his family to pay off the likes of Terry Boyle.

Boyle stepped back so Connor would have to raise his voice. "Did you say something, me bucko?" he asked, cupping his hand to his ear.

Connor clenched his fists. He wanted to smash those yellow teeth down the man's throat, but if he did, he knew he'd never work another day on the docks in New York City again. His heart pounded with fury and frustration. It wasn't right. A man shouldn't be treated this way.

He swallowed hard. "I need the work, Terry," he said in a louder voice. "I want to work."

Most of the men standing nearby had the decency to turn away from Connor's humiliation.

Boyle smiled, savoring his victory over the proud, stubborn Irishman. "Did you hear him?" he asked the men standing behind Connor. "He needs the work," he said in a bad impression of Connor. "He wants to work." He jerked his thumb over his shoulder with utter disgust. "Go in."

As Connor walked past, Boyle grabbed his arm. "I'll be watching you, Cavanaugh. See that you do a good day's work."

Connor pulled away. As he walked through the gate, he heard Boyle tell the rest of the men that there was no more work today. Stepping into the cavernous pier, Connor felt an uneasy mixture of shame and elation.

***

Connor stretched his back to relieve the dull ache from stacking crate after crate of heavy engine parts. He was so tired he'd slipped into that automatic mode where the body continues to perform long after the mind stops paying attention. Lift a crate from the forklift, carry it to the cargo net, stack the crate, go back for another one...and on it went.

Boyle had made sure that he was assigned to this back-breaking job, but Connor didn't care. It was almost quitting time and he was looking forward to going home and having dinner with Nancy and the kids. He'd been thinking about what she'd said and she was right. He should spend more time with them and he would do just that as soon as the farm was paid off. It occurred to him that, in the meantime, he should do something nice for them to make up for his absence. And then and there he made up his mind. If he could come up with the money, he'd take the family to the Christmas show at Radio City.

He was so engrossed in his own thoughts that he didn't notice the cargo net above. As the crane driver raised the net out of the ship's hold, one of the guy wires snagged on the ship's super structure. The net tilted precariously. The crane operator yanked the controls to the left to compensate for the load shift, but the strain snapped the other guy wire and the net swung in a wide arc, out of control.

Neil Cullen saw the net swinging toward Connor, who at the moment was carrying a crate over to a pallet, unaware of the danger. Neil yelled a warning, but Connor didn't hear him over the whine of trucks and cranes. Like a giant, lethal pendulum, the cargo net was swinging directly at Connor.

Neil jumped off the forklift, raced toward Connor and tackled him just as the cargo net smashed into the pile of crates just above their heads. The crates came crashing down around them.

There was a stunned silence. Then, Connor pushed a crate off his chest, looked around and muttered, "Jasus, Mary, and Joseph…!"

Neil sat up wide-eyed, shaking with fright. "You…eejit!" he sputtered. "Are you walking in your sleep, man?"

***

Darcy's Bar & Grill on Eleventh Avenue was a longshoremen's house of refuge. The paint was peeling off the walls, the windows were opaque from years of accumulated dirt and smoke, and the food was mostly inedible. But the dock workers who came here weren't looking for ambiance or sustenance. They were looking for a welcoming haven where they could knock down a few beers and shots and unwind from another grinding, grueling day on the docks.

Connor pulled Neil by the sleeve through the crowd and made a place for them at the smoke-filled bar. The bartender wiped up a spill in front of them with a filthy rag. "What'll it be, gents?"

"A beer for me," Connor said. "No. On second thought, make that a whisky."

"Are you celebrating then?"

"I am. What'll you have, Neil?"

Neil, still shaken by the accident, sat down unsteadily. "Ginger ale."

Connor made a face. "Ginger ale? For the love of God, what kind of Irishman are you?"

"One that doesn't drink."

"We're celebrating my life, man. You can't do that with ginger ale."

"All right, then. I'll have a beer. But just one."

As the bartender left to get the drinks, Neil continued the nagging that had started before the last crate had stopped rolling.

"You have to keep your wits about you on the pier. You know that. What were you thinking?"

"Ach, let it go. Sure I never look where I'm going. Doesn't Nancy say that all the time?"

"You're wearing yourself out with that other job. That's what you're doing. Why don't you just give it up?"

Connor ran his hands through his hair. "I can't," he said automatically. "The debt isn't paid yet."

Neil shook his head. "I don't understand this madness over a patch of dirt."

Connor looked down and saw that his hands were shaking and jammed them into his pockets. "Sometimes I don't understand it myself," he muttered.

The bartender brought the drinks and Connor raised his glass. "To my best friend, Neil, who this very day has saved my miserable life."

Neil, embarrassed and unaccustomed to praise, brushed the accolade aside with the wave of his hand. "You'd have done the same for me."

Connor certainly hoped he would do the same thing, but the truth was you never knew what you'd do under those circumstances until you did it. Neil had been tested and he'd met the challenge. And his act of courage had won the admiration and respect of Connor and every man who was working on the pier that day.

After they'd had their "one" drink, it took them nearly an hour to get out the door because every one of those men who had seen the near fatal accident insisted on buying them a drink.

***

Outside, Connor and Neil started up Eleventh Avenue toward the subway, hunched against the bone-chilling wind coming off the Hudson River. The rain had finally stopped, but the streets were still glistening from the all-day downpour. On the West Side of 11th Avenue, the hulking shapes of old wooden piers, standing cheek by jowl and stretching uptown all the way to 57th Street, were closed down for the night. Without the din of trucks, forklifts, cranes, and shouting men, the piers were strangely silent, almost ghostlike. Only solitary night watchmen in their dimly lit wooden shacks stood sentinel in front of their respective piers.

The clicking heels of the two men's boots reverberated off the pier's massive metal shed doors as they walked. Neither man spoke, for men like Connor and Neil were not men of words. Neither was capable of expressing the overwhelming emotions that came from a near death experience, but they were thinking the same thing: One of them had almost died today. When they reached the entrance to the Independent subway line, Connor blurted out, "Neil, if something should happen to me, promise me you'll take care of Nancy and the kids."

Connor's odd and completely unexpected request caught Neil off guard. He'd never considered the possibility that he might be called upon to take care of Connor's family. Of course he was godfather to Maureen and technically, according to the church, he would be responsible for her in the event that Nancy and Connor died. But that was a remote possibility which he'd never seriously considered. Now Connor was asking if he would take care of Nancy and the kids if something happened to him. There was no question that he would. He was thirty-two, single, with no family of his own. Connor, Nancy, and the kids were his family. Sure hadn't he been with Connor that very first night when he'd met Nancy at the dance? Still, his friend's request had made him feel uneasy.

"Don't be daft," he said, trying to shake the feeling. "Sure you'll live to be a hundred."

Connor squeezed his arm. "Promise me. If anything happens to me, you'll look after them."

Neil was baffled by Connor's demeanor. He'd never seen his friend so serious. Earlier, in the bar, he'd made light of the accident, but it was clear that it had shaken him all the same.

"Of course I will. But just watch where you're walking you damn fool."

As Connor skipped down the subway stairs, he turned back to look at Neil. "Oh, I almost forgot. Nancy wants you to come to dinner Sunday. Are you free?"

"I am."

"Good. Oh, and don't tell her about the accident today. Promise?"

Neil shook his head in exasperation. "All right. For the love of God, I promise."

***

Every Sunday, Nancy dressed the children in their finest clothing and she, Connor – when he wasn't working the second job – and the children went to ten o'clock Mass at St. Stephen's. Then it was home to the traditional breakfast of eggs, bacon, pan bread, and tea.

Sunday was an especially pleasant interlude for Connor and Nancy and others of their class. It was truly a day of rest. There would be no ironing, no cleaning, no shopping – all the stores were closed on Sunday – no work of any kind was permitted on the Lord's day. Sunday gave them an excuse to stay dressed up all day and forget for just a little while that they were simple working-class people. For one day in the week they could pretend they were genteel folk who could afford to spend the day in such unprofitable and idle pursuits as reading the newspaper and listening to the radio without feeling guilty.

The children, on the other hand hated Sunday, especially Patrick. Before the breakfast dishes were done, he was begging his mother to let him get out of his suit. But Nancy held her ground.

"Your Uncle Neil is coming to dinner and you don't want to be looking like a ragamuffin."

"What's that?"

Connor scooped Patrick up in his arms and held him over his head. "A dirty, filthy, little street urchin. Is that what you want to be?"

"Yes," Patrick cried out in delight. "I want to be a dirty urch."

Connor dropped him into a chair. "You can change after dinner."

Nancy shot a reproving look at her husband. "You're spoiling that child."

"Ach, it's pure torture for a boy to stay dressed up like little Lord Fauntleroy all day."

"And I suppose that goes for you, too?"

"I wouldn't mind taking off my tie."

"You'll do no such thing."

Connor put his arms around Nancy. "You're a hard woman, Mrs. Cavanaugh."

Nancy kissed him. "And you've a hard life, Mr. Cavanaugh."

***

Neil arrived at two in the afternoon with his usual offering— packs of Chiclets for the kids and a quart of Breyer's chocolate ice cream for dessert.

Nancy made Neil's favorite dinner of leg of lamb, mashed potatoes, and her special gravy because she was worried about him. He was too thin, no doubt the result of living in that slapdash rooming house off Third Avenue and eating the dreadful food of old Mrs. Sealy. Over the years, she'd tried to find a nice girl for him but, as a matchmaker, she'd been an abysmal failure. According to Neil they were either too young or too old, too tall or too short, or "just not my type" whatever that meant. Connor had told her to let it go, insisting that Neil was a confirmed bachelor, but Nancy didn't believe that. She knew that somewhere out there was the right woman for Neil, and by God, she would find that woman.

After he'd cleared his plate, she passed him the platter. "Have more lamb, Neil."

Neil patted his trim stomach. "I can't. Sure I'm as full as a horse."

That was Patrick's cue. The grownups were done eating. Dinner was now officially over. "Can I go now?" he asked.

"You may go," Nancy corrected. "Off with you all."

"And can I change? Daddy said so."

"Oh, all right. You may change."

Patrick and Fiona, glad to be free of the scrutiny of their parents and the confinement of the table, darted into the living room to listen to The Shadow on the radio. Maureen remained seated.

"You may go," Nancy said."

"I want to stay here and talk with you and Uncle Neil."

"We're going to talk adult stuff. You'd be bored."

"No, I won't—"

Connor pulled her chair out. "You heard your mother. Off with you."

Maureen left the table reluctantly.

"I'll come in to see you before I go," Neil called after her.

After she left, Connor said, "My little old lady. She loves to be with the grownups."

Nancy winked. "She loves to be around Neil."

Connor, smiling at Neil's obvious discomfort, said, "Does she have a crush on him then?"

"I believe she does."

Neil squirmed in his chair. "Don't be daft."

"It's true," Nancy said. "She gets so excited when she hears her Uncle Neil is coming over."

Desperate to change the subject, Neil said, "Do you think the war in Europe is going to affect us?"

Connor's upbeat mood suddenly evaporated. "I hope not," he scowled. "What's going on over there in Europe is not our fight. As far as I'm concerned, the bloody British can go to hell."

"Connor, what are you saying?" Nancy asked, shocked by the vehemence in his tone. "The Germans are bombing London."

"I know you left school early, Nancy, but surely you must know about the Irish Famine of eighteen forty-five. The bloody Brits tried to kill us all off. Over a million died of starvation and disease and more than two million were forced to leave Ireland for America and Canada. Am I supposed to feel sorry for those bastards?"

"Ah, that was a long time ago," Neil said, sorry he'd raised the subject.

"Oh, really? Then what about the Titanic?"

"What about it?"

"Did you know the White Star Line never christens their ships?"

"No, I didn't. So what?"

"So, when they were building that ship in the Belfast yards it was given a number that when read backwards spelled 'no Pope'. Those Protestant bastards who built that ship were anti-Pope and anti-Catholic, and that's why the ship went down."

Neil knew that Connor had dropped out of school in the sixth grade, as had Nancy, but Neil had completed high school and if he'd learned nothing else it was that nothing was that simple. It was true that the Irish Famine was a disgraceful, indelible blot on the conscience of England and it would remain there forever. No true Irishman would ever forgive them for that, but the Titanic story was nothing more than an old wives' tale.

Once again Neil tried to steer the conversation in another direction. "Speaking of ships, Connor, do you remember back in March when the Queen Mary docked at pier ninety?"

"Aye. I do."

"I heard she came to New York to avoid being bombed by the Germans. But just a couple of weeks later, painted a darkened coat of gray, she slipped out of the harbor and went back to England as a troop ship. Things must be getting desperate over there."

"And good riddance, I say. Let them keep their war in Europe."

"All the same, our government seems to take the European war seriously. Do you remember that business with the dummy mines in the harbor?"

Connor grinned. "Aye, I do. It was great fun watching all those Navy ships racing up and down the harbor looking for those mines."

"I don't understand. What are mines exactly?" Nancy asked.

"They're floating explosive devices planted by the enemy, hoping that an unsuspecting ship will run into it," Neil explained. "I saw one of those dummy mines up close. There're about three feet in diameter with ugly protuberances sticking out of the top of the mine. I believe that's part of the detonation mechanism."

"I hear Customs is giving the Italians on the Brooklyn docks a hard time." Connor said. "Since Italy jumped into the war, Italian ships at the piers are being searched and Italian longshoremen carefully screened."

This was all too much for Nancy. She stood up and started to clear the dishes. "I don't like all this talk of war."

Neil jumped up. "Here, let me help you."

"I can manage. You and Connor go into the living room. I'll have the tea ready in a minute."

"You shouldn't be working so hard in your condition."

Connor took Neil's arm. "She's had three children, man. I think she can handle a few dishes."

For a moment, Neil stood there, undecided. Then he followed Connor into the living room, leaving Nancy to wonder how two friends could be so different. Connor was a good husband, but it would never have occurred to him to help her with the dishes. As far as he was concerned, that was woman's work.

It was almost nine o'clock by the time Neil got up to leave. Connor and Nancy walked him to the door.

"Thanks for having me over for dinner," Neil said.

Nancy waved her hand in dismissal. "Not at all. I hate to think of you eating your Sunday dinner at that Automat all alone."

Connor thumped Neil on the shoulder. "Maybe you're right, Nancy. Maybe he should get married so he can get some good home cooking."

Nancy swatted him with a dish cloth. "Is that all marriage means to you?"

Connor wrapped his arms around her and nibbled her neck. "No, that's not all."

Nancy pulled away laughing. "You're disgusting."

A flustered Neil pulled on his cap. "I'll be going."

"See you in the morning," Connor said, closing the door.

As Neil hurried down the stairs, the germ of a thought began to form in his head. It was a forbidden thought, a dangerous thought, and he refused to give it voice. But, like a virus, it grew exponentially until it completely filled his being. He pushed it back in panic, but it refused to die. Even his pragmatic nature was no match and the thought won the struggle. He stopped on the stairs, his chest heaving with exertion and panic as the thought crashed into his consciousness and screamed at him: You damn fool, you're in love with Nancy.

CHAPTER THREE

Every year around Christmas, Nancy hosted an informal gathering of a few friends. These were simple affairs with everyone chipping in with platters of cold cuts, potato salad, and pails of beer from the bar down at the corner. This year, because she was expecting the baby in late December, she decided to hold the party the Friday after Thanksgiving.

The entertainment at these get-togethers was as uncomplicated as it was fun. Rugs were rolled back, the radio was tuned to a station playing Tommy Dorsey or Glen Miller and everyone danced. Later, if someone played an instrument, it was hauled out and Irish tunes were played to enthusiastic hand clapping and foot stomping.

Erin and Tom Cassidy, who lived on the second floor, were the first to arrive. Erin, an exuberant redhead who was the same age as Nancy, came in carrying a platter of cold cuts. "What a treat to get away from the kids for a night out. Oh," she cackled, "I shouldn't say that, it makes me sound like a terrible mother."

"I understand perfectly," Nancy said, taking the platter from her. "A two-year-old and a three-year-old are a handful. Who's minding them?"

"My mother. She came in from Brooklyn for the weekend."

Her husband, a big, beefy man, rolled his eyes. "The whole weekend."

She poked him playfully. "Don't you be making fun of my mother, Tom. If she weren't here, you'd be babysitting."

"Me? What about you?"

"I need a night out more than you."

"Oh, and you think driving a great big double-decker bus on Fifth Avenue is a stroll in the park?"

"It's a lot easier than chasing after two little ones in diapers all day."

"You have a point there." He held up a pail of beer. "Connor, I need a drink. Have you a glass for me?"

As the men went off to the living room, there was another knock and Nora Rice, Nancy's best friend, burst in carrying a bowl of potato salad. She was a naturally pretty girl, but she had an unfortunate tendency to overdo it on the makeup and clothes. "Somebody take this potato salad away from me before I eat the entire bowl."

"Is your potato salad that good?" Erin said, taking the bowl.

"It's my best dish," she said, then added, "Though, truth be told, it's the only dish I make." She jerked her thumb over her shoulder. "Look what I met on the stairs."

Neil came in carrying a pail of beer. "You make it sound like you found a stray cat."

She squeezed his cheek. "Now don't be so touchy, Neil."

"Where are the men?"

"In the living room. We'll be there shortly," Nancy said.

***

Tonight there were no instrumentalists, but, fortunately, Tom Cassidy, who had a fine tenor voice, was on hand. A quiet fell over the small group of friends huddled in the tiny living room as Tom began to sing:

"Oh, Danny Boy, the pipes the pipes are calling..."

Except for Nora, everyone in the room was from Ireland and the beautiful words and melodious voice reminded them of home. Nancy sat contentedly on Connor's lap as Tom finished.

"...And all the valley's hushed and white with snow. For I'll be here in sunshine or in shadow, oh, Danny boy, oh, Danny boy I love you so."

There was a moment of silence, then everyone burst into enthusiastic applause.

Nancy was up next and, choosing a popular American song, sang *All The Things You Are*, all the while staring at Connor.

When she'd finished, she turned to Neil. "Your turn."

"Oh, no, I couldn't carry a tune in a bucket. But let's hear a tune from the kids."

"Good idea," Connor said clapping his hands. "Maureen... Fiona...Patrick... come in here and sing for your supper."

Shyly, the three children, who'd been playing in their parents' bedroom, came into the living room. Connor gently pushed Nancy off his lap and lined the children up. "All right, then," he said, rubbing his hands together. "How about that song I taught you? Let's hear it."

And on those words, the children began to sing Galway Bay.

"If you ever go across the sea to Ireland.

It may be at the closing of your day. You will sit and watch the moon rise over Claddagh, and watch the sun go down on Galway Bay..."

From across the room, Nancy's mellow mood gave way to mounting irritation as she watched her husband's face. Clearly, he was moved by the words and for some reason that bothered her. The children finished the song to loud applause. Nancy and Connor's eyes met, and his broad smile gave way to a look of guilt and he turned away.

When they'd run out of songs to sing, the women went into the kitchen to make coffee and put out the dessert. For the men left in the living room, the talk turned – as it inevitably did these days – to the war in Europe.

Tom poured himself another beer from the pail. "With the Germans in Paris, I guess it won't be long before Hitler invades Britain."

"That's fine with me," Connor said. "Let the Brits feel the yoke of oppression for a change."

"Connor, are you still on that kick?" a grinning Tom asked.

"I am. It's not just Ireland they've enslaved. What about India and all those colonies in South America, Africa, and the Caribbean? Do you think those people are happy being under the boot of the English?"

"What is it they say?" Neil mused. "The sun never sets on the British Empire."

"Well, it's high time it did."

"Personally, I'm more concerned with what's going on right here in the city," Tom said. "Last month I was driving the bus through Union Square and there was a hell of a commotion with cops and firemen everywhere. Later, I found out it was some sort of drill. Mayor LaGuardia had ordered simulated bombs to go off in all five boroughs."

"Didn't I tell you, Connor," Neil said. "First it was the fake mines in the harbor, now this. I think the government expects this country to be attacked."

"Don't be daft."

"I'm not. Just last week, didn't the Fire Commissioner order five hundred of us longshoremen to show up at the Grace Line on 15th Street?"

"What for?" Tom asked.

"To remind us to be vigilant. They said we should watch for anything that might ignite buildings. The piers do have lots of combustible stuff about, especially now that we're sending supplies to the war effort in Europe."

Tom nodded his head. "I think you're right, Neil. The idea that we might be attacked is not daft at all. The Germans already occupy France and most of Europe. If they invade England, what's next? Us."

"All I'm saying," Connor said emphatically, "is, it's not our war and we should stay out of it."

"Are you an isolationist then?" Neil asked.

"Call it what you will, but haven't the Europeans have been fighting among themselves for centuries? It's not our fight."

"What if Germany declared war on us," Tom asked, "would you two sign up to fight?"

Connor shook his head vehemently. "No."

"Well, I would," Tom said.

"Are you mad?" Connor asked, stunned by his answer. "You have a wife and two little ones."

"I know. But I would consider it my duty to defend my country."

"Your country is Ireland," Connor pointed out.

"Ireland is the country of my birth. America is my country."

"What about you, Neil?" Connor asked, still shaken by Tom's assertion that he would sign up to fight in the war. "Would you join up as well?"

Before Neil could answer that question, the women came back into the living room with the coffee and dessert.

Nora, sensing an air of tension in the room, decided the men were probably talking about the war. To lighten the mood, she said, "Did anyone see that new Abbott and Costello movie, 'Keep 'Em Flying'? It's hilarious."

That broke the mood and the party finally broke up around midnight, which was just about the time the beer gave out.

***

Connor came into the bedroom as Nancy was getting ready for bed. "Well, they're finally asleep."

Nancy didn't say anything, but by the way she furiously yanked down the bedspread, he knew that she was angry. "What's wrong, Nancy? Is it about letting the kids stay up late? Sure it's only once in awhile and they love it."

"It's not that," she said, slipping under the covers. "I heard you telling the kids about the farm again."

"Ach, what's the harm there?" he said, sliding into bed next to her. "They love hearing about it." He tried to put his arm around her, but she pulled away.

"Because you make it sound like a fairy tale, some magical place with little fairies and leprechauns prancing about."

"Nancy, they're just children—"

"They're old enough to know what Ireland is really like." She rolled over to face him. "Why don't you tell them about your drunken father, the back-breaking work, not enough rain, too much rain, dying and sick animals."

Connor stared up at a paint-peeling ceiling, stunned by the vehemence in her tone. "I don't understand you. Why do you hate it so much?"

"Because it's caused you nothing but grief. You're killing yourself to pay off the debt. In the name of God, why?"

He ran his fingers through his hair. "To save the family's reputation…" his voice trailed off.

"Reputation is it? A fine reputation Denny Cavanaugh had."

"It's not just for him," he said quietly. "I'm a Cavanaugh as well."

Nancy saw the hurt in his eyes and immediately regretted her outburst. She snuggled close to him and pulled his head close to her breast. "You're an honorable man," she said, stroking his hair. "It's one of the reasons I fell in love with you. I know you mean well, but the farm just isn't worth the trouble."

"I know it's just a miserable patch of land, but it's the only thing I'll ever own in my whole life."

"And in the name of God, Connor, what will you do with it?" she asked, knowing and dreading the answer.

"Maybe some day… we could go back there… you and me and the kids… and…."

She pushed him away and turned her back to him. "No. Never," she said, her tone surprisingly bitter. "I left Ireland when I was seventeen to find a better life for myself and I've found it here in America. I'll never go back to Ireland again. Never."

***

Just before seven the next morning, Connor slipped out of bed, grabbed his clothes and boots and quietly started to tiptoe out of the bedroom.

"Off to the other job are you?"

He turned and shrugged. "I'm sorry, Nancy. I didn't mean to wake you."

"What time will you be home?"

"I don't know. We knock off at four, but, you know, sometimes—"

"There's overtime. I know. And God forbid you should turn down the overtime."

When she took that tone, he knew it was best to say nothing. He shrugged again, and, as he turned to go, she said, "Well, aren't you going to give your wife a goodbye kiss?"

Connor crawled across the bed and kissed his wife. As their lips touched, she pulled him on top of her. The warmth and the smell of her body was almost overpowering. It had been months since they'd made love and though he tried not to think about it, it was all he thought about. For just a second, he thought of slipping back under the covers and the part-time job be damned. He knew they couldn't make love, but he'd be content to just lie in that warm bed with his body pressed against hers. But it was a daft idea. In a few minutes, the kids would be awake and they'd have no peace at all. Reluctantly, he got out of bed and dressed.

***

Outside, it was a bitterly cold Saturday morning, even for late November, but the sun was shining and there wasn't a cloud in the sky. Connor took the IRT subway downtown to 42nd Street. From there it was just a few blocks to his construction job. He enjoyed walking and avoided subways and buses whenever he could. He especially liked walking in midtown Manhattan on a Saturday morning because the streets and sidewalks were almost deserted. He'd been in New York almost twelve years now, but in that time he still hadn't gotten used to the terrible confusion of people, the horn-honking traffic, and the general bedlam that was the lifeblood of New York City.

And after all this time, he still missed Ireland. Not the loud, bloody, ceaseless rows with his father. Now that he could do without. What he missed was the quiet, peaceful countryside where he grew up, the distant Carragh Mountains, the rolling green fields, the lowing cows, the snorting pigs, the frantic chickens, and the smell of the earth freshly plowed. He even missed the rain, which for some reason always seemed to fall more gently than the rain here.

When he got to the construction site, he nodded to the gate watchman, an old Italian man from the Bronx. Every time he stepped onto the site he was reminded of what a truly terrible place the docks were. Here there was no shapeup, no Terry Boyle, and no fear that there would be no work today because of the whim of a hiring boss. To be sure it was hard, physical work here. In some ways, harder than the docks, but he didn't mind. They left him alone to do his job and that was the way he liked it.

Falcone, the grizzled old worksite foreman, called out, "Hey, Irish. Come with me."

Gripped with apprehension, Connor followed Falcone to the supervisor's shack. No one was called to the shack unless they were being fired. He knew he was a good worker, so he doubted he was about to be let go. But, still, times were hard, and he'd seen more than one good worker get laid off. The depression wasn't over yet. Jobs were hard to come by and he was lucky to have gotten this one. Where in the world would he find another? For more than two years, he'd been whittling away at the mountain of debt, but there was still more to be paid. He could feel the panic rising in him, making him almost physically ill. In the name of God, where would he get the money?

There was a man inside the supervisor's shack whom Connor recognized by sight. He was the only man on the site to wear a shirt and tie. Connor had often seen him dashing about the site with a bundle of building plans, which he poured over with groups of other men. Connor didn't know who he was or what his job entailed, but he seemed to be the top man in charge.

In an unaccustomed sign of deference, Falcone slipped off his cap and stuck it in his back pocket. "This is Irish, the guy I was telling you about, Mr. Henderson."

Up close, Connor could see that the man had the kind of leathery skin that comes from being outdoors all year around. He squinted at Connor through watery gray eyes. "What's your name, Irish?"

"Connor Cavanaugh, sir."

"Well, Connor Cavanaugh, Falcone tells me you're a good worker."

Connor's heart skipped a beat. My God, were they about to offer him a full time job? It was what he'd been hoping and praying for since he'd started here. It would be a dream come true. He'd earn more money, it'd be steady work, and best of all, he wouldn't have to put up with the likes of Terry Boyle anymore.

Henderson sat down at the desk and lit a cigarette. "You afraid of heights?"

"No, sir," Connor answered quickly, not knowing where this conversation was going.

Henderson squinted at him through a cloud of blue smoke. "I'm offering you a new job. Cavanaugh. It'd be temporary and you'll still be part-time. But it pays more."

Connor hid his disappointment. Then he remembered Nancy's constant admonishment to him to think positively. All right, so it was only a part-time job, but couldn't a part-time lead to a full-time one? "I'll take it, sir."

Henderson grinned, revealing a mouthful of uneven teeth. "You don't know what the job is."

"True, sir. But there's no job I can't do if I set my mind to it."

"Fair enough. This morning you start working with the sky walkers."

Connor thought he'd heard wrong. The "sky walkers" were Mohawk Indian iron workers, who had a reputation for utter fearlessness while walking on iron beams hundreds of feet above the ground. Often, as he carried bags of cement to the mixer, he'd pause and look up in wonder at those tiny figures hopping from beam to beam, seeming to defy gravity. Then it hit him: Henderson wanted him to work with that lot? Jasus! What have I agreed to? Then he remembered something that brought a queasy feeling to his stomach. Just last week, a young sky walker had plunged to his death. Connor hadn't been working that day, but he'd heard about it. There was talk that the man was drunk, but still… Jasus! Was he the replacement for the dead Mohawk?

He was about to tell Henderson that he'd changed his mind, but then he remembered something that Henderson had said. "I believe you said it pays more. Might I ask how much more?"

"Twenty cents an hour."

Connor was stunned. He was making twenty-eight cents an hour off the books now. That meant... he tried to do the math in his head, but he didn't have the mental tools. Well, anyway, that was a fearful amount of money. It would certainly shorten the time he'd need to pay off the farm debts. Nancy was growing more and more impatient with him and the part-time job, so the quicker he finished with the business of the farm, the better it would be for family peace.

"That seems fair," he heard himself say in an oddly calm voice.

Henderson nodded to Falcone. "OK. Take him to the chief."

***

Four grinning sky walkers stood in a claustrophobically small construction elevator that was more like a cage and stared at Connor. One of them, a dark complexioned man built like a cement mixer, beckoned, "Come on, Irish, it's fifty stories up and you don't want to walk it, do you?"

Connor squeezed into the elevator as the others nudged and winked at each other, thoroughly enjoying his discomfort. The big man, whom the others called "Chief", was the foreman of the gang. He unscrewed a flask, took a swig, and offered it to Connor. "What does your tribe call it, a wee bit of the courage?"

Connor forced a grin. "Aye, we do. But at eight in the morning, it's a wee bit too early for a wee bit of the courage."

Chief slammed the gate shut, yanked a control handle, and the wire mesh elevator shuttered and wheezed into motion as it started its rickety ascent to the roof fifty floors above the streets of midtown Manhattan. By the time they'd reached the tenth floor, Connor was almost paralyzed with fear and he could hardly swallow. When he could force himself to look, he marveled at how the pedestrians down below looked like scurrying insects and the cars and buses looked like so many children's toys.

He'd never been higher than the roof of his barn back home and that couldn't have been more than thirty feet high. Still, in spite of his terror, he was awestruck by the sweeping panorama all around him as the elevator continued to rise. He'd never in his wildest dreams imagined the city looked like this. He could see clear over to New Jersey on the west and behind him to the east, Queens and Brooklyn. To the south, the Empire State and Chrysler buildings soared above the landscape.

***

Connor stepped off the elevator onto a floor of wood planks. Now that he'd gotten over the fright of being so high up, he realized two things. One, it had been cold on the ground, but it was positively freezing up here. And two, the wind was blowing so hard, he had to hold on to a beam to keep from being swept off the roof. How in the name of God did he expect to walk on those skinny beams without falling to his death?

The Chief pointed to a bucket of rivets. "It's time to earn your extra twenty cents, Irish. Take that bucket out to Beaver."

A moment earlier, Connor had watched stunned as the man they called Beaver had strolled cool as you please across a six-inch beam, while looking over his shoulder and having a conversation with another man.

Connor picked up the heavy bucket and was consoled with the thought that at least the extra weight would keep him from flying off the beam. But that consolation was soon dashed when he realized that at some point the bucket would be empty and he would have to come back across the beam with it.

Beaver was sitting on the end of a thirty-foot beam five hundred feet above the street swinging his legs with no more concern than if he was sitting on a fence. "Come on, Irish, we haven't got all day."

Connor took a deep breath and took a step forward. The Chief yanked him back by the collar. "No, that's not the way to do it. There's only one rule up here. Don't look down. Heed that rule and it's a walk in the park."

Connor took another deep breath and stepped onto the beam. It was freezing cold, but beads of sweat trickled down his forehead.

Don't look down, he repeated over and over again. He concentrated on looking at Beaver, who was grinning at him. After what seemed like an eternity, he made it across and placed the bucket down.

Beaver picked up a rivet and inspected it. "Hey, Chief, they're the wrong size."

The Chief scratched his head and tried to hide a grin. "I'll be damned. All right, Irish, bring the bucket back."

Connor looked around and realized that they were all laughing at him. Forcing down his rage, he made his way back across the beam. He put the bucket down in front of the Chief, and then, without warning, punched the big man in the jaw. The Chief stumble backward, falling over a pile of cement bags.

"Don't ever make sport with my life again," he hissed, as he stood over the prostrate man. He bunched his fists and braced for the fight that he knew would come. But he didn't care. He was so livid he was ready to fight one of them or all of them or the whole damn Mohawk tribe at once.

Instead of coming off the ground in a rage, as Connor expected, the Chief pulled himself on one elbow, rubbed his chin, and then broke out in a wide grin. Puzzled and wary, Connor looked around at the other men. And they, too, were grinning and giving Connor the thumbs-up sign.

***

The Chief clinked glasses with Connor. "No hard feelings, Irish. We do that to all the new men."

Connor grinned sheepishly. "I didn't know. I apologize for hitting you."

"Apology accepted. You're now an official sapling sky walker. You did good today. You've got real sand."

They were sitting in a blue-collar bar near Grand Central Station and this was part of the Mohawk's typical Friday routine. In a little while the Chief and the others would board a train that would take them back to their homes and families in upstate New

York. Monday morning, they would be back to repeat the whole process.

The bartender who'd been serving these guys for years, refilled their glasses. "You guys are nuts. It's a suicide job you've got. They don't pay you enough for what you do. Don't you know they're taking advantage of you?"

"Not me," Connor said. "I'm only going to be doing this for a little while."

The bartender grunted. "That's what Little Otter said."

Connor realized that was the name of the man who had fallen to his death last week. The Chief downed his whiskey and slammed the empty glass on the bar. "And Little Otter was right, wasn't he? He only did it for a little while."

While the next round of drinks was being served, Connor said, "Chief, I don't understand how I got this job. I thought only Mohawks did this."

"You're just temporary. We've got one of our men coming down from Canada, but it'll be a few weeks before he gets here."

Connor was disappointed with that news. "So I only have a few weeks?"

"Maybe six at the most. Why?"

"I can really use the money. I don't suppose there's any chance that I could work with you lads full-time."

The Chief slapped him on the back. "Love to have you, Irish, but you're from the wrong tribe. Your tribe's destiny is to run New York politics. We Indians have to take what we can get. There's an old saying back from reservation days: 'When the white man came, we had the land and they had the Bible. Now, we have the Bible and they have the land'."

Connor wasn't happy with the Chief's response. But he understood. Since he'd come to this country, he been puzzled by a huge contradiction. Everyone told him that America was the land of the free and that everyone was equal. But that wasn't really true. His experience was that Italian bosses didn't hire the Irish, Irish bosses didn't hire Germans and Poles, and no one hired the Negroes. So if the Mohawk Indians managed to get a toehold on ironworking, well, more power to them. He would take the few

weeks and be grateful for it. He calculated that if he worked
Saturday and Sunday for the next few weeks he just might make
enough to pay off the last of the debt.

CHAPTER FOUR

It was late afternoon by the time Nancy and the kids got back from Central Park. Today was Sunday, and Christmas was just three days away and still no baby. It had been an unseasonably mild day and Nancy had decided that a good walk and some fresh air might hasten things along a little bit. Besides, the kids, especially Fiona and Patrick, were more rambunctious than usual, and, hopefully, an hour or two in the playground would tire them out.

As she approached their apartment building, she took a deep breath and inhaled the wonderful scent of pine, not something usually encountered on Amsterdam Avenue. But every Christmas season, the luncheonette on the ground floor of her walk-up rented out the sidewalk to tree sellers and now there were a hundred Christmas trees of various sizes arrayed under a string of bare electric light bulbs—a miniature forest surrounded by a sea of concrete and asphalt.

Her upstairs neighbor, a seventy-year-old widow, was critically examining a five-footer. She turned to Nancy and her eyes narrowed. "Ah, Mrs. Cavanaugh, guten tag," she said in a heavy German accent. She patted Nancy's enormous belly. "It has been weeks since I laid eyes on you, now look at you, big as a house. So when are you due?"

"Two days ago, Mrs. Krueger."

The old woman nodded in satisfaction. "It is going to be a Christmas baby."

"Oh, I hope not," Maureen said. "He'll get gypped on presents."

"I'm sure I'll have the baby before Christmas," Nancy said.

Mrs. Krueger violently slammed the scrawny tree on the pavement and a shower of pine needles cascaded to the ground.

"This man, this tree seller, he calls this a Christmas tree?" she whispered to Nancy. "Nein, it is so gaunt a dog would not trouble himself to pee on it." She nodded toward a weasel-faced man in a torn pea coat. "He is asking four dollars for this tree. This is outrageous. Milk is thirty-four cents a gallon and bread is eight cents a loaf. Everything is getting so very expensive. Where, I wonder, will it all end?"

Without waiting for an answer, she turned to the tree seller. "Mister, I will give you three dollars and not a penny more and you will be happy to get it. Just look about you. You must have a thousand trees here and only a few days to sell them. By Christmas Eve it will be nothing but firewood."

"All right, all right. Three it is," he said, deciding it was worth three dollars to just get her to go away.

"Ya, danka. You will be so good as to wrap it with the cord, but be careful you do not break anymore branches off the pitiful thing. I am an old lady. Perhaps you would be good enough to carry this tree upstairs to my apartment. I live right here."

The tree seller looked at her suspiciously. "What floor?"

"The fifth."

He shook his head in defeat. "All right, all right."

She turned her attention to Nancy. "Do you have your tree yet?"

"Yes, Connor put it up a couple of days ago. What with the baby coming at any time, he might not have another chance."

Fiona and Patrick were running in and out of the trees, pretending they were in a forest. Mrs. Krueger studied them with squinty eyes. "Who will watch the little ones when you go to hospital?"

"My friend, Nora. She lives just around the corner."

Mrs. Krueger grunted. "Ah, she is the pretty little blonde girl who likes to use too much lipstick, is this not so? Well, if you get stuck – you know how unreliable some young people can be – I am always just upstairs."

"Thank you. You're very kind." Nancy suppressed a smile. When the question of who would babysit the kids when Nancy went into the hospital, the children had told her that under no circumstances was she to allow mean old Mrs. Krueger to be their babysitter.

The old lady, who missed nothing, glanced over Nancy's shoulder. "Is that not Mr. Cavanaugh coming?"

Nancy turned to see her husband, a big grin on his face, literally running across the street. Just then a brown United Parcels truck turned onto Amsterdam Avenue. Connor didn't see the truck and the driver didn't see Connor. Nancy closed her eyes at the sound of screeching brakes. She opened them, expecting to see Connor dead under the truck, but he'd made it to the sidewalk and was happily waving to the furious fist-shaking driver.

Unperturbed by his near mishap, he rushed up to Nancy, panting for air.

"Will you never look where you're going, Connor Cavanaugh?"

"Ach, you know me. I'm used—"

"—to cows in the street, not bloody automobiles," Maureen finished the sentence proudly.

Nancy's eyes widened. "You watch your mouth, young lady."

Connor picked up Nancy and whirled her around.

"Will you put me down you eejit, or I'll have the baby right here in the street."

Connor nodded to a thoroughly befuddled Mrs. Krueger. "Nice to see you, Mrs. Krueger. If you'll excuse us." Connor led Nancy away from the old busybody.

"What's got into you, Connor?"

"In my pocket I have the last payment for the farm."

Nancy's heart pounded in her chest. "Then you'll quit the construction job?"

"I already have." He didn't tell her that his replacement from Canada was going to be here next weekend and that his laborer's job had also been eliminated. But it didn't matter. In the last few weeks he'd been able to work every Saturday and Sunday and the money had just poured in.

Tears welled up in Nancy's eyes and she threw her arms around Connor. "Oh, thank God. Now I have my husband back."

***

Shortly after dinner, the kids, worn out from the playground, went to bed early. As Nancy was doing the dishes and Connor was reading the newspaper, she suddenly grimaced. She turned off the water and wiped her hands on her apron. "It's time," she said quietly.

"Time for what?" Conner asked, absentmindedly scanning the sports page.

"The baby's coming."

Connor bolted out of his chair. "Jasus, Mary and Joseph. Let's go, woman. Don't be standing there."

"I'm almost done with the dishes…"

"Never mind the dishes. Let's go."

"I will not. I won't leave a dirty kitchen behind me. It'll just take a minute—" She felt a sharp pain and doubled over. "All right. Maybe we'd better go. Get Nora."

While Connor raced around the corner to Nora's apartment, Nancy went into the children's bedroom. By now they had heard all the commotion and they were half awake. She sat down on the bed that Maureen and Fiona shared. "Now I want you children be good for Nora and your Dad, hear me? When I come home you'll have another little brother or sister. Isn't that exciting?"

"If it's a boy," Maureen announced, "he's going to be named Donal, and if she's a girl she's going to be named Nora, after Aunt Nora. Right, Mommy?"

"That's right, Maureen."

"I don't want another brother," Fiona said, rubbing her eyes.

"I hate you," Patrick said, yawning.

***

For some women, it seems the more children they have, the faster they give birth. But for Nancy, every birth had been long and difficult and this one was no exception.

Outside in the waiting room, Connor, nervously paced the tiny room and looked at his watch again. It was almost two in the morning. She'd been in the delivery room since eight. He stuck his head out the door and saw a nurse approaching. "Oh, nurse, can you give me any word on my wife. She's been in the delivery room for over six hours."

"And you are…"

"Connor Cavanaugh."

"Your wife is doing fine, Mr. Cavanaugh. The doctor will be out to see you as soon as the baby is born."

"When will that be?"

The nurse grinned and patted his arm. "I expect that's pretty much up to the baby."

It was close to three when the doctor came into the waiting room.

Connor jumped up. "Is the baby born? Is the baby all right? Is my wife all right?"

"Everything's fine, Mr. Cavanaugh. Congratulations. You have a healthy son. And your wife's doing just fine."

Connor slid back into his seat. "A son. Imagine that."

"You're first?"

"No. I have two girls and a boy."

"Now you have two and two. Wait here. You'll be able to see your wife in a few minutes."

***

Nancy was sharing a room with two other mothers, both of whom were asleep. An exhausted Nancy looked down at the baby in her arms. "You're a lucky little man, Donal Joseph Cavanaugh," she whispered. "Born just two days before Christmas."

Connor was sitting in a chair by the bed. "Maureen will be greatly relieved."

"I know. She was so worried he'd get gypped out of his Christmas presents."

"She's an old woman, that one." Connor stood up to get a better look at his son. "Will you look at the size of him? How many pounds is he?"

"Ten pounds thirteen ounces."

"He'll make a fine, strapping farmer."

Nancy looked up sharply. "He'll not be a farmer, Connor. He'll not work with his hands."

"It's how I earn my living. There's nothing dishonorable in that."

"No, there's not. But Donal Joseph Cavanaugh is going to get the education you never had."

Before Connor could respond the nurse came in. "I'm sorry, Mr. Cavanaugh, you'll have to go. Time for the young mother to get some sleep."

Connor leaned over and kissed his wife. "I'll be back tomorrow."

***

It was a very different, almost somber, Christmas than Connor was used to. It was true that they'd just had a baby and that was certainly a happy occasion, but it was the first time that the whole family was not together and the kids missed their mother. So did he. Their good friends Tom and Erin Cassidy had come through and invited them down for Christmas dinner. Erin was a good cook, but not as good as Nancy. But at the least the kids had a chance to play with the Cassidy kids and that helped to take their minds off the fact that their mother wasn't there.

They'd gotten back to the apartment around six and Connor went into the bedroom to change. He came into the living room knotting his tie. Patrick was playing with his new red fire truck and the girls were playing with their new dolls. "I'm off to see your mother and little Donal as soon as Nora gets here."

Maureen pulled him into a chair and climbed up on his lap. "While you're waiting for Aunt Nora, tell us about the farm again."

Patrick and Fiona made a mad dash to see who would occupy the other knee. Patrick won, but after some fidgeting and adjusting, and a good deal of pushing and shoving, Connor managed to get all three on his lap.

"Well, first you come to this fine iron gate. And there, just beyond the gate there's this fine—"

"—Loaning," Fiona said. "That's like a driveway," she said to Patrick with a smirk.

"I know," Patrick said, rolling his eyes.

Connor continued. "Then, as you come up the loaning, before you get to the house—"

"—There's a big old tree where you had a swing," Patrick chimed in.

"Right. And then you see the house—"

"—And it's all white with a slate roof and there are rose bushes outside the door," Maureen said dreamily.

Connor grinned at his three children. "I think I've been telling this story too much."

"No, no," Maureen said, adjusting his tie. "We love to hear about the farm."

"Are we going to go live there, Daddy?" Fiona asked.

Connor turned pensive. "That would depend on your mother."

"Tell us about the cows and the horses."

Connor brightened up. "It's a fact, Patrick. There are more cows on the roads in Ireland than automobiles. And the horses—"

He's interrupted by a knock at the door. "That'll be your Aunt Nora."

Connor slipped into his overcoat. "Thanks for watching the kids, Nora. Especially on Christmas night. I really appreciate it."

"Go on with you. To tell you the truth, it's depressing to be home alone on Christmas night. Besides," she said, rubbing Patrick's hair. "I love these little guys. How's Nancy and the baby?"

"They're both good." He looked at his watch. "I'll be back by nine."

"Take your time."

He kissed each of the children. "You kids be good. I'll tuck you in when I get back. Any messages for your mom?"

"Tell her to hurry home with Donal," Maureen said, rubbing her hands together. "I can't wait to see him."

"And are you anxious to see your new little brother as well, Fiona?"

"I guess so. He probably won't be as bad as Patrick."

Patrick responded by sticking out his tongue.

"Don't do that," Connor warned, "or it might freeze like that."

"Be careful out there, Connor," Nora said, handing him his cap. "It's raining cats and dogs."

***

Sheets of cold rain pelted Connor as he headed down Amsterdam toward the subway. He'd planned to take the subway to 86th Street and then catch a cross-town bus to the east side. But when he reached the subway station, he changed his mind. It was Christmas night and the subways and buses would no doubt be as scarce as hen's teeth. He decided he could probably get there quicker on foot. Besides, the walk would do him good. He'd been cooped up inside the Cassidy's overheated apartment all day and he was in desperate need of some fresh air.

He pulled his collar up against the wind and turned west on 97th Street toward Central Park. In spite of the wind and the rain, he started to whistle softly. And why not? Didn't he have much to be thankful for? It was Christmas night and he was on his way to see his wife and new son. She was fine. The baby was fine. The farm was finally paid off. He could hardly believe that. When he'd started to pay off the mass of debt, he'd though he'd never be done with it. Next weekend would be the first time in ages when he wouldn't have to go to the second job and he was looking forward to spending a quiet weekend with the kids.

He crossed Central Park West and went into the park. Central Park was one of his favorite places in all of New York City and he went there every chance he got. He liked walking there because it was the only patch of real estate in the entire city that reminded him of Ireland. About halfway across the park, the rain started to come down harder and harder and he began to regret his decision to walk. But there was nothing to be done now. Besides, he was more than halfway to the hospital already. By the time he emerged from the park, wind gusts were blowing the rain in waves of blinding sheets across Fifth Avenue.

CHAPTER FIVE

Sheets of rain also cascaded across the windshield of a Bentley sedan moving south on Fifth Avenue, practically blinding the driver. Skip Van Twiller, a nervous seventeen-year-old, dressed in white tie and tails, clutched the steering wheel and squinted through the blinding rain. His father, Douglas Van Twiller II, a stern man in his early fifties, also in white tie and tails, sat ramrod straight next to him, staring straight ahead.

In the back seat, Skip's mother, pulled her mink coat protectively around her and peered anxiously out the side window. "Douglas, Skip shouldn't be driving in these conditions. He doesn't even have his driver's license yet. And this rain is terrible. I can't see a thing."

"You don't have to see, Agnes," her husband said, dismissively. "You are not driving. Besides, Skip has to learn how to drive in all types of weather. You can handle it son, can't you?"

"Certainly, Father," the son answered unconvincingly.

"Well, at least slow down in these conditions."

"He's doing fine, Agnes." The father looked at his watch. "We're late as it is. You know how Aunt Abigail is about being punctual for her dinner parties."

Suddenly, in the blurry glow of the headlights and a blinding cataract of water, Skip saw a faint shape in the street in front of him. He squinted hard. What was it? And then he saw—a man! And behind and above him – a traffic light. And it was red... The young man's eyes widened in sheer terror. He slammed on the brakes. The brakes locked, but the tires planed on the slick surface and the momentum carried the car inexorably forward. He yanked at the steering wheel, but nothing happened. The shape loomed larger and larger. Then there was a sickening thump and the shape flew across the hood and a face – Connor Cavanaugh's face – smashed into the windshield. And then he was gone.

The Bentley came to a rocking stop, jerking the occupants' heads forward. For a moment there was utter silence save for the whoosh, whoosh of the windshield wipers. Then Agnes Van Twiller screamed.

Her husband spun around in a fury. "For God's sake, Agnes. Get hold of yourself."

He turned toward his son. He was still gripping the steering wheel, but he was hunched over it and hyperventilating in the throes of an oncoming asthma attack.

"Listen to me carefully the both of you," he said quietly. "I was driving. Is that clear?" Skip shook his head. He turned to look at his wife. "Is that clear, Agnes?"

Mrs. Van Twiller nodded.

Van Twiller took a deep breath and yanked open the door. He stepped out of the car and was immediately soaked through to the skin. He looked behind him and saw what looked like a pile of clothes lying in the street. As he got closer, he saw it was a man and there was a great deal of blood pouring out of a large wound to his forehead. He heard a gagging sound and turned to see his son vomiting in the street.

"Skip, get back in the car and don't come out until I tell you to." He watched his son stagger back toward the car. "Not the driver's side, you fool. The passenger side."

Just then a taxi pulled up next to Van Twiller. "What's up? An accident?"

"Yes. This man ran in front of my car."

The taxi driver squinted through his blurry windshield. "He don't look good. I'll take a run down Fifth Avenue and look for a cop."

"Thank you."

Van Twiller watched the taxi speed off. By now, a few pedestrians had gathered and someone from a nearby apartment had come out to throw a blanket over Connor.

He crossed the street to a phone booth and dialed a number. A man answered. "Hello?"

"Walter, this is Douglas. There's been an accident and I'll be needing your services."

"That's why you have me on retainer, Douglas. What happened?"

By the time Van Twiller finished briefing his lawyer on his version of the accident, he saw the flashing red light of a police car fast approaching from the south. "The police are here. I have to go Walter."

"All right. But be careful what you say to them. Admit nothing. I'll meet you at the police precinct. Don't worry, Douglas, everything is going to be fine."

Van Twiller hung up just as the two police officers jumped out of their car. The younger of the two went to Connor, the other cop approached Van Twiller. "You the driver?"

Van Twiller reached for his wallet. "Yes, I am officer. I suppose you want to see my driver's license."

Although Patrolman John Flanagan was a rookie and just on the force for less than a year, he'd handled dozens of vehicle accidents, but they'd all been fender benders. Nothing like this. As he approached the body lying in the street, he could see that the man was badly injured. A stream of blood, mixing with the rain, poured toward the gutter on the west side of Fifth Avenue. He knelt down and pulled the soaked blanket up around Connor's neck. "Hey, buddy, can you hear me?"

Connor's eyes fluttered open. "...bloody cows..." he whispered.

Flanagan leaned in closer. "What? Did you say something about cows?"

"...bloody cows...I'm used to bloody cows in the street..."

***

Unlike his rookie partner, Patrolman John Murphy had over twenty years in the department. He was what other cops in the police department called a "hair bag" – someone who'd been around a very long time. He'd seen and done it all and in those twenty years he'd survived by developing a sixth sense about danger – not only physical danger – but career danger as well. He'd seen more than one cop give a ticket to the wrong person, or lock up some big shot's kid and end up pounding a foot post in Staten Island. He vowed he would never make that mistake and right now he realized he was in one of those situations. All the signs were there. Van Twiller and the kid in the car whom he assumed was his son were dressed up like Fred Astaire in The Gay Divorcee. The old lady was decked out like the Queen on her way to a state dinner. Then, there was the car – a Bentley – that cost more than he could hope to make in a lifetime. He examined Van Twiller's license and recognized the Fifth Avenue address. The building was prime real estate on the upper east side only about ten blocks south of here. The building was loaded with blue blood types and came with uniformed doormen and dog-walking elevator operators. Everything about this guy spelled money – and trouble. He reminded himself to pull his dopey rookie partner aside and clue him in.

"So what happened, Mr. Van Twiller?"

"It all happened so fast, officer. We—that is—I was driving south. As you can see, the conditions are very bad, so I was driving at a very low rate of speed. Suddenly, this man jumped out in front of my car. I immediately hit the brakes" – he shrugged helplessly – "but there was nothing I could do."

Murphy said nothing, but he knew Van Twiller was lying. He'd already reconstructed the accident in his mind. Judging by the smashed windshield, he could imagine the trajectory of the body. The pedestrian got hit when he was directly in front of the vehicle. On impact, a man standing there will fly up onto the hood, crash into the windshield, and fly over the top of the car and land behind it. Murphy turned around and saw Flanagan kneeling over the body. They were at least fifty feet behind the car. If Van Twiller was going as slow as he said he was, the guy would have rolled over the car and landed no more than ten feet away. Van Twiller, he decided, was full of crap. He may not have been speeding, but he was certainly going way too fast for these conditions.

He glanced at the son, who was standing by the car, wheezing and making weird noises. "What's the matter with your son."

"Asthma. He has asthma."

Murphy noted that Van Twiller's tone was one of utter disgust, like his kid had leprosy or something. Murphy decided the old man probably didn't like to see weakness in his son. Murphy felt sorry for the kid. He'd met this family just five minutes ago, but he had them pegged. Van Twiller was a bully who got his jollies by intimidating his weak-willed son and his doormat wife. But, what the hell, none of that was his business. The rich may be different, but they can be just as screwed up as the rest of us.

The son came up to Murphy, coughing into a handkerchief. "Officer, do you know who he is?"

"No, I don't know. My partner will get that information."

"Is he going to be all right?"

Murphy turned and looked at Connor's motionless body. "It doesn't look good. We'll see."

The young man choked back tears. "Oh, my God…"

"Skip," the father said in a stern tone. "Get in the car and wait there."

Murphy turned as Flanagan came toward them. He had a pained expression on his face, which he always did when things were not going according to procedure. The kid was a stickler for procedure, but sooner or later, he would learn that nothing ever went according to what they told you in the police academy. "Take it easy, kid," Murphy said. "I just put in another call in for an ambulance. They'll be here any minute."

"Don't bother," Flanagan said in a flat tone. "He's gone."

The young man sagged to the ground. "No….no…no…."

The mother, who'd rolled down the window and been listening to the conversation, covered her face with her hands. Only Van Twiller seemed to be in control. "So, what's next officer?"

"Right now, we have to classify this as a vehicle homicide. My partner will drive you to the precinct. The detectives will want to talk to you."

As Van Twiller turned toward his car to tell his wife he would have to accompany the patrolman to the police station, Flanagan said to Murphy, "It was the damn

dest thing, John. He kept mumbling something about cows in the road."

Van Twiller whirled around. "What? What did you say?"

"I said the guy was mumbling something about cows in the road. I didn't know what he was talking about."

Van Twiller grabbed Murphy's sleeve. "Don't you see, officer? Obviously, the man was drunk. He saw cows in the road. No wonder he ran in front of my car."

"Well, I don't think you can make that assumption…"

"Really? May I point out to you, officer," Van Twiller said in his most withering tone, "that there are no cows on the streets of New York."

Murphy heard the career alarm bells ringing furiously. He was in dangerous territory and he had to be careful.

"I'm telling you, he was drunk," Van Twiller said emphatically. "And I insist you make a note of that in your report."

"Wait a minute," Flanagan said, reacting to Van Twiller's arrogant tone. "That's not proof he was drunk. The man was hit by a car, for God's sake. He had a head injury. He can't be responsible for what he said."

Murphy grabbed his partner's sleeve and pulled him aside. "Listen to me, asshole," he hissed. "Your future is on the line, right here and now. Tell him you're going to put it in the damn report or you're going to be rattling doorknobs on the graveyard shift in Staten Island for the rest of your time on the job."

Flanagan glanced at Van Twiller and finally got it. He saw the fancy clothes, the expensive car, the attitude. Murphy was trying to tell him that this was a guy you didn't want to cross. He pulled away from his partner. "All right." He shot Van Twiller a contemptuous look. Knowing he was about to give up something very important to him, he muttered, "I'll put it in the report."

***

"That man will be late for his own funeral and that's a fact," Nancy said to her roommate, Maria Balbone, a mother of six and at forty-three was the oldest woman in the maternity ward. "It's Christmas night and it's almost the end of visiting hours and where is he?"

"You know he'll be here, Nancy. He comes every night like clockwork."

Then they both perked up as they heard footsteps coming down the hall.

"See," Maria said, "didn't I tell you?"

Nancy, excited at the prospect of seeing Connor, ran her fingers through her hair, adjusted her nightgown, and smoothed the bed covers. Then she stared at the doorway expectantly as the steps grew louder and louder. Suddenly, she was gripped by a fear she couldn't explain, a sort of premonition of disaster. One thing she did know. Those were not the footsteps of her husband.

Just then, a solemn-faced patrolman appeared in the doorway. He looked down at a piece of paper in his hand, and then at Nancy. "Are you Mrs. Connor Cavanaugh?"

Nancy stared at the police officer, too stunned to answer, as her eyes welled up with tears.

CHAPTER SIX

Dead?

She looked at the ashen-faced patrolman, scarcely able to comprehend what he'd just said. Surely, he couldn't have said that. Not dead. "Did you say he was dead?" she asked in a quiet, flat voice.

The patrolman nodded. "Yes... Mrs. Cav... Cavanaugh..." he stuttered. This was the young patrolman's first death notification. "Your husband... was struck by a car and died of his injuries less than an hour ago. I'm... sorry for your trouble..."

Without warning, a tsunamic wave of abject fear, terror, and bottomless despair crashed over Nancy, physically causing her head to snap back. She saw the patrolman's lips moving, but the only sound she heard was an enormously loud rushing sound in her ears. She tried to focus on the patrolman, but her vision had narrowed to a small cone of light, and in that cone all she saw was the metal badge pinned to his uniform and the badge number—2870. For one terrifying, disorienting moment, she couldn't remember her name, or why she was here in the hospital, or even why she was feeling this terrible dread. But then, slowly, the wave receded from her mind leaving a detritus of confused fragmented memories and thoughts swirling about her.

Dead. She knew she should cry. She wanted to cry, but the tears wouldn't come. And somewhere in the dim recesses of her mind, she understood why. There was no time for tears. Not now. There was too much to do. But exactly just what she had to do, she couldn't begin to sort out in her head at the moment.

But there was one thing she could do – one thing she must do.

She pulled the covers aside. "I've got to get home to my children," she said in a flat voice.

A nurse, standing in the doorway, rushed forward and gently, but firmly, pushed Nancy back into the bed. "Now, now, Mrs. Cavanaugh. You must not get out of bed. It's too soon."

Nancy struggled to get free of the nurse's strong grasp. "Are you insane, woman? I can't stay in bed. I have to go home to my children."

The nurse called out. "Doctor. You're needed in room twenty-six right away."

Nancy's mind was suddenly a racing, screeching, tumultuous kaleidoscope of terrifying images and thoughts. There was so much she had to do, so much she couldn't do, so much that would never be done. She heard hysterical screaming and was surprised to realize it was coming from her.

The doctor rushed into the room with a hypodermic needle in his hand. "You're going to be fine, Mrs. Cavanaugh," he said in a maddeningly calm voice as he stuck the needle into her arm.

"What's that?" Nancy asked.

"Just something to help you sleep."

"I don't want to sleep, you eejit," she screamed. "I want to go home to my children."

"They're being taken care of by your friend Nora," the tense patrolman said. "I just came from your apartment. She said she will stay with the children as long as necessary."

"No. I've got to get home." Nancy tried to get up again, but she'd lost all her strength and she was suddenly very sleepy. She felt lightheaded, like that time she'd had too much to drink at Erin's wedding. She fell back on the bed. The doctor was saying something to the nurse, but his voice sounded very far away.

Suddenly, Neil Cullen appeared in the doorway. Was she dreaming? Was he an apparition? She raised herself up. No, he was no apparition. He was really there, looking so very sad and dreadfully pale with tears in his eyes.

"Nancy… I'm so sorry…. Don't worry about the children. Nora is with them." He patted her hand. "Don't you worry about a thing. Just get some rest."

Don't worry about a thing. Did he just say that? Nancy began to laugh, a giddy, wild hysterical laugh. Even in her shock and grief, she recognized the irony of that statement. She had three young children at home, a brand new infant, and a dead husband. Don't worry about a thing? At some level she knew her response was inappropriate, but she couldn't stop laughing. And that's the last thing she remembered, for she quickly fell into a drug-induced sleep.

It was almost five in the morning, when she awoke with a start. "My God, she whispered. "What a terrible nightmare." Then her stomach twisted in a knot – and she remembered. It was not a nightmare. Connor was dead.

***

The next day, against the doctor's orders and dire predictions of internal bleeding and other bodily damage, she signed herself and Donal out of the hospital. Neil was there to meet them and took them home in a taxi.

She climbed the three flights slowly, her whole body aching. When she got to the apartment door she froze, dreading this moment.

"Neil, what do I say to three little children who have just lost their father?"

Neil shrugged helplessly. "I don't know, Nancy. I don't know."

She took a deep breath and opened the door. Nora was standing in the kitchen about to take a sip of tea. She put the cup down and came to Nancy and hugged her. Neither spoke.

In the living room at the end of the hallway, Nancy saw her children. Patrick was playing with his fire truck and the girls were playing with their dolls. It all looked so – normal. She handed Donal to Nora.

Maureen was the first to see her mother. She stood up and walked slowly toward her in her usual quiet and solemn way. Now Patrick and Fiona saw their mother as well and, hand in hand, they followed their sister down the hall toward the kitchen. Holding hands? Nancy's eyes filled with tears. They never did that. At the last moment the three children, tears streaming down their faces, rushed to their mother. Nancy dropped to her knees and hugged her children. And in that moment she realized there was nothing she had to say. At least not now. Later, when they'd gotten used to what had happened to them, she would try to explain it to them.

After a while, the children, with the enviable resilience of youth, drifted back to the living room to resume playing. Nora made tea for Nancy and Neil and they all sat around the table.

Neil broke the awkward silence. "Nancy, as you requested, I've been to the funeral parlor. The wake will be tomorrow. Do you still want just one day?" He'd been surprised that Nancy only wanted a one-day wake, for it was customary to hold a three-day wake.

"Yes. Except for my Aunt Ellen, neither Connor nor I have any relatives in the city, so one day is enough. Besides, I don't think I could hold up for more than that."

Neil scowled. "Do you think that old biddy will come traipsing in all the way from her grand home in Sands Point Long Island?" he asked.

Nancy sighed. "Yes, I do. But, oh, God, I hope not."

Aunt Ellen, the younger sister of Nancy's mother, had come out to America in the early twenties. She was a mean-spirited, pinch-faced woman who had a talent never to see good in anyone. Her first husband, a Broadway Line trolley conductor had drunk himself to death after ten years of childless, married hell. A few wags said he'd done it just to get away from her. But Ellen, cunning and clever as she was, somehow always managed to land on her feet. For some strange reason, which no one who knew her could fathom, she'd ended up meeting and marrying Quentin Faraday, an extremely wealthy railroad executive from an extremely wealthy Long Island family. From all reports it was a troubled, loveless, and also childless marriage and it didn't last long. Two years into their marriage, Quentin dropped dead of a massive heart attack, leaving his entire fortune to Ellen.

"I just don't like that woman," Neil said.

Nancy assumed it was probably because her aunt had once called Neil a "dirty bog runner" to his face.

Neil recovered his train of thought. "Well, anyways, the burial will be the next day."

Nancy patted his hand. "Thank you, Neil." She felt so sorry for him. He seemed to be taking it harder than she was. And that was not unexpected. After all, he was Connor's best friend and he'd known Connor longer than she did.

***

It rained the day of the funeral, but it lacked the fury of the rain on the night of the accident. It was a small group that gathered around the open grave in the sprawling Brooklyn cemetery. Besides, Neil, Nora, the Cassidys, and a few other friends, there were a handful of men who had worked with Connor on the docks. Neil had introduced them, but in her emotional haze, she'd immediately forgotten their names. She did notice that there was an unusual looking dark-skinned, barrel-chested man, standing apart from the others. Neil hadn't introduced him and she wondered who he was and how he'd known Connor.

The priest, standing at the head of the open grave, had been reading from the Bible, but Nancy wasn't able to concentrate on what he was saying until he said, "To dust thou art, and unto dust shalt thou return."

He closed the Bible and grimly nodded to four cemetery workers. Slowly, Connor's casket was lowered into the open maw of the cold earth. When the coffin reached the bottom, Nancy, accompanied by the children, stepped forward and each one of them tossed a single red rose down into the hole.

And just like that, it was over.

As they walked back to the car that Neil had borrowed for the day, the dark-skinned man approached Nancy. "I'm sorry for your loss, Mrs. Cavanaugh."

"Thank you. You were very kind to come. Did you work with my husband?"

"Yes. On the construction site."

Nancy had almost forgotten about that damn part-time job. It seemed like he'd done that ages ago.

"Your husband was a very brave man, Mrs. Cavanaugh."

Nancy was puzzled. "I don't understand. Brave? How brave did he have to be to be a laborer at a construction site?"

"He was a sky walker," the man said proudly. "It took a lot of courage to do that."

Nancy was more puzzled than ever. "I'm afraid I don't know what a sky walker is."

"Iron worker. We're the ones who walk on the beams as the building goes up."

"Oh, of course." Last year, Nancy had been downtown and she remembered stopping at a construction site to watch iron workers – sky walkers, apparently they were called – hopping from beam to beam hundreds of feet above the ground. The mere sight of them had made her stomach queasy.

"Connor did that?"

"Yes. Just for a few weekends. But it took a lot of courage."

Nancy smiled. It would be just like Connor to not tell her that he was doing dangerous work. She shook the man's hand. "Thank you for coming. You've told me something about my husband that I didn't know."

As she walked back to the car, she was struck by a sad irony. Connor had defied death by walking on thin beams hundreds of feet above the ground, but he couldn't get across Fifth Avenue alive.

***

Most of the people who'd attended the funeral came back to Nancy's apartment afterwards. A steady stream of neighbors and friends came in carrying cooked dishes, cakes and pies, and cold cuts for sandwiches. There was enough food in the icebox that Nancy wouldn't have to cook a meal for at least two weeks. The woman crowded into the small kitchen drinking tea, talking softly, and saying with the best of intentions all the wrong things.

"Ah, at least he went quick…."

"Connor's gone, but you do have a brand new baby …."

"It's the way of the world. One comes in, another goes out…"

"The Lord works in mysterious ways…"

"You still have your family…"

The men gravitated to the living room to drink their beer and smoke their cigarettes. Occasionally, there would be a loud belly laugh, but it was quickly stifled as the laughter remembered where he was and why he was there.

Much to Nancy's dismay, Aunt Ellen had indeed come all the way in from Long Island to attend the funeral. When they got back to the apartment, Nancy had offered to take her very expensive mink coat, but the aunt demurred, saying the apartment was on the chilly side and she'd just as soon keep it on, thank you very much. Nancy knew that was just an excuse. The old lady wanted everyone to see her fine mink coat.

Nancy did her best to avoid the tedious woman, but when she went into the bedroom to get a handkerchief, the aunt followed her.

"Nancy, I have to speak to you in private," she said, closing the door.

"Yes, what is it, Aunt Ellen?"

"Tis a terrible thing that's happened, what with your Connor dying and all." She pulled her mink coat up around her neck as though she'd suddenly felt a fierce arctic wind blowing through the bedroom. "He didn't have insurance, did he? No, of course not. Men like that never think of providing for their families."

Nancy was almost speechless, but she managed to sputter, "Insurance is very expensive, Aunt Ellen."

"Aye. And so is the drink. But the men always find a way to pay for the pint, don't they?"

"Connor wasn't a big drinker."

"Well, that's what you say." She brushed an imaginary piece of lint from her mink. "Everything is so dear these days. Do you know my broker tells me my entire portfolio is down fifteen percent?"

"I'm so sorry to hear that, Aunt Ellen."

The sarcasm was lost on the old woman who nodded in acceptance of the commiseration. "Just so you understand, Nancy, I won't be able to give you any money. So there's no use in asking."

Nancy was jolted out of her haze of grief. She didn't know whether to laugh of throw the old biddy and her mink coat out of her apartment. "Aunt Ellen," she said, very quietly, "I don't need your help. I will take care of myself and my family."

"Well, that's easy for you to say. But mind, the authorities will take those children from you in an instant if they don't think you can raise them proper."

Nancy could feel the anger rising in her and she fought mightily to keep it in check. "No one will take my children away from me," she said in a firm voice.

***

It was after six by the time the last of the mourners had gone. Nora and Erin stayed to clean up and then they left. Only Neil remained. Nancy made a fresh pot of tea.

"Thank God that's over," she said, pouring the tea.

"You shouldn't have gone to all this trouble. No one expected it."

"It was the right thing to do."

"I saw your Aunt Ellen trap you in the bedroom."

"Oh, please don't remind me. If I never see that woman again, it'll be too soon. Do you know she had the audacity to tell me that I shouldn't expect her to give me money?"

"Ach, she's an old skinflint and that's a fact. Pay her no never mind."

"I don't. And besides, it doesn't matter. The children are my responsibility now."

Neil furiously stirred his tea, trying to decide how to broach the subject. Finally, he blurted out, "Nancy, I want to help you."

"You have, Neil. And I really appreciate all that you've done for me and the children."

"No, I mean, I want to be a meaningful part of your – I mean you and the kids lives."

"That's sweet, Neil, and I really value your friendship. But you have your own life to lead."

"No." He slammed the cup down so violently that it spilled tea onto the table. He lowered his voice. "I mean, I want to do this very much."

Nancy was taken aback by the passion in his voice.

Neil wiped up the spill with a napkin. "Nancy," he said in a quieter tone, "Connor said that if anything should happen to him, he made me promise that I would look after you and the kids. And I said I would." He took an envelope out of his pocket and put it on the table. "This is for you." It was all of Neil's savings. "It's just something to tide you over."

"I truly appreciate that, Neil. You were Connor's best friend and you're always welcome in this house." Without looking inside the envelope, she slid it back toward him. "But I will provide for my children."

"In the name of God, how? Look at you. You're a twenty-eight-year-old woman with four young ones. What will you do?"

Neil's harsh, if accurate, assessment stunned her as though he'd thrown a bucket of cold water in her face. Up until this moment, she hadn't thought about what she would do. "I'll get a job," she blurted out. But as soon as she said it, she realized that was no answer. Get a job? What would she do? More to the point, what could she do? As soon as she'd said that, the full impact of being on her own hit her. My God. I haven't worked a day since Connor and I were married. I have no education. I have no skills.

"What will I do, Neil?" she asked, plaintively.

"Ach, you'll find something," he said, wishing he'd kept his big mouth shut. "Anyway, it will only be until you win the lawsuit."

"What lawsuit?"

"From the accident of course."

"What are you talking about? It was an accident."

"Sure it was, but that's why wealthy people like the Van Twiller's have insurance. He's got to take some responsibility for Connor's death."

"My God, that does sound grand, but it'll never happen. I would need a lawyer and God knows what else. Where would I ever get the money?"

Neil's optimism quickly faded. He hadn't thought of that. Winning a lawsuit meant hiring a lawyer and going to court. All of that had to be massively expensive. She was right. Where would she get the money?

"Well, maybe there will be no need of a lawsuit. Those big insurance companies are always afraid of the lawsuit. They'll make a settlement. I'm sure of it. And it won't cost you a thing. Think of it, Nancy. With the settlement money you'll be able to put the kids through college and maybe even buy yourself a nice little house in Queens."

"That's a lovely image, Neil. But in the meantime, I have to find a job."

CHAPTER SEVEN

The next day, Nancy took the Broadway trolley to an employment agency in midtown Manhattan that specialized in low-end service jobs. Nora had to work, and there was no one else available to watch the children, so Nancy had no choice but to bring them along, including Donal in a baby carriage.

Filling out the employment application was a dispiriting exercise. There were so many areas that she had to leave blank and there were so many questions she had to answer no to that she wondered if it was all a complete waste of time. Mortified, she gave the form to a woman at the front desk and sat down to wait for her name to be called. Forty minutes later, an officious older man with slicked down gray hair, came out of an office. "Mrs. Cavanaugh?"

Nancy and the children followed him into a cramped office containing nothing more than a couple of chairs and a small, paper-strewn desk. She motioned the children to sit on three chairs lined up against the wall and gave them a stern look, which they understood was a reminder to be quiet. She prayed that Donal wouldn't wake up and cause a fuss, but she was pretty sure he wouldn't. Before they'd left the house, she'd given him a bottle and she hoped that would hold him. She felt guilty about the bottle. She'd breastfed her three other children, but since Connor's death, she hadn't been able to give milk.

She sat down at the desk and anxiously watched him read her application. He said nothing, but his eyebrows kept rising and falling and there was a slight nodding his head from side to side. Absentmindedly, she straightened a brass name plate that said his name was Harold Miller.

Finally, he looked up. "Exactly what kind of employment were you looking for, Mrs. Cavanaugh?"

"I don't know. I need work. I know I don't have much experience—"

"You don't have any experience," he said, peering at her application again, as though magically expecting some evidence of experience to materialize on the sparsely completed form. "Left school in the sixth grade, mill work…" He looked at her over his wire rimmed glasses. "Where was that?"

"Ireland."

"I see. And you were a domestic for three years in Connecticut. Is that about the sum total of your work experience?"

Nancy nodded.

Miller tossed his glasses on the desk and rubbed the deep indents on either side of his nose caused by the glasses. "I have only two job openings that fit your – limited qualifications. One is for a live-in full time domestic." He glanced over her shoulder at the children who were sitting very still, as they'd been instructed. "Obviously, that is not a job that a woman with children could take. The only other job I have is a cleaning lady position in a building in midtown."

"I'll take it," Nancy said with great relief. She'd half-expected him to laugh her out of the office. Being a cleaning lady wasn't exactly what she had in mind, but beggars couldn't be choosers, could they?

***

When they came out of the building, Maureen said, "What were you doing there, Mommy?"

"Looking for a job."

"Why do you need a job?" Patrick asked.

"Because Daddy's dead and we're poor," Fiona said.

"We are not poor, Fiona," Nancy said fiercely. "I don't ever want to hear you say that again. Do you understand?"

Fiona started to cry and Patrick took her hand. "Don't cry, Fiona."

Tears welled up in Nancy's eyes. She had been noticing that since Connor's death, those two had become thick as thieves.

Nancy pulled her daughter close. "I'm sorry, love. I didn't mean to yell at you. But I want you children to understand something. We are not poor. We'll never be poor because I will always take care of you."

"How Mommy?" Maureen asked.

"I just got a job in there. Starting tomorrow, I'll be earning money."

Fiona wiped the tears from her eyes. "But who will take care of us when you're working?"

"Your Aunt Nora probably. I'll work something out."

But the truth was, she had no idea what she would do about a babysitter. She had pitifully few options. Nora, she knew, was more than willing to watch the children, but she had a full time job and her own life to live. Neil would gladly help, but he, too, worked full time. Besides, babysitting was not man's work. Paying a babysitter was out of the question.

Suddenly and without warning, a wave of anxiety overwhelmed her, and she felt the nausea welling up in her. Not again! Please God, not now. At least now she knew what to expect. First came the light-headedness, then the pounding of the heart as though it would rip right through her chest. She clutched the handle of the baby carriage, terrified that she would faint right there on the street.

Since Connor's death, she'd had several of these—she didn't know what to call them. Attacks? Bouts? Fits? All she knew was that one minute she was fine. Then, suddenly, there was that wave of anxiety and a feeling of black, all-encompassing desolation would overcome her, leaving her feeling utterly hopeless, dejected, and frightened.

"But when will we see you?"

The tone of panic in Patrick's voice, wrenched her out of her trance-like state. She rubbed her clammy hands on her coat and forced a smile. "It's a night job, Patrick. I'll go to work after you children are in bed and I'll be back before you wake up."

Tears welled up in the frightened little boy's eyes. "I want to go to Ireland with the horses and cows."

"I'll hear no more talk about Ireland," she snapped. "You're Americans and this is where we'll stay."

"But what about the farm?" Patrick persisted.

"Enough about the damn farm. I don't want to ever hear you mention it again. Do you understand?"

"But Daddy told us—"

Fiona tugged at Patrick's sleeve and whispered, "Patrick, be still."

They rode the trolley uptown in silence. Nancy gazed out the window, ashamed of herself. She'd been snapping at the children too much and it had to stop. They had enough to cope with without a shrew of a mother. When they got off the bus, she took them to the candy store and bought them ice cream cones.

***

The next night at exactly seven forty-five, Nancy walked into the lobby of a midtown office building on 43rd Street. A middle-aged, sour-faced woman was waiting for her. She looked Nancy up and down with open disdain. "Mrs. Cavanaugh?"

"Yes."

"I'm Mrs. Reardon, the supervisor of the cleaning staff. For the first six months, you will be on probation. That means that if you don't show up for work, or you are late, or you don't do the tasks assigned to you, you will be fired. Is that clear?"

An intimidated Nancy could only nod.

Mrs. Reardon led Nancy down to a basement locker-room where she was issued a uniform and a cleaning cart. Then she followed the supervisor onto an elevator and rode it to the fifteenth floor. The doors opened to reveal the largest office area Nancy had ever seen. It was as big as an airplane hangar with row upon row of desks that seemed to go on forever.

"This is your floor, Cavanaugh," the supervisor said. "You will dust every desk top. Be careful you don't disturb any papers. Empty the garbage cans – mind there's no half-filled coffee containers inside. They'll spill and you'll have to clean that up as well. The floors are washed every night, waxed every second week.

The rugs are vacuumed every other Wednesday, the windows once a month." She turned to Nancy. "Any questions?"

Nancy looked around, bewildered and overwhelmed. "No, I don't think so," she said in a small voice.

"Right. Get started. I'll be back to check on you."

***

It took Nancy almost four months to get into the rhythm of the job. It was daunting at first, especially with Mrs. Reardon always looking over her shoulder, but eventually she developed a system and the work went smoothly. It was physically hard work, but she didn't mind, for it kept her busy and the time went by quickly.

The babysitting issue ultimately sorted itself out as well. Even though Erin Cassidy generously offered to babysit, Nancy couldn't bring herself to inflict four more children on the mother of two young ones. She decided she would avail herself of Erin's offer only in the event that no one else was available. Nora babysat when she could. Even Neil insisted on babysitting, and that was great help. Still, even with everyone's help, there were times when she had to leave the children alone. She felt guilty about it, but she dared not miss work. Her only consolation was that she could put Maureen in charge. She'd always been mature for her age, but since her father's death, her oldest daughter seemed to sense that she had to take on more responsibility. She was especially good with Donal and treated him like he was her own child. Nevertheless, she gave Maureen strict instructions to go immediately to Erin's apartment if anything happened.

To supplement the meager income from the cleaning job, Nancy had taken the job of superintendent in her own building. In addition to a small stipend, the landlord agreed to give her free rent in exchange for washing down the hallways once a week, putting out the garbage, and keeping the coal furnace in the cellar stoked at all times.

***

Saturday morning, Nancy came back from her weekly shopping with her children. She opened the mailbox and found an official-looking letter from the law firm of Bossart & Bossart, requesting her to contact their office for a meeting.

Later, that evening, she showed the letter to Neil. "What do you think?"

"This is good. I think they want to make a settlement. Didn't I tell you?"

"And I won't have to hire a lawyer?"

"No. They'll offer you a sum of money and that will be that."

"Well," Nancy said cautiously, "that would be grand. Maybe I'd be able to quit the cleaning job."

"I'm sure you will," Neil said confidently.

***

The following Wednesday morning, Nancy dropped the kids off at Erin's apartment. With mounting apprehension and not knowing what to expect, she climbed aboard the Broadway trolley and headed downtown to the lawyer's office located at 233 Broadway. Neil had offered to come with her, but to his dismay, she'd refused his offer. She couldn't articulate it, even to herself, but somewhere deep inside her, she knew that this was something she had to do by herself.

When she arrived at 233 Broadway, she was taken aback at the grandeur and opulence of the building's lobby. It was no accident that the law firm of Bossart & Bossart had chosen the Woolworth building as their headquarters. The neo-Gothic style building, constructed in 1910, was one of the tallest buildings in New York City. Resembling a European Gothic cathedral, it had been labeled "The Cathedral of Commerce" during its opening ceremony. The law firm had chosen the Woolworth building as a not too subtle way to impress clients and intimidate the opposition.

At the twenty-fifth floor, the elevator doors opened revealing a world of magnificence and finery that Nancy had never experienced in her entire life. Enormous gold letters on the wall behind the receptionist's desk spelled out Bossart & Bossart, Attorneys at Law. The wall-to-wall carpet, seemingly miles of it, was soft as sheep's down. There were live plants everywhere and paintings – real paintings – not the sort of shoddy reproductions you could find in a Woolworth's.

The young, elegant receptionist looked up. Even she looked like a movie star in a wonderful silk dress and a string of pearls. Nancy was suddenly aware of her own shabby coat and pulled it tightly about her. "Yes? May I help you?"

"I'm Mrs. Nancy Cavanaugh," Nancy stammered. "I'm here to see Mr. Bossart."

The receptionist consulted an appointment book. "Yes, of course. Won't you please be seated. Mr. Bossart will be with you momentarily. May I get you a cup of coffee? Tea?"

Nancy looked down at the lovely, expensive carpet. "No, thank you," she said, horrified at the thought that she might spill something on it.

Fifteen minutes later, an elderly distinguished gentleman with wavy, silvery hair came out to the reception room and approached her with a kindly smile. "Mrs. Cavanaugh, I'm Walter Bossart. Thank you for coming. Won't you please step into my office?"

At her cleaning job, she'd been inside some very large offices that belonged to the big shots who worked for the insurance company that occupied most of the fifteenth floor, but Mr. Bossart's office was by far larger than any of them. And it had a splendid view of lower Manhattan. Nancy was delighted to see that she could actually see the Statue of Liberty. She was surprised at how small it looked out there in the middle of the harbor.

"Mrs. Cavanaugh, may I offer you a cup of coffee? Tea?"

"Thank you, no." The carpet in this office was even finer than the one in the reception area and she couldn't take the chance of a spill.

Walter Bossart sat down behind a huge antique desk. "And how old is the baby now?"

"Almost four months." Nancy was getting a good feeling about this man. He seemed kind and understanding, not like that horrible Mrs. Reardon. She began to relax. This was not going to be the ordeal she'd been expecting.

"I have two of my own," Bossart said. "They grow up so fast. Both of them are at Yale."

His demeanor became serious as he opened a folder. "Mrs. Cavanaugh, let me say on behalf of my client how terribly sorry we are for the loss of your husband."

"Thank you."

"After careful consideration of all the exigent circumstances surrounding this most unfortunate matter, my client is prepared to offer you a generous settlement."

Nancy had to remind herself to breathe. This was like some lovely, wonderful dream. It was nothing like she expected. Neil had been right. There would be no need for a fight in court, no need for lawyers, and, best of all, there would be no crippling expenses, which she couldn't afford anyway.

Bossart slid an impressive set of documents across the desk. "Now if you'll just sign on the bottom indicated by the X, we can have the monies transferred to your bank today. It's as simple as that." With a kindhearted smile he handed her a beautiful gold fountain pen.

Unaccustomed to reading fancy lawyer's documents and not wanting to appear to doubt Mr. Bossart's word, she leaned over the document, about to sign it, but then her eyes fell on a sentence near the bottom. In consideration of the above, party of the first part will remit to one Mrs. Connor Cavanaugh, the sum of...

Nancy looked up, stunned, unbelieving. "My God, Mr. Bossart, is that all you think a man's life is worth?"

Bossart looked pained. "I know it's difficult to put a price on something like this, Mrs. Cavanaugh, believe me I know, but there were, how shall I say it, extenuating circumstances."

"Extenuating... I don't understand."

"Mrs. Cavanaugh, believe me, this is most difficult for me to discuss. Nevertheless, I must tell you – it appears your husband was drinking the night of the accident."

"That's a lie. He was with my children all day and all evening until he left for the hospital."

"Well, I must tell you that the police officer on the scene said your husband was muttering something about cows in the street. It's all in the police report, which I can get a copy for you if you wish."

Nancy's eyes filled with tears, hardly able to believe her ears. How many times had she heard Connor say, 'sure I'm used to cows in the road, not bloody automobiles'? "And that's why you think he was drunk?"

"I think I need not remind you that there are no cows in the streets of New York."

Nancy slowly rose out of her seat and slammed his elegant fountain pen on the desk. "Mr. Bossart," she said, in a quietly measured voice, "you are a great eejit."

"Mrs. Cavanaugh" – the kindly smile was gone and the tone had become hard – "let me remind you that this is a very generous settlement, which can be withdrawn at anytime. You have young children to think of. A lawsuit will be very expensive and you're bound to lose."

But his threats were of no use. Nancy had already left the office.

CHAPTER EIGHT

As Nancy hurried away from the building with tears blinding her, a slight, bald headed man in shirtsleeves chased after her. "Mrs. Cavanaugh, please wait."

"No. I won't sign that paper. I'll never sign that paper."

The man looked around, guardedly. "You're right. You shouldn't sign it," he whispered.

Nancy turned and faced him. "Who are you?"

"My name's not important, but I work for the firm. If they knew I was talking to you, I would lose my job. All I'm saying is don't sign anything until you see a lawyer."

"But I can't afford a lawyer."

"You must have representation. You're no match for them."

"But I don't know any lawyers—" Then she remembered something. "Wait. Maybe I do…"

***

That night, Nancy came to work early. Hoping to avoid the meddlesome Mrs. Reardon, she changed quickly, grabbed her cart and slipped onto the elevator. On the fifteenth floor, she hurried down the corridor and stopped in front of a door marked Isaac Kaplan, Attorney at Law. From cleaning his office every night for the past few months, she'd come to know him. He was kind and considerate, unlike some executives who, if they were still working, would brusquely tell her to come back later, even if that meant that she couldn't wax the floors according to her schedule. She knew he usually worked late and she was relieved to see a light coming from under the door.

Isaac Kaplan, a slightly balding man in his late thirties, was hunched over a desk overflowing with papers. He looked up. "Hi, Nancy. Either you're early, or I'm late."

"I'm a bit early, Mr. Kaplan."

"OK. Don't mind me. I'll be out of here in a little while."

As Nancy went about cleaning the office, she kept shooting furtive glances his way, trying to work up the courage to speak. Then she saw him start to pack up his briefcase. In another minute he'd be gone and she didn't think she would be able to summon up the courage to speak to him again. It was now or never.

"Mr. Kaplan," she blurted out. "May I speak to you for a moment?"

Kaplan sat back. "Sure. What's up?"

"I have a problem. A legal problem."

By the time she finished telling Kaplan her story, he was pacing the office, getting angrier by the minute. "Those bastards – oh, sorry, Nancy. They're going for a quick settlement and they're taking advantage of you."

"What should I do?"

"Don't take their settlement. Hire a lawyer and take them to court."

"I don't have that kind of money."

He waved a hand dismissively. "There are plenty of lawyers who will take the case on contingency."

"What does that mean?"

"It means they'll take the case without any money upfront. If there's a settlement, they get a percentage." He saw her doubtful expression and added, "Don't worry. It's all on the up and up."

"Would you do that?"

"Me? I'm too busy, Nancy. Besides, it's out of my area of expertise. I do workman's compensation cases. And furthermore, Bossart and Bossart is the biggest and most influential law firm in the city. They're what we call a "white shoe" law firm. Been around forever. I just don't have their resources. It'd be like David and Goliath, except I wouldn't even have a slingshot."

As he'd been speaking, he'd been pacing up and down the small office, trying to convince himself as much as her that he couldn't possibly take the case. The reality was, he was afraid of these guys. What'd he told her was true. They were a real powerhouse law firm and they would crush him like a bug. Then his eyes went to the photo of his wife and son on his desk. "How's the new baby?"

"Donal is good. He's a happy baby."

"How old?"

"Almost four months."

"My Ben is almost six months."

Kaplan looked around his cramped, shabby office. How did I get here? he asked himself. I went to law school to right the wrongs of the world, to seek truth, justice, and the American way – just like Superman. So what am I doing defending guys with imaginary back problems?

He fell into his chair and put his head in his hands. "God help me," he muttered. "All right, Nancy. I'll take the case. I'll talk to them tomorrow."

"About what?"

"About being reasonable."

"And if they're unreasonable?"

"Well, if they turn out to be unreasonable, we'll sue the asses off those guys."

***

It was the end of the workday and Neil and the other exhausted longshoreman streamed off the pier, some to go home, others to stop off for a quick beer and a ball at Darcy's on 11th Avenue.

Scotty, a fellow longshoreman, sidled up to Neil. "Jasus, it was a terrible day loading all those heavy machine parts onto the ship. What the hell's in all those crates anyways?"

"Parts for airplanes, trucks, and tanks."

"What in God's name do the English do with all that stuff?"

"According to the papers, the Germans blow up a lot of it."

"I'm telling you, Neil, this damn European war will be the death of me yet. My back is killing me. I miss the old days when the heaviest freight we handled were crates of bananas from Honduras."

"Aye, but at least no one got hurt on the job today."

"True enough. Did you know there's been a fellow in Darcy's the past two nights buying drinks and asking questions about Connor?"

Neil stopped. "No. You know I don't go there. What kind of questions was he asking?"

"He wanted to know how much Connor drank, did he have a girlfriend, did he gamble. Was he honest. That sort of thing."

"Who is he and why would he be asking those questions?"

Scotty shrugged. "I don't know. Old Darcy thinks he's probably a private eye."

"But why would a private investigator be asking questions about Connor?" Then he remembered: Nancy's lawyer had filed a lawsuit. This man, whoever he is, must be working for the other side.

"Are you going to Darcy's now?" Neil asked.

"Aye."

"I think I'll go with you."

***

They came into the crowded, smoke-filled bar filled with dozens of dockworkers. "That's him," Scotty said, nodding toward a heavy-set man seated at the bar. There was a pile of money in front of him and he was surrounded by a swarm of men hoping to get a free drink.

"So how well did you know Cavanaugh?" he asked one of the drunks who shaped up every day, but never got picked to work.

Before the man could answer, Neil said, "Who wants to know?"

The heavy-set man spun on his bar stool and studied Neil with small, pig eyes. He was over six feet and had the busted nose and the hulking body of an ex-prize fighter. "Who wants to know who wants to know?" he asked in a gravelly voice.

"I'm Neil Cullen. I was Connor Cavanaugh's best friend."

"Then you're just the man I want to talk to. What are you drinking, pal?"

"I'll take nothing from the likes of you."

"Then fuck off, donkey."

Neil threw a roundhouse that took the big man right off his stool. But the man had been hit before and he came off the floor surprisingly fast for someone his size. He swung at Neil and hit him a glancing blow to the side of his head. Neil saw stars and his ears started to ring.

Clearly, the heavy-set man could handle himself, but he was a lot older than Neil, and no match for an enraged man on the side of the angels. Neil charged the much larger man, fists windmilling. He missed more than he hit, but he connected with enough blows to send the bigger man crashing against the bar. With blood gushing from his nose, he grabbed a bar stool for support, but his wobbly legs wouldn't hold him and he sagged to the floor pulling the bar stool on top of him.

Neil towered over the fallen man, wide-eyed and panting for breath. "You want to know about Connor Cavanaugh? I'll tell you all you need to know. He was a decent man, a hard-working man, a family man." Neil grabbed the pile of bills from the bar and threw them in the man's face. "Take your filthy money and get out of here. There's no one here wants what the likes of you has."

The heavy-set man lurched to his feet and angrily tossed the bar stool aside. The Mick had gotten in a couple of lucky punches, but he knew he could take him. He was about to charge Neil, but then he noticed that the atmosphere in the bar had suddenly changed. Dozens of angry men surrounded him. He was the outsider. He knew he could take the donkey, but he couldn't take them all. There would be no buying drinks for this crowd. Not now. He scooped up his money and stumbled out of the bar.

***

Late in the afternoon of the next day, Nancy and Neil went to see Kaplan. When Neil finished telling Kaplan his story about the man in the bar, he said, "So who do you think he was?"

"He was probably a private investigator."

"Why would they hire a private investigator?" Nancy asked.

"They're trying to find something damaging in your husband's background so they can knock down the settlement or maybe even not pay you."

"Well, he won't be coming back to the docks again. I know that much," Neil said, rubbing his sore hand.

"Perhaps, but I'm afraid there are other places to dig."

"They can dig all they like," Nancy said, indignantly, "but, they'll find nothing and that's a fact. Connor Cavanaugh was a good husband and father."

The phone rang. "Kaplan, here." He listened for a moment and hung up. "Speaking of the devil, that was Bossart's office. They want a meeting tomorrow."

"That's good news, isn't it?" Neil asked.

Kaplan shrugged. "We'll know tomorrow."

Nancy looked at the clock on Kaplan's desk. "Oh, my. Look at the time. I've got to go to work."

***

Mrs. Reardon came into the locker-room as Nancy was telling two coworkers, Betty and Doris, about her pending meeting with the lawyers.

"So you're going to the lawyers tomorrow," Mrs. Reardon said.

Nancy nodded. She'd have preferred that the nosy supervisor didn't know her business and she was sorry she'd even mentioned the lawyer to her coworkers.

"She'll be rich, she will," Betty said. "So what'll you do with your fortune, Nancy?"

Nancy saw the look of naked envy on Mrs. Reardon's face, and now she really regretted telling the others about the lawyer. From the beginning, Mrs. Reardon had had it in for her and she couldn't understand why. She always got along with people and she did her job, better than most if truth be told. But no matter what she did, Mrs. Reardon was always on her about something. Early on, Nancy decided that the best course of action was to avoid the old biddy as much as possible.

"There won't be a fortune," she said, trying to defuse the situation. "But if there's enough, I would love to buy a little house in Queens."

The supervisor smiled, but there was no warmth in it. "Are you giving your notice then?"

"Well… no, I…"

"Of course she is," Doris said. "Do you think she's doing this dirty work because she loves it? Tell her, Nancy."

"Well, I guess I will be leaving if…"

"Then you're giving your two weeks' notice?"

Nancy was confused by the way the conversation was going and intimidated by the supervisor's insistent tone. "Well, yes... I guess so."

Mrs. Reardon nodded in smug satisfaction. "Your notice is accepted. Now get to work the lot of you."

***

At exactly three o'clock, Walter Bossart walked into his well-appointed conference room followed by three assistants. Nancy and Isaac Kaplan were already seated. Nancy realized with a start that one of the assistants was the same man who had warned her about getting a lawyer. He studiously avoided eye contact with her and she did the same.

The courtly Bossart bowed to Nancy. "Good afternoon, Mrs. Cavanaugh."

"Good afternoon, Mr. Bossart," she replied in a voice tight with tension.

Kaplan stood up to shake hands with Bossart. "Good afternoon, Mr. Bossart. I'm Isaac Kaplan and I'm representing Mrs. Cavanaugh."

Bossart smiled. "I don't believe I've heard of your firm," he said in a tone that a sensitive person might take for sarcasm.

But Isaac Kaplan was not the sensitive type and he recognized Bossart's opening gambit. What he was really saying was what he'd told Nancy earlier — I am Goliath and you are a very, very small David.

Kaplan smiled back at him. "I'm only a one-man shop, but we both adhere to the same laws, don't we? So I guess that makes us equal." Let the games begin, he thought as he slipped into a well-appointed chair.

Bossart held his hand out and an assistant handed him a folder. "Let's get down to business, shall we? I don't want to take up any more of your time than is absolutely necessary." He opened the folder and studied it for a moment. "Mrs. Cavanaugh, after careful consideration and due deliberation, we are prepared to offer you a revised settlement, which we believe is fair and more than generous."

He slid a document across the table toward Nancy, but Kaplan snatched it up and studied it. He shook his head. "I don't understand. This is almost the same as your first offer."

"Well, in light of the new developments, we think this is a fair settlement."

"What new developments?"

Bossart held out his hand and another assistant handed him a second folder. Kaplan rolled his eyes. This was lawyerly theater at its worst.

Once again, Bossart studied the file, as though refreshing his memory. But Kaplan knew that was all for show. A lawyer like Bossart would have memorized the contents of that folder.

Bossart looked up at Nancy. "Mrs. Cavanaugh, did you know your husband entered this country illegally through Canada?"

Nancy's head snapped back as though she'd been struck in the face. "What? No… I don't know anything about that…"

"I'm sure you didn't." Bossart's tone was reassuring. "But it does raise some troubling questions about the status of your children."

Kaplan slammed his hand on the highly polished desk. "This is bullshit, Bossart, and you know it. Connor Cavanaugh's legal status, whatever it might be, has nothing to do with the status of his children."

Nancy clutched Kaplan's arm. "What's he talking about? Can they do something to my children?"

"No." Kaplan saw she was about to come to pieces. He jumped up. "I need a moment to confer with my client."

Bossart nodded, the picture of understanding. "Of course. Of course." He turned to one of his assistants. "Roderick, please show Mrs. Cavanaugh and Mr. Kaplan to the small conference room."

***

Livid, Kaplan led Nancy into the conference room and slammed the door. The bastard had blindsided him. He looked at Nancy, trembling with tears in her eyes. And now his client was a basket case. He took Nancy by the shoulders and gently pushed her down into a chair.

"He's bluffing, Nancy," he said, softly. "Listen to me. It doesn't matter if Connor was legal or not. It doesn't matter if he came from Timbuktu. The kids were born in this country and that makes them United States citizens. Period."

Nancy looked up at him. "Mr. Kaplan, I'm afraid."

"Of what?"

"I have four children, no husband, and I barely earn enough to get by."

"So?"

How could she explain it to him? When Bossart said that Connor had entered this country illegally, she immediately remembered Aunt Ellen's words in the bedroom. "Mind, the authorities will take those children from you in an instant if they don't think you can raise them proper."

"Mr. Kaplan, if what Mr. Bossart says is true, and the authorities investigate, maybe they'll think I'm not a fit mother. My God, maybe they'll take my children away from me."

"No, no, Nancy, that won't happen. Believe me."

Nancy looked Kaplan in the eye. "Can you guarantee that Mr. Bossart can't make trouble for me?"

Kaplan fell into a chair next to her. "No, Nancy. I can't guarantee what someone with unlimited money and resources will or will not do to you. All I can say is, they're using this illegal immigrant issue, which we don't even know is true, to scare you into settling for a lot less money than you and your children deserve."

Nancy stood up and wiped the tears from her eyes with a handkerchief. "Then I can't take that chance. My children mean more to me than all the money in the world."

Slowly Kaplan rose from his chair. He couldn't believe it, but it was over. Just like that. He could almost sympathize with that Nazi bastard Max Schmeling, who was knocked out by Joe Lewis in the first round of their second fight a couple of years ago. He could imagine the fighter coming into the ring expecting to win, and then – bang – just like that, he's down for the count.

It wasn't supposed to be that way. Once he'd made up his mind to take on this case, he'd jumped in with both feet. And it felt good to be working on a case that had some meaning, a case that cried out for justice. He'd diligently researched case law and was sure he was on the winning side. His client was a young mother with four small children, no insurance, and a dead husband who'd been struck by an auto driven by a very wealthy man. Nancy could never be made whole, but at least there would be a substantial settlement, enough to give Nancy and her children a comfortable lifestyle that didn't entail waxing floors in an office building at night. What Bossart was offering wouldn't provide anything remotely close to that. Where was the justice? Where the hell was the justice?

"I understand where you're coming from, Nancy. But for the record, I have to say that I think you are making a very bad mistake. And as your lawyer, I have to advise you that you should not accept their settlement offer."

Nancy patted his arm. "I know you want the best for me and I truly appreciate all that you've done. Mr. Kaplan, I don't understand all this legal business. All I know is that I'm afraid Mr. Bossart or Mr. Van Twiller will make trouble for me and I just can't take that chance."

Kaplan nodded and for the first time in his life he hated the profession of law and he hated being a lawyer. The law was simply not supposed to be this way.

"Before we go back in there and you accept his offer, I want you to understand exactly what you'll be agreeing to. That sum will be divided into five parts. You'll get one-fifth and your children will each receive one-fifth, which will be placed in a trust fund and held there until they turn twenty-one."

"You mean I won't be able to touch any of it?"

"Only your share. As far as the children are concerned, the law allows for withdrawals for certain things, such as clothing and emergency medical expenses. But all request for funds from their accounts would have to be approved by a trustee of the court."

"That doesn't seem right, Mr. Kaplan. I thought I might use that money to buy a small house in Queens. It would be for the children as much as me."

"I understand. No one questions your personal integrity. I know you would never use that money for your own personal gain. But believe me, Nancy, there are plenty of parents who would burn through that money in a year if they could get their hands on it. The courts recognize that and to protect the interests of children their money must be placed in a trust fund supervised by a trustee of the court."

Nancy shrugged in resignation. "If that's the way it has to be, I guess I'll manage."

***

Nancy and Kaplan came back into the room, where Bossart was conferring with his assistants. He stood up. "Well, Mrs. Cavanaugh, have you made a decision?"

"You know she has," Kaplan said, not even trying to hide his utter contempt. "Mrs. Cavanaugh has decided to accept your very generous offer."

A smiling Bossart slid the agreement and a pen across the table. "Excellent. Mrs. Cavanaugh, I'm glad we have come to an agreement."

Nancy picked up the pen and looked at Kaplan. The lawyer blinked away tears of frustration as he watched Nancy sign the document.

***

Nancy and Isaac Kaplan came out of the Woolworth building into the bright, if thin, sunlight of an early April afternoon and stood on the sidewalk, silently and mindlessly watching traffic move up and down Broadway. Nancy was still bewildered. She tried to digest exactly what had happened up there, but none of it made sense. Somehow events had overtaken them and the result was nothing like she thought it would be. Nancy hoped that in the fullness of time, she would someday understand, because at some point she would have to explain it to her children. One thing she did know was that her dream of quitting that awful job, of buying a small house in Queens, of sending her children to college, was now nothing more than a cruel delusion. But she comforted herself with the thought that at least now there would be no more talk of illegal immigration and deportment.

As bad as she felt, she felt even worse – and not a little guilty – for involving Isaac Kaplan in this affair. She'd thought it was going to be so simple. Kaplan had said that lawyers were only paid if they won. And she was convinced that they would win. Win what? Or how much? She had no idea. But now everything had changed. She'd signed the settlement. And that was that. It was a pitifully small sum and she couldn't get the one question out of her mind: "Is that all a man's life is worth?"

Nancy squeezed the lawyer's arm. "Mr. Kaplan, I'm so sorry. Your fee won't amount to much."

Kaplan shook his head violently. "There's nothing to be sorry about, Nancy. And forget about the fee, I won't accept it."

Nancy felt the anger rise in her. Charity was something she would not countenance. "You will take it, Mr. Kaplan. You earned it."

"That's not the point."

"Yes, it is—"

Kaplan took her by the shoulders. "Listen to me, Nancy. You owe me nothing. There's something that lawyers are required to do from time to time. In Latin it's called pro bono publico, what most people know as pro bono, which means 'for the public good'. Lawyers are supposed to donate some of their time to people who need the services of a lawyer, but can't afford it. And that's what I've done. You owe me nothing. And, besides, in the Jewish religion the Torah talks about something we call a mitzvah, an act of human kindness. It's me who should thank you. I got a two for one here."

Tears welled up in Nancy's eyes and she hugged him. "Thank you, Mr. Kaplan."

"No, thank you, Nancy. We didn't win, but you made me feel like a lawyer again, and that's something I haven't felt in a long, long time." He turned away from her and tried to convince himself that the tears in his eyes were from the wind. "So, what's next for you?"

"I don't know. I guess— Oh, what time is it?"

"Five-thirty."

"My God. I've got to go or I'll be late for work."

Isaac Kaplan stood on the sidewalk and watched Nancy Cavanaugh rush up Broadway to catch the subway to her job in midtown Manhattan. Tonight, he realized, she'd be cleaning his office again.

***

Nancy was never happy going to work, but tonight she especially dreaded it, for she would have to tell Mrs. Reardon that she'd changed her mind. Would the peevish supervisor allow her to continue to work, or would she hold her to her word? Had she already found a replacement? Nancy's stomach knotted as she considered the possible consequences. What would she do if she lost this job? With her limited experience, where would she get another?

When Nancy came into the locker room, Doris, and Betty were already there changing into their work uniforms. Mrs.

Reardon was seated at a table, flipping through a movie magazine. Nancy groaned inwardly. It was bad enough she would have to beg for her job back, but now there would be witnesses as well.

"Mrs. Reardon, could I speak to you."

Mrs. Reardon looked up. "Well, what is it?"

Nancy shot a glance toward the other two women. "I wonder if we could talk in private."

Mrs. Reardon rolled her eyes. "What can you say that would be such a big secret. Get on with it, Cavanaugh."

"I've... I've changed my mind. I won't be leaving after all," she whispered.

"What did you say? Speak up, woman."

Nancy leaned in closer and was surprised to smell beer on the woman's breath. "I said… I've... changed my mind and I won't be leaving after all."

Mrs. Reardon smiled grimly. "So. You're not going to be the rich lady living in your fine home out in Queens. Is that it?"

"No, I'm not."

"Did you hear this, ladies?" Mrs. Reardon said to the other two.

Betty and Doris had heard what Nancy said and they were embarrassed for her. They busied themselves carefully tying shoelaces and buttoning dresses.

But Mrs. Reardon was enjoying Nancy's discomfort too much to stop. "It seems Mrs. Cavanaugh will have to continue working just like the rest of us poor, deprived souls. Isn't that wonderful news?"

"I'm glad you're staying," Betty said, trying to break the tension in the room.

"Me, too," Doris added quickly.

Nancy looked at Mrs. Reardon uneasily. What would her answer be, yes or no? The supervisor had an odd look on her face. Unless Nancy was misreading her, it seemed to be one of relief. But that couldn't be.

But it was. Mrs. Reardon was relieved. Less than an hour earlier, she'd been summoned to the office of John Kean, the manager of custodial services for the building.

"I've just heard that Nancy Cavanaugh is leaving," he said, barely able to control his anger. "Since she's started working here, I've gotten nothing but good reports from the tenants about her, which is remarkable to say the least. Typically, I only heard from them when something is wrong. Now Mrs. Reardon, I think I know why she's leaving. It's you. You seem to have a knack for driving good workers out of the job. Well, I'm here to warn you that the turnover rate is unacceptable. Tonight, you will talk to Mrs. Cavanaugh and do everything in your power to convince her to stay. Your job, and your future with the company, depends on how you handle it. You may go."

Mrs. Reardon had left Kean's office visibly shaken. She had to admit that everything he'd said was true. She had done her best to drive Cavanaugh out of the job because she hated her, and her kind. She was young, she was pretty, and she was proud, too proud. She enjoyed tormenting her type and watching them squirm. They never fought back because they were afraid of losing their jobs, and that made it even more fun. But her little entertainment had backfired on her. If she couldn't get Cavanaugh to stay, she would be the one to lose her job.

Up until the moment when Nancy had asked for her job back, she had no idea how she could convince Cavanaugh to stay. And now that problem was solved. She looked up at an anxious looking Nancy Cavanaugh and allowed herself to enjoy the young woman's discomfort for just a moment longer, then she said, "Suit yourself. You got ten minutes to get dressed."

CHAPTER NINE

For the end of November, it was a reasonably mild Saturday morning. Nancy, as she did every Saturday, took the kids food shopping at Gristede's on 96th Street and Columbus Avenue. Christmas was still a month away, but much to her dismay, the stores had already started to put up seasonal decorations. All of which made Nancy extremely ill at ease.

"Look, Mommy," Patrick said, pointing to a three-foot cutout of Santa Claus. "Santa's coming soon. When we go home we have to write our letters."

His two sisters clapped their hands in happy agreement.

To distract them from anymore talk of Christmas, she hurriedly gave ten cents to Maureen. "Here, take your brother and sister and buy something from the candy store next door and wait for me outside."

As she watched them rush off, excitedly telling each other what they wanted from Santa, she wondered how she was going to get through Christmas this year. All year she'd been dreading December. For the rest of her life December would always represent a painful fusion of joy and heartbreak – Connor's death and Donal's birth.

***

As they approached their apartment building, Patrick tugged at Nancy's coat. "Mommy, I want to open the mailbox."

"No, it's my turn," Fiona protested. "You did it yesterday."

"Did not."

"Did, too."

Nancy handed the mailbox key to Patrick. "Here, this is a reward for not sticking your tongue out at your sister."

Up until recently, Fiona and Patrick had been inseparable, going so far as to insist on sleeping in the same bed. While Nancy was pleased to see them become so close, she was also saddened, because she knew that the bonding was their way of dealing with the grieving process. Then, the day before Thanksgiving, she heard them fighting and felt a great sense of relief. The day after Thanksgiving, when Patrick announced that he wanted his own bed back, she was positively delighted. It meant that they had finally come to terms with their sorrow.

Maureen, her serious, mature-beyond-her-years daughter, was another matter. Her method of coping with the loss of her father was to become a surrogate mother to Donal, and she devoted her every waking moment to him. She insisted on feeding him, clothing him, even changing his diapers.

And for that Nancy was eternally grateful. At some level, she sensed she was floundering in a sea of despair and she needed all the help she could get from whatever source. Since Connor died, life had become mind-numbingly difficult and more arduous than she ever thought possible. Every day since his death, she'd been consumed with a pervasive, but unnameable, dread. It was not something she could put her finger on, but it was always there every hour of every day.

There were days when she simply did not want to get out of bed. She just wanted to bury herself under the covers and not think of anything – not the past, not the present, not the future, and certainly not how she was going to take care of four small children. Bed became an uneasy sanctuary, but it was not a place of peace. It was more like a state of oblivion, a place where she could just – exist. There were days when it was only the thought that she had four children to take care of that she managed to summon the strength to get out of bed.

Bed had become the focal point of her life. At every opportunity, she took to it, not quite understanding why. Before all this, she had never taken a nap in her life, but now it seemed that no matter how much sleep she got, she was always exhausted. It certainly wasn't that bed was any comfort. Hardly a night went by when she didn't experience one of those attacks which would rip her from a restless sleep, gasping for breath as she tried to shake the sense that she'd been slipping into a dark, bottomless pit of hopelessness and despair.

She also worried about how Connor's death was affecting the children. Patrick and Donal had no father as a role model. Would she be able to fill the void? She was guilt-ridden at the thought that she was not a good mother. She snapped at them too often, ignored their needs too often, and she was ashamed of herself because she didn't seem to be able to stop her downward spiral of despair. Under it all was a sense of foreboding, a sense that she was just barely hanging on.

Patrick came out of the lobby waving an envelope. Nancy recognized the stamp. It was a letter from Ireland.

Maureen saw her mother stiffen. "What is it, Mommy?"

"It's a letter from Ireland. From your Aunt Eunice."

Nancy ripped open the envelope and read the short letter.

Dear Nancy,

As we approach the first anniversary of my dear brother's death, God rest his soul, I'm having a Mass said in his honor. Hope all is well with you and yours. By the way, Billy and me will be moving to the farm now that Connor has no further need for it.

Your loving sister-in-law,

Eunice.

Nancy angrily crumpled the letter and stuffed it in her handbag.

"What's the matter, Mommy?"

"Nothing, Maureen. Nothing."

***

That night, Nora and Neil came over for dinner. She waited until the children went off to listen to the Green Hornet on the radio, and then, while they were having their tea in the kitchen, she showed them the letter.

When she'd finished reading it, Nora said, "What do you make of it?"

"At first I was so mad I couldn't see straight. Who was she to have the farm after what Connor went through to pay off the debts? But then I calmed down. I don't want anything to do with that damn place. She's welcome to it."

"There might be a problem," Neil said.

"What kind of problem?"

"They say possession is nine-tenths of the law."

"What does that mean?"

"It means if she moves in there she can eventually claim full title to the farm. A similar thing happened to my late uncle."

"Did your sister-in-law help with the debts?" Nora asked.

"Not a red cent. She said the farm was Connor's and it was his responsibility. Do you really think she could get the farm, Neil?"

"Aye. I do."

"Well, I won't let that happen. I don't give a tinker's damn if she lives there, but that farm belongs to my children. It's the only legacy they have from their father. What should I do?"

"Maybe you should talk to that lawyer who helped you," Nora suggested.

Nancy nodded. "I think I will."

***

Monday evening, Nancy arrived at work early. She wasn't worried about Mrs. Reardon anymore. Since Nancy had asked for her job back, the supervisor had been almost pleasant to her. Nancy didn't understand what that was all about, but she welcomed the change. Now, without the old biddy on her back all the time, working wasn't half bad.

As usual, Kaplan was working late. Nancy showed him the letter. "I don't mind if she lives on the farm, but Neil thinks that if I let her move in, she could eventually claim it as hers. Can she do that?"

"I don't know anything about Irish law. I'll have to do a little research. Why don't you come back Friday? I should have something for you by then."

***

Nancy was on pins and needles all week. Every day, she imagined her sister-in-law moving to the farm, and Nancy, three thousand miles away, could do nothing about it. Finally, Friday came and Nancy, taking no chances that Kaplan might leave early, arrived at his office at four p.m.

"You asked me if she could move to the farm and eventually claim ownership by dint of possession," Kaplan said, referring to his notes. "Well, there is no simple yes or no answer. I know everyone talks about possession being nine-tenths of the law. It's not actually a law, but it does come from common law and it has some weight in the courts. The belief is, if you actually possess something, you have a stronger legal claim to owning it than someone who merely says it belongs to him or her. The common law states that failure to exercise and defend his or her property rights may result in permanent loss of the landowner's interest in the property. That's the short answer, but it can get very complicated. Again, I don't know Irish law, but whether or not she could claim title to the farm would depend on a lot of things. For instance, is there an actual title to the land? Was it assigned to Connor through a will or other legal codicil?"

"I've never seen or heard of any such document."

"I'm not surprised. In many European countries, Ireland being one of them, it's the custom to leave the farm to the eldest son. Now here's where it gets complicated. Connor didn't leave a will and your sister-in-law could contend that as his only living blood relative, the farm should revert to her."

"Never," Nancy snapped. "I won't allow it."

"Remember, Nancy, I said *could*. It doesn't mean she would prevail. It depends on how good her lawyer is and the arguments he makes."

"Lawyers took advantage of me once," Nancy said, in a quiet, steely voice, "but no one will ever again take advantage of me. I'll fight in the courts if necessary."

"It looks like that is what you'll have to do. But there is one problem"

"What's that?"

"You'll have to go back to Ireland to do it."

Nancy fell back in her chair, feeling a wave of panic coming over her. "Go back to Ireland? No, no, that's not possible. I don't ever want to go back there again."

"I'm afraid you have no choice, Nancy. The Irish courts will not allow you to make your case from three thousand miles away."

"But I can't. I just can't go back there."

Kaplan was puzzled by the tone of vehemence and panic in her voice. "Why can't you go back? Was it so terrible?"

"It was… it's a long story."

The lawyer patted her hand. "All right. You don't have to make a decision right away. Think about it."

***

The morning of December seventh was partly cloudy and rather cold with temperatures in the mid-thirties. It wasn't the ideal weather for a trip to the cemetery, but Nancy had decided to go today, because she knew it would have been too painful to visit Connor's grave on the actual anniversary of his death.

Together with Neil and the four children, they took the BMT subway out to the cemetery in Brooklyn. At the grave, Nancy took Donal out of his carriage and held him in her arms. He was getting so big. She could hardly believe he was going to be a year old this month. From the beginning, she'd been afraid that the tragedy surrounding his first year of life might turn him into a sullen, withdrawn baby, but thank God, that wasn't the case. To Nancy's delight, he'd become a happy, outgoing one-year-old. Nancy attributed most of his sunny disposition to Maureen, who from the beginning had tended his every need.

She watched Maureen, Fiona, and Patrick solemnly place flowers on the grave. They, too, seemed to be faring well. Occasionally, she glimpsed a fleeting sadness in their eyes when they mentioned their father, but on the whole, they seemed to have adjusted quite well to his death. Once again, she thanked God for the merciful resiliency of youth.

Neil placed a rose on the grave and came to stand beside Nancy. "Almost a year. I still can't believe he's gone."

Nancy nodded, not trusting herself to speak. This was her first trip to the cemetery since Connor's funeral. She'd wanted to come sooner, but she just couldn't bring herself to do it. But now she made up her mind. For the sake of the children, she resolved to bring them here again, maybe in the spring, when the flowers and trees were in bloom and it wouldn't look so sad.

***

On the way back to the subway, Neil bought ice cream cones for the kids. As she watched them sitting on a park bench, devouring their cones, Nancy said abruptly, "I'm going back, Neil."

"Going back? To Ireland? That's just daft. You've got four kids, and Donal not even a year old." He was taken aback by her abrupt about-face. They'd spoken about it after her visit to the lawyer and he'd gotten the impression she had no intention of going. "When did you come to this decision?"

"About fifteen minutes ago, standing by Connor's grave. I thought about how hard he worked for those two years in the middle of a depression to pay off the debts. I know he did it for me and the children. I have to go, Neil. I can't let him down."

"How long will you be gone?"

His desolate tone escaped Nancy. "It shouldn't take more than a few months to sort everything out."

"Where will you live?"

"With my parents at first."

"But you told me they were the reason you came out here."

"I know, but it'll just be until I can get the farm cleaned up and livable. A week at the most. I think I can deal with my parents for a week."

Neil lapsed back into a glum silence as he tried to digest what she'd just said. His mind was a jumble of conflicting thoughts. He didn't want her to go and tried desperately to think of a good reason why she shouldn't. He didn't know how long it would take her to sort out the farm ownership problem, but he was pretty sure it would take a lot longer than a few months.

"How will you pay for the fares?"

"I'll use my settlement money."

"But that'll be almost all of it."

"Don't you think I know that," she said, apprehensively. "Neil, I have no choice. I must do this."

***

It was almost four-thirty when they came out of the subway station at Broadway and 96th Street. A large crowd was gathered in front of an appliance store on the corner. Several women were crying and all the men looked stunned and angry.

"What's going on?" Nancy asked Neil.

"I'm sure I don't know."

As they came closer, they heard a radio announcer's voice over a loudspeaker. "…Japs have attacked Pearl Harbor, Hawaii, by air, President Roosevelt has just announced. The attack also was made on all military and naval operations on the principal island of Oahu."

Nancy turned to Neil, confused. "Did he say a tax on Pearl Harbor?"

Neil shook his head. "No, he said *attack*."

The announcer continued. "To repeat… the Japanese have bombed Pearl Harbor. All service personnel are to report immediately to their duty stations."

"Where is Pearl Harbor?" Nancy asked.

"It's an American naval base in Hawaii," a man in the crowd said.

The announcer continued, "The Japanese Imperial headquarters announced at six a.m. their time, and four p.m. eastern standard time, that a state of war existed among these nations in the Western Pacific, as of dawn."

"Does that mean we are at war with Japan?" Nancy asked.

Neil shrugged, trying to digest what he'd just heard. "I guess so."

"Damn right it does," the man said, savagely. "And I'm going down to the recruitment station tomorrow and sign up to kill every goddamn Jap I can get my hands on."

Nancy and Neil looked at each other, hardly able to comprehend what they'd just heard. Neither said a word, but they both knew one thing: Nancy would not be going to Ireland anytime soon.

CHAPTER TEN

Before they even made it back to Nancy's apartment, just two short blocks from the subway, the mood in the city had erupted into a heightened state of irrational hysteria and rumor. They passed a newsstand dealer on 97th Street who bellowed, "Japs land on the coast of California! Los Angles under attack! Read all about it."

A frenzied tailor two doors down stood on the sidewalk outside his store and babbled to anyone who would listen, "A Jap sub has been spotted no more than two-hundred yards off the Brooklyn Navy Yard…" he muttered over and over again.

As soon as they got back to the apartment, Nancy turned on the radio just in time to hear Mayor LaGuardia say in his peculiarly high, squeaky voice, "Toughen up. Look out for murder by surprise. The situation is one of extreme crisis with anything to be expected."

Fascinated, but at the same time frightened, by the tone of hysteria coming over the airwaves, they huddled around the radio all day and into the night. They heard that the FBI had sent guards to protect Croton Dam and the Brooklyn Navy Yard where the battleships Iowa and Missouri were under construction. Regular programming continued all day, but there were frequent interruptions with bulletins ranging from anti-aircraft guns being set up in Prospect Park and Fort Totten to the Port of New York Authority canceling all vacations and leaves, and assigning extra guards at its bridges and tunnels.

Nancy and Neil were shocked to hear that large numbers of Japanese nationals in New York had been taken into custody. At the end of Walter Winchell's news program on NBC Blue that night, they listened in stunned silence as he said in his instantly recognizable staccato style, "Persons who arouse suspicions by their conduct, speech, or deed, are inviting microscopic examination, perhaps prison."

Just after eleven, Nancy had had enough disturbing news and shut the radio off. "My God, we're at war. What's to become of us?"

"We'll be all right," Neil answered, none too convincingly. "They hit us with a sucker punch, but by God we'll whip them in the end."

***

The next day, Nancy and Erin, who'd stopped by to drop off a pot of soup, sat transfixed around the radio – along with millions of other Americans – to await President Roosevelt's address to a joint session of Congress. At 12:30 p.m., President Roosevelt came on and they heard him utter those famous words: "Yesterday, December 7, 1941 – a date which will live in infamy – the United States of America was suddenly and deliberately attacked by naval and air forces of the Empire of Japan."

At the conclusion of the broadcast, Nancy turned the radio off. She'd finally accepted the fact that the country was at war, but she still had so many questions. "How long do you think it will go on?" she asked.

Erin shrugged. "I don't know. I've heard it could be as long as a year."

From the moment she'd heard about the attack on Pearl Harbor, she'd known that going to Ireland was out of the question. In a way it was a great relief. She didn't want to go back in the first place and the war gave her the perfect excuse. But she did feel a twinge of guilt that a war, which would inevitably take thousands upon thousands of lives, had become her excuse not to go. Although that decision had been taken out of her hands, it didn't solve her real problem: How to stop her sister-in-law from moving to the farm. "Do you think a year is long enough to establish nine-tenths possession?"

Erin looked up from stirring her tea. "That's a question for your lawyer, isn't it?"

***

The following evening, Nancy spoke to Kaplan about her concerns and he promised to look into it. Three weeks later, she came in to clean his office and he said, "I've been in contact with a Mr. Owen O'Donnell, a solicitor in Ireland – that's what they call their lawyers. It's all fairly technical, but the bottom line is he found a magistrate who, due to the exigent circumstances of the war, has agreed to issue what amounts to an order enjoining your sister-in-law from moving to the farm."

"Oh, that's wonderful news, Mr. Kaplan."

"It's not all wonderful, Nancy. The order will expire within six months of the end of the war. So, if you wish to pursue the case, you'll still have to go back to Ireland to do it."

Nancy nodded thoughtfully. "Well, at least I'll have a year or so to prepare myself."

Kaplan grunted. "I'm afraid you'll have a lot more than a year."

"You think the war will last longer than that?"

"Without a doubt. Germany and Italy have declared war on us. The whole world is at war. God knows when – or how – it will all end."

***

Saturday morning, Nancy was coming up from the cellar after tending the boiler when she came across Mrs. Krueger hysterically crying in the foyer. Her clothing was disheveled and her always carefully coiffed hair was in total disarray.

"Mrs. Krueger, what's the matter?"

The old woman fell into her arms. "Oh, Nancy… I have never been so… so humiliated in my life."

"What happened?"

The old woman could barely catch her voice. "I was… I was in Gristede's, doing my weekly… shopping… I…" At that, she completely broke down.

Nancy guided her up to her own apartment and made her sit down while she made tea. By the time Nancy poured the tea, Mrs. Krueger had regained her composure.

"So, Mrs. Krueger, what happened?"

The old woman grasped her tea cup with two shaky hands and took a sip. "It was terrible, Nancy. Just terrible. I was in Gristede's doing my weekly shopping and talking to that nice Mr. Braccia, the butcher, about a roast, when I was suddenly aware of voices around me. I turned. There was a woman standing behind me. I did not know her name, but I knew her from sight. I had seen her often in Gristede's. She was the kind of person you nodded to, but never really spoke to. She was talking to three other women. At first I did not understand what they were saying, but then I heard. I understood. They were saying terrible things about me. 'Why is this Nazi bitch shopping here?' one said. Then another one said, 'Why doesn't she go back to Germany to be with those filthy Nazis murderers.' Well, I protested most vehemently. 'I am not a Nazi.' I said. 'I am an American citizen.' 'You are a damn spy,' the third one shouted. 'You probably send signals to those murdering German submarines that are sinking ships off the coast of New Jersey.'

"'Nein, nein,' I said. 'I despise that man Hitler and his Nazis.' I could not listen to any more of that. Mr. Braccia had wrapped a nice roast for me. Reluctantly, I put it back on the counter and turned to leave. As I headed for the door — could you believe it, Nancy — a woman slapped my face? Then another spit on me. Spit on me. And then they physically pushed me out of the store. I fell down and tore my stockings."

The old woman looked up at Nancy with tears in her eyes. "Why did they do that to me? It is true that I was born in Dusseldorf, Germany. It is true that I speak with a German accent. But I have been in this country for more than fifty years. The proudest moment in my life was when I raised my hand to become a citizen of the United States of America. I have taught history in the New York City public school system for over forty years. In all that time, I always stressed to my students the terrible wrong that Germany did in starting World War One. Nancy, I am a citizen of the United States, the same as those women in Gristede's. How do they have the right to treat me like that?"

Nancy had no answer for the frightened old woman. She was stunned and perplexed by Mrs. Krueger's experience. Weren't she and Mrs. Krueger living in the United States of America, the land of the free, the home of the brave? How could something like that happen to a harmless old woman like Mrs. Krueger? And – Nancy felt a sudden surge of fear – if that could happen to an elderly German woman who was a naturalized American citizen, what could happen to an Irish immigrant woman?

***

In her travels to and from work, Nancy passed newsstands on almost every corner. She tried to ignore the frightening headlines, but she couldn't help seeing them. Day after day, The New York Times, The Daily News, and the other two dozen city newspapers, blasted shocking headlines in large, bold black print:

MACARTHUR UNITES HIS LINES FOR CRUCIAL STAND...

HITLER REPORTED ON EAST FRONT TO STEM ROUT...

U. S. BANS SALES OF AUTOMOBILES AND TRUCKS...

JAPANESE BOMBERS RAID WAKE ISLAND...

JAPANESE FORCES ENTER MANILA...

SOVIET FORCES LAUNCH COUNTEROFFENSIVES ALONG THE WHOLE GERMAN/RUSSIAN FRONT...

She had never heard of most of the places mentioned, but from the accompanying maps, it was clear that Isaac Kaplan was right. The whole world seemed to have gone mad and was intent on destroying itself.

***

Nancy had just put the kids to bed when there was a frantic knock at the door. She opened it to a hysterical Erin Cassidy.

She put her arm around her friend. "Erin, come in. What's the matter?"

"It's... it's Tom..." she sobbed, falling into a chair.

"Oh, no." Nancy assumed it was some kind of accident with the bus. "Has something happened to him?"

"He's... he's..." Erin's breathing was so jagged she was hiccuping. "He's... joined the Army," she blurted out.

"What? How can that be? He's a married man with two young children. They wouldn't draft him."

Erin slammed her fists on the table. "They didn't draft him. He joined."

"You mean voluntarily?"

"Aye.

"Why in the world would he do that?"

Erin took several deep breaths to bring her breathing back to normal. "I don't know what's gotten into him," she said in a shaky voice. "Since Pearl Harbor, he's been a madman, ranting day in and day out about the sneaky Japs and Hitler and the Nazis and God knows what else. He told me tonight after dinner. He said he wanted to wait until the kids were in bed." Erin sneered. "'I'm surprised you remembered you have children,' says I to him. Of course he was full of apologies, but he said it was something he had to do. He said he would feel like a coward if he stayed home while other men went off to fight the war. Nancy, what am I going to do?"

Being a woman, Nancy was at a complete loss to understand such insane behavior. Since Pearl Harbor, she'd been hearing one dismaying report after another on the radio about how thousands of men were flooding the recruiting offices, clamoring to enlist. Men with gray hair insisted they were "about thirty," while others with severe hearing loss or poor eyesight or worse debilitating ailments adamantly insisted they could function as fighting soldiers. This mad dash to go fight a war made no sense to her whatsoever. Nancy did what she always did when she was angry, sad, or confused: She made tea. By the time it was ready, Erin had calmed down.

"How will you take care of the children when he's gone?" Nancy asked, pouring the tea.

"Tom says he will send his pay, which includes a family allotment, to me. He says I should be able to get by on that."

Nancy didn't know what to say and she lapsed into silence. The radio had been on in the background all the time they'd been talking. In the ensuing silence, she suddenly heard Mayor LaGuardia's distinctive voice: "We have never had a war by a foreign enemy brought to the streets of our city. And right into our homes. The truth is that we are in serious danger. If our enemies have an opportunity to bomb our city they will do so."

Erin looked up at the radio with a defeated expression. "We're at war, aren't we, Nancy? We're really at war. And Tom is going off to fight in it."

Nancy squeezed Erin's hand. Until now, all this talk of war and men going off to fight had been so much background noise to her. But now, looking at her heartbroken friend, it had come home to her and she finally realized that the war was eventually going to touch all of them.

***

That Sunday night, Neil came to dinner. But he wasn't himself. He was exceptionally quiet, he barely ate and, unusual for him, he hardly interacted with the kids. Over tea, after the children had gone off to argue over whether or not they should listen to Superman or the Green Hornet, she said, "I think you hurt Maureen's feelings."

"How? What did I do?"

"You barely paid any attention to her. You know how she dotes on you."

"I'll apologize. I meant no harm."

"Neil, what's the matter? You're not yourself. Is there trouble on the docks?"

"No, no. We've never been busier. My God, Nancy, you wouldn't believe the amount of freight we're been loading onto the ships. It's all war goods, the kind of stuff our boys need to fight the Germans and the Japs. The docks are so busy, they've put on extra shifts. The shapeup is a thing of the past. Nowadays, everybody who wants to work gets hired. Even the drunks. Of course they try to keep them out of harm's way, but the place is a beehive of activity twenty-four hours a day."

Nancy smiled ruefully. "It's too bad Connor wasn't here to see the end of the shapeup. He hated that part of the job."

"Aye, indeed he did."

"Tom Cassidy joined the Army," Nancy blurred out, much to her surprise. She'd planned on mentioning it at some point, but not at this moment.

"He did?"

"You don't seem surprised."

"Well, he did mention it once. In fact, right here in your apartment before Connor died. At the time, I thought it was just the beer talking."

"Well, I think he's being totally irresponsible. He has a wife and two young children. He has no right to go off and fight a war and leave them to fend for themselves."

"But that's what's happening all over the country, Nancy. Men, young and old, married and single, are responding to the call."

"I suppose I can understand all that. But I don't like the idea of young men going off to fight a war and leaving behind wives and children."

Neil's whole demeanor changed and he became more serious than she'd ever seen him. "Nancy, this is war. It's not a sport where only the young participate. Our way of life in this country, our very existence, means we must fight the Germans and the Japs with everything we have until we crush them."

Nancy was stunned by the unexpected vehemence in Neil's tone. Clearly, the war had profoundly affected him as well. Neil was pensive for a long moment, and Nancy thought he might have been thinking about Connor, but then he blurted out his own announcement, "I've joined the Marines."

Nancy put her cup down so suddenly, it spilled onto the table. "In the name of God, you did what?"

"I joined the Marines, I did."

"You, too? Why would you go do a thing like that?"

"It's my patriotic duty, isn't it? This country has been good to me. Better than Ireland ever was."

Neil would never tell her, but doing his patriotic duty wasn't the only reason he'd joined the Marines. In the beginning, after Connor died, he'd convinced himself that the only reason he was spending so much time with Nancy was because he was simply doing what Connor had asked him to do, which was to look out for her and the children. But as the months went by, he realized it was something more than that. He'd tried to deny it, ignore it, excuse it, but the honest-to-god truth was that he was in love with her.

Since he'd had that shocking epiphany in the hallway a year earlier, he'd done his best to keep that thought out of his head, but he couldn't do it anymore. He'd tried desperately to work out a solution to his dilemma, but nothing was satisfactory. At first, he thought maybe he could just go on the way he'd be doing and... No, that would not work. Being so close to her without being able to tell her what he felt about her was becoming too painful to bear. Then for a time he'd convinced himself that he would just tell her how he felt and ask her to marry him. Yes, that would be best. But.... What if she said no? Worse, what if she expressed shock and horror that he could have such a mad idea? He was, after all, Connor's best friend and she was the wife of his best friend. What could he have been thinking?

The acceptable solution finally came to him the day they heard the announcement that the Japs had just bombed Pearl Harbor. When that irate man in the crowd said, "I'm going down to the recruitment station tomorrow and sign up to kill every Jap I can get my hands on," he realized that was the solution. It was the perfect excuse to get away from her. It would give him – and hopefully her – time to decide how they felt about each other. He hated leaving her, but he consoled himself with the thought that it would only be for a year or so.

The sound of Nancy's voice pulled him out of his musing. "But aren't you too—" Nancy stopped and bit her lip, but Neil knew what she was about to say.

"Too old to fight? That's what the recruiting station said, too. Right now they're just taking the younger ones, but that'll change soon. I told them I was only thirty-three, in fine condition, single, and ready and willing to go over there and kill those bastards. They signed me up."

"But why the Marines, Neil? Nora's gone out with a few of them and she said they were all daft."

Neil looked a little sheepish. "Ach, there were lines for all the services, but the line for the Marines was the shortest. You know how I hate standing in line."

Nancy laughed in spite of herself. "I suspect you'll be standing in a lot of lines for some time to come."

Neil grinned. "Aye. I suppose I will."

"When do you go?"

"Five o'clock Sunday morning I'm to be at Penn Station to board a train to some place called Camp Lejeune."

"In the name of God, where is that?"

"North Carolina, I think. Or is it South Carolina? I'm not entirely sure. Anyways, it's going to be interesting," he said, trying to put a brave face on it. "Do you know I've been in this country almost twelve years and I've never been outside New York City once? It's going to be a great adventure I'm going on."

***

After Neil left and she'd put the kids to bed, she went into the kitchen and made herself another cup of tea. On nights when she was at home, away from the cleaning job, she savored the quiet time, because it was a time when she could be alone with her thoughts without fear of being interrupted by the clamor of the children or the intrusions of the outside world.

Allowing herself this time of reflection had been a long time in coming. For months after his death, she would not permit any thought of Connor or their past lives to intrude into her consciousness. It was simply too painful. But as the months went by and the pain dulled, she slowly permitted those thoughts to return. She had even come to enjoy them.

These quiet times allowed her to reflect on her life – to think about where she was now and to think about where she would be in the future. It was also a time to remember the most tender memories of her life with Connor. Mostly she strove to recall the good times in their lives, but sometimes questions that were cruel and lacerating welled up in her. And those questions always centered around his last night on earth. Why, she would ask herself, did he decide to walk to the hospital on such a terrible night? And then the other questions would inevitably follow. Why didn't he take the subway? Why didn't he leave two minutes earlier? Or two minutes later? A couple of minutes either way and he would never have collided with that car on Fifth Avenue. And when she was feeling especially dispirited, she would ask the final cruel, accusatory question – how could he have done this to her and the children?

But tonight, she was thinking about other things. She sipped her tea and tried to sort out the muddle of emotions she was feeling. She was still ambivalent about going back to Ireland, and that had been uppermost in her mind, but now she had to contend with Neil's shocking announcement. He was going off to war.

Of course she knew thousands of men were joining the services, but for some reason she'd just assumed that he would always be here. How long would he be gone? she wondered. What if he didn't come back? What if he died in one of those exotic-sounding places whose names she could barely pronounce or for the life of her pick out on a map?

It occurred to her that since Connor's death, she'd come more and more to rely on Neil. Sometimes it made her feel guilty, because she knew he wasn't getting any younger and instead of spending all his time with her and the children, he should have been out looking for a nice young girl to marry and settle down with. It was selfish on her part, she knew, but he was a great comfort to her – calm, steady, always ready to lend a helping hand. Up until now, she'd considered him a good friend and counted herself lucky to have him, but now, tonight, for the first time, she had to face what she'd been hiding from herself for a long time. Tears welled up in her eyes. "I'm sorry, Connor," she whispered softly, hardly able to believe what she was saying, "but I think I've fallen in love with your best friend."

CHAPTER ELEVEN

Early Sunday morning, Nancy went with Neil to Penn Station to see him off. He didn't want her to come, but she'd insisted. Even at this hour, the cavernous train station was surprisingly crowded and bustling with activity. Mostly it was men in the uniforms representing the Marines, Army, Navy, and Coast Guard who hurried toward trains that would take them to their bases and ships. Here and there in the crowd were men in uniforms Nancy didn't recognize. She assumed they were soldiers from our allied countries.

A Marine, guarding the entrance to the track, snapped to attention and said, "Sorry, ma'am, only authorized ticketed personnel permitted beyond this point."

Nancy was relieved. It would be easier saying goodbye here. She had seen too many movies with tearful train station goodbyes and she knew she would not be able to keep from crying.

"Well," she said, straightening his tie. I guess this is it."

"Aye." Neil watched a group of men, suitcase and bags in hand, streaming past him and showing their tickets to the guard. He assumed they were all going where he was going. He couldn't help noticing that they all looked a lot younger than he did and he began to wonder if he'd made a mistake.

An announcer said, "Final boarding on track twelve for Washington and points south. All aboard."

Neil picked up his suitcase. "Well. I guess I'll be going then."

Nancy kissed him. "Neil, you take care of yourself."

"I will."

"And write."

"I will."

"And make sure you eat."

"I will."

And then he was gone. She watched him race down the track and board the train. She stood there for a long time after the train pulled out of the station. She'd promised herself she wouldn't cry, but, nevertheless, tears streamed down her cheeks.

***

On the way back from Penn Station, Nancy bumped into Erin Cassidy outside their walk-up. Tom was gone only a couple of weeks, but Erin looked terrible. She'd always been outgoing, exuberant, someone ready for a good laugh. But in just two short weeks she'd changed dramatically, becoming extremely quiet, almost morose. Nora noticed the change, too, and had offered to babysit the kids so Nancy and Erin could go to a picture show to take her mind off her husband going off to war, but Erin always begged off, citing a headache or some other made-up excuse. It was almost as though she didn't want to – or, in her mind, shouldn't – have fun as long as her Tom was off fighting the war.

Nancy hugged her. "Erin, how are you doing?"

"I'm all right, Nancy, really, I am." But her wan smile belied her true feelings. "My Mom came in from Brooklyn to spend the weekend with me and the kids. She's been great. I'm so blessed that I have a mother who would…" Her eyes filled with tears. "Oh, Nancy, it's so hard getting used to Tom being away. I wake up in the middle of the night and reach out to him, but he's not there in bed next to me and I…"

Nancy pulled her close. "I know, I know. It must be so difficult." But of course she couldn't know how difficult it was. Neil wasn't gone more than an hour and she missed him already. But she couldn't imagine what it must be to have a husband go off to war. "Have you heard from Tom?"

"No, and I'm concerned."

"Oh, I wouldn't worry about it. He's probably so busy with the training and such. I'm sure you'll hear from him as soon as he can find the time."

"You're right. I'm sure he will." She wiped the tears from her eyes. "So what are you doing up and about so early?"

"I've just come from Penn Station. I was there to see Neil off."

"Neil? Where is he going?"

"He joined the Marines. He's off to some camp in North Carolina."

Tears welled up in Erin's eyes. "Oh, no…. Another one gone off to war. Nancy, when will this madness end?"

That was a question that Nancy had been asking herself with no satisfactory answer forthcoming. "Neil thinks a year or so." She patted Erin's hand. "Sure it'll be over before you know it and when Tom and Neil come home we'll have a great party. Won't that be grand?"

Erin's smile was wistful. "Aye, that'll be grand."

"Erin, as long as your mother's here to watch the children, why don't you come by tonight and have a cup of tea with me and Nora?"

"Oh, I'd love to, Nancy, but I have to write a letter to my sister in Chicago."

"Oh, all right. Maybe another time."

"Aye. Another time."

As Nancy went into the vestibule of her apartment building, a thought occurred to her: I never heard Erin mention a sister in Chicago.

***

When Nancy came into the apartment, Nora was giving her three, very unhappy children breakfast in the kitchen.

"Did Donal eat?" she asked.

"Yes, he did. Maureen gave him his morning bottle and now he's asleep."

Maureen looked up from her cereal, her eyes moist with tears. "Is Neil gone?"

"My God, Maureen, you make it sound like he's dead. He's on the train to North Carolina and he's fine."

"Is he going to die?" an ashen-faced Patrick asked.

A lump stuck in Nancy's throat. She knew he was thinking about his father. "No, Patrick, Neil is not going to die."

"He knows how to take care of himself, doesn't he Mommy?" Fiona asked with heartbreaking hopefulness.

"Yes, he does. Besides, he's just gone into the service and there's a whole lot of training he's going to get before they send him anywhere. So don't worry about him."

Initially, Neil's announcement that he'd joined the Marines had come as a complete shock to her personally, but now she worried about the effect his going away would have on the children. For as long the kids could remember, Neil had always been there, the favorite uncle, the one who brought them Chiclets and played with them. After Connor died, she noticed a subtle change in their behavior. Slowly, quietly, they began to look upon Neil as their surrogate father. Nancy saw no harm in it. After all, they could certainly use a male adult figure in their lives, but she never dreamed that he would leave them to go off to war. She knew the children would miss him terribly, perhaps even more than she would.

Anticipating their sense of loss at Neil's leaving, Nancy opened her purse and took out a map she'd bought on the way home. She spread it out on the floor. "Look at this. It's a map of the world. I'll pin it to a wall and when we find out where Neil is going, we'll stick little pins on the map so we can keep track of where he is. Now go see if you can find Germany and Japan."

The children excitedly grabbed the map and ran off to the living room.

Nora poured Nancy a cup of tea and sat down opposite her. "Well?" she asked with a slight smirk.

"Well, what?"

"You know perfectly well what I'm talking about. Did he ask you to marry him?"

"Are you daft?"

"You were expecting him to ask, weren't you?"

Nancy shrugged. "I was expecting nothing of the kind. He's never even hinted at such a thing."

"He doesn't have to hint. Just one look at him and you can tell he's madly in love with you."

"You have an overactive imagination, Nora."

The truth was, she wasn't expecting him to ask her, but she wouldn't have been too surprised if he had. Still, she decided it was best this way. She knew a lot of young people were getting married before the men shipped overseas. But she thought that was a bad idea. What if they were killed? The thought was too appalling for Nancy to contemplate. She couldn't imagine living through the death of another husband.

***

It was early February and Nancy had just gotten the kids off to school when there was a frantic knocking at the door. She opened it to a wide-eyed Erin Cassidy.

"Have you heard the news?" she said breathlessly.

Nancy's heard sank. "No... What news?"

"It's been on the radio. A great big ship over on Pier 88 was set on fire and it capsized right there at the pier."

Nancy breathed a sigh of relief. She'd thought it might be something to do with Neil. "Oh, my. Do they know what started the fire?"

"They were converting the ocean liner to a troop ship. There're saying it was sparks from a welding torch, but I don't believe that." She lowered her voice and actually looked over her shoulder. "I think it was sabotage."

"Really?" Nancy was becoming alarmed at her friend's behavior. She was becoming increasingly obsessed about anything to do with the war, seeing intrigues and plots everywhere. "Why do you say that, Erin?"

"Didn't a German submarine torpedo and sink a passenger freighter just a couple of hundred miles off Cape Hatteras in North Carolina? Who's to say there aren't more German saboteurs crawling all over the city like rats just waiting to set fire to another ship or blow up a bridge or do whatever it is that they've been trained to do."

"Well, I'm sure the FBI will thoroughly investigate the fire."

"I hope so." She seemed to find that reassuring. Then she remembered something that set her off again. "Nancy, did you know they have Mickey Mouse gas masks for children?"

"No, I didn't."

"They do. So children won't be afraid of them." Tears welled up in her eyes. "What's to become us? Mickey Mouse gas masks for children? What's next? Little machine guns?"

Nancy laughed. "I don't think so."

"Well, what about those identification tags the children have to wear to school? They're like little dog tags. Do you know why they have to wear them?" Tears slid down her cheeks. "In case the school is bombed, they'll be able to identify the little bodies."

Nancy squeezed her friend's hand. "Erin, it's all just a precaution. There's a great big ocean between us and the Germans. No one is going to bomb our children or our schools."

"That's what I pray for night and day." She sniffed and stood up. "Well, I've got to get back downstairs. I just wanted to tell you."

"Thank you, Erin."

After Erin left, Nancy put the radio on to get the latest news. The lead story was about the ship fire. The announcer said, "Today the ship, SS Normandie caught fire on a Manhattan pier and eventually capsized. Officials say sparks from a welding torch ignited a stack of life vests filled with kapok, a highly flammable material. It's been reported that the ship capsized due to the heavy volume of water pumped into her from fire boats."

Nancy turned the radio off when she found herself wondering if the "officials," whoever they were, were telling the truth. The war, she decided, was making everyone paranoid.

***

It had been almost a month since Neil left and she was finally getting used to him not being there. But she did miss him, more than she thought she would. There were times when she would have sworn she heard his footsteps on the stairs only to discover it was someone else. More than once on the street, she thought she'd caught a glimpse of him in a crowd, but, of course, it wasn't him. Slowly, Nancy slipped back into her routine of tending to the children and working. At least working conditions were better now that Mrs. Reardon had left for a better paying job in a factory in New Jersey. The new supervisor was a much kinder woman.

Since Pearl Harbor, Nancy had tried her best to block out news of the war. It was just too depressing and far too confusing. But it proved to be impossible. Every store she went into had their radios tuned to the news. Even the movie theaters gave regular reports, sometimes interrupting the picture to do it. And if she missed a news bulletin, she could count on someone like Nora or Erin to come rushing breathlessly into the apartment to give her the latest update.

During the month of February 1942, judging from the newspaper headlines, the progress of the war was not good. The Japanese had bombed Java. It took Nancy and the kids almost a half hour to find Java on the map. Later that month, much to her distress, President Roosevelt ordered the detention and of all west-coast Japanese-Americans. What did that mean for the Irish? She had heard that Ireland was neutral, but others said it was pro-German. Much to her relief, a smiling Isaac Kaplan assured her that Franklin Roosevelt had no intention of locking up all the Irish in the United States. And then there were the frightening events right here in the states. She'd heard reports that a Japanese sub had fired on an oil refinery in Ellwood, California. Nancy hardly knew what to make of it all.

***

It was early in the spring of 1942 when Nancy opened her mailbox and saw an official-looking envelope from the federal government. And her heart stopped. On Kaplan's advice, she'd never followed-up on that dreadful lawyer's allegation that Connor had entered the country illegally. Kaplan had assured her that Connor's legal status had absolutely no bearing on her or her children and now that he was dead it was a moot point. Still, since then, she'd been troubled with the feeling that someday the government might come after her. With mounting dread, she tore open the envelope and heaved a sigh of relief when she saw that the letter was from a federal agency called the U.S. Office of Price Administration. The contents of the letter perplexed her. Something called "rationing," the letter informed her, was about to begin.

A week after she received the letter, Nancy, along with Nora and Erin, who'd received the same letter, reported to the newly opened Rationing Board downtown. After a great deal of confusion and misdirection to endless lines, they were issued ration books. To Nancy's surprise, Erin and she were issued separate books for each of the children, even Donal.

Back at the apartment, the three women sat around the kitchen table examining the strange books filled with twenty-eight little stamps with pictures of tanks and airplanes and boats.

Erin studied her stamps with a puzzled expression. "It doesn't say what the stamps are for. Shouldn't they have little pictures of meat and sugar on them? I'm not planning on buying a tank or an airplane."

Nancy shrugged, as puzzled as her friend.

Nora read from a list of instructions that came with the rationing card. "It says here that a can of peas is sixteen points. That sounds very dear, but I don't care. I don't like peas anyways."

Nancy was reading her instructions. "But you like peaches, don't you?"

"I do."

"Well, that's twenty-one points a can."

"Oh, for God's sake."

Erin's eyes swept down the list. "It looks like everything is going to be rationed – sugar, coffee, meat, nylons—"

"Nylons!" Nora exclaimed. "Now they've gone too far. The nylons I have are in shreds. What am I to do?"

"I heard some girls are staining their legs with tea juice."

"That's disgusting." Nora examined the back of her ration card. "Look at these little red and blue things. What do you think they're for?"

"They're ration coins."

"How do you use them?"

"I think it's like change," Erin said. "If you don't use the entire coupon, you get these little things as change."

Nora shook her head. "This is all too complicated for me."

"Well, you'd better get used to it," Nancy said, a bit overwhelmed herself. "I think we'll be doing this till the war is over."

***

And that was just the beginning of rationing. As the war proceeded, more and more food and material was needed to feed the insatiable engine of the war. Soon, just about everything was rationed. The point system for buying food and goods became so complicated that newspapers began to publish charts to help the average person navigate the increasingly byzantine rules and regulations of the Office of Price Administration.

By June of 1942, things finally started looking up on the warfront. Nancy was heartened by the news that the Japanese were defeated at the battle of Midway, which all the papers said was a turning point in the war. It was the first good news she'd heard since the start of the war.

It took her and the children only fifteen minutes to find Midway on the map. She was getting much better at geography. But just when she was beginning to feel good about America turning the tide of the war, she read in the papers that the FBI had captured eight Nazi saboteurs from a submarine off the coast of Long Island. Long Island? My God! That was less than thirty miles from New York City!

At the end of June, she got her first letter from Neil. He'd been away for six months, and she'd been a little more than disappointed that he hadn't written. But he explained that his unit was under blackout orders and they were not permitted to write letters. He did tell her that his unit was shipping out to a Hawaiian island called Maui for additional training. Her heart skipped a beat. My God, the Hawaiian Islands, she realized, was where Pearl

Harbor was. With a sinking feeling, it occurred to her that he was moving closer and closer to the war and into harm's way. Masking her anxiety, she called the children together and told them that Neil was on his way to Hawaii. Together, they found Maui and stuck in their second pin showing where Neil had gone.

With his finger, Patrick traced the path from North Carolina to Maui. "Wow, Uncle Neil has traveled a long way."

"He has," Nancy said. "Over six thousand miles."

After the children were asleep, Nancy tiptoed into the girl's bedroom and examined the map more closely. The Hawaiian Islands were a small, insignificant cluster of dots in the middle of the vast Pacific Ocean. She was relieved to see that Neil was completely isolated, thousands of miles from anywhere dangerous. But then her eyes swept west and her stomach turned. Suddenly, it was as clear to her as the nose on her face. The western Pacific was a series of islands, some of which, like Midway and Wake, had already been the center of great battles. But there were more – the Marshall Islands, the Marianas, Guam, Guadalcanal in the Solomons. And like stepping-stones, these chains of islands led to one place – Japan. With an eerie, almost supernatural prescience, she saw the future of the war in the Pacific. The Marines, with Neil being one of them, would have to fight their way across all those islands until they could get to Japan. Lord, she wondered, how could he survive all that?

***

In early August of 1942, Donal was four months shy of two. He was too young to understand anything about the war, but he was fixated on one thing – the ration books. The colorful stamps and tokens fascinated him. One day Nancy came into the kitchen and was horrified to see a grinning Donal sitting on the floor surrounded by stamps that he had methodically torn from the ration book, thereby rendering them worthless. To prevent black-marketing, the Office of Price Administration had established an ironclad rule: Stamps must be torn out of the book in the presence of a shopkeeper. Otherwise they were invalid. That day, Nancy spent the better part of an afternoon at the Rationing Board Office explaining what Donal had done. After much discussion and consultation, she was issued another ration book and instructed to see to it that it was kept away from mischievous little hands.

CHAPTER TWELVE

A new word began popping up on the radio and in the newspapers – recycling. As the war progressed, civilians were asked to collect all kinds of metal – from old ice skates to frying pans – for scrap metal drives.

Maureen, Fiona, and Patrick, now eight, seven, and six, had gotten right into the spirit of scrap collection. Weekly, Maureen organized her brother and sister and they set out through the neighborhood on scavenger hunts to collect old newspapers, bits of rubber, and tinfoil, which they turned in to the neighborhood scrap collection center. Patrick's enthusiasm for collecting tinfoil knew no bounds and before long he had a ball of tinfoil the size of a grapefruit.

***

Sunday afternoon, Nora arrives for tea feeling very sorry for herself. "Nancy," she lamented, "this war is ruining my life. I go to the dances, but I don't know why I bother. The men I meet are either too old, too married, or too stupid. All the good ones have gone off to war."

Nancy sympathized with her. There were times when she felt sorry for herself, being a young widow with four small children and unable to go out once in a while to have a good time. But listening to Nora, she was happy to be away from that sort of thing.

The kids came into the kitchen buttoning their coats. "We're off to collect newspapers," Maureen announced.

"Use it up, wear it out, make it do, or do without," Patrick announced.

"And where did you hear that?" an amused Nancy asked.

"It's on the radio. Everybody says it."

"Sunday's the best day," Fiona said. "The Sunday papers are always bigger."

"All right," Nancy said, helping Fiona button her coat. "Be back here no later than four."

Nora listened to the fading sound of the children's footsteps on the stairs. Then she said suddenly, "Do you know where Neil is?"

"No, I don't. The last I heard he was in Hawaii."

Nora took a copy of the New York Times out of her bag and slipped it across the table. "It's from last Tuesday."

Nancy scanned the headlines. American Forces Make Landings in Solomons. "That place sounds familiar, but I'm not sure where it is. I'll have to look for it on the map." Then she saw a smaller headline underneath and her stomach turned. Marines On Shore. "Oh, my…"

Preferring The Daily News and The Daily Mirror, she was not a Times reader and the layout of the front page confused her. There were a whole series of headlines one on top of the other with the print getting smaller and smaller toward the bottom, which seemed peculiar to Nancy, because the message these headlines conveyed was anything but small. Fighting Is Heavy After Surprise of Japanese in Tulagi Region. And then the next one, which took her breath away – Price Is High, King Warns. "Who is King?"

"I think he's some kind of admiral or something. I can't keep track of all the names and places. It hurts my head."

Feeling a numbness come over her, she read the final smaller-print headline. Admiral Says U.S. Loss May Be Severe. Nancy studied a drawing accompanying the story showing a long and skinny island called Guadalcanal. It didn't look like much and she wondered why in the world the Marines would bother to attack it.

Nancy and Nora went into the girl's bedroom to look for it on the map. She was getting much better at finding things. At least now she knew to look in the Pacific Ocean instead of the Atlantic.

And when she found Guadalcanal she realized that her intuition was correct. It was the first stepping-stone to Japan.

Nora looked over her shoulder. "Do you think Neil is there?"

"I don't know. I hope not." But she had a nagging feeling that that was exactly where he was. The question was: Was he dead or alive?

***

It was a crisp, fall afternoon in late September of 1942, when Nancy and the kids got back from the local Rationing Board with five new books. She was finally getting the hang of using the books' complicated point system, but at the Rationing Board she received bad news. In January a new rationing book would be issued with all new rules.

As they approached the apartment building, Fiona tugged at Nancy's handbag. "Mommy, give me the mailbox key, it's my turn."

With key in hand, Fiona ran ahead. By the time Nancy and the other kids came into the foyer, Fiona had opened the box and was waving an envelope in the air. "You have a letter, Mommy."

Nancy glanced at the return address. It was from Neil, but her stomach knotted when she studied the handwriting. It wasn't his. She stuffed the envelope into her handbag.

"Who is it from?" Maureen asked.

"It's nothing. Just a letter."

All day long, Nancy could think of nothing else but the letter, but she dared not open it in front of the children for fear that it might be bad news. His name was on it, so obviously he was alive, but if he didn't write it, he must be terribly injured. In spite of herself, her mind conjured up the most horrible injuries imaginable – he'd received terrible burns... he'd lost an arm or leg... or even worse, he'd had a severe head injury and his mind was gone....

Finally, after dinner she couldn't take it any longer. Ignoring their loud protests and whining, she made the children go to bed a half hour earlier than usual. When she was sure they were asleep, she made herself a cup of tea, forced herself to remain calm, and with shaking hand opened the letter.

Dear Nancy,

I hope all is well with you and the children. As you can probably tell, this is not my handwriting. Nurse Milano was kind enough to write it for me, as both my hands are wrapped in bandages. Don't worry. I'm all right. I was standing too close to a tank that got blown-up and I was burned – mostly my hands. It's not a million-dollar wound – that's the kind of wound that is serious enough to get you sent back to the States, but not serious enough to make you a cripple. No such luck. Whatever happened to the luck of the Irish, I wonder? The doctors tell me I will live to fight another day, but will probably be in the hospital for a few more weeks. I'm sorry, but I'm not allowed to say where I was or where I'll be going. The Marines have a fearful amount of rules, but I'm with a good bunch of guys. They call me "Pops". Can you imagine that and me only thirty-four? Well, anyway, I'll close now. You can write me at the return address on the envelope. Give my love to Maureen, Fiona, Patrick, and Donal. He must be getting as big as a barn.

Love, Neil

Nancy read the letter several more times, but her eyes always stopped at the words both my hands are wrapped in bandages and I was burned. It sounded as though he was all right, but she knew him. If he wasn't all right, he would never say so. Now she wondered should she tell the children the truth or just make up something?

The next morning at breakfast, she split the difference. "That letter was from your Uncle Neil," she said, casually. "He told me he burned his hands on a hot engine. They put him in the hospital for awhile, but he'll be good as new in no time."

To her immense relief they accepted her story without question.

***

Nancy awaited the approach of Thanksgiving with growing trepidation. This was going to be the first Thanksgiving the children would have with neither their father nor Neil present. She so wanted to make a festive meal for them, but it proved to be impossible. Every day the shortage of food grew worse. Having ration stamps was no guarantee that you would be able to find what you were allowed to buy. Fresh vegetables were out of the question. She hadn't seen them in the stores in months. People who owned their own homes or who had access to a little patch of dirt planted "Victory Gardens" where they could raise their own vegetables. More and more, Nancy found herself thinking about the farm in Ireland. And not without a little irony. Connor had said it wasn't a big farm, but at least there she could have planted a garden and fed her children fresh vegetables, instead of the watery and tasteless stuff that came out of a can.

It was impossible to buy a turkey, but Nora came through with a scrawny chicken. She was very mysterious about the circumstances of how she came into possession of the bird and Nancy assumed she'd gotten in on the black market, the same place she got her nylons.

Dinner was a meager and sorry affair, but the children didn't seem to notice. After Nora had gone home and the children were in bed, Nancy made herself a cup of tea. She glanced at the calendar over the stove and her heart sank. In less than two weeks it would be December again. Last December was pure madness, what with her deciding on the spur of the moment to go to Ireland and then not being able to go because of the war. What, she wondered, would this December bring?

***

December brought neither tragedy nor joy, just the same aching loss of Connor that seemed more acute in the month that he died. And it also brought those same accusatory questions that always seemed to arise late in the night. For the sake of the children, Nancy was determined to stay positive and cheerful. But it wasn't always easy. Since Nora had shown her the Times article about Guadalcanal, she'd gotten into the habit of stopping at the corner newsstand every day and reading The Times' front page. Mostly the headlines were about places in Africa and Europe that she'd never heard of, but on December 7th, the first anniversary of the attack on Pearl Harbor, her eye caught a small headline that made her heart pound: Nimitz Looks to Taking War into Home Waters of Japan.

Would Neil be part of that? She understood the reasons why he was not allowed to say where he was going, but, still, it was maddening not knowing where he was. Since that first letter, he'd written her at least twice a week. The letters were always optimistic, but they were exasperatingly vague. He was getting better, he'd said, but the doctors had decided to keep him in the hospital "a while longer." She studied those letters, looking for hidden answers. Why were they keeping him in the hospital? Was he in pain? Was he permanently crippled? But it was no use. Try as she might, she couldn't sift any clues from his bland words.

***

On New Year's Day, Nora dragged herself into the apartment looking tired and hung-over. She had tried to talk Nancy into going to Times Square to ring in the New Year, but Nancy, even assuming she could have found someone to watch the kids, was in no mood for celebration.

Judging by the way Nora looked, Nancy was glad she hadn't gone. "So how was Times Square last night?" she asked, slightly amused at her friend's hangdog appearance.

"Very odd. You were right not to come. If I'd had any sense, I'd have stayed home myself. There was a mob of people, and an awful lot of teenage boys and girls. I didn't go there to meet teenagers; I can tell you that. It was all very sad, actually, to watch everyone blowing on old, second-hand horns with no gusto at all."

"They shouldn't have had those horns. They should have gone to the recycling center." Nancy was surprised by her severe tone. Her children had become sticklers for recycling everything and it was rubbing off on her.

"There was no gayety," Nora said, glumly. "I suppose that's to be expected, what with the war and all. Still…"

"Did you stay to see the ball come down?"

"I did. And it didn't."

"What do you mean?"

"Well, there it was. Midnight. The entire crowd stood breathless, waiting for the glowing white ball to come down the flag staff on top of the New York Times tower. But it never did."

"What happened?"

"Instead of the glowing white ball, silent bands of lights from plane-spotter stations around the edge of the city crisscrossed their beams in the sky. This, mind you, happened just at the stroke of midnight. Well, we didn't know what to make of it. We just stood there, mouths agape, absolutely silent. It took a few seconds for us to finally realize what those searchlights meant. There would be no ball drop. The searchlights would have to do. Well, you wouldn't believe the god-awful din of horns and cowbells that followed. Later, I heard someone say that last night was the first New Year's Eve since 1908 that no ball fell to signal the end of the old year and the beginning of the new." Nora smiled ruefully. "I suppose you could say I've witnessed an historic event. So maybe it wasn't a total loss after all."

The smile faded. "Nancy, what happened next was so moving, it made me cry. Over a loudspeaker, a man in a radio station's sound truck asked for ten seconds of silence for our young men serving overseas." Nora squeezed Nancy's hand. "It was a sight to behold. All the horn-tooting and cowbell noise stopped immediately. Men took off their hats and the women quit their laughing. But farther away, on the outer fringes of the crowd, they didn't hear the announcement. The horns kept blowing and the bells kept ringing. It seemed so disrespectful, but of course they didn't hear the announcement."

Nora's eyes filled with tears. "And then, a woman's beautiful, clear voice started singing The Star-Spangled Banner. Everyone joined in. It was absolutely stunning."

Nora snapped out of her reverie and she dug into her handbag. "Oh, I almost forgot." She pulled out a copy of The Journal American.

Nancy bit her lip and stared at the newspaper, wondering if it was something that might concern Neil.

"Look, Nancy," Nora pointed to an ad in the classified section of the paper, "they're hiring women to work in a factory in College Point."

"Where's that?"

"Queens."

"What kind of work?"

Nora read from the ad. "It says here the plant manufactures mess kits."

Nancy shook her head. "What's a mess kit?"

"I have no idea, but the pay is grand. Who cares what they make."

Nancy studied the ad and her eyes widened. The salary they were offering was more than twice what she was making as a cleaning woman. And now she understood what had been happening at work. It had started with Mrs. Reardon, but now, almost every night she went to work, she heard that another of her coworkers had left for a better paying job in a factory. With the men off to war and production increasing to twenty-four hours a day, employers had to turn to women to fill the worker gap.

"Well, Nancy, what do you think?"

"I think we should it."

CHAPTER THIRTEEN

Monday morning, right after Nancy took the three older kids to school and left Donal with Erin Cassidy, she and Nora took the subway and the bus out to College Point. It was almost a mile walk from the bus stop to the factory located in a rundown industrial section. They stopped in front of a dreary red-bricked building and looked up uneasily.

"Is this it?" Nancy asked, doubt creeping into her voice.

Nora checked the address in the paper. "It is."

"It's very dirty, isn't it?" Nancy noted.

"It is. It looks like the windows haven't been cleaned since the last war. What do you think?"

"Well, we're here. We might as well go in and see what the job is all about."

The guard at the front gate placed a call and soon a short, grim looking man appeared.

"I'm Mr. Carboy, the assistant factory manager." He eyed the two prospective employees with undisguised misgiving. "Are either one of you currently working in a defense-related job? Because if you are, I can't hire you. It's against the law."

Nancy shook her head.

"I don't think waitressing at Schrafft's qualifies as defense-related work," Nora said with a big smile.

Carboy grunted, failing to see the humor. "Very well. Come with me."

Nancy and Nora practically had to run to keep up with the little man, who led them down a long dark hall and into a cramped office. From behind his desk he studied them through thick wire-rimmed glasses, trying to decide if they'd lied to him about the defense work. Finally allaying his suspicions, he said, "Have either of you ever done assembly line work?"

"I'm a waitress," Nora answered hopefully.

"That's hardly assembly line work, is it?"

"It is where I work," she said, giving him her best grin.

Carboy grunted again and turned to Nancy. "What about you?"

"Cleaning. I clean offices in a building downtown."

He shook his head in dismay. "It's too bad neither one of you have any experience. Assembly line work is hard. You stand all day, it's noisy, it's a nine-hour-day with a half hour for lunch. I don't think you women are suitable for such a job."

Nancy couldn't help but notice that he practically spat out the word "women." She'd heard women at her cleaning job complain about not getting hired for a factory job because it was clear that the men doing the hiring wanted only men for the job. One had even gone so far as to point out that a woman's place was in the home, not the workplace. It seemed ridiculous to Nancy. There was a war on and most of the men were in the service. If they didn't want to hire women, who would they hire?

Just then the door opened and a man with bushy black hair came into the office.

Carboy jumped up as though he'd just gotten an electrical shock. "Oh, Mr. Kane. I was just using your office to—"

"That's all right, Stanley." He looked at Nancy and Nora in a boldly appraising way. "Who have we here?"

Out of the corner of her eye, Nancy saw Nora preening herself. Obviously, she found him attractive. Nancy had to admit he was reasonably good looking – in a sleazy sort of way. Like one of those Hollywood slimy types who always treated the girl badly by the end of the movie. She'd noticed him while they were following Carboy to his office – or rather Mr. Kane's office – he'd been talking to three men at the other end of the hallway, but he'd followed them with his eyes.

"I was just telling them that they're not suited for the job, Mr. Kane."

Kane shook his head. "Stanley, Stanley, this is now what, the fifth and sixth woman this month that you have found not suited for the job?"

"But they've never done assembly line work," Carboy protested.

"Stanley, we need to fill the slots and these two young ladies look more than able. They're hired." He offered his hand to Nancy. "I'm Ralph Kane, the manager of the plant."

There was something about him that made Nancy suddenly uncomfortable. Was it her imagination or did he hold her hand a bit longer than necessary? Up close she also noticed that he was older than he'd first appeared and she was sure his hair was dyed.

"Stanley, show these young ladies around the plant."

Clearly defeated, a tight-lipped Carboy muttered, "Follow me."

She'd just gotten the job, but already Nancy was beginning to have doubts. Would Carboy give her trouble the way Mrs. Reardon had when she'd first taken the cleaning job? Her new supervisor, Mrs. Booker, was very kind. On the other hand, this job paid a lot more. In the end, it wasn't much of a dilemma. Of course she would take the higher paying job. She'd just have to deal with Mr. Carboy.

He led them onto the factory floor. Nancy thought he'd been exaggerating about the noise, but he wasn't. The cavernous room was a frightening clamor of hissing stamp presses, rhythmic rivet punchers, and clanging metal. A conveyor belt snaking across the factory floor was manned by dozens of busy workers — almost all men.

Up until now, Nora had not said a word. Nancy couldn't tell if she just was overawed by it all or she had nothing to say, which was not like her. Finally, she shouted over the din, "Mr. Carboy, what is a mess kit?"

Carboy, rolling his eyes, snatched a metal, oval-shaped item off the conveyor belt. "We make these for the Army and the Marines," he bellowed. He snapped the device open and they saw that it consisted of two halves. The deeper half formed a shallow, flat-bottom. To Nancy and Nora's surprise, it looked very much like a frying pan with a handle.

"This is the M-1942 divided pan-and-body stainless steel system. It comes with utensils – a knife, a fork, and a spoon." He pointed at another conveyor belt. "As part of the complete kit, we also produce a stamped cup especially molded to fit over the bottom of a military standard one-quart canteen."

Nancy looked over the busy floor at the noisy, hissing machines moving up and down, bewildered. "What will we be doing?"

"I'll start you both off in the packing section. As the kits come off the assembly line, you pack them into boxes. You should be able to handle that," he added dismissively. He glanced at his watch. "I have to go. You start Monday. Be here nine o'clock sharp."

***

"What do you think?" Nancy asked, when they finally got on the subway to Manhattan.

"I think he's real dreamy."

"Who?"

"Mr. Kane."

"I was talking about the job."

"Oh, that. I don't like it, but it's better than waitressing at Schrafft's. Since the war, we haven't been as busy and tips are really bad."

"I'm not nuts about the job either. The pay is very good, but I don't like that Mr. Carboy one bit."

"He doesn't like you either – or me. Come to think about it, I don't think he likes women period. Not like that dreamy Mr. Kane."

"Nora, I have an odd feeling about him and I'd stay away from him if I were you."

"Well, fortunately, you're not me. Nancy, for God's sake, he's the first man I've seen in a dog's age who wasn't old or queer. My love life is a complete shamble."

Nancy said no more. She knew once Nora got something in her head, there was no talking her out of it.

***

That night, Nancy went to her cleaning job feeling apprehensive and guilty. The cleaning crew had been shorthanded for months because so many women – as Nancy was about to do – had left for higher paying factory jobs. She dreaded telling Mrs. Booker she was leaving. The woman had been so kind to her, even allowing her to go home early that night Donal got sick. That was something that Mrs. Reardon would never have allowed.

When she came off the elevator in the basement, she saw Mrs. Booker talking to Mr. Kean, the manager of custodial services for the building. She'd seen him from time to time, but she'd never spoken to him.

Kean looked up. "Ah, Mrs. Cavanaugh, we were just talking about you."

***

Nancy sat in Mr. Kean's office and stared at both of them in disbelief. Her mind reeled as she tried to absorb what he'd just told her. "So, Mrs. Booker is leaving," she said, trying to make sure she'd heard him correctly. "Is that what you're saying, Mr. Kean?"

"Yes. She's going to babysit her grandchildren while her daughter goes to work. And I'm offering her supervisor's position to you. It'll pay twenty percent more an hour. You're a good worker, Nancy, and you deserve the promotion."

Good God! In her wildest dreams, she would not have expected this. Tonight, her only concern had been how she was going to break it to Mrs. Booker that she was leaving. She never dreamed that she would be offered a supervisor's job. Could she do the job? Of course she could. There was not a doubt in her mind. But that wasn't the question. The real question was: Did she want to do it? And there was no easy answer to that one. As a supervisor, the pay would be much better, but it was still not as good as the factory job making mess kits. It was certainly easier to get to work here – just a subway ride downtown. The factory job meant a subway and a bus each way. And then there was that business of the unpleasant Mr. Carboy. Would he leave her alone or would he constantly harass her the way Mrs. Reardon had done? But despite all the pros and cons coursing through her mind, it kept coming back to one overriding factor – money. With her janitor's work and pay as a cleaning lady – even as a supervisor – she could barely skimp by. The money from the factory job would make things so much easier. How many nights had she sat at her kitchen crying in utter frustration while she held in her hands the precious stamps that would allow her to buy shoes for the children, but didn't have the money?

"Thank you so much for the opportunity, Mr. Kean." It was her voice, but she could hardly believe what she was saying it. "But I can't accept your kind offer. Tonight I was going to tell Mrs. Booker that I was leaving. I'm taking a job at a factory and the pay—"

"—Is a lot better," Kean said, disappointed, but not surprised. "I know. Well, good luck, Mrs. Cavanaugh."

Nancy was still feeling troubled as she rode the subway home that night, nagged by the thought that she'd made a mistake, that she'd given up a good job for an unknown one. But she reminded herself that she'd made her decision based on what was best for her family and she had to let it go. Now the next real worry was – what to do with the kids while she was at work?

***

The solution to that problem turned out to be surprisingly easy. She knew she couldn't ask Erin. She already had her hands full with her own two children, and besides, more and more Erin was acting erratically and she didn't want to leave her children with her if at all possible. Her only hope, slim as it was, was Mrs. Krueger who lived on the top floor. The children weren't crazy about having the old woman as their babysitter, but as Nancy

pointed out to them at a family sit-down, she had no other
alternative.

Not holding out much hope of success, she'd gone to see Mrs.
Krueger to broach the idea of babysitting Donal. To her
astonishment, the old woman readily agreed to watch him, claiming
it was her patriotic duty to care for the little tyke while his mother
was off working to defeat that Nazi bastard Hitler.

Now that Donal was taken care of, it was time for Nancy to
have a talk with the other three. From time to time, she would have
serious sit-downs with the four of them. Usually, it was because
they were getting out of hand, or they weren't doing their share of
the chores. Since Connor's death, disciplining the children fell to
her exclusively. It wasn't a role she relished, but it was something
that had to be done.

After dinner, as the kids were about to bolt from the table,
Nancy held up a hand. "Wait. I want to talk to you kids about
something very important."

The children, recognizing the serious tone in her voice,
slipped back into their chairs.

"You know Mommy has a new job that I start next Monday.
It's a day job, so I have to figure out what to do with you until I get
home. Today I spoke to Mrs. Krueger—"

At the mention of her name, the three eldest groaned in
unison. "No, Mommy," Patrick said, in a near panic. "You can't
leave us with her."

"What is it with you kids and Mrs. Krueger?" Nancy asked in
exasperation. "She's never done anything to you."

"She's old," Fiona answered with the perfect logic of an eight-
year-old.

"So what? You're all going to be old someday." For some
reason the children thought that was hilarious. Even Donal
laughed, although he wasn't sure why.

"OK, here's what I've worked out. When you three go off to
school, Mrs. Krueger will watch Donal until you come home.
Then" – Nancy couldn't believe what she was about to say.
Maureen was only nine, but, thankfully, she was a very responsible
nine-year-old – "when you come home Maureen will collect Donal

and take him back to the apartment, where you will all stay until I get home. If there are any problems, Maureen, you're to go straight up to Mrs. Krueger. Is that clear?"

They nodded, relieved at the reprieve.

Nancy wasn't sure that they understood the importance of what she'd just said and it was vital that they did. "Listen to me," she said in a low, serious voice. "Everything you children do reflects on me. I'm a widow with no husband. If you do anything wrong, the authorities will come and take you away from me."

Maureen burst into tears.

"Maureen, what's the matter?"

"Mommy," she said, sobbing breathlessly, "you're always saying the authorities will come and take us away from you. You scare us when you say that."

She rushed to her daughter and hugged her. "Oh, no, Maureen, no one will ever take you away from me. No one will ever take any of you away from me. Never."

"But you're always saying they will," Fiona said, tears welling up in her eyes.

Always saying? Nancy was stunned by the accusation. She hadn't been aware she always said that. Seeing her children cry broke Nancy's heart. Unintentionally, she'd allowed her own fears and vulnerabilities to terrify her children. Even Donal, who barely understood what was going on, looked fearful. My God! What have I done?

Nancy loved America. She appreciated everything the county had given her, especially the opportunity to leave Ireland, especially that. But since Connor's death, she'd been consumed by a powerful, all-encompassing feeling of insecurity. Deep down she knew it was irrational, but the truth was, she was afraid of the government and the authorities. If they chose to come after her for any reason, what could she do? She was no match for them. She was just an uneducated immigrant with four small children. In all her time in this country, she'd had only one contact with the law and it had brutally come down against her. Even she knew that what had happened in Bossart's office wasn't justice, and she wondered if it were possible for someone like her to ever get justice in this country. Since that meeting in the lawyer's office, almost three years ago, she couldn't get out of her head the words of that awful Mr. Bossart— "It does raise some troubling questions about the status of your children."

And that had been her abiding nightmare ever since, something she obsessed on. What if they decided she was not a fit mother? She was not a citizen of the United States. They could do whatever they wanted, including taking the children away from her. They could deport her to Ireland. She'd shared her fears with Nora, who dismissed them out of hand. This was America, Nora had assured her. Everybody, even immigrants from Ireland, have rights under the Constitution. Then why had Japanese-Americans been rounded up and put in camps? Nancy had asked. And it wasn't just them. What about the Germans? What about the Italians? Nora had no answer for that. Neither did Nancy.

She stroked Maureen's hair and promised herself that from now on she would keep her fears to herself.

CHAPTER FOURTEEN

The first week in the new job proved to be wildly chaotic as she struggled to fine-tune her new routine. Every morning she got up extra early to make sure the kids had a good breakfast before the three older ones went off to school. Then she dropped Donal off at Mrs. Krueger's apartment and met Nora at the train station on 96th Street. The subway and bus rides were long and tedious, but what choice did she have? As she pointed out to a complaining Nora, there were no good paying factory jobs on Amsterdam Avenue. Every night she came home completely done-in from standing all day packing endless boxes of mess kits and fell into bed as soon as she tucked the children in.

At least twice a day, during that first week, Carboy would appear at their packing station and shake his head in grave tight-lipped disapproval. On Wednesday he said, "You women have got to work faster than that. We have government quotas to meet, you know. Our boys overseas are anxiously awaiting these mess kits. There's no time for lollygagging."

"So if they don't have one of our lovely mess kits, do the soldiers eat out of their hands or what?" Nora asked, after the annoying little man had gone. She winked at Nancy. "Can you picture all those soldiers standing at the docks on the European shore as the ship comes and pleading, 'Oh, please, sirs, do you have our M-1942 divided pan-and-body stainless steel system mess kits?'" She shook her head in disgust. "The man's pitiful."

All joking aside, Nancy and Nora redoubled their efforts to speed it up, but their best was never good enough. Then that Friday, Nancy saw Kane pull Carboy aside. She couldn't tell over the noise of the machinery, but it looked like Kane was yelling at him. From that day on, much to Nancy's immense relief, Carboy stopped harassing them.

***

It wasn't until the end of March that Nancy finally began to feel comfortable with the job and her home routine. She'd had her doubts about how Donal and Mrs. Krueger would get along. He was a good boy, most of the time, but he was, after all, just two. And children that age, she knew from experience, could be a handful. To Nancy's delight, Mrs. Krueger and Donal got along famously. Not surprisingly, Maureen fulfilled the role of surrogate mother in Nancy's absence with great composure. Of course, there were the occasional complaints from the others about how she bossed them around, but all in all, everything ran smoothly.

Nancy and Nora were still in the packing section which, she'd been told by the small handful of female coworkers who worked there, was the worst work station and the one that Carboy reserved for newly hired women.

***

It was late one afternoon towards the end of June, when a smug Carboy announced to Nancy, "Mr. Kane wants to see you in his office right away. Go."

Fighting back panic, she hurried down the hall to the manager's office. This couldn't be good. Usually, if someone was called into the office, it meant that they were being fired. She knew she wasn't as fast as some of the other more experienced women in the packing station, but she was getting better at it. At least she was better than Nora. Of course that wasn't saying much. Nora spent more time looking for a glimpse of Kane than packing. The only other thing she could think of was that Mr. Carboy had been saying bad things about her. My God, what would she do if she lost this job?

Kane was sitting behind his cluttered desk. He motioned
Nancy into a chair. "So, how are you getting along with the
work?"

"Fine, Mr. Kane. I think I'm really getting the hang of it," she
said, trying her best to sound confident and upbeat.

Kane nodded in an understanding way. His eyes were locked
on her and it made her uncomfortable. She forced herself to look
away and dusted an imaginary spec of lint from her dress.

"Have you ever done any filing, general office work?"

"No, I haven't."

"Well, it's not all that difficult really. If you know the
alphabet, you can file. As for the rest of it, it's just common
sense."

Nancy didn't know where he was going with this. There had
been a girl working in the office, a pretty young thing, but she'd left
about a week ago unexpectedly. Everyone wondered what had
happened to her.

"I've decided you will be my clerk," Kane said.

Nancy wasn't sure she'd heard him correctly. The clerical
position was considered the cushiest job in the factory and there
wasn't a woman there who wouldn't have killed for it. There had
been a lot of talk about who would fill the opening and it was the
general consensus that it would go to the woman with the most
seniority.

"Mr. Kane, I don't know how to type or—"

He waved a hand in dismissal. "No typing necessary. I told
you, it's strictly clerical – filing, answering the phones, that sort of
thing." He flashed a toothy grin. "I know you can do it."

Nancy's mind was reeling. What a wonderful opportunity!
She remembered her humiliation when she'd gone to that
employment agency and wasn't able to list any experience. She
remembered the look of distain on the interviewer's face. She
couldn't believe her good fortune. How often would a woman
with a sixth grade education get a chance to be a clerk in an office?
She was being offered an opportunity to get real work experience.

Ah, but…but…

She couldn't quite put her finger on it, but there was something about this man that made her uncomfortable. He was always touching the women – patting them on the back or rubbing their arms. But, truth be told, it was nothing more than that. She had to admit he was always a perfect gentleman with her. Perhaps he was just being friendly. Perhaps she was making a mountain out of a molehill. Still, she wasn't sure she wanted to work in this cramped office with him nine hours a day.

"The job pays ten-cents more an hour," he said.

A raise? She'd been here only six months, but already she'd seen an extraordinary change in her financial condition. True, it was still hard to get certain things, even if you had the proper stamps. But on the occasion when those things were in the stores, at least now she could afford to buy them. Just last Saturday she'd proudly taken the children to Klein's department store in Union Square and bought each of them brand new shoes. It was the first time in a long time that she'd felt that happy.

Much to her amazement, she noticed that she began to actually have a surplus at the end of the week. But, as Nora pointed out, that was true of most working people who earned any kind of a decent wage. After all, what with the chronic shortages, there wasn't much to spend your money on. Nancy began to buy war bonds with the money that was left over after she paid for her necessities. It was a good way to save money and it made her feel patriotic.

She heard his words again—*I've decided you will be my clerk*—and allowed herself to fantasize about the future. If she could keep this job after the war, someday she might be able to save enough for a down payment on a little house in Queens, maybe somewhere near College Point. That would make the travel a lot easier. Putting all doubts aside, she said, "I'll take it. Thank you, Mr. Kane."

"Don't thank me. I've had my eye on you. You're a good worker, Nancy. You'll be an asset to the company."

Nancy didn't know how to break the news to Nora. She knew her friend was keen on Mr. Kane, but in six months he hadn't shown the slightest interest in her even though she shameless flaunted herself every chance she got.

On the subway ride home that day, it was Nora, much to Nancy's relief, who brought up the subject. "So what did Kane want?"

Nancy decided it was best to just come out with it. "He offered me the clerk job and I accepted it." She studied her friend's face for a reaction and was relieved to see a big grin.

Nora grabbed Nancy's hands. "That's terrific. You've got four little ones at home. If anyone deserves the job, it's you."

"You're not mad at me?"

"Why should I be mad at you?"

"Well, I thought you fancied him."

"Are you kidding? All right, I'll admit I was taken with him at first, but… Do you know he dyes his hair?"

"I suspected as much."

"And he's a lot older than he looks."

"Yes, I think he is."

Nora's voice dropped to a whisper. "Nancy, I have an odd feeling about him and I'd stay away from him if I were you."

Nancy nodded solemnly, trying not to laugh. Those were the very same words of warning she'd spoken to Nora six months earlier.

***

It was the beginning of another December, the year – 1943. This was the fourth December since Connor's death and with each passing year, mercifully, the pain of December slowly dissipated. She still thought of him all the time, but not with the heart wrenching ache of previous years.

But otherwise things were the same. The war in Europe and the Pacific raged on. Much to everyone's dismay, it was now entering its third year. Every day she scoured The Times headlines for news of the war in the Pacific. In November, the name Bougainville appeared. She used her map to discover that Bougainville was part of the Solomon Islands. Then a few days later, there were headlines about an island called Tarawa and her eyes locked on a statement from an admiral: "Our invading forces met only moderate resistance on Makin, but on Tarawa, main Japanese stronghold in the Gilberts, the enemy fought back fiercely."

Nancy studied the map with a sinking feeling. Her theory was holding true. American forces were moving from island to island, getting closer and closer to Japan. She shuddered, thinking of how many men would die when the American forces finally attacked the mainland of Japan. It was exasperating not knowing where Neil was, but in her heart she was certain he was on one of those islands.

Despite the war and her ongoing concern for Neil's safety, she was cautiously optimistic about the coming year and pleased with the way her life was going. She had a job she enjoyed and one that paid well. And it was so much easier than she'd imagined. The position of clerk had always seemed so mysterious to her. In the classified ads, they required a high school diploma, something way beyond her reach. And now here she was doing that very job, and doing it well, according to Mr. Kane.

Still, in her soberer moments, her contentment was marred by feelings of unnamed guilt and anxiety. For better or for worse, she was a product of her Catholic upbringing in Ireland. Imprinted indelibly in her psyche were visions of parish priests in their pulpits endlessly thundering the words of Proverbs: "Pride goes before destruction, and a haughty spirit before a fall." Even with her sixth grade education, she'd read enough Greek mythology to know what hubris meant. She couldn't shake the feeling that if she were too happy, something bad would surely befall her.

That feeling of guilt became manifest when she saw Mrs. Krueger and Donal together. The old woman had adopted Donal as the grandchild that she never had and the feeling was mutual. The joy of seeing how well they got along, however, was tempered by pangs of regret. There were times when it seemed that Donal was closer to the old woman than he was to her, and she felt deep remorse about not being home enough with him and his brother and sisters.

***

It was the end of the day on Friday, and Christmas was just two weeks away. Nancy was packing up to leave when Kane came into the office. The usually self-possessed factory manager looked uncharacteristically preoccupied.

"Oh, Nancy, I'm glad I caught you before you went home. Do you think you could stay an extra hour or so? I've just came from a meeting at the War Office Procurement Section and I need you to help me pull a list of documents for an audit they're going to do next week. With these guys it's always at the last minute. I hate to ask you, but I'm really in a bind."

Nancy didn't really want to stay. On the way home, she'd planned to stop off at Macy's to buy some presents for the kids. Toy trucks and dolls were scarce, but Nancy was determined to make this the best Christmas the children had ever had. She knew she was partly guided by guilt for leaving them alone so much, but she did want to see them happy.

She was going to tell him that she had other plans, but he'd had been very good to her and she felt she couldn't refuse his request.

"All right, Mr. Kane. I'll ask Nora to stay with the children."

"Good girl."

He gave her a list of documents to pull and she spent the next hour retrieving them from the files. He was rummaging through a file cabinet behind his desk, when he looked up exasperated. "Nancy, I'm looking for last month's invoice from Atkins, but I can't find it."

"It should be there, Mr. Kane. I remember filing it."

Nancy had to squeeze between him and the desk to get to the file cabinet. It was then that she noticed that his breath smelled of alcohol and his eyes were glassy. She wondered if the audit was more serious then he'd let on and he'd stopped off for a couple of drinks to calm himself down.

As she bent over the file drawer, he moved beside her and put his hand on her back. "Do you see it?"

Nancy stiffened, but she didn't say anything. He started to rub her back and she stood up. "Mr. Kane, please."

He stepped back. "What? What'd I do?"

Now Nancy felt foolish. Was she overreacting? "I'm... sorry..." she stammered. "It's just that it's tight quarters here. If you give me a little more room..."

Suddenly, he put his hands on her shoulders and violently slammed her against the file cabinet. "But that's just the point," he said in a husky voice. "I don't want to give you more room."

Nancy was frightened by the strange, unfocused look in his eyes. She tried to pull away, but he was much stronger than she was and he had her pinned against the file cabinet. He slid his hands down her sides, grabbed her hips and pulled her toward him.

She jerked her head to the side as he tried to kiss her. "Stop it, stop it."

"Oh, come on, Nancy," he whispered in her ear. "I know you're a widow. How long has it been since you've made love to a man?"

She shoved him away. "Get away from me, you great fool."

"Don't play coy, Nancy. You know I've wanted you since that first day I saw you. And you wanted me."

"You're out of your mind. I'm going home."

As she tried to push past him, he grabbed her again. She stepped back and smacked his face as hard as she could. He stumbled back, more stunned than hurt. The outline of her hand was clear on his flushed face.

Overcome by fright and rage, it took her a moment to realize something was amiss. He looked somehow – different. Distorted in some way. Then she realized what it was. He was wearing a toupee and her smack had dislodged it. Unaccountably, she began to giggle and pointed to his head.

"What?" He put his hands to his head. "Jesus..." Frantically, he tried to adjust the wig, but he only succeeded in making it worse. Now it was on backwards. Nancy couldn't contain herself. She burst out laughing hysterically and kept pointing to his head.

His face grew darker with rage as he tried to get the wig on straight. Finally, in exasperation, he hurled it to the floor. His head, mostly bald, was covered by a few wispy strands of gray hair. "You think that's funny?" he roared. "I'll tell you what's funny, you bitch. You're fired. You hear me? Fired! Now get out! Get out!"

Unable to control her laughter, Nancy pushed past him and fled down the stairs and out onto the street. It was only when she was safely away from him that the laughter turned to tears.

CHAPTER FIFTEEN

"That bastard!" was Nora's reaction when Nancy told her what had happened.

Nancy poured the tea and sat down. "I blame myself, too."

"In the name of God, why? You did nothing wrong."

"There were signs that all was not right. He was always touching me, not inappropriately, but you know, the hand on the arm, the quick back rub, bumping into me in that cramped office, that sort of thing. Sometimes I'd look up and see him staring at me. I have to accept that it was partly my fault. I shouldn't have ignored the signs. I should have…" Nancy's eyes welled up with tears. "I'm so ashamed of myself. You know why I ignored his behavior, Nora? Because I didn't want to lose the job. And now I have."

"What are you going to do?"

Nancy shrugged helplessly. "Try to get my old cleaning job back."

"Ah, that's terrible work. You have experience as a clerk now. Why don't you try for that kind of job?"

Nancy shook her head ruefully. "What kind of reference do you think Mr. Kane would give me?"

Nora slammed her hand on the table. "That does it. I'm going to quit tomorrow. I'm going march into that old bald headed, sleazy lecher's office and tell him exactly what I think of him."

"You'll do no such thing, Nora. You'll end up jobless, just like me. And he'll give you no reference either."

***

The next day, an anxious Nancy rode the elevator up to John Kean's office on the fifteenth floor. She'd left the cleaning job for the best of reasons – to earn more money for her family. Nevertheless, quitting the job had seemed to her an act of ingratitude, and now she was mortified that she was about to ask for her old job back. She'd heard that hope springs eternal, and she held out hope, as slim as it was, that she would not only get her job back, but maybe even the supervisor's job. Perhaps he hadn't filled it. Possibly it had just become available again. As the elevator doors opened, she shook her head to clear it of such optimistic nonsense.

Kean seemed genuinely glad to see her when she appeared in his office doorway." "Mrs. Cavanaugh, right? Come in. Come in."

When she was seated he said, "Well, what can I do for you?"

"Mr. Kean, I don't want to take up your time. It's just that… I've come to ask for my job back," she blurted out.

Kean's smile faded. "I see. What happened?"

Nancy looked away from his penetrating gaze. "I'd… rather not say."

Kean said nothing, but inside he was seething. He'd seen this so many times before. Attractive women like Nancy Cavanaugh had left for better paying jobs in the defense industry only to come back to him looking for their old jobs, sometimes after as little as a week or even a whole year later. He had no illusions about the women who worked for him and what they did. A cleaning lady's job was just about the bottom of the barrel. If a woman had a choice, she would always opt for something better. But he hired what he could get and it was usually uneducated immigrants with no other work skills. That's why he'd offered her the supervisor's job. He recognized in her a first-rate worker and he'd hoped that the offer of a supervisor's job would entice her to stay. He'd been sorely disappointed when she'd left, but he couldn't blame her.

He also suspected that she'd quit her new job for one of two reasons – she'd either had the misfortune of working for an ignorant misogynist who believed that a woman's place was in the home and she had no business trying to do the work of a man, or she'd gone to work for a man who believed that any woman who was willing to work among men was really just looking for a man, and he was the one to satisfy her needs. He knew both types flourished in the current market place. As the father of three teenage girls, it infuriated him to think that these lowlifes would take advantage of his daughters under similar circumstances.

Kean found it hard to look at Nancy, seeing the humiliation and mortification in her face. He wanted to end the interview as quickly as possible. "Mrs. Cavanaugh," he said, trying to sound positive, "as it turns out, I do have an opening. I'm sorry it's not a supervisor's position, but I can start you off at the salary you were earning when you left."

Nancy felt a sharp ache in her stomach. She was immensely grateful that he was willing to hire her back, but she did a quick calculation and realized that her salary would be almost fifty percent less than she'd been making. In the blink of an eye, her whole life had changed. From now on there would be no surplus money at the end of the week, no more buying war bonds, no more buying goods that she had stamps for. She would have to get serious and tighten her belt. With dismay and sadness, she realized that the merry Christmas she'd planned for her children was lost and gone forever.

"Thank you, Mr. Kean," she said in a voice drained of all emotion. "Thank you for taking me back."

***

Christmas was a quiet and somber affair, not the cheerful time Nancy had planned. Nora came to dinner full of apologies. She'd looked high and low, but there was not even a scrawny chicken to be had for all the stamps in her ration book. By the end of '43, food, especially meat, had become more and more difficult to find. And so the main course for Christmas dinner that day was a meat that was both cheap and plentiful – Spam. Since the start of the war, Spam had been the butt of jokes, called everything from "mystery meat" to "the ham that didn't pass its physical" by soldiers. What had Neil called it in one of his letters? "Meatloaf without basic training." Nancy found it wasn't half bad if it was fried. At least the kids seemed to like it. And when she tucked the children into bed that night, she was eternally grateful that there had been not one complaint because the wartime Santa had left them only one present each.

***

By the start of 1944, Nancy had become a work-hardened veteran. Since the war, she'd had three jobs and had experienced more than her share of missteps, poor decisions, and one harrowing experience with the lecherous Mr. Kane. But in that time her initial timidity had given way to a self-confidence that she didn't think she possessed. Thinking back, she could hardly recognize that shy girl who had allowed herself to be terrorized by that horrible Mrs. Reardon. Perhaps her newfound self-confidence had something to do with the fact that in a few months she would turn thirty. The very thought astounded her. She didn't feel thirty. How, she wondered, did she go from being a young, naïve housewife to what she'd become in a few short years? The war, she decided, had accelerated the pace of everything. And nothing was the same. She wondered, sadly, if anything would ever be the same again.

Her new supervisor was neither as harsh as Mrs. Reardon nor as kind as Mrs. Booker, but she was fair and let Nancy and the other women do their work, and that's all that Nancy wanted. It was easier the second time around to quickly slip into her cleaning routine. Her first night back, she stopped in to see Mr. Kaplan.

As usual, he was at his desk hunched over a thick folder when she came in. He looked up and his smile of recognition quickly turned in to a frown. "Nancy, what are you doing back here?"

When she'd finished telling him about her encounter with Kane, he didn't seem surprised. "What happened to you was terrible, Nancy, but not uncommon I'm afraid. Just last week I went to a bar meeting and the subject of what you, and women like you, are going through came up. No one knew what to call it, so someone suggested calling it 'female pestering.' Kind of an awkward phrase, but it hits the mark. Anyway, it was the general consensus that until the war, women were employed in typical women's jobs – secretary, stenographer, that sort of thing. With the advent of war, women were suddenly thrust into doing what had been men's work – assembly line, truck driver, even flying military airplanes. There are a lot of men who can't bear the thought that women can do a man's job."

"So what's the answer?"

"I think it will sort itself out once the war is over," he said confidently.

"How?"

"Because women will go back to being housewives or whatever they were doing before the war."

Nancy was stunned by his offhanded answer. "Not me. I'll continue working. I have to. I have a family to provide for."

Kaplan seemed genuinely taken aback by her response. "Well, I guess in your case—"

"Not just my case, Mr. Kaplan. My friend Nora is single, but she's earning a nice wage on the assembly line making mess kits. She won't want to give that up. What for? To go back to being a waitress at Schrafft's?"

"But what about all the men when they come home from the war? They'll be looking for jobs, jobs that women have been doing."

"Well, they'll just have to go find their own, won't they?"

Kaplan shook his head. "I'm afraid you're wrong there, Nancy. When the war is over and the men come back home, women will be forced out of those jobs.

"But that's not fair."

"Fair or not, that's the way it's going to be."

On the subway ride home that night, Nancy mulled over what Kaplan had said and she was fearful of his vision of the future. She didn't want to spend the rest of her life cleaning offices. She'd had a taste of a better life and she liked sitting in an office and filing and answering the telephone and maybe even the chance of doing something even better. But if what Kaplan had said was true, that wouldn't be possible. She would be condemned to spend the rest of her life cleaning offices.

***

Notwithstanding the ongoing war, life in the Cavanaugh family settled into a relatively steady, comfortable rhythm. One positive aspect of being fired from the factory job was that now Nancy was able to be home during the day with Donal, and she took that opportunity to become reacquainted with her youngest son. She was astonished by how much the three-year-old knew. But of course she realized it was due to Mrs. Krueger's constant attention and her natural born abilities as a teacher. Much to Nancy's astonishment and delight, even the other children had fallen under her spell. What they'd initially perceived as sternness and aloofness in the old woman was really a very witty, dry sense of humor. Now it was the children who would insist that Mrs. Krueger babysit them when Nancy went off to work. And that was a great relief to Nora. Much as she loved the children, nine hours at the factory job was exhausting enough for one day.

***

It was early afternoon. Nancy had just come up from the cellar after banking the furnace when she heard a blood-curdling scream in the hallway. She raced up two flights of stairs and saw two men in Army uniforms hovering over Erin, who was slumped on the floor screaming hysterically.

Thinking they were trying to assault her or rape her, Nancy yelled, "Stop that! Get away from her or I'll call the police!"

One of the men, a major, turned to Nancy. "Who are you, ma'am?"

His tone was so quiet and reassuring that Nancy realized she must be mistaken. "I'm Mrs. Cavanaugh and I'm Erin Cassidy's friend."

The other man, a captain, was helping a dazed Erin to her feet. She was screaming and crying at the same time and Nancy couldn't quite understand what she was saying. Then she started to pick up a word here and there. Dead... Tom... Dear God... No...." And suddenly, she understood. "Is Tom Cassidy dead?" Nancy bleakly asked the major.

"Yes, ma'am. We just notified Mrs. Cassidy that her husband, Sergeant Thomas Cassidy, was killed in action."

Erin screamed again and her legs buckled. With the help of Nancy, both officers carried Erin into the apartment. She led them into Erin's bedroom and they gently placed her in bed. Nancy pulled a comforter over her and sat down next to her. What should she say – what could she say – to a woman who had just found out that she'd lost her husband? She remembered her own experiences after Connor's death. Many well-meaning people had said things, hoping to comfort her, but they only made it worse. And Nancy realized that, right now, there was nothing to say. She took Erin's hand and squeezed it.

Nancy stayed with her until she finally fell into a fitful sleep about fifteen minutes later. When she came out to the kitchen, the two officers were still there.

"What happens next?" Nancy asked the major, painfully aware that one day she might be confronted with the same situation.

"Tomorrow, Mrs. Cassidy will be contacted by a Casualty Assistance Officer, who will advise her of the Army's various options, benefits, and allowances available. Until then please advise your friend that she should delay making any decisions on care and preparation of the remains until she has been fully briefed by the Casualty Assistance Officer."

"There are children," the captain said. "Where are they?"

"Oh, my God!" Nancy brushed away a tear. "I forgot all about the children. Yes, there are two of them and right now they're in school."

"Is there anyone who can notify the principal and pick them up?"

"I can do that... Oh, but someone should stay with Erin."

"Is there anyone else who could pick up the children?"

Nancy immediately thought of Mrs. Krueger. "Yes, there is someone."

"Very good. Well, we must be getting back to Fort Dix."

As they were leaving, Nancy said, "Major, where was Tom killed?"

"Anzio, ma'am."

"Anzio? Where is that?"

"Italy, ma'am."

"Oh, thank you. I'll have to look that up on my map," she said, immediately realizing it was an idiotic thing to say.

That night, Nancy stayed with Erin while Nora stayed with her four. Several times during the night, Erin woke up screaming. Around three, she finally fell into a restless sleep.

Tom's remains arrived two weeks later. Nancy accompanied Erin to LaGuardia airport to receive the flag-draped casket. At Erin's instance, there was no wake and Tom's body was buried in a cemetery in the Bronx. The only ones in attendance were her two children, Nancy, Nora, and Mrs. Krueger. Later, they went back to Nancy's apartment for tea.

***

Throughout the early months of 1944, Nancy continued to watch the war unfold in the headlines of The New York Times. She had been getting better at finding battle locations in the Pacific, but now she was confronted by an array of new, strange-sounding places like Kwajalein Atoll, Truk Island, the Admiralties, and a place called Hollandia, which she thought must surely be in Holland, but turned out to be in of all places – New Guinea! All the names and locations made her head spin and her map was becoming a veritable pincushion of multicolored pins. Nancy's initial plan was to use red pins to show Neil's whereabouts and use blue pins for everything else. But, much to her frustration, after all this time there were only two red pins on the map – North Carolina and Maui.

She still didn't know where he was. It had been months since she'd received a letter from him. She knew his unit was somewhere in the Pacific, so she assumed that he must be fighting on one of those strange-sounding places and she prayed he was

safe. With mounting dread, there was one thing she did notice.
The contested islands and battlefields were moving the armed
forces closer and closer to Japan. Over time, the daily headlines –
with their endless litany of islands and battles – had a numbing,
hypnotic effect on her. Headlines about one exotic location
blended into another.

Then everything changed on June 6th.

The New York Times headline screamed:

ALLED ARMIES LAND IN FRANCE IN THE HARVE-
CHERBOURG AREA; GREAT INVASION IS UNDER WAY

Nancy had been hearing the rumors for months about a
coming invasion. Everyone had been talking about it. A major
assault of Europe was being planned, but of course no one knew
where or when it would occur. And now, finally, here it was – the
long awaited invasion of Europe. Nancy's heart pounded as she
dared to hope that if the invasion was successful, the war would
soon be over.

But it wasn't soon over. It took until late July before the allies
could even move off the beaches of Normandy and begin their
slow slog toward Berlin. Optimism had been running high after the
Allied landing in Normandy on D-Day. Every day, Nancy read in
the newspapers and heard commentators on the radio state
emphatically that the war would be over in a matter of weeks.
Those prognostications proved to be wildly optimistic. Germany
would not surrender for another eleven months, and in that time
war would continue to unleash its deadly venom. Germany
bombed Britain with V1 bombs, the Allies entered Paris, the Allies
invaded Germany, and – Nancy noted with great interest – the
Marines landed on Iwo Jima.

***

Less than a month before the war's end, an unexpected
tragedy befell the American people. On April 12th, around five
p.m., Nancy and Erin were in the kitchen having tea. The kids –
Erin's and Nancy's – were in the living room gathered around the

radio listening to Tom Mix when an announcer broke in. "We interrupt this program to bring you an important bulletin…"

The children jumped up and ran into the kitchen.

"Mommy, Mommy," Patrick yelled. "The president is dead. President Roosevelt is dead."

Erin's hand shot to her mouth. "Oh, my God, the Germans have assassinated the president."

Nancy switched on the kitchen radio just in time to hear an announcer say, "At approximately one o'clock this afternoon, President Franklin Delano Roosevelt, the 32nd President of the United States, died as the result of a cerebral hemorrhage."

Erin violently shook her head. "I don't believe that for one second."

Nancy was stunned by the wild intensity in her voice and the fierce look in her eyes. For a while now, Nancy had been growing increasingly worried about her. Since Tom's death, she'd been harboring bizarre thoughts and acting strangely.

"OK," she said, "you kids go back to your radio." When they'd left, Nancy said gently, "Erin, why would they lie?"

"Because they've been lying to us since the war started, haven't they? The newspapers never print true causality counts. A lot more of our servicemen are dead than they're letting on. Mind, you'll see, when this war is over, the number of dead is going to be staggering and there will be hell to pay. That's why Roosevelt is dead. It's God's judgment on him."

"Why would you say that?"

"He knew the Japs were going to bomb Pearl Harbor," she said with a smug self-assurance. "Everyone knows him and Churchill wanted the Japs to attack us so we would get into the war and save England. They knew all about it before it happened."

"Erin, those are nothing more than rumors. There's no truth to any of it."

Erin let out a hollow laugh. "Think what you will, Nancy. But I know better."

Over the next several days, the radio and newspapers continued to report in greater detail the cause of the president's death, but still, Erin stubbornly refused to accept their explanation.

***

Less than a month later, on May 7th, Nancy heard the news that she'd been waiting for since December 7th. Germany, finally, surrendered.

The war in Europe was over.

That evening after dinner, Patrick took up his station by the window to watch the firehouse across the street. Suddenly, he called out excitedly, "Mommy, Mommy. Come see what's going on."

Nancy and the other children rushed to the window to behold an unbelievable sight. Swarms of grinning, crying, deliriously happy people spilled onto Amsterdam Avenue blowing horns and banging on pots and pans.

"They shouldn't be out in the middle of the street," a disapproving Maureen observed.

Nancy pulled her daughter close to her. "It's all right, Maureen," she said through her tears. "They're just happy the war's over."

Motorists on the avenue were blocked by the dancing, swirling throng, but they didn't care. They jumped out of their vehicles, honked their horns, and cheered along with everyone else. Across the street, someone threw a bucketful of shredded newspapers out the window.

"Look, Mommy," Donal said in awe. "It's snowing."

Before the confetti hit the ground, others had gotten the same idea and soon the air over Amsterdam Avenue was a swirling blizzard of confetti and people were dancing in it ankle-deep.

"They shouldn't be wasting all that newspaper," Patrick said curtly.

Nancy tousled his hair. "It's all right, Patrick, the war's over. There's no need to save newspapers anymore."

"Can we throw newspapers out the window?" Fiona asked.

"You certainly can. Gather up all the newspapers you were saving for the scrap drive."

Nancy sat by the window alternately watching the revelers below and her gleeful children spread out on the living room floor shredding newspapers. It was a bittersweet moment. She was thinking of Connor and Neil and wishing they both could be here. Connor, or course, would never be here again, but Neil? Would he come home from the war alive? As the children tossed handfuls of shredded newspapers out the window, Nancy released all the tension that had been building for so many years.

And she let the tears flow.

CHAPTER SIXTEEN

Nancy let the children stay up late to watch the merrymakers on the street. After all, it was the end of the war and exceptions should be made. Since the start of the war, Nancy had been heartsick, worrying about how the war was affecting her children. She watched and listened to them carefully and was gratified that she saw no sign that the war was frightening them. Mercifully, they were too young to understand exactly what was going on, but they did know that men were dying. They'd seen that right in their own building with the death of Tom Cassidy, and at school some of their friends had lost fathers and uncles. Someday, when they were older, they would look back on this day, the day that the war ended, and Nancy wanted them to remember it as a special, happy occasion.

Out on the street, someone had hooked a speaker to a car radio and the music of Glen Miller and Benny Goodman blared out into the night. By ten o'clock, there was no sign that the party was about to end anytime soon, so she dragged her loudly protesting children away from the windows and sent them off to bed.

She was about to go to bed herself when there was a knock at the door and her heart skipped a beat. Every time she heard a knock at the door late in the night, she immediately conjured up a fantasy-nightmare scenario – it was Neil, home alive, or two solemn-faced Marines to tell her that Neil had died in combat. But it was only Nora, flushed from dancing.

"I've had the best time," she said, falling into a kitchen chair. "I must have danced with a hundred different men. It was wonderful."

Nancy put the kettle on. Clearly, Nora was all wound up and it was going to be a long night. "I thought you'd be in the middle of that crowd," she said.

Nora didn't answer. Her mind was in another place. "Isn't it fantastic, Nancy. Think of it. The war is over. It's over!"

"It's wonderful," Nancy agreed. "But you know..." She was suddenly overcome with a flood of memories of nights when she'd awakened with a start only to find herself wallowing in a sea of depression, overwhelmed with a feeling that she would never survive, that the country would never survive. "God help me, Nora," she said softly. "There were times when I thought it would go on forever or that we all would die."

"So did we all."

The two friends sat at the kitchen table, saying nothing, just looking at each other and grinning wildly and stupidly. But then, the import of what had just happened hit them and they both jumped up and hugged each other. Not a word was spoken. They let the tears wash away the detritus, fears, and anxieties of the past four years.

***

The next morning the children dragged themselves into the kitchen bleary-eyed and yawning.

Nancy shook her head at the sight of them and grinned. "Well, if it isn't the four party-goers. It's not as easy as it looks, is it?"

Maureen slid into her seat, still half asleep. "Mommy, I didn't dream it. The war is over, right?"

"Yes, it is, honey."

"Oh, goody," she said, brightening up. "Then that means we can go to Ireland."

The other children joined her in clapping their hands in delight.

Nancy's stomach knotted and she stepped back as though she'd been slapped in the face. Ireland! My God. She hadn't thought about the farm or Ireland for a very long time. When

Kaplan assured her that her sister-in-law couldn't move to the farm, she'd pushed all thoughts of going back out of her mind. That was something she wouldn't have to think about until the war was over. Well, now the war was over and the clock had started ticking. Kaplan said she had six months after the war to get to Ireland and make her case. She would have to start making plans to go back immediately. But there were so many questions. What would she do with the furniture? The apartment? How would she get there? Would her parents agree to take them in for a short time? So many questions, so few answers.

***

The war was over only in Europe. Nancy and the kids continued to track the war in the Pacific. Through the rest of '44, the Marines continued island-hopping toward Japan. She and the children dutifully placed pins identifying battles on Saipan, Guam, and Peleiu Island. In vain, every day she checked the mailbox looking for a letter from Neil, but none came. She consoled herself with Nora's reminder: No news is good news. Neil had listed her as next of kin. If anything happened to him, for better or for worse she would be the first to know.

***

At the beginning of 1945, to Nancy's dismay, it looked as though this year promised to be much like the last three years. When would it end? The routine continued. The kids went to school every day, and she went to work every night. And nothing else changed. On the warfront, battles continued to be fought in the Pacific. The allies appeared to be moving closer and closer to Tokyo, but she wondered why it was taking so long.

Then, on August 6th, a B-29 dropped something called the atomic bomb on Hiroshima and President Truman came on the radio and promised the Japanese government "a rain of ruin from the air the like of which has never been seen on this earth." Nine days later, the Empire of Japan surrendered to the Allies. Nancy read her final New York Times' war headline with tears in her eyes:

JAPAN SURRENDERS; END OF WAR!

After almost four years, the guns of war fell silent around the globe. She, like every other American, was ecstatic. But, unlike most Americans, the end of the war posed special problems for her. Now that the war was truly over, she had to start answering all those unanswered questions she'd pushed out of her mind. The next day, she stopped by Kaplan's office to discuss it with him.

"The magistrate said his injunction would end six months after the war. Are we talking about the war in Europe or the war in the Pacific?" Nancy asked.

"I had the same question. I wrote the solicitor to clarify that. The clock started ticking on August 15th. That means you have until February 15th to get to Ireland and file your motions."

Nancy relaxed. "Well, at least I'll have six months to work something out."

"Not quite, Nancy. The North Atlantic is not a place you or your children want to be in the winter. I'm told the storms can be fierce."

"So what are you saying, Mr. Kaplan?"

"If I were going to cross the Atlantic Ocean with my child, I would not go any later than November. I would not risk crossing in December, January or February."

Nancy's heart dropped. "Do you think the ship would sink?"

"No, not at all. I'm talking about the chance of extremely rough conditions. You don't want to expose yourself, or especially your children, to that. They could be seasick for days on end."

His remarks changed everything. She'd thought she had six months to plan this trip, but he was telling her she really had only three.

***

One by one, she dealt with the thorny questions. The most important one being: Would her mother agree to take her and her kids in for a short period of time? Given her history with her

mother, it was painfully difficult for her to write the letter. She
agonized over it for several days, but finally, she wrote:

Dear Mother,

*For reasons, which I will explain to you when I get there, I must come
home for a short period of time. I intend to live on Connor's farm, now mine
and the children's, but I'm sure it will take a week or so to get it into a livable
condition, as it's been abandoned for so many years. I'm writing to ask you if
we could live with you and Father for that short period of time. I assure you, we
will be no trouble.*

Your loving daughter,
Nancy

***

Mrs. Krueger usually came to babysit the children about 15
minutes before Nancy left for work, but today she came earlier
because she has something she wanted to talk to Nancy about.

Nancy opened the door. "Oh, Mrs. Krueger, you're early.
Please come in."

The old woman was barely seated before she got right to the
point. "Nancy, what is this I hear about you going back to
Ireland?"

"That's right, I am."

"*Gott in Himmel.* Why would you go there now?"

"You know the story, Mrs. Krueger. I told you about the farm
and my sister-in-law."

"*Ya*, but that was a long time ago and I thought by now you
would have come to your senses. What are you thinking, child?
You should not be trekking off to Ireland with four young
children."

"What choice do I have?"

"You have many choices, Nancy. But, if you must go, why
not leave the children with me."

"Oh, no, Mrs. Krueger, I couldn't ask you to do that."

"Why? Do you think I am too old?" the feisty old woman
asked. "When I was teaching, I had classes of thirty or more
unruly children. Believe me, they gave me no trouble."

Nancy grinned. She had no doubt that the no-nonsense Mrs. Krueger could handle twice that many.

"So your four would be no bother at all. Besides, they are good children. You raised them well, not like the little street scamps I see roaming the neighborhood these days. I am sorry. Those children are not being brought up, they are being dragged up. It is a disgrace."

Nancy had thought of leaving the children with someone, but she'd quickly dismissed the thought. She planned to be in Ireland for only a few months, but she couldn't bear the thought of being separated from the kids for even for that amount of time, especially after all the times she'd had to leave them alone while she was working. She was still working on that guilt.

"I appreciate your offer, Mrs. Krueger. And I know you would take good care of them, but I want us to be together."

The old woman sighed in resignation. "*Ya*. I understand," she said, even though her expression said otherwise. "But if you change your mind, I am here."

"Thank you."

The old woman glanced around the apartment. "And what will you do about the apartment?"

"Give it up."

"Give it up? Are you mad? You said yourself you will only be gone for a short while. Apartments are becoming as scarce as hens' teeth what with all the men coming back from the war. You will not be able to find one when you come home. You and the children will be living homeless in the street, mark my words."

Nancy knew only too well that the old woman was right about the scarcity, and she'd agonized over her decision for a long time. She wanted to keep the apartment, but in the end she realized she had no choice. "I know you're right, Mrs. Krueger, but I simply can't afford to pay rent while I'm gone."

At least the problem of what to do with the furniture turned out to be no problem at all. With all the servicemen returning from overseas, there was a serious shortage of apartments in the city. It was against the law for landlords to sell their apartments to the highest bidder, but there was a loophole. The landlord could pretend that the money he received from the perspective tenant was simply for the furniture in the apartment. Even dilapidated furniture that wouldn't fetch more than a few dollars at a thrift shop went for hundreds of dollars. Given the times, it was a fiction that both landlord and tenant readily accepted. When Nancy offered to sell her furniture to the landlord, he was delighted to buy it all.

Nancy looked at the clock. It was almost time to leave for work and she hoped the old woman was finished with her well-intended interrogation, but she wasn't.

"Have you booked passage yet?"

"No, but that shouldn't be a problem," Nancy said with exaggerated confidence, hoping her tone would head off any more questions. "Now that the war's over, they'll be plenty of ships leaving from New York."

The old woman smiled at her sweetly. "I am ever amazed at your misplaced optimism, Nancy Cavanaugh."

***

It turned out Mrs. Krueger was right. Booking passage proved to be a lot more difficult than Nancy had thought. She made a list of all the passenger steam ship companies in the city. The next morning, as soon as the children went off to school, she headed downtown to the Cunard White Star office, one of the world's largest shipping companies.

A middle-aged man with a pinched face, looked up from his desk with an air of mild annoyance. "Yes, may I help you?" he asked with a slight British accent.

"I'd like to inquire about booking passage to Ireland in October or November."

The clerk's eyebrows arched. "That's not possible. The government has requisitioned all suitable ships to serve as either troop transport or hospital ships."

"But the war is over."

"Perhaps, but these ships are still being used to transport servicemen back to their respective countries," he said, as though that should be evident to her.

Ignoring his patronizing tone, she persisted. "When do you think ships will become available for civilian passengers?"

"I'm sure I have no idea. That's a decision for the government and I am not privy to its deliberations."

Discouraged, but undeterred, she visited the rest of the shipping companies on her list, but, to her dismay, the responses were the same. The clerks at the other companies were politer and understanding, but the answers were still the same. No ships would be carrying civilian passengers until further notice.

With each discouraging response, Nancy's cautious optimism gave way to despair and panic. It was mid-September. If Kaplan was right about the storm conditions in the Atlantic, she had less than ten weeks to book passage, pack, and be ready to go. But the weather was the least of it. By now, based on the responses she'd gotten, she was prepared to go in December or January, if necessary, storms be damned. No matter what, she had to get back to Ireland by February 15th. Kaplan had written the solicitor in Ireland requesting an extension, but the magistrate would not, under any circumstances, extend his moratorium.

It was late afternoon by the time she got to Oceans Ltd., the last shipping company on her list. She got the same answer here as well. As a disheartened Nancy was leaving, the elderly woman clerk said, "Have you tried Emerald Star Lines?"

Nancy consulted her list. "I've never heard of it."

"That's because the line is primarily a freight carrier, but I think they have one of two small passenger ships. You might want to try there."

***

Nancy thanked the woman and went directly to the offices of Emerald Star Line on 11th Avenue. As she approached the address, she was taken aback to discover that it was directly across the street from the piers. The pier where Connor had worked was just a few blocks south of there. She stopped in front of the address and looked up at the building in dismay. She checked the address that the woman had given her again. Could this be it? It was an old dilapidated building with a saloon on the ground floor – Darcy's Bar & Grill, according to the old, rusty sign swinging over the front door. On the sidewalk outside the bar, the stench of stale beer and cigarette smoke permeated the air. Nancy was surprised to see that although it was barely four in the afternoon, the bar was already crowded.

As she looked up at the building, she was overcome with misgivings. *Do I really want to trust my life and the lives of my children to a shipping line that's housed in such a squalid building?*

Utterly discouraged, but realizing this might be her last chance, she climbed the rickety stairs to the second floor office and went inside. The interior was nothing like the other companies she'd visited. None had been exactly plush, but none of them had such a musty odor of age and dampness hanging heavily in the air. Exterior light came from a single grime-encrusted window through which she could barely see, which didn't matter because the only view was of an ugly brick wall. There was a wood-gouged counter piled high with invoices and manifests that looked as though they hadn't been touched in weeks.

Nancy decided this was a great waste of time. As she turned to leave, a wizened old man shuffled out of a back office.

"Yes, yes. What is it?" he asked impatiently. "Are you looking to book passage?"

Taken aback, she turned around. "Why, yes. How did you know?"

He looked at her over his spectacles. "I got call from a colleague at Ocean Ltd. She said I should expect you."

"Oh. Yes, I'm looking for passage for me and my four children to Ireland in October or November. Do you have a passenger ship going there?"

"Well, we do and we don't."

"I don't understand."

"Katherine Mary," he said elliptically.

"Who's that?"

"Not who, she."

Nancy could feel herself getting irritated with this old man who seemed to enjoy talking in circles. "Sir, your name is—?"

"Barnes."

"Mr. Barnes, I'm having a hard time following you."

"The Katherine Mary is a ship," he said with a touch of irritation in his own voice. "She's our only passenger ship."

"I see. Can I purchase tickets for October or November?"

"No."

Nancy roller her eyes. "Because?"

"Because right now, even as we speak, she's on her way back from Europe with a boatload of drunken soldiers. In fact, she's due to dock in a few days."

"And then what?"

"Ah, that's the question, isn't it? She may be sent back to collect more soldiers or she may be returned to us to use as a passenger ship again."

Nancy's heart leaped. "When will you know?"

The old man took his glasses off and rubbed them furiously with a soiled handkerchief. "Who knows?"

"Well, who does know?" Nancy asked, now totally exasperated.

He put his glasses back on and blinked at her. "The War Office's Naval Shipping Procurement… something… something or other."

Nancy decided to give it one last try before she left. "So, when do you think they will tell you?" she asked, speaking the words very slowly.

"Could be days, could be weeks." He slid a pad in front of her. "Write down your name and address. I'll let you know."

Nancy went home feeling utterly dispirited. It seemed her only chance of getting to Ireland was the Emerald Star Lines, but even that seemed doubtful. If they sent the ship back for more troops, she would certainly miss the deadline. But then she had a more troubling thought – what if we do sail on the Katherine Mary? She recalled the ramshackle condition of that office and prayed there was no correlation between it and the Katherine Mary.

She didn't relish crossing the ocean in storm season on a decrepit ship that had just carried – what were his words? – "a boatload of drunken soldiers."

***

When she got home, Maureen rushed to meet her at the door waving a letter. "This came for you, Mommy."

Nancy was hoping it was a letter from Neil, but it was from her mother. She stared at the familiar tight, constricted script, wondering what was inside. Would she agree to take them in or not?

"Who's it from?" Maureen asked.

"It's no one."

She tossed the unopened letter on top of the icebox. She'd had enough bad news for one day. It could wait.

But it couldn't wait. As she prepared dinner, she kept glancing at the letter. At dinner, the kids talked about their day at school. It was a time Nancy treasured, because it gave her a glimpse into their lives. But this time, she couldn't listen. Her mind was on that damn letter. On pins and needles, she waited until the children were in bed, then she rushed into the kitchen, grabbed the envelope and ripped it open.

Dear Nancy,

I received your letter two weeks ago. It has taken me this long to decide what is best for us. And it has not been easy. When you left you made it clear that you would never return, so, as you can imagine, your request comes as a great shock. That aside, your father and I are not getting any younger and the thought of four noisy, wild children mucking about the house is not something in all honesty we would look forward to. Also, you should know that because of the war, everything has become very dear and I don't see how we would be able to feed five more mouths. And so for these reasons, I am letting you know that you will not be able to stay with us. I'm sure you understand. I hope this letter finds you and yours in good health.

Your loving mother

***

Later that evening, Nora came over for tea. Nancy handed her the letter. When she'd finished, she tossed it on the kitchen table. "Bitch! Oh, sorry, Nancy, I didn't mean—"

"It's all right, Nora. I wouldn't exactly put it that way myself, but I understand the sentiment."

"I know you were counting on your parents to take you in until the farm was ready. My God, what are you going to do now? Don't you have brothers or sisters you could stay with?"

"I have a brother and two sisters, but they all went to England a long time ago. There's no one left in Ireland but my parents. Believe me, if there was any other choice, I'd have taken it."

She scooped up the letter and stuffed it back into the envelope. "God help me, I hate to say it about my own mother, but she's a greedy old woman with a great need to control things, especially me." Nancy handed Nora a letter. "Here's what I've written in response."

Dear Mother,

I hope this letter finds you and Father in good health. I received your letter and I feel I must respond. First, I can assure you that my children are not noisy and do not run wild. I guarantee that they will be perfect children in your house. Secondly, as for the cost of feeding five extra mouths, I have always had every intention of paying my way for me and my children and, in addition, I planned to give you a few pounds for your troubles. I hope you will reconsider your decision. I must come home, but I promise my stay with you will be for a very short period of time, just until we can move to the farm.

Your loving daughter,

Nancy

When Nora finished reading Nancy's response, she looked up. "You think she'll buy it?"

Nancy's smile was sad. "I'm afraid she will. The promise of money will change everything."

CHAPTER SEVENTEEN

By the beginning of October, Nancy was a nervous wreck. Her entire life was now focused on just two things – the calendar and the mailbox. Each morning she anxiously crossed off yet another day on the kitchen calendar, knowing that with each passing day she was drawing closer and closer to February 15th. Each afternoon she checked the mailbox and each day it was empty. Still no letter from her mother. Still no letter from Emerald Star Line. Still no letter from Neil.

What if her mother refused to let them live with her? Well, they could stay in a hotel, couldn't they? No. What was she thinking? That would be prohibitively expensive. Worse, what if she couldn't get on a ship before February 15th? She knew she had done everything she could, but, still, she couldn't shake the nagging feeling that there had to be something more that she could do.

In desperation, she'd started praying to Connor. Every night when she got into bed she would say, "Connor, you've got to help me get to Ireland. I'm doing this for you and the kids. Please help me get back to your farm." One night, when she was feeling especially disheartened, she resorted to recrimination. "This is all your fault, Connor. You've got to help me." She blinked away tears and shook her head. "No, Connor, I'm sorry. I didn't mean that. Just see what you can do."

She'd become so obsessed with receiving a letter that she'd learned the mailman's schedule and would wait in the vestibule for him to arrive. Seeing him every day, it was inevitable that they would become quick friends, and eventually she confided in him the importance of the letters. Every day, he would come into the vestibule and shake his head sadly, as though it were his fault that there was no letter. "I'm sorry, Mrs. Cavanaugh, no letter for you today."

"Thank you, Mr. Nachi. Maybe tomorrow."

The afternoon of the second Monday in October, as she did every afternoon, she went downstairs to wait for the mailman. This time he came in with a broad grin on his face. "I have a letter for you, Mrs. Cavanaugh."

It was from Neil. She checked the return address and was disappointed to see that he was somewhere called Camp Pendleton in California. She'd hoped he was somewhere a lot closer than three thousand miles away. She tore it open and read it right there in the vestibule while Mr. Nachi went about filling the mailboxes.

Dear Nancy,

I hope this letter finds you and the children well. I apologize for not writing, but as you can imagine, things have been hectic since the war ended. Here at Camp Pendleton, a major decommissioning center, it's been one great SNAFU. It seems odd being able to mention where I am, another sign that the war is truly over. It's taken me a while to accept that fact. The camp is packed to the gills with Marines who have come in from all over the Pacific and we're all anxious to get home. There is some kind of insane point system that decides who goes home when. It has something to do with time in the service, time overseas, medals, and God knows what else. I don't understand the half of it. All I know is I want to come home. My CO tells me I have a lot of points, so I expect to ship out for New York soon. That's all I can tell you right now. I'll tell you more as I find out myself. Give my love to Maureen, Fiona, Patrick, and Donal. They must be all so big now, I'm sure I'll not recognize any of them.

Love, Neil

She was so engrossed in the letter that she didn't notice that Mr. Nachi had been standing there the whole time anxiously watching her.

"Is it good news, Mrs. Cavanaugh?"

"Yes and no. He's well and that's good. But he's in California and he's not sure when he'll get back to New York."

"Well, at least you've heard from him. I have so many women on my route who still have not heard from their husbands and boyfriends. It's so sad, really. Anyway, I'm glad that you've heard from your man. Maybe tomorrow I'll have a letter from your mom or the shipping line."

"Thank you, Mr. Nachi."

***

Two days later, she did receive a letter from her mother.

Dear Nancy,

I hope this letter finds you and yours well. I received your letter and after careful consideration, I do believe we will be able to put you and your children up, as long as it's not for too long and, as you promised, they will be quiet and no bother. Needless to say, with everything so dear nowadays, the extra money will be greatly appreciated and will be a great comfort to me and your father, who is retired and living on a meager pension.

Sincerely,
Your mother

Nancy felt a great weight lift from her shoulders. Finally, things were starting to fall into place. Now all that remained was to get a letter from the Emerald Star Line telling her that they had a berth for her and her family.

She looked up at the ceiling. "Connor, are you working on this?"

***

The initial euphoria Nancy felt from getting a letter from her mother quickly faded when she realized that none of it mattered if she couldn't get back to Ireland. She immediately slipped back into her obsessive behavior—checking the calendar and the mailbox. Every morning after the children went off to school, she would cross off yet another precious day.

Today was Monday, October 22nd. She stared at the calendar, hardly able to believe how quickly time was passing. She'd long since stopped worrying about sailing before the storm season. It was too late for that. All that mattered now was that she sail in time to get to Ireland by February 15th.

Disheartened, she went downstairs to await Mr. Nachi. He was late, which was not like him. And that set her mind ablaze with wild speculation. Was he sick? Would his replacement misplace the letter? Was he too ashamed to show up with no letter? The more she thought about it, the more bizarre her thinking escalated. Just as she was imaging he'd been hit by a bus and the contents of his mail bag had spilled into a sewer and had been swept out into the Hudson River to be lost forever, he burst into the vestibule with a big grin on his face. "Mrs. Cavanaugh" – he bowed deeply – "I have for you a letter from the Emerald Star Line."

Nancy tore the envelope open and read the short letter.

Dear Mrs. Cavanaugh,

I am pleased to inform you that the Katherine Mary has been released by the government and returned to civilian service. Accordingly, she is scheduled to sail to Belfast, Ireland at 4 p.m. on November 2, 1945 for a complete refitting. If you wish to reserve a berth, you must remit the total cost of passage no later than October 26, 1945.

Yours truly,
Walter Barnes
Emerald Star Lines Agent

Nancy hugged the surprised and flustered mailman. "Mr. Nachi," she said, tears cascading down her face, "I'm going to Ireland! I'm going to Ireland!"

***

It wasn't until she got back upstairs and reread the letter that it finally sunk in – *she was going to Ireland.* Her stomach knotted as she experienced that familiar and sickening anxiety she hadn't felt since she left Ireland fifteen years earlier. And with that, all the elation seeped out of her. In a more somber frame of mind, she read the letter again and her eyes locked on the sentence: If you wish to book passage, you must remit the total cost of passage no later than October 26, 1945.

Her eyes shot to the calendar. "Oh, my God!" she muttered. "That's only four days away. And we sail in eleven days!" She started to feel the onset of a panic attack. Stop it. Stop it, she told herself. There's no time for that. There's too much to do. But what should she do first? She'd have to write her mother and pay for the tickets and notify the school that the children would be leaving and pack and… Her mind reeled with the enormity of it all.

***

The next four days were a blur of activity. Not sure a letter to her mother would get there in time, she sent a Western Union telegram. Then she agonized about Neil. She hadn't seen him since he'd left almost four years ago. She wrote him telling him they were leaving, hoping the letter would get to him before they left, and praying that he might get home before she left.

She made a trip to the Emerald Star Line office to find out how much the tickets were and was pleasantly surprised when Barnes showed her the invoice.

"Not that I'm complaining, Mr. Barnes, but the fares seem very inexpensive."

"About half what it should be," the old man agreed. "You're lucky, Mrs. Cavanaugh. The ship has been out of civilian service since the start of the war. She's in bad shape and she's heading back to Cork for a major overhaul."

Nancy didn't like the sound of that. "Bad shape?" she repeated, looking around the disheveled office and imaging the ship looking like this. "Is there a chance that she might sink?"

The old man shook his head as though that was the craziest thing he'd ever heard. "No, not at all. Not at all. Cosmetics and a few coats of pain is all she needs."

***

By November 1st, much to her amazement, Nancy had accomplished everything on her seemingly endless list of things-that-must-be-done. She was ready to go. After her initial panic about the sailing date, she'd forced herself to calm down. Later that night, after the children had gone to bed, she made herself a cup of tea and wrote out another list of minor, yet vital, things that had to be done. As the days ticked she methodically crossed out the items one by one.

Now, on the eve of sailing, she crossed off the last chore – pack. She slammed the steamer trunk shut and locked it. "There. Done."

Nora flopped down on the trunk and shook her head. "Nancy, you're a wonder. I don't know how you did it."

"Necessity, as they say, is the mother of invention."

"I'm exhausted just watching you this past week. You're a whirling dervish you are. What time do to you sail tomorrow?"

"Four o'clock."

Nancy sat down on the other steamer trunk and the two old friends sat there in the middle of the living room saying nothing. They'd agreed that it would be too emotional to say goodbye at the pier, so this was going to be the last time these two friends would be together for a while.

"So, when do you think you'll be back?"

"A few months, maybe six at the most. At least that's what I'm hoping."

"It's too bad Neil didn't get back here in time. He'll be sorely disappointed."

"Aye, it is too bad. The children keep asking if he'll be here before we go." She shrugged. "I told them maybe. I didn't know what else to say."

Nora stood up. "Well, it's getting late. You must be exhausted and you have a busy day ahead of you tomorrow."

"Yes, I do."

Wordlessly, they hugged each other for a long time. At the door, Nora said, "Now write me as soon as you get there. Promise?"

"I will."

"You're going to be fine."

"I will."

"Come back as soon as you can."

"I will."

"I miss you and the kids already." With tears in her eyes and unable to say anything else, Nora turned and rushed down the stairs.

***

Fifteen minutes later, Nancy was getting ready for bed when there was a knock at the door. Thinking Nora must have forgotten something, she opened the door and standing there were two Marines in full dress uniform. Nancy's heart stopped and she thought she would faint. Since those two officers had come to Erin's door, Nancy had been dreading something like this. She knew next of kin were usually notified by telegram, but sometimes they came to the door in person, as they did for poor Erin Cassidy. Nancy's mind raced. How could this be? Tom Cassidy had died in the war. Neil had survived the war. Oh, dear God, could it be possible that he died in some kind of stupid, insane accident?"

"Nancy...?"

Nancy struggled to fight the panic off. I know that voice. She studied the two Marines in the dimly lit hallway. Their faces were blurry, but then, slowly they came into focus and she saw... "Neil...?"

And then she fainted.

When Nancy came to, she was stretched out on the living room couch and an anxious Neil was standing over her holding a glass of water. "Are you all right?"

"What happened?"

"You passed out."

"Oh, I'm so embarrassed."

He patted her hand. "Don't be. It's not often I have that kind of effect on women."

The other Marine laughed and Nancy turned to look at him.

"Oh, Nancy, this is my buddy, Ray Fazio."

Nancy sat up, feeling light-headed. "Hello, Ray."

"Hi Nancy" he said, awkwardly. "Pleased to meet you. I'm sorry we scared you."

"No, no. It's all right." She stood up. "I'll make tea."

The two men looked at each other and grinned. "How about you make tea for yourself," Neil said. "We've brought something for ourselves."

By the time the tea was made, her head was clear and she'd recovered from the shock of Neil's sudden appearance. She studied him more carefully in the bright light of the kitchen. He was terribly gaunt, but otherwise he looked pretty much the same, allowing for the intervening four years. But yet, there was something about him that was different. It was his eyes, she decided. There was a profound sadness and wariness in them that had not been there when he'd gone away. She could only imagine what he'd seen and done to make him look like that. Maybe someday he would tell her.

And there was another change that surprised her. He'd become a drinker. She remembered how Connor used to tease Neil about his tea totaling ways, calling him a disgrace to the Irish. She wondered what Connor would think now if he could see his best friend sloshing whisky into a water glass and drinking it down neat. When he raised his glass to his mouth, she was startled to see that his hand was terribly scarred. So was the other one. In fact, he kept slipping his left hand into his pocket.

"What are the steamer trunks for?" he asked.

"We're going to Ireland."

Neil paled. "When?"

"Tomorrow."

"Tomorrow? I... I didn't know. Why didn't you tell me?"

"It all happened so fast. I did write you."

He shook his head, irritated. "Damn it. The letter probably passed me somewhere in the middle of the country. Tomorrow is it?"

"Neil, I wrote you about the February deadline a long time ago." She was surprised to find herself getting irritated and decided that it was because of his accusatory tone, and she didn't like it. "This ship is the only one taking civilian passengers to Europe. I was lucky to book passage. I have a deadline to meet. You know that. I must get back by February 15th."

"Yes, I guess you must."

Nancy noticed another change in him that she didn't like. There was an undercurrent of hardness and bitterness in his tone. He was no longer the sweet young man who had gone off to war four years ago. But, of course, she chided herself, that was to be expected. The men fighting the war had seen and done so much and allowances would have to be made. Still, she wondered with a sinking feeling, how else had he changed?

Ray, uncomfortable with the sudden tension, downed the rest of his drink and stood up. "Well, I think I'll be going. Thank you for your hospitality, Nancy. It was good meeting you."

"And where the hell are you going?" Neil said.

"To find a hotel—"

"Don't be a jackass."

"Don't call me a jackass, you jackass."

"You know damn well there's not a hotel room to be had in the city. Sit down. You're not going anywhere."

"Neil," Nancy said, taken aback by the unexpected belligerence in his tone. "Don't talk to your friend like that."

Neil sat back as though she'd slapped his face. He looked around the kitchen, as though realizing where he was for the first time. He pushed the half-full glass away from him. "I'm sorry, you're right," he said, softly.

"It's all right, Nancy," Ray said. "Neil and me go back a long way."

"I don't care." Nancy stared Neil down. "No one will speak with that tone of disrespect in my house. Is that clear?"

Neil shook his head. "You're right. It's been a long day and… I'm sorry we barged in on you like this. The train was supposed get in at noon, but we kept getting sidelined and we didn't get into Penn until almost eleven. Ray lives in New Jersey and it was too late for him to catch a bus, so…"

"It's all right. There's no need to apologize."

Nancy wanted to cry. For almost four years she'd been waiting for him to come home, fantasying about this moment. But she never envisioned this kind of reunion. It was all wrong. She was leaving for Ireland tomorrow and he was acting like a damn fool. What was the matter with him? Had she been wrong all these years? Had she invented in her mind a man who never really existed? Was it her? Was it him? Was it the damn war?

A forlorn and frustrated Neil stood up. "Come on, Ray, maybe we can find a hotel room."

Nancy began to panic. Everything was spinning out of control. This was supposed to be a happy occasion. It was something she – and she assumed he – had been looking forward to for so many years. After all the packing and getting herself and the four kids ready for an ocean voyage, she was so exhausted she couldn't think straight. It had been one long week of nothing but pressure and stress. She didn't have the strength to deal with this now. It would have to be sorted out tomorrow.

"You will both stay here," she said with a forcefulness that surprised her. "Neil, take Donal out of his bed and put him with Patrick. You'll sleep in his bed. Ray, you will sleep on the living room couch. I'm really tired. Let's go to bed."

Nancy handed Ray a blanket and, as he was told, he went into the living room, fell on the couch and was instantly asleep. Neil came out of the bedroom that Patrick and Donal shared. "I put Donal in with Patrick. He never woke up. Nancy, I can't believe how big those two are."

"I can. You should see how they eat."

"My God. Patrick looks just like his father."

"Yes, he does."

He stroked her hand tentatively. "So, how are you doing?"

"All right. I'm doing all right." Her eyes welled up with tears. This was the gentle man she remembered. "How are you doing, Neil?"

"Oh, I'm adjusting." He looked away. "Nancy, since I've come back to the States, I can't believe the utter nonsense I hear coming from civilians. Every place I go, they pat me on the back and tell me what a great job I did, how I defeated the Japs and the

Nazis. And wasn't that a wonderful thing. Well, what did they do? Those goddamn useless men who stayed safely at home, making money, far away from the bullets and the bombs and the carnage and bloodshed of war…"

He shook his head violently and fell silent for a moment. "Nancy, I'm so sorry about tonight. That's not the way I wanted it to be. If that damn train had come in on time, Ray would have been off to New Jersey and I, well…"

She pulled him close and kissed him lightly on the lips. "Let's go to bed, Neil. Tomorrow's another day." As she turned away, she said, "Oh, I have a question. What does SNAFU mean?"

"It means situation normal, all – fuc... – fouled up"

"Kind of like tonight," she said.

"Yeah, kind of like tonight."

***

Neil got into Donal's bed, but he couldn't sleep. He stared at the ceiling and kept rehashing what had happened earlier in the evening, wondering where it had all gone so wrong. He hadn't meant for their first meeting in so many years to be like that. But, somehow, events overtook him – the train delays, Ray... He punched his pillow. Well, damn it, he had to bring him along, didn't he? He had nowhere else to go.

His restless eyes fell on the pin studded map on the wall and he remembered she'd written him that she and the kids were tracking the war in the Pacific. He got up to take a closer look. They'd done a good job. Nancy and the kids had pinned every battle. He wondered if, when she put pins in Guadalcanal and Tarawa and Tinian and Iwo, she had any idea that he was fighting on those islands.

He turned to look at Patrick and Donal sleeping in the other bed. Patrick was nine and Donal would be five in December. He'd missed so many years of their lives already and now she and the kids were going away again. For how long? At the most, six months, she'd said. But he had a feeling it would be longer than that. He was certainly no judge of time. Hell, hadn't he thought the war would be over in a year?

CHAPTER EIGHTEEN

The next morning, Nancy was awakened by the sound of the children screaming, "Uncle Neil is back! Uncle Neil is back!"

When she came into the living room, the kids were holding Neil's hands and dancing round and round with him, while a perplexed Ray Fazio peeked out from under a blanket.

"Hush, you kids. Uncle Neil's friend is trying to sleep."

Ray sat up. "No, it's time to get up anyway. I have a train to catch."

Nancy went into the kitchen to make coffee. A moment later, Neil came in putting on his great coat. "I'll go get bagels."

"Bagels? Since when do you eat bagels?"

"Since I started eating a lot of things besides boiled potatoes. Have you ever heard of sushi?"

"No."

"It's raw fish. I had it in Hawaii. It's very good."

"It sounds disgusting."

"I'll admit it's an acquired taste. Where's the closest bagel shop?"

"I'm sure I don't know. I don't eat bagels."

"Well, you're in for a treat. Is there a Jewish deli nearby?"

"There's one on 98th street."

"Be right back."

A yawning Ray came in and sat down. "Thanks for putting me up for the night."

She poured him a cup of coffee. "Please, it was no bother."

Patrick came marching into the kitchen draped in Neil's tunic, reminding Nancy of Mickey Mouse as the Sorcerer's Apprentice.

He rubbed the three stripes on the sleeve. "Mr. Fazio, is Uncle Neil a sergeant?"

"Yep. A platoon sergeant."

"What do all these neat ribbons mean?"

Ray knelt beside Patrick. "Well, a lot of them are routine. For example, see this red ribbon with the blue stripe? That's a good conduct medal. Most of us got that, although I'll be damned if I know why." He winked at Nancy. "But now this one is special." When he pointed to the navy blue ribbon with a white vertical stripe, his playful tone suddenly changed and he became almost reverential. "That's the Navy Cross," he said quietly. "Your Uncle Neil got that for pulling three men out of a burning tank while taking machine gun fire from a Jap pillbox even after he'd been shot in the leg."

"Wow."

Nancy started. "What? He told me he was standing next to a tank that exploded."

"Well it did, just after he got those tankers out. His hands got burned real bad. We figured it was a million-dollar wound, but we heard he bugged the doctors so much that they sent him back to his unit just to be rid of him. That Neil, he's some character."

Nancy slid into a chair. "Where did that happen?" she asked, suspecting that she knew the answer.

"Guadalcanal. Boy, that was one hell of a fight." He turned back to Patrick. "And this one" – he pointed to a purple ribbon with white vertical stripes at the edges – "is the Purple Heart he got for getting wounded."

Nancy was still trying to digest what he'd just said. "Ray... where... where else did you fight? He wasn't allowed to tell me."

"Tell me about it. Not for nothing, but those damn censors would barely let you put a date on a letter. Let's see, from Guadalcanal we went to Tarawa, then Tinian, and finally Iwo. Now that was really one hell of a fight."

"Did Uncle Neil kill a lot of Japs, Mr. Fazio?"

"Patrick!"

"I just want to know, Mom."

"You don't need to know that."

Fazio, seeing that Nancy was upset, tousled Patrick's hair. "Well, there was a lot of shooting going on, Pat. It's hard to tell who shot who. For all I know your Uncle and me only shot up a bunch of palm trees."

Ray Fazio left after breakfast and when he put his uniform on, Nancy noticed that he, too, had a purple heart. The kids went out to say goodbye to their friends for the last time, and Nancy and Neil were finally alone.

She poured him another cup of coffee. "How'd you like the bagels?" he asked.

"Very good. Kind of like a roll."

"There a lot more versatile than rolls. You haven't lived till you've had bagel and lox with a smear."

"What in the world is that?"

"You take a bagel, smear it with cream cheese, then add the lox – that's salmon."

"You've become quite the gourmet since you've been away."

"After eating all those C and K rations in the field, when I got R and R, I was ready to eat damn near anything."

Nancy studied him, realizing she'd discovered yet another thing that was different about him. Before the war neither he nor Connor would touch spaghetti or Chinese food, or any ethnic food, come to that. They were content to eat their potatoes and beef or lamb. "How'd you sleep?" she asked.

"Like a top," he lied.

"I don't see how. Donal's pillow is like a marshmallow. But he won't give it up. He insists it come to Ireland with us."

At the mention of Ireland, they both fell silent. It was a topic they both wanted to avoid talking about.

"Too close to an exploding tank?" she asked, finally breaking the tense silence.

"What are you talking about?"

"Ray said your hands got burned pulling men from a burning tank. And you were shot."

Neil turned away from Nancy's penetrating gaze. "Ray Fazio is a real yenta."

"A what?"

"Yenta. Somebody who can't keep his big mouth shut."

"Was it bad over there, Neil?"

"I don't want to talk about it, Nancy."

"But maybe if you talk about it—"

He slammed his cup on the table, sloshing coffee onto the table. "I said I don't want to talk about it."

He immediately busied himself wiping up the spill with a napkin. Damn it! He'd done it again. He hadn't meant to snap at her like that. Outbursts like that were beginning to bother him. Sometimes he said things or did things that were not like him. It was as though, at times, someone else was in control of his mind.

"I'm sorry, Nancy. I didn't mean to—"

"It's all right."

She went to pat his hand, but he pulled it away and slipped it under the table. "Is there any coffee left?"

She stood up. She had hoped that the tension would be gone this morning, but it was still there. "Sure."

***

By the time Nancy packed the last few articles, including Donal's pillow, it was time to leave for the pier.

Neil hailed a cab, and he and the cabdriver hauled the two steamer trunks down the stairs. The children were frenzied at the thought of going on a sea voyage to Ireland and they couldn't stop talking on the drive to the pier.

"Maybe we'll see whales," Maureen said.

"Or sharks. They eat the whales," Patrick said with relish.

"No they don't. Whales are stronger than sharks," Fiona pointed out.

"Are not."

"Are too."

"I want to see a U-boat," Donal announced.

Patrick made a face. "The war's over, dopey. There are no U-boats left."

"Don't call your brother dopey," Nancy admonished her son.

***

When they got to the pier, a grizzled old private security guard was directing a clog of taxis and cars away from the entrance. "I'll be damned," Neil said, pointing to the guard. "Old Charlie is still here."

Neil got out of the cab and approached the guard, who didn't seem to recognize him at first. Then with a big grin, he embraced Neil in a bear hug. Neil came back to the cab and got in. "It's OK," he said to the cab driver, "you can drive on to the pier."

A grinning Charlie raised the gate, motioned the cab forward, and snapped a salute as the taxi drove onto the pier. The cavernous, shed-like building was bustling with forklifts conveying steamer trunks and cargo to the other end of the pier. Off to one side, out of danger of rumbling trucks and forklifts, a stream of passengers made their way down the length of the pier.

At the far end of the building were two huge sliding doors leading to the exterior pier. "Drive down to the doors," he instructed the cabbie.

When Neil got out of the cab, several stevedores who were loading steamer trunks onto flatbeds, recognized Neil. "Neil Cullen," a fat balding man shouted. "Will you look at you all dressed up like a fancy Marine."

The men surrounded him, patting him on the back and shaking his hand. He could only get away from them by promising to meet them later at Darcy's for a drink.

After turning the steamer trunks over to the stevedores, Neil, Nancy and the kids walked through the open doors and got their first look at the Katherine Mary.

"Oh, my God," Nancy muttered. "We're to sail the ocean in that thing?" she whispered to Neil.

She'd seen plenty of ocean liners docked at the piers over the years – the Queen Mary, the Queen Elizabeth, the Mauritania. Compared to them, the Katherine Mary was pitifully small. It had only one smoke stack, unlike the Queen Mary, which had three. And it didn't look like it had been maintained very well. There were streaks of rust running down the sides of the ship and everywhere she looked she saw peeling paint.

Neil saw the shaken look on Nancy's face. "It's not too bad," he whispered, trying to sound positive. "I've sailed in worse, and through Pacific typhoons as well, with a thousand Marines aboard."

"Well, that's all very well," Nancy snapped. "But we're not Marines, are we?"

"The shipping agent did say she was going back to Belfast for a refitting," Neil pointed out. "She's been ferrying troops for almost four years. You can't expect her to be in apple-pie order, now can you?"

"And as I remember, he also said all she needed was a little cosmetics and a few coats of pain. I think she needs a great deal more than that."

Donal yanked on Nancy's coat. "I want to go on the boat. Please, please, Mommy."

Neil nodded toward the gangway and whispered in Nancy's ear. "Look at all those other passengers going onboard. They don't seem to have a problem with the way she looks."

Nancy had to admit he had a point and she was comforted by the sight of a steady stream of men and women and a smattering of children moving up the gangway onto the ship. They looked like sober, sensible people who would have the good sense not to sail on a coffin ship.

Nancy shrugged in resignation. "We've come this far. In for a penny, in for a pound. We'll manage."

***

The children raced down the interior corridor of the second deck, vying to see who would be the first to find their cabin. Fiona won. "Here it is, Mommy. "Here's our cabin. Two thirty-three."

With trepidation, Nancy opened the door and gasped. She expected the cabin to be small, but the confined space was more closet than room. With two sets of bunk beds on either wall, and a cot against the other wall, there was barely room to turn around.

How in the world, she wondered, would they live here for the days and weeks to come? The children didn't seem to mind. Patrick scrambled up on to one of the upper bunks. "This is my bed," he announced. "I'm sleeping here."

Donal tried to climb up the other upper bunk, but he was too small. He started to cry. "I want to go up there."

Nancy pulled him to her. "You can't, sweetheart. You're too little. Fiona you'll take the other top bunk. Maureen, you'll take this lower, I'll take the other lower, and Donal, you get to sleep on your very own cot. That seemed to mollify him. With a grin, he flopped down on the cot and bounced up and down. "I like this bed, Mommy."

"All right, now that that's settled, let's go back up on deck and say goodbye to Uncle Neil."

Neil was waiting for them on deck, looking pale and restless. "Well, how are your accommodations?"

"It's very small."

"You'll get used to it. When we left Pendleton for Hawaii, our bunks were stacked eight high. There was barley room to turn over. I remember—" He stopped talking when he saw the expression on her face. "You're right. I was in the Marines and we were at war. Well, then. Do you have everything?"

"You've asked me that a thousand times, Neil. Yes."

Neil was a study in perpetual motion. One moment he was at the rail looking down at the people still making their way up the gangplank. The next he was looking up, studying the smoke stack.

"Neil, why are you so jittery? It's me and the kids who have to cross the great ocean in this rust bucket."

"I'm fine. I'm fine." He looked at his watch. "It's almost time." He knelt down. "Hey kids, come here." They gathered around him. "Uncle Neil is going to say goodbye to you kids now so that you can be up at the bow when the ship pulls away from the dock. That's the best view. As you go down the Hudson you'll see the Statue of Liberty on your right. It's a grand sight." He handed each of them a packet of Chiclets. "This is probably the last Chiclets you'll see for a while. When you come home, I'll have another box for each of you. OK?" He kissed the girls and solemnly shook hands with the boys. "Now make sure you write. All of you. You, too, Donal."

Maureen took his hand and there were tears in her eyes. "Don't worry, Uncle Neil. I know you're going to miss us, but we won't be gone long. We'll be home real soon."

"I know you will, Maureen. OK, now off with you all. The bow's that way." He watched them run along the deck, then he turned to Nancy. "At least they're going to enjoy the voyage."

She watched them disappear around a bulkhead and smiled. "I think they will. They're kids. Everything's an adventure to them."

Neil, suddenly pale and very serious, took Nancy's hands in his. "Nancy, I want to ask you something."

"What is it?"

"Will you—"

Suddenly, the ship's horn blared, drowning out his words. Nancy leaned close. "What did you say?"

"I said, would you—"

The ship's horn sounded again.

Nancy started to laugh. "I can't hear a word you're saying with all that racket."

"Will you marry me." In the sudden silence his booming voice carried over the deck causing other passengers' heads to turn.

Nancy stared at him, incredulous. She hadn't been expecting this. When she finally found her voice, she said, "You pick this time to ask me?"

"No. The first time was December 7, 1941, the day we went to the cemetery. I thought a year was a decent time for you to mourn Connor. I was going to ask you that night. And then – well, there was Pearl Harbor and I was off to war. Since the end of the war, all I could think about was getting home and asking you to marry me. I'd planned to ask you last night, but there was the damn train delay and Ray and… and an anger and tension between us that I still don't understand."

A voice crackled over the loudspeaker. "All ashore that's going ashore."

Neil anxiously glanced at his watch. "The children need a father, Nancy. I know I can't replace Connor and I won't try. But I'll do everything in my power to make you and the kids happy."

"Last call. All ashore that's going ashore."

"Well?"

Nancy's head was reeling. "Neil, this is so sudden. My mind's a muddle. I need time to think about it."

And that answer stunned her. A week ago she would have said yes in an instant. But after last night, she was no longer sure she wanted to marry him. He was different. The war had changed him. But how much? How much of the old Neil was still there? Would she be able to love the new Neil? She didn't know. She just didn't know. She would need time to think about it, but she had no time. They were about to sail for Ireland.

Neil glanced over the rail anxiously. They were bringing up a forklift to lower the gangplank. "When will you give me an answer?"

"When I come home."

"But that's months away."

"It's November. I'll be home by the spring."

A purser hurried by. "Sorry, Sergeant, you have to go. They're about to lower the gangplank."

Neil pulled Nancy close to him and kissed her. A shutter went through her body. She hadn't felt the passion of a man since Connor died. With a start, she realized it was the first time Neil had ever really kissed her. He looked into her eyes. "When you come home, you'll give me an answer?"

"I will. When I come home."

"OK. I'll hold you to it."

He turned and raced down the deck. Nancy hurried to the rail and looked over the side. Oh, my God. The gangplank was already away from the ship. Then she heard confused shouts. The forklift stopped for a moment. Then it turned and reset the gangplank against the ship. Neil ran down the gangway to the cheers and applause of the dockworkers standing by.

A moment later, Nancy felt, rather than heard, the engine's increased vibration as the ship propellers engaged.

Two tugs, tethered to the Katherine Mary, gently pulled her away from the pier. Nancy leaned on the rail and saw Neil standing quietly among the bustle of men and machines who had just completed their tasks of servicing the ship. Their eyes locked on each other and she stayed there on the deck, watching him until, as the ship's bow slowly swung south, he was just a small dot on the dock. The ship's horn sounded twice and there was a noticeable surge as the ship's twin propellers engaged and the two tug boats disengaged.

Trying not to think about what Neil had just asked her, Nancy walked toward the bow to be with her children when the ship passed the Statue of Liberty.

The voyage had begun.

CHAPTER NINETEEN

As Neil promised, they did indeed see the Statue of Liberty as the ship sailed down the Hudson River towards the Verrazano Narrows. By the time the ship came abeam of the statue, it was dusk and it was truly a magical sight. To their right, the statue's lighted flaming torch thrust into the dark sky, while on the left, the bright star-like twinkling lights of Manhattan skyscrapers lit the night. There was a gentle swell coming in off the ocean and the ship's bow slowly dipped and rose in a quiet, gentle rhythm. Nancy thought it a pleasant sensation, but she wondered what it would be like in the North Atlantic if a storm blew up.

Unpacking and storing clothing in the tiny cabin was a real challenge. There was precious little storage space and Nancy quickly ran out of places to put clothing. Recognizing defeat, she announced that for the duration of the trip they would live out of the steamer trunks. At least the children thought that was a grand idea.

She'd barely finished unpacking when a voice came over the loudspeaker. "Good evening, this is the captain speaking. As per Coast Guard regulations, we are required to conduct a lifeboat drill. On the back of your cabin door you will find a card indicating the location of your assigned lifeboat station. Please don your life jackets and proceed immediately to your assigned station."

Maureen read the card on the back of the door. "We're number six, Mommy."

"Good." She looked around the cabin. "Now, I wonder where the life jackets are?"

"Up there," Patrick said, pointing to the vests stuffed into an upper closet shelf. After several false starts, they finally managed to get into their life jackets and adjust all those confusing straps and belts.

Up on deck, it was completely dark. The only lights visible in the distance were a string on faint lights along the New Jersey shore. It was also very chilly and Nancy hoped the drill wouldn't take too long. She was uncomfortable, but at least she was comforted by the actions of the crew. With keen interest she watched them go about their assigned tasks with quiet efficiency. One by one, the crew inspected each passenger to make sure all life jackets were worn properly. But then it occurred to her – they'd had plenty of practice. The Katherine Mary must have made countless voyages across an ocean infested with German submarines. Of course they would be well trained in abandoning ship.

At least the kids were enjoying themselves, laughing and pointing to each other and saying how silly they looked.

And then it was over. The captain came on the loudspeaker. "This concludes the drill. You may return to your cabins. Thank you for your cooperation. Dinner will be served in the dining room at seven-thirty."

***

The ship's rather small dining room was nothing like the pictures she'd seen of the elegant dining room on the Queen Mary. But, of course, how could it be? She had to keep reminding herself that the Katherine Mary was little more than a glorified tramp steamer. From what she saw on deck during the drill, Nancy estimated that the ship was carrying no more than a hundred or so passengers.

The chief steward directed Nancy and the children to a table where a distinguished-looking gentlemen with long, slicked-back gray hair was already seated. He stood up and bowed formally to Nancy.

"Good evening, dear lady," he said with an accent that Nancy took to be German because he sounded a little like Mrs. Krueger.

"My name is Victor Haas and it seems I am to be your dining companion for the duration of the voyage."

"I'm Nancy Cavanaugh," she said, shaking his hand, "and this is Maureen, Fiona, Patrick, and Donal."

He bowed to the girls and, treating the boys as if they were men, he shook hands with them. "May I say, it is a pleasure to meet such a lovely family."

"Thank you, Mr. Haas."

"Please, Mrs. Cavanaugh, you must call me Victor. That is not the European way, I know. We always address people by their last names, but I've been in the States since the start of the war and, God help me, I've picked up many of the American ways. I must say, I like it."

"Well, then you must call me, Nancy."

He bowed. "Very well, Nancy."

Nancy breathed a sigh of relief. Mr. Haas seemed completely unfazed at the prospect of spending an entire voyage sitting at a table with four small children. One of her many worries about the voyage was how other passengers would react to her kids. Over the years she'd had several unpleasant experiences getting on buses, subways, even going to the movies with four kids. The looks on some people's faces registered everything from mild alarm to abject horror that one of these children might actually sit next to them. A few of them even fled their seats rather than face the prospect of sitting next to someone like – Maureen? Nancy was always tempted to say something, but she held her tongue. After all, she, herself, had seen her share of unruly children whom she wouldn't want to sit next to either. She had to forgive those people. They couldn't know that Nancy had raised her children to be polite and well-behaved. It was all part of that fear, she realized ruefully, that if she was not perceived to be a fit mother, they could take her children away from her.

Nancy looked around her, pleased by the seating arrangements. They were at a table for eight, but everyone appeared to be seated. She liked the idea that the nice Mr. Haas – Victor – would be their only dinner companion.

Just then there was a commotion at the door. A flustered heavyset woman in her early sixties was in animated conversation with the head steward. After a few moments they seemed to sort out whatever difficulty there was. But then, much to Nancy's dismay, the head steward led her directly to their table.

Haas stood up and bowed as he had for Nancy. "Good evening, dear lady. Victor Haas at your service."

She flopped down into a chair next to Donal, rapidly fanning herself with a lacy handkerchief. "Funny, you don't look like a servant to me."

Haas's bushy eyebrows shot up. He opened his mouth to speak, but he closed it and he sat down slowly.

"Sorry, I'm late, folks. But for the life of me, I couldn't get out of that damn life jacket. It was like wrestling with an octopus. They show you how to put it on, you'd think they'd show you how to take it off, wouldn't you?"

She addressed this question to Donal who could only nod wide-eyed at the strange lady.

"Anyway, I'm Cora Ingram, pleased to meet you all."

"I'm Nancy Cavanaugh, and this is Maureen, Fiona, Patrick, and Donal."

"Oh, what a cute bunch of kids. Hi, kids."

"Hello, Mrs. Ingram," they mumbled in unison.

"Oh, no. I'm not a missus, never have been. I'm a miss, but just call me Cora. That'll do just fine." She looked at Victor, who was still recovering from her whirlwind entrance. "Victor Haas, right? I know you're no servant." She waved a hand at him. "That was just a joke."

Victor nodded and smiled tentatively.

After the soup was served, Cora said, "So where are you going, Donal?"

"We're going to Ireland."

"No kidding. I've never been out of the States myself, but I hear that's a beautiful country. I'm going to Scotland."

"We're going back to live on my Dad's farm and fight my aunt in court because she's trying to take the farm away from us even though it belongs to my Dad and he paid off all the farm debts and—"

"Donal." Nancy interjected, trying to steer Donal away from giving away all the family secrets the first night of the voyage. "Eat your soup. Do you have family in Scotland?" Nancy asked, hoping to change the subject.

"Well, it seems I had an aunt I never knew I had. She died last year. And that's why I'm going to Scotland. It's the craziest thing. I got a letter from a solicitor telling me that this aunt, she was twice removed or something, died and left me a castle! Can you imagine that?"

"A real castle?" Victor asked dubiously. "I ask only because we Europeans have been known to exaggerate one's status by creating imaginary titles and describing one's modest county home as a manor. Or a castle."

"No, it's a real castle all right. He sent me pictures. It's got towers and everything."

"Wow," Patrick eyes widened. "A real castle."

"Yep. Hey, you guys can come visit me."

The children clapped in delight at the thought of visiting a real castle.

"What will you do with it?" Nancy asked.

"I have no idea. I'll have to take a look at it. I hear those castles can be nasty, drafty things. So from what Donal tells me, I gather your husband is dead?"

Nancy was taken aback by the abrupt change of topic and the directness of her question. "Yes, he is."

"The war, uh?"

"No. He died before the war. He was hit by a car."

"Oh, my. That must have been awful for you."

Nancy nodded uncomfortably. She didn't really want to discuss Connor's death with this total stranger.

"I lost my wife as well," Victor interjected.

"Oh, I'm sorry to hear that," Nancy said, getting the distinct impression that he'd said that to ward off any further questions from Cora Ingram. She was grateful for his intervention.

Cora turned her attention to Victor. "Oh, really? How'd you lose your wife?"

Victor signaled the steward. "I don't think this is an appropriate topic of conversation for dinner," he said, glancing at the children.

Cora fanned herself again. "Oh, of course. You're absolutely right."

When the steward came, Victor said, "May I see the wine menu?"

"I'm sorry, sir. We have no wine cellar in place for this voyage. But we do have several bottles of prewar French Cabernet."

Victor grimaced. "Well, I guess that will have to do. Please bring your best bottle."

"Very good, sir."

When the steward came back, Nancy watched, fascinated, as the steward screwed off the cork and offered it to Victor. He smelled it and nodded. Then the steward poured a dribble of wine in his glass. Victor swirled the wine, held it up to the light, sipped it, and made a face. "*C'est la vie.* Very well," he said to the steward. "You may pour."

Nancy was speechless. She'd never seen anything like that outside of a Fred Astaire movie.

"Ladies, will you join me in a glass of wine?"

Cora flipped her wine glass over. "Sure."

Nancy didn't know what to do. She was ashamed to tell him that she'd never tasted wine in all her life. The sum total of her knowledge of alcohol consisted of beer and the occasional rye and ginger ale highball.

He turned her glass over and poured wine into it. "I think you will like this," he said.

He held up his glass. "To a wonderful voyage."

Nancy and Cora clinked glasses. "To a wonderful voyage."

Nancy took a tentative sip. It was different. It tasted a lot like grape juice, but not quite. There was something different about it, something exciting that she couldn't quite explain. After the third sip, she decided she liked wine.

After dinner, Victor invited her and Cora for an after dinner drink in the lounge, a small room off the dining room. Nancy begged off. She was wiped out. The previous weeks' craziness had finally caught up to her. In her mind-fogged state, she could hardly believe that they had just set sail at four o'clock this afternoon. It seemed as though they'd been a sea for so much longer than that.

***

The next morning, they went to the dining room for breakfast which, Nancy was informed, was "open seating" meaning, the steward explained, that they could sit wherever they wanted. She looked around but she didn't see Victor or Cora so they sat down at a table with an old couple who hardly said a word to them or to each other all through breakfast.

After lunch, which was open seating as well, Nancy and the kids set off to explore the ship. It was chilly on deck and overcast. There were a handful of deck chairs scattered about the deck, a few of which were occupied by hardy souls wrapped in blankets. Nancy gazed anxiously out at the dark green sea which, thankfully, was relatively calm. Her only previous ocean voyage was when she'd come to America. That ship was small as well, even smaller than the Katherine Mary, and she'd shared a tiny cabin with four other women. A gale had blown for three days straight and she'd been deathly sick the entire time. She prayed she wouldn't have a repeat of that experience.

Below decks, they came across a small room which had been turned into a recreation room for children with an assortment of toys ranging from blocks and hobby horses for the little ones to board games for the bigger kids. Nancy had been concerned that the children would have nothing to do for the entire voyage and would be bored to death, so she was pleased to see that there were about a dozen children of various ages playing in the recreation room.

"Can we go in there?" Patrick asked.

"Sure. Why don't you all go in and make friends with the other children."

***

Left to explore the ship alone, Nancy made her way to the stern where the lounge was located. As she approached the room, she heard the most beautiful piano music coming from inside. She assumed it must be a recording, but when she came into the lounge, she saw a man sitting at the piano and was delighted to see it was her table mate, Victor Haas.

Cora, who was seated at a table near the piano, spotted Nancy and beckoned to her. Nancy slipped into a seat next to her.

"My God, he plays beautifully."

"He should," Cora said out of the side of her mouth, "he's a world-renown concert pianist."

"Oh, I'm so embarrassed. I probably should have recognized him."

"Don't be. If you're anything like me, I'm sure your tastes run more to Frank Sinatra and Benny Goodman. I, myself, have never had much exposure to that long-hair stuff."

Victor finished to enthusiastic applause. After pulling away from a cluster of well-wishers, he sat down with Nancy and Cora.

"That was beautiful," Nancy said.

"It would sound much better if the piano were in tune."

"What was the name of that song?"

"That was Franz Schubert's *Impromptus for Piano*. Have you heard of it?"

"Oh, no. But it was beautiful. Cora tells me you're a concert pianist."

"Yes, that is how I came to be stranded in the States. I was on a concert tour when the Japanese bombed Pearl Harbor. The very next day, my agent tried to book passage to Europe, but, alas, it was too late. As you know, all commercial shipping was suspended for the duration of the war."

"Where's home?" the ever questioning Cora asked.

"Vienna."

"Really? I took you for a kra...— I mean German."

Victor's smile was tight. "An understandable mistake. However, calling an Austrian German, is tantamount to calling someone from Mississippi a northern Yankee."

"Yikes! As a born-and-bred Tennessean, Victor, I get your analogy. My most sincere apologies."

"Please, there is nothing to apologize for." He signaled the steward. "Will you ladies join me in a glass of sherry? Assuming, of course, that they have sherry."

Nancy's mind was reeling. She felt as though she were floating in a dream world. So far, the voyage was so much more enjoyable than she'd ever thought possible. Her concerns about the small size of the ship turned out to be part of the Katherine Mary's charm, creating a cozy, intimate atmosphere. Since she'd come on board, her whole experience had been one marvelous experience after another – being served all her meals in a dining room with the likes of Victor Haas, drinking wine, and now, the offer of sherry – was more than she could digest.

"Nancy, will you join us in a glass of sherry?" Victor asked.

The sound of his voice brought her back to reality. She would love to have a glass of sherry – whatever that was – with Victor and Cora, but she heard herself say, "Thank you, no. I have to see to my children."

Cora shot her a baleful look. "Nancy, you're on board a ship in the middle of the Atlantic Ocean. Where in the world could they possibly go?"

And it hit her. Cora was absolutely right. Where could they go? For as long as she could remember, she'd been so used to taking care of her children or providing a babysitter that her natural reaction was to round them up and take them under her protective wing. But she didn't have to do that, did she? Not here. They were on board a ship. They couldn't get lost. They knew where their cabin was and the ship was small enough that they could always find her in the event of an emergency. She sat back and breathed a great sigh of relief, feeling a wonderful sense of freedom.

"I've changed my mind, Victor. I would love a glass of sherry."

Nancy took a sip of her sherry. It was sort of like wine, but different somehow. She decided she liked sherry, too.

"I must apologize for my behavior at dinner last night," Victor said. "That business about the wine was uncalled for. I keep forgetting that the war is just over and there are still shortages. When I sailed on the Queen Mary—"

"You sailed on the Queen Mary?" Cora asked, wide-eyed.

"Oh, many times. Of course that was before the war."

"Wow. I'm impressed. It must have been wonderful."

"Let's just say," he said with a smile, "that it was something a little more than the Katherine Mary."

"I'll bet. So, how'd your wife die?" Cora asked, stunning both Victor and Nancy with yet another abrupt change of subject.

"You're a very direct woman, aren't you?" Victor asked.

"I am. God help me, I can't help it. I'm just so damn inquisitive and I have a big mouth, too. Guess what I do for a living?"

"I couldn't begin to imagine," Victor said, with just a hint of sarcasm in his voice.

"What do you think, Nancy?"

Nancy shrugged. "A school teacher?"

"Naw. I'm a librarian. Can you believe it?"

"No," Nancy and Victor said in unison.

"It's true. Instead of me telling people to shut up in the library, they're always telling me to shut up. Is that a hoot or what?" She took a sip of sherry. "This isn't half bad. Victor, you don't have to talk about your wife if you don't want to. Don't mind me."

Victor's pleasant smile faded. "She died during an Allied air raid on March 12, 1945." He took a sip of his sherry and stared off into space. "She sought shelter in a block of apartments just across the street from the State Opera House. The buildings collapsed from the bombs, burying everyone. There were no survivors. I'm going home to see where she is buried."

Nancy's eyes welled up with tears and she felt a stab of shame. During the war, all she thought about, worried about, were men like Neil and Tom Cassidy and the husbands and boyfriends of her girlfriends. But she never really considered the millions of innocent people all over Europe who suffered and died as well.

"I'm sorry for your loss, Victor," she said quietly.

"Thank you." He slapped his knees. "Well, I think I shall play the piano."

"What will you play?" Cora asked.

"Oh, I think Bach's *Prelude and Fugue in C.* It was my wife's favorite piece."

As soon as the opening progression of arpeggiated chords sounded, everyone in the lounge lapsed into respectful silence, except for Cora, who leaned over to Nancy and whispered, "I'm such a jerk."

CHAPTER TWENTY

Thanks to open seating at breakfast and lunch, Nancy and the kids got to sit with a lot of different passengers. Within a few days, she knew almost everyone onboard. She learned that no one was there for a leisurely transatlantic cruise. For most of them, like Nancy, the war had disrupted their lives and now they were desperate to restore some semblance of normalcy to their lives by cleaning up unfinished business.

She met an American man from Ohio who was going back to reunite with his wife and daughter who had been trapped in war-torn Germany since 1942; a woman who was going back to England to look for her missing sister; and a grief-stricken man who wanted to visit the grave of his son who had been killed in the Battle of the Bulge. Everyone on board – like herself – was anxious to return to Europe for a variety of personal and sometimes tragic reason. The final destination for some was Ireland. But for others, like Victor Haas, Ireland was just a dropping off point to Europe and beyond.

The children quickly made friends with children their own age and Nancy was delighted that she saw them only at meal times in the dining room and at bedtime, where they would excitedly regale her with descriptions of their day's activities. Having most of the day to herself, she enjoyed walking the deck or bundling up on a deck chair, quietly contemplating the vast, soothing ocean. She discovered the ship's small library and began to read – and enjoy – novels, something she hadn't had time to do since the birth of Maureen.

One afternoon, Nancy and Cora were in the lounge listening to Victor play when the kids came rushing in. Nancy hushed them and made them sit down and listen. When he was finished, he called the children up to the stage. "Does anyone know how to play chopsticks?" They shook their heads in the negative. "Well, then I must teach you. Who wants to learn first?"

The three older ones were too shy to answer, but Donal piped up. "I do."

Victor sat him down on the seat next to him and held his little fingers on the keys. "Ready?" And with that, he and a giggling Donal began to play chopsticks. That's all the other kids had to see.

"I want to go next," Patrick said.

"No, me," Fiona said.

Victor looked at the reserved Maureen. "What about you?"

"I would like to learn. But they can go first."

In less than an hour, under Victor's expert tutelage, each of them learned to play chopsticks, which Nancy and the other passengers would regretfully hear ad nauseam for the rest of the voyage.

***

As the days passed, Nancy continued to revel in the unexpectedly wonderful and glorious idyllic pleasure of the voyage. She thought back to her initial reservations and wondered – what had she been so afraid of? She'd just been silly. Everything was fine. Even the weather was agreeable.

But, then, on the sixth night at sea, around three in the morning, Nancy was awakened from a sound sleep by the ship's violent rolling. She grabbed onto the bunk for support and felt the bow of the ship rising, rising, rising… and then with a violent thud that made the entire ship shudder, it came crashing down into the sea. And she knew immediately. They'd sailed into the kind of violent North Atlantic storm that she'd been dreading. She listened intently to hear if the children were awake, but, thankfully, all she heard was their soft, rhythmic breathing.

Nancy remained awake the entire night. Around seven, the children began to wake up. "Wow," Patrick said. "This is like a roller coaster."

"I want to go up on deck," Donal said.

"I don't feel so good," Maureen said.

The trip down the corridor to the dining room was made with great difficulty. Every time the ship rolled, they were thrown against the opposite wall. By eight o'clock, the dining room was usually full, but this morning there weren't more than a dozen people.

To prevent dishes from sliding off the tables during violent rolls, the dining room stewards had installed wooden grids on the tabletops consisting of eighteen-inch squares.

Carefully and with great effort, they slid into their seats. Donal thought it was hilarious watching his plate slide back and forth, bouncing from one side of the grid to the other. But for some of the other passengers who had made it to the dining room, the sight of plates and glasses sliding around the table sent then scurrying back to their cabins.

For two days, the ship rolled in heavy seas and high winds. Most of the passengers remained in their cabins, too seasick to venture out, including Victor and Cora. But much to Nancy's relief, none of the children – nor herself – succumbed to seasickness.

***

The rest of the voyage was uneventful and life aboard ship quickly returned to normal, including Victor's daily afternoon impromptu concerts in the lounge. On an afternoon when the ship was about two days out of Belfast, Nancy was in the lounge with Cora and a dozen other passengers listening to Victor play a Chopin nocturne. Suddenly, the ship's engines stopped and a moment later, a voice came over the loudspeaker. "Attention please. This is the captain speaking. This is not a drill. Please secure your life jackets and proceed to your assigned lifeboat stations immediately. I repeat, this is not a drill."

At first people didn't know what to make of it. They looked at each other, puzzled. Then a few got up and hurried out of the lounge. And suddenly, everyone was on the move. Nancy's first thought was that she didn't know where the children were. As she hurried out of the lounge, she breathed a sigh of relief when she saw Patrick and Fiona skipping down the corridor laughing. Apparently, they hadn't heard the message.

"Where's Maureen and Donal?"

"I think they're up on deck," Fiona said.

For the sake of the children, Nancy forced herself to remain calm. "All right. Listen to me carefully. I want you both to go to the cabin right away. Put on your life jackets and wait for me there."

Nancy hurried up on deck, which was already swarming with passengers moving to their assigned lifeboat stations. Nancy began to panic. With all the activity on deck, how was she supposed to spot two small children? She stopped an officer. "Mr. Keel, have you seen my children."

"No, I haven't Mrs. Cavanaugh, but you must get into your life jacket immediately."

Ignoring him, she pushed him and ran down the length of the deck through an ever increasing throng of people. She was close to being overwhelmed with panic – and then she saw them. Maureen, serious and pale clutched Donal's hand as they hurried along the deck. She spotted Nancy and ran toward her, relief spreading across her face.

"I heard the announcement, Mommy. We were on the way to the cabin."

"Good girl. Come on, let's get down and get our life jackets on. Fiona and Patrick are waiting for us there."

Five minutes later, Nancy and the kids were up on deck at their assigned lifeboat station. Crew members had already released the lifeboats from their davits and had lowered them to deck level. The crowd was abuzz with rumors that ranged from the truly frightening – the ship was sinking, to the preposterous – a U-boat had been spotted.

A voice over the loudspeaker boomed. "Attention please. This is the captain speaking. A mine has been spotted off the starboard bow. We are in no immediate danger, but as a precaution the ship has been stopped while we assess the situation. Please remain at your lifeboat stations until you are given the all clear."

Victor, who was standing next to Nancy, pointed out to sea. "Look, there it is."

All eyes turned in the direction he was pointing. About a quarter of a mile from the ship, Nancy saw a small, black object floating in the sea. Even from this distance, she could make out the ugly spikes protruding from the sphere.

"I don't get it," Cora said. "If we can see the damn thing, why can't we just go around it?"

"Because there might be more than one," Victor said.

There were a few gasps and everyone immediately scanned the sea looking for more mines. It had been relatively mild for a November day on the Atlantic, but now as the sun was going down, the wind picked up and the temperature dropped.

"I'm cold, Mommy," Donal said, shivering. "I want to go inside."

"I know, honey. But we have to wait here a little while longer."

Nancy watched anxiously as the seas began to pick up. When they'd come topside, the ocean had been calm, but now whitecaps were popping up everywhere. She was horrified at the thought that she and the children might have to climb into those tiny lifeboats and bob about in a storm-tossed ocean God knows how many miles from land.

"How long do you think we'll have to stay here?" Cora asked plaintively.

No one had an answer. Silently, everyone anxiously focused their attention on the bobbing mine and the surrounding sea.

Twenty minutes later, a voice on the loudspeaker boomed, startling everyone. "Attention please. This is the captain speaking. The emergency is over. You may leave your lifeboat stations now. Thank you for your cooperation."

As Nancy took the children downstairs to their warm cabin, the engines started up and she felt an almost imperceptible movement as the ship got underway again.

After the adventures of the Atlantic storm and the mine sighting, everyone on board began to feel that they were now seasoned sea voyagers. Fortunately, nothing else happened to test their newfound confidence.

***

At dawn on the tenth day, Nancy was awakened by Patrick shouting, "Ireland! I see Ireland!"

Maureen and Fiona scrambled out of their bunks and rushed to the porthole to see what Patrick was looking at.

"Oh, I see it, too" Maureen said.

Fiona pushed Patrick aside. "Let me see. Oh, there it is."

Donal jumped up and down, but he was too short to see out the porthole. "I can't see. I can't see."

Nancy got out of bed and held Donal up to the porthole.

"I see Ireland too, Mommy. See?"

Nancy did see. In the dim light of the dawn the green headlands of Ireland rose up from the ocean, backlit by the glow of the morning sun rising beyond it. It was a truly breathtaking sight. But its beauty was lost on her. For most of the voyage, she'd been able to put this day out of her mind, but now it was here and she felt that old, uneasy churning in her stomach.

***

It was just after one in the afternoon when the Katherine Mary came into Belfast harbor. As Nancy and the kids stood at the railing, watching the dock men catch the large hawsers and secure the looped ends onto the mooring bollards, she was filled with a renewed sense of apprehension and doubts. Did she do the right thing taking the kids back here? Was the farm really worth fighting for?

Maureen looked down at the sea of faces gathered on the pier. "Do you see grandmother and grandfather?"

Nancy scanned the crowd. "No, not yet. They're probably—" She stiffened. There they were. At the first sight of her parents, terrible memories flooded her mind, reminding her why she left Ireland in the first place. They'd aged, but they hadn't changed. Her mother still pursed her lips in perpetual disapproval and she still dressed in black from head to toe as though she were in permanent mourning. And she still wore her hair in a severely tight bun. Her father, tall and austere, looked as remote and forbidding as ever. Watching them, they seemed like total strangers to her and she could scarcely remember ever being their daughter. The thought made her want to cry. They spotted Nancy, but neither one of them smiled.

Gazing down at them, Nancy was reminded of a photograph of a painting she'd once seen in a magazine. It was called *American Gothic* and it depicted a grim-faced man and woman. Her parents reminded her of those two. Irish Gothic. She would have laughed, if she hadn't felt so tense.

***

Nancy and the kids went down to the lounge to wait with the other passengers for permission to disembark.

Victor bowed to Nancy. "Nancy, it was so nice meeting you and your lovely family. You made what I thought would be a long, arduous journey most pleasant."

"Thank you, Victor, for introducing me to wine and sherry. Oh, and thank you for teaching the children chopsticks."

"It was my pleasure. They're all quick learners, but I'd keep my eye on your little Donal. I think he has some serious musical talent."

"Oh, really? Thank you."

He handed her a card. "Here is my address. The next time I tour the States, I would like you and the children to be my guests."

"Thank you, Victor. That's very thoughtful of you."

Just then, Cora came barging into the lounge trailed by a distraught purser and two stewards. "I don't know where the damn tags are," she said to the purser. "Just put the bags on the pier. I'll find them."

"Madam, that's not possible. Government regulation state that every bag must have a tag."

"Well, I'm telling you, I never received any damn tags."

"Miss, Ingram, if you would please look in your disembarkation papers one more time."

"Oh, all right." Cora opened the packet and shuffled through it. I don't see anything here."

"There," the purser said.

"There what?"

"There are the tags."

"You mean these little things?"

"Yes, Miss Ingram. Those little things."

"Oh." She handed them to the purser. "Here are your precious tags."

Victor chuckled and whispered to Nancy, "I suspect the purser and crew would rather face a German U-boat wolf pack than another voyage with the redoubtable Miss Ingram."

"I suspect you're right."

Cora spotted them and hurried over. "Well, I guess this is it, folks. Hey, it was a lot of fun traveling with y'all."

"I never thought I would say it," Victor said, "but it was a lot of fun traveling with you, too, Cora."

"You have to come visit me in my castle."

"I would be delighted," Victor said.

"So would I and the kids."

"Good then it's settled. I have your addresses and I'll be in touch."

A voice on the loudspeaker said, "Will Miss Cora Ingram please report to the gangway station."

"Oh, that's me. I told the purser in no uncertain terms that I must be off the ship in time to catch the afternoon train to Scotland."

After a round of vigorous hugs and kisses, Cora was gone.

"She was really a lot of fun," Nancy said.

"Yes, she was. But it's too bad about her castle."

"What do you mean?"

"She doesn't realize it, but owning a castle these days is quite out of the question. British real estate taxes are just too prohibitive and I doubt she could afford the upkeep on a librarian's salary. Even the aristocracy can't afford their castles and country homes anymore. Since the end of the last war, they've been selling them off or deeding them to the government."

"Oh, that's too bad. I feel so sorry for her."

"Don't. After all, how many of us can say that we once owned a real castle in Scotland?"

"That's true."

The voice on the loudspeaker said, "All passengers with names from A to D please report to the gangplank station."

"Well, I guess this is it." Nancy was genuinely sorry to see the voyage end. It had been one of the most pleasant interludes in her entire life and Victor had been a large part of it. "Thank you again, Victor, for everything."

He kissed her cheek. "Thank you. Remember to write me about tickets."

"I will."

Nancy and the children followed a stream of passengers up the stairs to the gangway station.

The voyage was finally over.

CHAPTER TWENTY-ONE

They came down the gangplank and the pleasant memories of her idyllic voyage quickly faded as the real world came crashing down on her. Her parents were standing off to the side. As she approached them, Nancy's apprehension increased. Images of her childhood, long forgotten or buried, flashed before her. She blinked them away. Even the children seemed cowed by the sight of her austere parents.

Her mother's piercing gray eyes studied them with undisguised coolness. Her father looked on with an aloof detachment that had always maddened Nancy. No one made a move to hug or kiss. The kids instinctively crowded close to their mother.

"How are you, Mother?"

"The rheumatism acts up around water."

"Sorry to hear that. How are you, Father?"

"Can't complain."

Her mother's gaze locked on the children as though they had just fallen out of the sky. Nancy introduced them. "This is Maureen... Fiona... Patrick... and Donal."

As Nancy had instructed them every day of the voyage, the girls curtsied and the boys shook hands. Nancy was relieved to see that everything was going well – until she saw Donal staring at the web of fine red veins on his grandmother's cheeks and she just knew he was going to say something. Fortunately, a passing horse carting a wagonload of luggage off the pier distracted him.

"The boys need haircuts," Mother said. "Don't they cut hair in America? And they're very skinny and wearing clothes that wouldn't keep a horse warm in summer."

"Och, leave off, Moira. They're yanks and don't the yanks always do the odd thing?"

Nancy's mother turned and started walking toward the exit. "Come on, then. The taxi's waiting. William, get the bags."

***

The two-hour-long drive from Belfast to Ballycastle passed in an uncomfortable silence, punctuated only by the occasional exclamation from one of the kids when they spotted a cow or horse in a passing field.

Nancy rolled the window down. Despite her growing anxiety, the fresh, clean smell of the air and the indescribable greenness of the grass brought back pleasant memories of her and her friends hiking through fields and filching apples from a convenient apple orchard. Ireland was a stunning contrast from the bustle and noise of New York City.

When Nancy left Ballycastle, it had been a medium sized town, bigger than a village, but smaller than cities like Dublin or Cork. From what she could see as they drove down Hillcrest Street – Ballycastle's main street – it hadn't changed very much. The old picture show house was still there, and so was the fish and chips shop, and – Nancy was delighted to see – Mr. Ranjini's candy store was still in business. The fact that an Indian from faraway, exotic India had chosen to open a candy store in Ballycastle had always been the subject of intense curiosity and speculation. Nancy loved to go into his store. He was so unusual, with his dark eyes, strange clothing and odd accent, but he had a wonderful sense of humor, which most of her friends never appreciated.

When the taxi turned into Cathedral Street, where she'd grown up, once again the bad memories came flooding back to her – the fears, the anxieties, the terrors. For a moment, Nancy thought she might be ill. My God, what am I doing here? Whatever possessed me to come back?

"Hey, where are all the cars?"

Patrick's question brought her back to the present. She realized Cathedral Street must be a strange sight to children used to the constant traffic on Amsterdam Avenue. In spite of its lofty name, Cathedral Street was a fairly narrow street bordered on both sides by rows of low slung, two story attached houses. The houses seemed oddly stunted, but that was because you stepped down into the kitchen, which took almost two feet off the elevation of the houses. There wasn't a car in sight, Nancy noted, just a milkman on a cart being pulled by a tired donkey at the far end of the street.

Her father and the taxi driver dragged the two steamer trunks into the house. Nancy hung back on the sidewalk to pay the driver. She stayed outside after he drove away, pretending to take in the sights. The truth was, she didn't want to go inside. Then, realizing she'd put it off as long as she could, she took a deep breath and stepped down into the past and into a house she hadn't seen in fifteen years.

It seemed so much smaller than she remembered. She didn't recall the kitchen ceiling being that low. It gave the room a dark, cave-like feel despite a double window facing out onto the street. The fireplace seemed half the size she remembered, but it still dominated the room. It was a working fireplace with a large black iron pot hanging from an iron swing arm. That black, scorched pot, she realized, was probably the same one from which she had eaten porridge and stew when she was a child.

Her mother picked up a poker and stoked the smoldering fire, sending an explosion of sparks up the chimney. "I suppose you'll be wanting tea?"

"Could I have a glass of milk, please?" Donal asked.

"Milk is it? This is not America, you know. Money doesn't grow on trees here."

Her sharp tone made Donal's lower lip quiver. He was about to cry, but then he glanced out the window and saw the milkman and his donkey pass by and his eyes widened. "Mommy, there's a donkey outside!"

Thankful for the distraction, Nancy said, "Why don't you all go outside and say hello to the donkey."

The kids rushed out the door, just as happy to get away from their grandmother as they were to see a real live donkey. The man had stopped in front of the house to fill a pail of milk from his aluminum milk urn for a woman across the street. The kids surrounded the drowsy donkey and gingerly petted him.

Inside, from force of habit, Nancy sat down on the same chair she'd occupied when the family sat down to dinner. She was overcome with a strange sensation. It was as though she'd never left. She watched her father take a key out of his vest pocket and, as he did every day, wind the clock hanging on the wall by the window.

He glanced out at the children standing around the donkey. "Look at them. They're staring at the beast as though it were some kind of exotic animal from darkest Africa."

Nancy saw their smiling faces through the lace curtains and her face brightened for the first time since she'd arrived in Ireland. They're just like their father, she thought. They think Ireland is some kind of magical place.

Her mother poured the tea into mugs and sat down opposite her. "So how long will you be staying here?"

"Just until I can get the farm cleaned up, Mother. A day or two, I would think."

The old lady grunted. "Your father will take you out there tomorrow. You can get started on the cleanup."

"First, I have to see someone."

"Who?"

"Eunice Dunne."

Her father closed the glass door on the clock face. "Isn't that the woman you're going to court with?"

"Yes, she's Connor's sister."

"Is that wise?"

"I have to try, Father. Maybe if we speak face to face, we can settle this without going to court."

Nancy fervently prayed that was true, now more than ever, given her feelings about being back in Ireland. If she could come to some arrangement with her sister-in-law, she could go back to the States immediately and erase this nightmare that she had gotten herself into.

***

Nancy's first night in her childhood home was a restless and uneasy one. Her mother had set her up in her old room, which she'd shared with her two older sisters growing up. Now she was sharing it with Donal, who slept in the same bed with her, and Patrick, who slept on a rickety cot. The girls were shunted off to a tiny room at the back of the house. The kids complained about the cramped accommodations, but Nancy assured them it wouldn't be for long.

For most of the night, she tossed and turned, but when she did fall asleep, she was troubled by a kaleidoscope of dreams centering around her childhood… and Connor… and Neil… and the farm. In a final dream that woke her in a breathless panic, the Katherine Mary was sinking and she couldn't find her children.

***

The next day was Sunday and Nancy was sure she would find her sister-in-law at home. Right after breakfast, she set out to find to home of Eunice Dunne. She stopped in front of a modest row house on Bridge street less than a mile from her parents' home. Once again, she was astonished at how small – and yet in some way, distant – Ballycastle was. She was born and raised here. Connor was born and raised in Kilgrin, a little farming village not more than ten miles north of Ballycastle. But they'd never met until that dance at that ballroom in New York City. The same was true of Neil who was born and raised in Knockanally, another farming village twelve miles in the opposite direction. Although they'd all lived in a fifteen-mile radius, they hadn't met until they came to America.

Nancy took a deep breath and thumped the large brass knocker. The door opened and gaunt woman in her late forties appeared. Nancy's breath was taken away when she saw how much Eunice resembled Connor.

"Yes?" the woman asked.

"Are you Eunice Dunne?" she asked pointlessly, already knowing the answer.

Eunice's face morphed in to a tight frown of suspicion. "I am."

"I'm Nancy Cavanaugh, Connor's wife—"

Eunice started to close the door.

"No, wait, please—"

"I have nothing to say to you."

"Please, can't we talk? Can't we work this out between us?"

"I told you, I have nothing to say to you. Talk to my solicitor," she said and slammed the door in Nancy's face.

For a moment, Nancy stood there feeling as though she'd been physically slapped. She'd just wanted to try to make peace, but, apparently, that was not going to happen. With a sinking feeling, she realized that the only way to settle this dispute was going to be through the courts. She's naively assumed that all this could be settled in a short period of time, but, witnessing the hostile intransigence of her sister-in-law, she began to suspect that maybe this would take longer than she'd thought.

***

When she got back to her parents' home, she was suddenly reminded of a long-forgotten ritual. Every Sunday afternoon, for as long as Nancy could remember, her father went into the parlor, a small room off the kitchen, to be alone and listen to records on his windup Victrola while her mother went upstairs for her afternoon nap. After all these years nothing had changed.

As he was going into the parlor, Donal said, "Where are you going, Grandfather?"

The old man looked down at Donal over his wire rimmed glasses. "To listen to music on my Victrola."

"What's a Victrola?"

"It's a machine you use to listen to records."

"Could I listen, too?"

"No. you would not understand the music."

"I know how to play chopsticks."

The old man grunted and wordlessly retreated into the parlor.

Nancy felt a sudden stab of pain as she suddenly recalled experiencing the same cold rejection as a child when she'd asked to listen to his records. A few minutes later, Nancy and the kids, quietly sitting around the kitchen table, heard the scratchy tenor voice of John McCormack singing "It's a Long Way to Tipperary". By the time grandfather had moved on to "The Minstrel Boy", the kids had become bored and went out to play. All except for Donal, who stayed behind. He sat on the floor next to the parlor door, listening intently. To Nancy's delight, he seemed to really enjoy the music, even when Margaret Burke-Sheridan sang arias from *Madame Butterfly*. She remembered what Victor Haas had said about his potential music talent. At the time, she'd thought he was just being kind, but maybe Donal did have some musical abilities. The thought pleased her.

The door opened and grandfather almost tripped over Donal. "What are you doing on the floor?"

"Listening to the music. It's good."

Grandfather poured a cup of tea for himself and went back into the parlor. A moment later, the door opened and he stuck his head out. "Come in, if you want to."

Donal scrambled into the parlor and the old man shut the door. Nancy was dumbfounded. In all her years growing up, neither she, nor her two sisters and brother had even been allowed to participate in that Sunday ritual, even though they dearly wanted to.

Inside, Donal got his first look at a Victrola and he was puzzled. They had a radio at home, but this looked nothing like that. It was taller than he was and the top opened and there was a handle on the side. Grandfather lifted him onto a chair and he saw a round turntable with a big needle-like arm. Grandfather put a record on the turntable and cranked the handle. To Donal's delight, the record began to spin faster and faster. Then he put the needle-like arm on the record and he heard music.

After a while, the music began to slow down. Grandfather said to Donal, "Crank the handle. Go ahead."

Donal did as he was told and to his delight, the music sped up again. "We don't have to do that with our radio back home," he said.

"This is not a radio. It's a gramophone. The sound comes from the needle and the record, not over the airwaves."

Donal nodded gravely, but he didn't understand a word his grandfather said. All he knew was he loved the sound of the music coming from the machine.

An hour later, grandfather looked at his pocket watch and lowered the lid. "That's all for today. Your grandmother will be getting up from her nap to make dinner now."

"Thank you for letting me listen, Grandfather. It was very good."

The old man grunted. "Which one did you like best."

"I liked that man the best."

"John McCormack?"

"Yes. That one."

The old man lowered Donal to the floor. "All right. Off with you."

***

The next day, Nancy's father borrowed a car and drove her and the children out to the farm in Kilgrin. She was excited, but at the same time apprehensive about seeing the farm, She'd seen only one blurry photograph of the farmhouse and she wasn't sure what to expect.

The countryside, however, was magnificent, full of lush green rolling hills dotted with farms, plowed fields, and grazing animals. And off in the distance, the craggy and majestic Carragh Mountains.

When she was a child, she and her friends would think nothing of walking for miles and miles in the countryside. Even thought she'd grown up less than ten miles from Kilgrin, she couldn't recall ever coming out this way.

The four kids sat in the back of the car with their faces glued to the windows, loudly shouting out the animals they saw.

"There's a cow…"

"There's a horse…"

"Look at all the sheep…"

Ten minutes later, Nancy's father pulled the car off the road and stopped in front of a rusty gate, half-hanging off its hinges.

"Well," he said, turning off the engine, "we're here."

With the engine shut off, there was a startling and unexpected silence. The happy smiles drained from the children's faces at the sight of the gate.

"Where's the fine gate that Daddy told us about?" Maureen asked.

Nancy tried to hide her dismay. "Remember, Maureen, no one's been here for quite some time. Some repairs will be needed."

Unable to drive the car up the narrow path choked with weeds, they got out of the car and made their way on foot.

"Is this the winding loaning?" Fiona asked, increasingly bewildered.

Nancy was too stunned to answer.

Patrick ran ahead. "I'm going to find the tree where Daddy had a swing." He ran to the top of the loaning and stopped when he saw a stump where the tree had been. "It's gone, Mommy."

Before they could digest that sight, Maureen pointed. "Oh…"

Everyone looked where she was pointing. It was the farmhouse. But it was no longer white with a fine slate roof. Now it was a grim, gray derelict building covered with the mildew and dirt of decades. Half of the slate shingles were missing.

"Where are the rose bushes?" Fiona asked, close to tears.

Nancy didn't know what to say. Like a sleepwalker, she approached the house. She pushed open the unhinged front door and stepped inside the darkened house and her heart sank. It was so much smaller than she'd imagined it would be and the inside was in even worse disrepair than the outside. A narrow staircase filled with rubble led to the second floor. In the kitchen, ceiling planks hung down haphazardly, exposing the support joists. Two window panes had been smashed and the glass scattered across the earthen floor littered with hay. It smelled like a barn and the petrified animal droppings everywhere attested that that was exactly what it had become. Animals have been living here.

Tears welled up in her eyes. I never should have come back here, she told herself. I hate this farm. I have always hated this farm. In the name of God, what was I thinking?

She backed out the door.

Outside, her father came to stand beside her. "Och, it's been abandoned for nearly twenty years. What did you expect?"

Nancy fought back tears. "Not this."

Patrick pointed to the field behind the house. "Look, Mommy. There are cows in the field. Do they belong to us?"

Nancy saw the cows grazing in the field, and in the next field over, crops had been planted. "No, son. Those cows belong to someone else, but they've been using our land."

She took another look at the farmhouse and her heart sank. She'd thought they'd be able to move in within a couple of days. Now she realized that would be impossible. Nancy clutched her children around her and wept for their spoiled dreams.

After a moment, she shook away the tears. There was no time for that. There was too much to be done, but her numbed mind couldn't begin to fathom where to start.

But there was one thing she could do. "Let's go," she said to her father. "I have to talk to my solicitor."

Herding her children in front of her, Nancy stumbled back down the weed-choked path.

CHAPTER TWENTY-TWO

The small, dark-paneled office of Owen O'Donnell smelled of stale pipe smoke and musty books. His desk was cluttered with a half-dozen large leather-bound books and case folders stacked in precariously high piles.

Owen O'Donnell, a small gnome-like man in his late sixties, sat behind this pile of books and papers stuffing his pipe with tobacco. "And how is that fine lawyer, Mr. Isaac Kaplan?"

"The last time I saw him he was doing fine."

"A real gentleman that."

"Yes, he is. Mr. O'Donnell, what progress are you making with my case?"

"I've filed the necessary documents, Mrs. Cavanaugh. Everything is proceeding lovely."

"Good. When will the trial begin?"

He put a match to the bowl and sucked in hard, releasing a cloud of blue smoke. The room was suddenly suffused with the smell of maple. "Well now, these things take time. You yanks are always in such a hurry."

"Yes, I am in a hurry, Mr. O'Donnell. I'm anxious to get back to the States, so I would appreciate it if you would move this case along as quickly as possible."

He nodded patronizingly. "Yes, Mrs. Cavanaugh, I will do just that. Have no fear." He stood up. "Now, if that's all—"

"No, there is something else."

O'Donnell sat down heavily. He'd hoped he was finished talking to this assertive young yank. "Yes, Mrs. Cavanaugh, what is it?"

"Someone has been planting crops and grazing cows on my land."

He stared at her for some time, as though trying to understand what she'd just told him. "I see. And your point is…?"

"My point is, that's my land and I have not given anyone permission to use it."

"But surely you have no use for the land at the moment."

Nancy was flabbergasted at his lackadaisical attitude. "Mr. O'Donnell, I'll admit I don't know anything about Irish law, but I'm pretty sure that even in Ireland there are laws against trespassing and stealing."

"Now, now, I wouldn't vex myself with any of this, Mrs. Cavanaugh. What's the harm in your neighbors using land that you yourself is not using?"

"Mr. O'Donnell," she spluttered, "that's why I'm here in the first place. To keep someone, my sister-in-law in this case, from occupying my land."

"Ah, but this is very different. Whoever is using your land is not a relative. They would have no claim."

"I don't care. I want whoever is using my land to either pay me or get off."

His eyebrows shot up and his eyes narrowed. "I wouldn't advise going to war with your future neighbors."

"I don't want to go to war with anyone," she said, finding his attitude maddening. "I just want them to pay me for the use of the land or leave."

"I see. And what would you have me do?"

"I don't know. File a petition, an injunction, something to stop them."

He shook his head gravely. "Well, here's the thing, Mrs. Cavanaugh. That might mean another lawsuit and right now my advice would be to marshal our forces for the important battle ahead, establishing superior claim to your sister-in-law's."

Nancy didn't know why, but for some reason, O'Donnell didn't want to get into the middle of this fight. She wished that

Isaac Kaplan were here. He'd have taken them on. She stood up. "All right, I'll deal with this myself."

"I would advise caution, Mrs. Cavanaugh. Getting into the middle of a dispute between farmers and the land can be a bad business."

"Thanks for your advice."

She stormed out of the office, certain her sarcasm had gone over his head.

***

Nancy hurried down Hillcrest Street, deeply troubled by what had just transpired in the solicitor's office. Kaplan had been the one to contact O'Donnell back in forty-one. Did he know anything about O'Donnell? He hadn't offered an explanation as to why he'd contacted that particular solicitor and Nancy hadn't thought to ask. But now, after meeting him, she had her doubts about how effective he would be. He just didn't seem like a fighter. The last thing she needed was a timid solicitor. Damn it, wasn't that what she was – a timid woman, always had been, always would be…? Suddenly she stopped in the middle of the busy sidewalk, and while streams of shoppers brushed past her, she had her own epiphany – she was a timid woman, but, by God, that would have to stop. And it would stop right now.

Armed with a renewed sense of purpose, she continued down Hillcrest Street, deep in thought, as she formulated a plan to deal with the farmers who were using her land. She wasn't paying attention to where she was walking and accidentally bumped into a man heading in the opposite direction.

"Oh, sorry."

The man stopped and turned around.

"Nancy? Nancy Delaney? Is that you?"

Nancy turned to look at the tall, good-looking man smiling at her. Her mind was still in a fog. Slowly, it cleared and she recognized him. Back then, he'd had bright red hair, but now it was a dark auburn. She decided that it suited him well.

"Sean Garrett…!"

He gave her a tentative peck on the cheek. "Nancy Delaney! When did you get home?"

"It's Nancy Cavanaugh, now. A few days ago. There's a problem with my late husband's farm and—"

"I heard." He shrugged at the surprised expression on her face. "Nancy, Ballycastle is still a small town. Everyone knows everyone else's business. It's not like your New York City with your millions of people and no one knowing the name of his neighbor." He took her arm. "How about a cup of tea?"

That was the best offer she'd had since she'd come back. She welcomed the thought of a few precious minutes away from her parents, Mr. O'Donnell, and even, God forgive her, the children. At the moment, she couldn't think of anything better than having tea with an old boyfriend.

***

He took her to a teashop at the other end of Hillcrest Street. It hadn't been there when she was a child, but she couldn't remember what had been on this site.

The waitress brought a pot of tea and a tray of scones.

"So what have you been up to since I went off to America?"

"A few years after you left, I married Mary Nolan. Did you know her?"

"No, I can't say I did."

"Ah, she was lovely. A better wife a man couldn't ask for."

"So, where are you two living?"

Sean turned away. "She's dead."

"Oh, my God, Sean, I'm so sorry. What happened?"

Sean's looked out the window, but his eyes were a thousand miles away. "A bus accident. It'll be two years ago next month. She was on her way back from a shopping trip in Dublin. The bus skidded off the road. She was eight months pregnant."

Nancy squeezed his hand. "Sean, I'm so sorry."

He shrugged. "Thank you. Since then, I've thrown myself into my work. It's all I do." He was quiet for a moment, then he remembered. "Oh, what's the matter with me? I'm such a fool, just thinking of myself. Nancy, I'm sorry for your loss as well."

"Thank you, Sean."

For a long time, they sat there silent, each thinking about their respective losses.

After a moment, he said, "I've heard you plan to live on the farm out in Kilgrin."

"I do. I was there this morning. It's a shambles. The ceiling is falling down, the windows are gone, it's been neglected for so long. There's so much to do, I don't know where to start."

"Sounds like it needs serious repairs."

"It does."

"Then you're in luck."

"Why?"

Sean waved for the check. "Because that's what I do for a living, Nancy. I have my own construction company. Tomorrow, we'll take a ride out there and see just how bad it is."

Outside the teashop, Sean said, "Come on, I'll drive you home, if you don't mind riding in a truck with 'Sean Garrett Construction Company' written on the side."

"I don't mind at all. Do you remember where I live?"

He stopped smiling and looked wistful. "Of course I do. How could I forget. Oh, before I take you home, I'd like to show you my house. It's not far, just outside of town."

Nancy had a feeling that she shouldn't go there, but he had been so kind and he had cheered her up. "Oh, all right."

Sean pulled his truck into the driveway of a fine brick house surrounded by tall trees and thick shrubs. Behind the house was a sweeping view of the Carragh Mountains no more than fifteen miles away. Between the mountains and his house was a pleasing crosspatch of stonewalled fields dotted with grazing sheep and cows. His nearest neighbor was a farm about a mile away.

"Oh, Sean, it's beautiful. The house, the view."

"I'm glad you like it. I built it myself."

They went through the front door and directly into the parlor, a cozy room with a large stone fireplace taking up most of one wall. On the wall facing the mountains, he'd done something she'd never seen before in an Irish house – he'd installed three very large windows. It looked odd to her, but she realized why he'd done it. It opened up the room to the splendid view of the mountains off in the distance. The comfortable parlor had a decidedly feminine touch. Obviously Sean's wife had been the one responsible for decorating the room.

Sean led her down the hallway to the back of the house. "There are three bedrooms and a bathroom," he said, sounding like a nervous real estate salesman. "I even installed one of those newfangled showers you yanks are so keen on."

As they walked by a closed door, Nancy said, "What's in here?"

Sean looked away. "That was to be the nursery."

Nancy moved on, sorry she'd asked.

They came back into the parlor and Nancy stood by the windows. "Sean, what you've done is absolutely beautiful."

"Thank you. I'm sure it's a lot bigger and more comfortable than the farm in Kilgrin."

She chuckled. "It is that." She studied Sean, puzzled by his odd behavior. Since they'd come into the house, she noticed that he seemed to be nervous, hyperactive and preoccupied.

He paced up and down the parlor. "As you can see, Nancy, there are three bedrooms and plenty of room for kids to play."

And suddenly, she understood. "Sean," she said quietly, "I think we should go."

He stopped pacing and faced her. "We should have gotten married back then and to hell with your mother," he blurted out.

Nancy turned away and pretended to study the landscape. Searing memories of that time so long ago came flooding back into her mind. She was just sixteen, he was nineteen. They both worked in the Ballycastle Mill, a dark, sprawling, oily, noisy, and ponderous thing dedicated to feeding Europe's insatiable appetite for wool, cloth yarn, and sewing thread. She worked in the warping room at a mindless job that entailed watching a winding machine take lengths of yarn and wind it onto warper's bobbins.

He was – what did they call him? – Mr. Fixit. And he was a wonder. He could repair any machine that needed fixing – from blending machines to carders to combing machines to drawing machines.

The first time she saw him, she immediately fell in love with him – as did every other girl in the mill. He was young and handsome with curly red hair and green eyes. And he had a fine sense of humor, always making the unhappy girls tethered to their machines laugh.

One day he saw her frantically struggling to reattach a string of yarn to her bobbin.

"Is it trouble you're having?"

"I am," she said, looking over her shoulder, terrified that she would lose her job. She'd been told by her strict supervisor in no uncertain terms that she should never let the yarn pull away from the warper's bobbins. But she'd been daydreaming and it had happened.

"Let me fix that." With sure hands and with a supreme confidence that awed Nancy, he quickly reattached the yarn. He smiled at her. "There. Done. And what's your name?"

"Nancy"

"A beautiful name that."

And with that, he was gone – no doubt off to rescue another machine and perhaps another inattentive girl – leaving Nancy positively breathless and speechless.

At the end of the day, he was waiting at the gate when she came out of the mill. He slipped up alongside her. "I think you owe me something, Nancy," he said.

She moved away from the cheeky boy. "I owe you nothing."

"Oh? Wasn't it I who fixed your bobbin?"

"Yes. But that's your job."

"Aye, but I'm supposed to notify my supervisor that there was a breakdown. I didn't do that because they'd been on you about letting the yarn slip off the bobbin."

He was right. If he'd reported the problem to a supervisor, she'd surely have lost her job. She did owe him – something – but she'd heard things about him and she was very worried about the meaning of "owe." "All right. Maybe I do owe you something. What is it that you want?" she asked cautiously.

"Come have fish and chips with me."

"Is that it?"

"Of course. What did you expect?"

She blushed. "Oh, all right."

And that fish and chips dinner led to a movie and then walks in the countryside. Soon Nancy and Sean were in love. Around that time, she'd been seeing in the movies and newspapers Hollywood stars bobbing their hair. Stars like Irene Castle with her "Castle bob" and other stars like Colleen Moore and Louise Brooks bobbed their hair. It was seen as a somewhat shocking statement of independence in young women, as older people were used to seeing girls wearing long dresses and heavy Edwardian-style hair. But Nancy loved the look. She, herself, had lovely long auburn hair, but she was sick of it and wanted to look like Irene Castle. She had a friend who fancied herself a hair stylist. One night Nancy went to her house and an hour later Nancy emerged with her version of a "Castle bob."

Her joy was short-lived. As soon as she walked into her house, her mother took one look at her and screamed, "You hussy! I always knew you'd come to no good in the end. Look at you. May God forgive you and your sinful ways."

"Mother, I'm sixteen. I have a right to cut my own hair."

"That you do not. You are in my house and you will do what I tell you."

With that, she rushed toward Nancy, fists flailing. Stunned by the onslaught, Nancy fell to the ground overwhelmed by the unexpected assault. Dazed, she tried to rise, but her mother grabbed her by her shorn locks.

"Do you think you can shame this family by acting like a common whore?" she said, dragging Nancy by the hair toward the coal bin. "You will not, by the merciful Jesus. You will rot in this coal bin before I will let you do that."

"No, Mother, please, not there. Please..." Nancy kicked and fought to avoid the dreaded coal bin, but she was no match for her crazed mother, who slapped and kicked her daughter into the small room under the stairs. Nancy stayed locked in there the entire night. In the morning, her mother unlocked the door and Nancy squinted up at her, blinded by the light.

"Come out, if you've learned your lesson." She pointed a bony finger at Nancy. "And mind, you will never see that Sean Garrett boy again or you will live to regret it. Mark my words."

Nancy turned away from the window, overwhelmed by a deep sadness. "That all happened in the past, Sean, and it's best forgotten."

"But Nancy, this could be yours, ours—"

"Sean, please don't say anymore."

"You're right. I'm sorry. I had no business—"

"It's all right. Can we go?"

"Of course."

Nancy took one last look around, bitterly wondering what might have been.

***

As usual, as soon as dinner was over, the kids rushed outside to be away from the repressive atmosphere of their grandparents' home. As soon as Nancy finished cleaning up, she put on her coat and went outside to see what they were doing. They were just standing on the sidewalk looking glum.

"What's the matter?"

"There's nothing to do," Patrick said.

Nancy felt a stab of guilt. She'd been so preoccupied with her own troubles that she was neglecting her own children. "Come on, let's take a walk."

At the top of the street, she stopped to point out a lamppost. "See the notch up there? When I was a child one of the boys would climb up there and tie a rope inside the notch. Then we would tie a loop at the other end of the rope and use it as a swing."

A puzzled Patrick scratched his head. "Where did you swing to?"

"Around the lamppost."

"Didn't you hit your head?" Maureen asked.

"All the time. But that was the fun of it, trying not to knock your brains out."

"That doesn't sound like very much fun," a dubious Fiona said.

Donal chimed in. "I like the swings in the park."

"There are no parks here, dopey," Patrick pointed out.

"Patrick, don't call your little brother dopey."

They continued walking. After a while, Maureen said, "What else did you do for fun?"

"Well, we played a game called stickwhack."

"What's that?" Patrick asked.

"Someone's father would take a square stick about seven-inches long and, using a hot poker, burn a different number of marks on each of the four sides. The game was to put the stick on the curb and whack it with another stick and then when it landed, count the number of burn marks facing up. The one with the most burn marks won."

She could see by their expressions that they didn't consider any of that very much fun. She decided she would save telling them about turning a bicycle rim into a hoop for another time.

They walked in silence for a while longer. Then, Maureen said, "When are we going to move to the farm?"

"Yeah, I want to move to the farm tomorrow. I don't like Grandmother."

"Patrick, that's not a nice thing to say about your grandmother."

"Why not?" Fiona asked. "She doesn't like us either."

"That's not true."

Maureen's eyes filled with tears. "Then why is she always yelling at us?"

"Look, I want you kids to understand something. She's an old lady and some old ladies become grouchy and impatient as they get older." What she didn't tell them was that she'd always been that way.

"What about Grandfather?" Patrick asked.

"He doesn't yell at you."

"Yeah, but if we make one little sound, he always gives you that stern look over his glasses."

"I'm afraid to move about the house," Maureen said.

"I don't like the food grandmother cooks," Donal said.

"And there's never enough either," Fiona said. "I'm always hungry."

Nancy had taken them for a walk hoping to boost their spirits, but it seemed she only succeeded in making them feel worse. She felt bad for them. It was true, they had nothing to do. If they were in school at least that would take up most of their day and they could make friends there. But she'd decided there was no point in signing them up for school because they would soon be moving to the farm.

They walked back down Cathedral Street and Nancy stopped in front of the house. She looked up and down the street. "That reminds me. Did I ever tell you about the Foot?"

Her serious tone immediately caught their attention. "No," Maureen said. "What's a foot?"

"Not what, Maureen. Who. The Foot was a ghost."

"No…" they said in unison.

"Yes. He's been around forever. Sometimes, late at night, you can hear the Foot walking along this very sidewalk." Maureen involuntarily stepped off the narrow sidewalk onto the street.

"What does he look like?" Patrick asked, wide-eyed.

"No one's ever seen him. You just hear him. It sounds like click, thump, click, thump. Legend has it he was a murdered sea captain with a peg leg and that's why he sounds like that."

"Have you ever heard him, Mommy?" Fiona asked.

"I have." Nancy pointed up at the bedroom window she was sharing with Donal and Patrick. "I used to sleep in that very front room. I heard him only one time. I was about fourteen. I awoke in the middle of the night, drenched in sweat, terrified. But I didn't know why. Then, I heard it – click, thump, click, thump."

"What did you do?" Donal asked.

"I pulled the covers over my head. I was sleeping with my sister, Peggy, but I was deathly afraid to say anything to her for fear the Foot would hear me."

"Then what happened?" Maureen asked.

"He passed the window and soon the sound got fainter and fainter." Nancy pointed toward the top of Cathedral Street. "He always starts up there and makes his way down the street and disappears that way," she said, pointing toward Hillcrest Street.

The children stared in the direction she was pointing as though they might actually see the Foot coming along the sidewalk.

Satisfied she'd entertained them with a great ghost story – albeit one she'd actually experienced – she said, "OK, it's getting chilly out here. Let's go inside. And remember, we won't be staying here long."

***

Nancy stood inside the farmhouse, anxiously watching Sean making notes on a clipboard as he went about assessing the damages. "How bad is it?"

He pulled a rotting ceiling beam down. It crashed to the dirt floor and a cloud of dust rose up. "Nothing that can't be fixed."

He glanced into the other room, which would be the bedroom. The floor plan was uncomplicated and simple, very much like any other small farmhouse built at the end of the last century. The building had been evenly divided in two. One half of the farmhouse was the bedroom, the other half was a combination of kitchen, dining room, and living room.

"How long will it take?"

"A few weeks, if I can get the supplies."

"A few weeks—?"

"Maybe longer. Nancy, the war's just over. It's still devilishly hard getting supplies." He saw the discouraged expression on her face. "Things still rough at home?"

"They are. Mostly, I feel sorry for the kids. They're always walking on pins and needles."

"I'll try to work as fast as I can."

"I appreciate it, Sean. How much will all this cost?"

"Don't worry about that."

"No," she said firmly. "I will pay you for your work. We will draw up a contract and I will pay you a fair price for your labors. That's the way it must be."

"All right. Whatever you say." He brushed a spray of dust from her shoulder. "You've become a headstrong woman, haven't you?"

"Yes, I have," she responded, not entirely satisfied with that answer.

Sean glanced around the room and grimaced. "Nancy, do you realize what you're getting yourself into?"

"I think so. Why do you ask?"

"You've lived in America for a long time. I'm sure you and the kids have gotten used to all the creature comforts that America can provide. You'll have little of that here."

He went over to an old cast iron stove and blew the dust off the top. "This is what you'll cook your meals on. It's not gas or electric, but it's a serviceable stove. It'll burn coal or wood and it will also be your source of heat for the house. You do know you have no running water."

"What?" Her eyes shot to the sink. She'd been so distracted by the sorry state of the place, she hadn't noticed that there was no faucet in the sink. "Where will I get water?"

He pointed out the window. "There's a stream at the bottom of the field. That's where I've been getting it. You, or the kids, will have to bring it up one bucket at a time."

Nancy rubbed the grimy window with the palm of her hand to get a better look at where he'd pointed. The stream all the way at the bottom of an elongated, sloping field. That, she realized, would be a long haul, and all uphill. "We'll manage," she said with more confidence than she felt.

"There's no electricity. Your only source of light will be candles and smelly kerosene lamps."

"Sean Garrett, are you trying to discourage me?" she asked, indeed, getting discouraged.

"No. I just want you to know what you're about to take on. Oh, and one more thing." He looked away, embarrassed. "There's no indoor plumbing."

"What? Oh, I... So what do we do?"

"You have a couple of choices. At some point I could build you an outhouse, but that could get pretty cold in the winter. The other alternative is a commode somewhere in the house that would need to be emptied every day."

"Some choices."

"What you are planning to do is not going to be easy, Nancy. I've worked for Americans who moved here with wildly romantic visions of living in a cute wee farm with a thatched roof and rose bushes. They were usually gone in six months."

"Sean, I have no illusions about any of that. I'm here to win my case, sell the damn farm, and go back to the States."

He looked a little disappointed at her response. "Of course, you know what's best for you and the children. I just want you to go into this with open eyes."

"Thank you, Sean. I do appreciate your concern."

As they went back to his truck, Nancy glanced over her shoulder at the grazing cows. "Sean, when is market day?"

"Tomorrow. Why?"

"There are a couple of men I have to see."

CHAPTER TWENTY-THREE

While Nancy was inspecting the farm with Sean, Patrick was standing in front of a lamppost on Cathedral Street. He'd found a length of rope and stared up at the lamppost, wondering how he could get up there and tie the rope around the notch. After several unsuccessful tries at climbing the post, he gave up and went back to the house disgusted. His sisters and brother had gone for a walk into the countryside and his grandmother was upstairs napping. He went out into the backyard intending to swipe a piece of rhubarb from grandmother's garden. It tasted bitter and he didn't much like it, but it helped fill the void in his stomach. He came into the backyard and was surprised to see his grandfather sitting by the shed, using a knife to carve a piece of wood.

Fascinated, Patrick sat down beside the old man. He'd never seen a grown man use a knife like that. "What are you doing, Grandfather?"

"Whittling."

"What's that?"

"Just what you see. Whittling. Have you never heard of whittling?"

"No."

Patrick watched in silence for awhile. Then, "What are you making?"

"You ask too many questions."

Patrick lapsed back in to silence and watched awhile longer. Then, bored, he got up and went back into the house.

Grandfather looked up and there was an expression that could have been regret or possibly longing. But whatever it was, it was soon gone and he went back to his whittling.

An hour later, Patrick was sitting on the curb outside the house waiting for his sisters and brother to come back from their walk. Grandfather came out and dropped a piece of wood in his lap. It was about seven-inches long and it had a different number of burned grooves on each of the four sides.

"When I was a lad, we called the game stickwhack." All you need now is to find a stick to whack it with."

"Wow. Thank you, Grandfather."

The old man grunted and went back into the house.

***

Tuesday was market day in Ballycastle. On that day, the farmers brought their wares to town to sell or barter everything from homemade butter to prize bulls and rams. There was a certain festive atmosphere about market day. It was an excuse for farmers, who usually didn't have time for idle conversation during the week, to get together on Tuesday and share gossip and the latest news. All sales, whether of prize bulls or spring lambs, were a chance for farmers to spit, shake hands, and take a wee draft of whiskey to seal the bargain. Today, the street was clogged with wagons full of animals and foodstuffs. Clusters of farmers haggled over the price of sheep, lambs, horses, and bulls.

It was a determined Nancy who marched into this Brugelesque scene.

"Excuse me," she asked a woman who was selling eggs off the back of a cart. "Do you know Mr. Tully from Kilgrin?"

"Kevin Tully? Sure. He's right over there about to cheat his neighbors into buying that sickly calf."

"His neighbors? Would they be Hogan and Whelan?"

"They are. The fat one's Hogan and the short one's Whelan."

Nancy was in luck. They were the very three she had come here to meet. She walked up to the men. "Are you Mr. Tully?"

The tallest of the men turned around. His weathered face made him look older than his fifty years. "Aye, that's me."

"And you gentlemen would be Mr. Whelan and Mr. Hogan?"

They nodded tentatively, suspicious of this strange woman.

"What do you want, missus?" Tully asked, apparently the spokesman for the group.

"I believe you gentlemen are grazing your animals on my land."

"Ah, so you must be Mrs. Cavanaugh? I'd heard you'd come home from America."

"I am and I have."

"Sure there's no harm done, missus. The cows are good for the soil."

"And is growing crops on my land good for the soil as well?"

"The land was going to waste," Whelan said, clearly irritated by her cheekiness.

"Well, not any more. Who owns the cows?"

"We all have cows in the field."

"And the crops?"

"They're my crops," Tully said.

"Well, if you want to use my land, you'll have to pay rent."

That announcement brought scowls to their faces.

Tully scratched his scruffy chin. "We'll have to give this some thought, missus."

"Fine. You have until Sunday to give it some thought."

And with that, she turned and walked away, leaving the three farmers to grumble among themselves.

***

The next afternoon Nancy went to the butcher's shop on Hillcrest Street to buy a chicken. There were several women in the store. Nancy picked out the best of the scrawny chickens displayed.

As he wrapped the chicken in brown paper, the pleasantly smiling proprietor asked, "Will that be all, missus?"

"Yes, that's it."

"Are you new to Ballycastle?"

"I grew up here, but I've just returned from the States."

"Oh, and you would be…?"

"Nancy Cavanaugh."

Suddenly, there was a decided chill in the air. The other women shoppers stopped talking and glared at her. A woman standing next to her moved away. Even the proprietor stopped smiling.

Nancy took her change and walked out of the store, ignoring the hostile stares of the other women. Sean was right, she thought. Ballycastle was still a small town and she'd forgotten how quickly news travels in a small town.

When she got home there was a letter from Nora.

Dear Nancy,

I miss you already. Some interesting news. I got fired from my job in the factory. But so did that bastard Mr. Kane. It all would have been very funny, if I wasn't in the middle of the whole mess.

The very day you sailed to Ireland, Kane called me into his office and offered me your job. After your terrible experience with him you'd think I would have the good sense to turn him down. But, I didn't. Like a fool, I took the job. It was more money and I was getting sick to death of packing mess kits. A poor excuse, I know. It took the heel just three nights to pull that old can-you-stay-late-tonight rubbish. I told him I would not. He got very upset and then he grabbed me and tried to molest me. But after your experience, I was ready for him. I hit him over the head with a staple gun. I can assure you he will not be able to wear that old dead animal wig for quite awhile. Well, as you can imagine, he fired me.

A week later I went back out to the factory to have lunch with some of the girls. They told me there had been quite a row the day before. Two big shots from the head office came in and they had a hush-hush meeting in Kane's office. The upshot was they fired Mr. Kane. And good riddance to him I say. It seems the girl you replaced finally complained to someone in the head office. I guess they saw a pattern – that girl before you quitting, then you getting fired, then me. They offered me my old job back, but I turned them down. To tell you the truth, since the war ended, there's not much call for the M-1942 divided pan-and-body stainless steel system.

We thought the factory would close, but they started making a whole new line of products – tents and poles and little alcohol stoves for something called the "Camping Industry." Can you imagine anyone paying good money to buy equipment so they can go out and sleep in the woods like some wild animal?

Well anyways, I'm back at Schrafft's. Business has picked up and so have the tips.

Oh, one sad note. Mrs. Krueger, God rest her soul, died. They said her heart gave out. If you ask me, I think she died of a broken heart over that Hitler and Nazi business. Even though the war is over, there are some people here who still hate the Germans and Japs. I don't personally know any Japs, but I know a few Germans and they've told me they've had similar experiences as old Mrs. Krueger did.

Well, anyway, I must close. Give my best to the kids. Come home soon!!!!

Love, Nora

***

That night during dinner, Nancy told her parents about her experience in the butcher shop.

"Back only a few days and already you're making enemies," Mother chided her.

"I'm not trying to make enemies, Mother, and I'm not trying to go to war with my neighbors as Mr. O'Donnell believes. I just want what's right. It's my land and I should be paid for its use. God knows I could use the money."

Her father shook his head. "Still and all, it's a bad business and you didn't handle it well."

Nancy lapsed into silence, sorry she had brought it up.

After dinner, the other kids went outside to play. Maureen stayed behind to help clear away the dishes. As she turned to go to the sink, she bumped into grandmother.

"Will you look where you're going, you clumsy girl," the old lady snapped.

Maureen started to cry.

Nancy patted her cheek. "It's all right, Maureen. You go out and play with the others." She waited till her daughter had gone. "Mother, she was only trying to help."

"Sure there's not enough room for a body to move. They're always underfoot. When will you be moving to the farm?"

"Very soon, I hope." But not soon enough, she thought.

***

The next day, Nancy and the kids took the bus out to Kilgrin. She was disappointed to see that the rusty gate still had not been painted or repaired. The loaning looked more usable, but that was only because Sean's truck, driving back and forth, had beaten down the weeds.

A dismayed Nancy stood in front of the farmhouse with Sean. "Hardly anything's been done."

"I'm having the devil of a time getting supplies. I've pulled most of the ceiling down, but I have no new planks to put up. Can't get paint either. I'm doing my best."

"I know you are."

Nancy watched the children petting the cows in the field. "I see Tully and his friends haven't taken the cows out of my field." She realized that today was Saturday. "Tomorrow's the deadline. Either they pay me or they clear off."

"I'd go easy there if I were you."

"Why is everyone always telling me to go easy," she said, exasperated. "I'm the wronged party here."

"I know, but you don't know this crowd. They're a clannish lot and they can be spiteful."

"I don't care. What can they do to me?"

"You seem upset, Nancy. Trouble at home?"

"I get nothing but complaints, Sean. According to my mother, the kids are a constant din, they have bottomless stomachs, and she has no privacy. None of it is true. The children move around the house like ghosts. The poor things are afraid to make a sound. I don't know what to do, Sean. I thought we'd just be there for a couple of days. It's been two weeks, but it feels like two years."

"I'll talk to my suppliers again."

"Thanks, Sean. You're a good friend."

"It's nothing. Oh, I hear you met the ladies at the butcher shop. I'm sorry."

"I don't care about those old biddies. It's the children I'm worried about. I've got to get them out of my mother's house and out here where they can make all the noise they want. Where they can act like children again."

***

The next day was Sunday, Nancy's imposed deadline. She'd heard nothing from Tully and the others and decided it was time to confront them.

Sean drove her and the children out to the farm.

"What are you going to do?" Sean asked anxiously.

"I don't know." And that was the truth. She didn't know what she was going to do and she was not looking forward to a confrontation. "Try to reason with them, I guess."

Sean nodded approvingly. "That's the ticket. Remember, you catch more flies with honey than vinegar."

***

Nancy was hoping the cows would be gone and there would be no need of an altercation, but they were still there, quietly and contentedly grazing on her grass.

"Mom, the cows are still here. Are they ours now?" Patrick asked, hopefully.

"No, son, they are not."

For a moment, Nancy studied Tully's farmhouse two fields away. After a moment, she came to a decision and started off across the field.

Sean saw a look in her eyes that he didn't like. "Nancy, where are you going?"

"To meet my neighbors."

Sean chased after her. "Remember what I said about the honey and the vinegar..."

But she wasn't listening. By now, she was practically running across the field. Sean and the kids chased after her.

Tully was repairing a thresher in front of his barn when Nancy, the four kids, and Sean appeared. He looked up. "Is there something you want, missus?"

"I'm here to collect the rent for the use of my land, Mr. Tully."

"Och, things have been hard. Sure I don't have the money to—"

"I know things are hard, Mr. Tully. I have four children to feed."

He waved a hand in dismissal. "Ach, you rich yanks don't know what hard is."

Nancy was incensed by his flippant attitude. How dare he dismiss her. What did he know about her life? What did he know about coping with the loss of a husband and working in demeaning jobs just to put a roof over the children's heads and food on the table? She was fed up with men like Tully and Bossart and Kane, who looked upon her as someone not worthy of respect or attention.

"Mr. Tully," she said in a low, controlled voice, "I've tried to be reasonable, but you give me no choice."

He shrugged, indifferent to her implied threat.

Nancy turned and walked away.

***

Back at the farmhouse, Nancy rummaged through the debris that Sean had piled in the front yard. She found a large piece of wood and wrapped a rag around it.

"Nancy, what are you doing?" a nervous Sean asked.

She didn't answer. She opened a can of naphtha and soaked the rag. "Sean, do you have a match?"

"Be careful, Nancy, that stuff's very flammable. What are you going to do?"

"Sean. Just give me a match."

Reluctantly, he tossed her a box of matches. She struck one and put it to the rag, which immediately burst into flame. The four kids stood back, wide-eyed and stunned, not sure if they should laugh or cry.

With black smoke streaming from her improvised torch, she opened the gate to the first field and shooed the cows out. They didn't need much encouragement. The flame from the torch and the black smoke almost caused a stampede.

Tully's fourteen-year-old son was leading a horse up from the spring when he looked across the field and saw a sight he'd never seen in his life. "Jasus, Mary, and Joseph!" he muttered. Leaving the horse to fend for itself, he raced back to the barn. "Da, Da, see what the crazy yank woman is doing!"

Tully stood up and saw cows spilling out of the field, and a determined Nancy holding a billowing torch belching black smoke moving toward the crop field. "Get Whelan and Hogan," he shouted to his son, as he raced off toward his crops.

Nancy stood amidst the crop plants, the torch burning and hissing above her head.

"For the love of God, don't do it," Sean begged her.

"I'll let no one take advantage of me—"

"Stop! For Jasus' sake," Tully shouted, breathless from the sprint across the field. "Are you a madwoman all together?"

She turned to look at Tully and saw Whelan and Hogan racing across the fields toward them. It was good that all three of them would be here to see what was about to happen. "I'm just clearing my land, Mr. Tully." She dipped the torch toward the first plant.

"No—!" Tully shouted. "For the love of God, all right. We'll pay."

By now Whelan and Hogan had arrived and they stood beside Tully, wide-eyed, out of breath, and speechless.

Tears welled up in Nancy's eyes. She stood there for a moment, reveling in her triumph, then she jammed the torch into the ground and it sputtered out. "Good. I'm glad we've come to an arrangement. I'll have my solicitor draw up a contract. Good day, gentlemen."

***

The ride back to Ballycastle passed in an uneasy quiet. The children seemed stunned by their mother's behavior and they didn't know what to make of it. They didn't even play their look-for-the-animals game.

Finally, Sean said, "You've become a tough woman since last I knew you, Nancy Cavanaugh."

She couldn't tell if his tone was one of admiration or disappointment. "All the time I was married to Connor, I was happy to let him make the decisions. My job was to stay home and take care of the children. But now he's gone and I have to do both." Nancy glumly stared out the window, wishing it wasn't that way.

***

That night, Sean went back out to the farm to deliver some lumber that had just come in. On his way back, he decided to stop at Logan's Pub, Kilgrin's only pub. It was basically a hole in the wall, almost an afterthought, squeezed between a feed grain store and O'Malley's general store. The ceilings were so low that everyone reflexively ducked their heads when they came in. Like most nights, the pub was smoky and crowded with farmers.

Sean stepped up to the bar. "What'll you have, Sean?" the bartender asked.

"A pint, Mr. Logan."

Tully, Hogan, and Whelan were sitting at the other end of the bar, watching him.

"We don't see much of you in here anymore, Sean Garrett."

"I've been busy."

"I'm surprised the widow's handyman has time for a pint," Tully said loudly to his companions. "Always chasing after her the way he does."

Sean glanced over at them with undisguised disdain. He didn't like them any more than they liked him. He'd heard that they were unhappy with him because he was restoring the Cavanaugh farm. To their minds, taking the side of a yank against his own people was an unforgivable act of disloyalty. And they had to be in a black mood after Nancy's humiliation of them this afternoon.

Sean put his beer down and turned to face them. "You thought you were so clever, putting one over on a woman. But if Connor Cavanaugh was here, you wouldn't dare cheat him. You're nothing but a bunch of cowards."

Four farmers who were sitting between them at the bar, sensed a fight coming on. They took their pints off the bar and retreated to a table in the corner.

"I've been busy," Tully said, in a bad imitation of Sean. He winked at his companions. "I'll bet you are."

Hogan and Whelan snickered.

Sean stood up. "What's that supposed to mean, Tully?"

Tully took a swig of his pint and wiped his mouth on his sleeve. "I'm sure the young widow Cavanaugh must be very lonely at night."

More snickers from the other two.

Sean lunged at Tully. His first punch knocked Tully off the barstool. As the farmer got to his feet, everyone backed away, making room for them. Both men were about the same height. Tully had him by a few pounds, but all-in-all it was a fair fight. At least it would have been a fair fight, but the three farmers weren't looking for that. They all jumped Sean. At first he held his own. He put Whelan down with a roundhouse right, bloodying the man's nose. Then Hogan grabbed him in a bear hug and, as Tully was moving in with fist raised, Sean reared up and with both feet kicked Tully in the chest, sending him crashing into a table.

But it was still three against one and he couldn't fight all of them. As Sean was struggling to get free of Hogan's bear hug, Whelan, blood streaming from his broken nose, grabbed a pint mug off the bar and smashed it over Sean's head. He fell to his knees and like jackals the three were on him, punching and kicking him until he was knocked senseless.

***

The children and her parents had long gone to bed. Nancy sat at the kitchen table, moodily staring into the fire. She was glad she had stood up to Tully and his friends and got what she wanted, but she wasn't happy that she'd acted like a crazy woman. Would she have really set the crops on fire? She still didn't know.

There was a soft knock at the door and it startled her. She glanced up at the wall clock. It was after ten. Who would be out this time of night? She opened the door and her hand shot to her mouth when she saw the bloodied Sean standing there. "Mother of God, what's happened to you?"

She helped him to the kitchen table and put the kettle over the fire. A few minutes later, she was dabbing a rag dipped in hot water on his cuts.

"What happened?"

"I was in Logan's. Your man Tully and his friends were there. They said things about you that I couldn't stomach. And well – there was a fight."

Nancy's distress at seeing him like this quickly turned to anger. She dabbed at his cuts aggressively. "Sean Garrett," she hissed. "I will fight my own battles, not you."

"Ow! Easy there," he said, flinching. "That hurts."

"Sorry." She waved the bloodied cloth in his face. "Promise me you'll never fight for me again."

"I'll promise no such thing."

"My God, you are one thick-headed Irishman."

Sean gingerly touched the swelling lump under his eye. "Aye, and a good thing, too."

Nancy sat down heavily, overcome by a wave of anger and frustration as she considered her sorry state of affairs. What was she doing here in her mother's house tending to the wounds of a man who had gotten into a bloody brawl in a pub over her? Dear God, when will this be over?

CHAPTER TWENTY-FOUR

They'd just sat down to eat dinner when her mother said, "Your behavior out at the farm is all over Kilgrin and Ballycastle."

"Really? I think the good people of Kilgrin and Ballycastle have entirely too much time on their hands."

Her mother waved a fork at her. "You can make light of it, but, mark my words, you're getting a reputation."

"For what? For standing up for myself? Because I'm a woman? Tully and his cronies wouldn't have dared do what they did if Connor were here."

"Well, he's not here, is he? You don't seem to understand, you never did. You were always such a head-strong, willful girl. I tried to knock—" She stopped and jabbed at her potato. "All I'm saying is, there is man's work and there is woman's work. And you don't seem to know the difference."

The rest of the meal was conducted in an uncomfortable silence, save for the scraping of utensils on plates. At one point, Donal reached for his water glass and knocked it over.

"Och, don't be so clumsy," his grandmother hissed.

"He didn't mean it!" Fiona shouted.

Grandmother's head jerked back, as though the water had been thrown in her face. She turned purple with rage. "Don't you talk to me in that tone of voice."

Nancy saw her mother raise her hand to strike Fiona and it suddenly triggered horrifying images of her own childhood, long repressed. Now, flashing through her mind with dizzying rapidity were images of her being beaten with a poker... being locked in the dark, scary coal bin for hours on end for reasons she never knew... being forced to take ice-cold baths for wetting the bed...

compelled to wash the bed sheets of her brother who had wet the bed…

Nancy's hand shot out and she grabbed her mother's wrist in a vice-like grip. "Don't you dare," she said in a steely tone, "ever raise your hand to one of my children."

***

The next day, Sean was on a ladder replacing slate shingles, when he heard Nancy's voice. "Hello, Sean."

He turned around and saw her and the kids standing at the foot of the ladder with two steamer trunks at their feet. "What's this, then?"

"We're moving in."

"Are you mad? You can't. I'm not close to being done here."

"Doesn't matter. We're here to stay. Besides, now you'll have five more helpers. The work will go faster. "

"There are no beds, Nancy. No furniture."

"We'll sleep on the floor. I've left my mother's house for good, Sean. There's no going back."

Sean was thinking that Nancy had lost her mind. She and four children couldn't possibly stay in a half-renovated house with no furniture. Where would they sleep? Where would they eat? Then, he remembered. "Did you know old Mrs. Lally?" he asked. "She lived in that little cottage just outside Ballycastle on the Killeen road."

"No, I can't say that I do."

"Well, she died a few weeks ago. Her son wants me to completely renovate the house."

"And what has this to do with me?"

"You're in luck. He asked me to get rid of all the furniture."

***

That afternoon, Sean and two of his workers moved three beds, a couch, a kitchen table, a few side tables, dishes, and pots and pans into the farmhouse. It wasn't much and it was old and worn, but at least they would have the bare essentials – beds to sleep in and a table to eat from.

Nancy was delighted with the couch, a red velvet chaise lounge. It was completely out of place in the little farmhouse, but it did brighten up the room. Nancy nudged Sean. "This thing looks like it belongs in a bordello."

Sean tried not to grin. "I'm sure I wouldn't know anything about that."

Later, as Nancy was unpacking, she pulled out a calendar and stared at it wide-eyed. Oh, my God! Christmas is only eight days away. She'd been so preoccupied with the farm, her mother, and her troublesome neighbors that she'd completely lost track of the time. It didn't help that Christmas was not the big holiday that it was in the States. When she'd gone into the shops, there had been no Santa or reindeer cutouts to remind her that Christmas was just around the corner. With sadness, she realized that this Christmas there would be no presents for the children. The effects of the war were still evident in Ireland. Dolls and trucks, as well as most other toys, were just about non-existent in the shops and the few available were prohibitively expensive.

***

The first day in their new home was an endless source of excitement for the kids. For the first time since they'd landed in Ireland, they could whoop and shout without getting reproachful looks from their grandparents.

Unlike back home, they weren't confined to sidewalks, away from the deadly flow of cars, trucks and taxis on Amsterdam Avenue. They spent the day freely exploring the countryside, climbing over stone walls, jumping over brooks, and at one point running away, giggling in fright and excitement, when a cow – which they took for a bull – came trotting toward them.

For Nancy, it wasn't so much fun. Her first task was to get the stove going, a daunting chore at best. It took her almost an hour just to get it lit. Then she tried to make pan bread in a skillet on top of the stove and burned it to a crisp. The rest of the day she spent removing the accumulation of twenty years of dirt and grime, and sweeping out the hay and desiccated animal droppings.

In the afternoon, she took a much needed break and for the first time explored her property. Besides the farmhouse, there were three other buildings – a large barn, a chicken coop with a partially-collapsed roof, and what looked to be a storage building for farm tools. She went into the barn and was immediately assailed by the familiar odor of cow droppings mixed with hay. It brought to her mind a flood of pleasant childhood memories. Her father had been a baker by trade and had never been a farmer, but some of her friends' families owned farms and she'd enjoyed many a summer day racing through hay lofts and horse stalls in endless games of hide and seek.

Slowly, she walked to the back of the barn and stopped in front of a dirt-encrusted stall and her eyes filled with tears, imaging Connor sitting on a stool milking a cow. She touched a gate handle. He must have touched that very handle thousands of times. He had been in this barn. He had lived in that farmhouse across the yard. She could feel his presence everywhere and it gave her comfort. She didn't know how long she'd spent in the barn, but the joyous shouts of the children coming up the loaning brought her out of her reverie. They were home from their great adventure.

***

By bedtime, she was completely done in. Thankfully, so were the kids who'd tired themselves out crisscrossing the countryside all day.

Nancy tucked Patrick into his own cot, then the girls, who shared a bed. Nancy climbed into her own bed which she shared with Donal.

Just as they were slipping into the sleep of the weary, something bumped into the side of the house. Nancy's eyes snapped open.

"What was that, Mommy?" Patrick asked with a quivering voice.

Suddenly Nancy regretted telling them about the Foot, and worse, all those Irish ghost stories she'd told the children during the crossing. They'd been entertaining on the ship, but in a remote country farmhouse in the middle of the night, the last thing these kids needed was to be thinking about banshees, fairies, and leprechauns.

"It's nothing," she said.

There was another bump.

Donal pressed in closer to his mother. "I'm scared," he whispered.

"It's all right, Donal. It's nothing."

Then they heard an eerie groaning sound.

Patrick was out of bed like a shot. He vaulted over his sisters' bed and dove into bed with his mother. Maureen and Fiona would happily have followed, but they were too terrified to risk the six-foot journey from their bed to their mother's.

Suddenly, Nancy was outraged by a thought: Could this be Tully and his dim-witted friends trying to scare me?

"You kids stay here," she said getting out of bed. "I'll go see what it is."

Ignoring the children's panicky protests, Nancy threw a coat over herself, slipped into her shoes, searched the kitchen for a weapon and had to settle for a broom. Slowly, she opened the door and stepped out into a chilly, pitch-black night. Holding the broom like a baseball bat, she moved around to the back of the house, barely breathing. She saw nothing. She heard nothing. Then... something – or someone – rustled in the bushes.

"Tully, is that you?" she shouted, trying to keep the panic out of her voice. "Show yourself you cowardly bastard. Come out or I'll brain you with this broom."

The bushes parted and a huge face with large, black eyes loomed out of the darkness. Nancy screamed. She turned to run, but she fell over a log and sprawled onto the ground. Rolling over and holding the broom like a spear, she braced for the attack. A cow lumbered out of the gloom and ambled past her.

By now Nancy was hyperventilating and unable to catch her breath, but finally, when she did, she began to laugh.

She came back into the bedroom to find all four saucer-eyed children in her bed.

"Was it a leprechaun?" Patrick asked, peeking out from under the covers.

"No, it was only a cow."

The four kids exhaled in relief.

"All right, everybody back to bed."

No one moved.

Sighing, Nancy climbed into bed with them. "Just this once you can all sleep with me. Good night."

After a few minutes, Fiona said, "I can't sleep."

"Neither can I," Patrick said.

"Neither can I," Maureen echoed her brother.

"Me, too," Donal said.

Nancy was exhausted, but she knew she would get no sleep until they went off. She began to sing softly, "Give my regards to Broadway remember me to Herald Square..."

Maureen joined in. "Tell all the gang on forty-second street..."

Patrick and Fiona came in together. "That I will soon be there..."

And finally, Donal, singing loudly, "Tell them of how I'm yearning to linger with that old time throng..."

Now they were all singing at the top of their lungs. "Give my regards to Old Broadway and tell them I'll be there er' long."

When they finished the song, all the kids had great big smiles on their faces, but tears rolled down Nancy's cheeks. Of all the songs they knew, why had she chosen that one? She didn't need a reminder that they were three thousand miles away from home, living on a godforsaken farm with no electricity, no heat, no running water, and no indoor plumbing. Once again she asked herself: What in the name of God am I doing here?

***

The next morning, there was a knock at the door. Thinking it was Neil, she opened it laughing, "How formal. You don't have to— Oh…"

It wasn't Neil. It was a smiling woman in her early fifties and she was holding a basket. "Good morning, I hope I didn't wake you?"

"Oh… No, not at all."

"I'm Mrs. Rose Crossan, your neighbor. Our farm is just west of you." She held out the basket. "I brought you fresh eggs and butter."

Nancy was completely flustered. "Oh… come in. Please come in. I'm Nancy Cavanaugh."

After her run-in with Tully and his friends, as well as the episode in the butcher's shop, she didn't think there was a neighbor within miles who would talk to her.

While Nancy made tea, Rose looked around the kitchen. "You've done wonders with the place."

"Thank you. It was a real mess, but it's coming along."

"Well, it's been abandoned for a long time. You know, I remember your late husband, Connor."

"Do you?"

"Oh, yes. I was born on our farm. My husband, John, married into the family. I was about fifteen when your Connor was born, but I remember him growing up. He was a very nice young man."

Nancy was charmed and delighted to talk to someone who actually knew Connor when he was a little boy. She poured the tea and sat down.

"It was very kind of you to come by and introduce yourself. I'm afraid I've not made much of a favorable impression on some of my other neighbors."

Rose made a face. "Pay no mind to Kevin Tully. The man's a damn fool. Always was and always will be. And so are those other damn fools, Hogan and Whelan."

"They were using my land," Nancy said, feeling the need to offer an explanation.

Rose nodded vigorously. "Of course they were. My John had words with them. They were stealing, he told them. But they wouldn't listen." Rose's eyes lit up mischievously. "I hear you threatened to set the fields on fire."

"Well, I'm not sure that was a very good idea—"

"Nonsense. Good for you. They had no right to do what they did."

"Tell me what you remember about Connor.'"

"Well, as I said, I was young, but, as I remember, he was a happy child. How many times would I see him running about the countryside, examining birds and animals and anything else that he took a fancy to?" Rose's smile faded. "Of course, that was when he was a little boy. By the time he was ten or eleven, his father—"

"Denny Cavanaugh?"

"Yes, old Denny. He wasn't a bad sort most of the time, but when he had the drink in him, well, he was the devil's own creation. A complete madman all together. He used to—" Rose put her hand to her mouth. "Oh, God forgive me, I shouldn't speak ill of the dead."

"No, please, Rose, I would like to know everything I can about my husband. He never talked much about his life in Ireland."

"He made your Connor work in the fields like he was a common laborer, and him only ten. He made him drop out of school, he did. I remember your Connor talking to me about birds and crops and horses and cows. There was nothing that didn't catch his interest. I always thought he would go off to university. Of course that was highly improbable, being the son of a farmer, but still, occasionally, some church or social group would come along and rescue lads like him from the life of a farmer. But, of course, that never happened."

Rose looked outside. "My, it's getting on. Well, I must be going. If you need fresh eggs or butter, send one of the children over. I've got more than enough."

Nancy was so happy with this wonderful woman that she wanted to cry. "Thank you, Rose. Thank you for being so kind."

"It's nothing. Well, good luck here in Kilgrin. In spite of what you may think, it's really a lovely village and there are some good people here."

CHAPTER TWENTY-FIVE

By the time Christmas Eve arrived, conditions in and around the farm had improved greatly. In the past week, Sean had been able to buy whitewash and Nancy and the kids spent a day whitewashing the exterior. Even though some of the kids managed to get more whitewash on themselves than the walls, Nancy had to admit it didn't look half bad. Sean finished replacing the rest of the roof slates, and he'd been able to buy enough planks to at least cover the kitchen portion of the ceiling.

Late in the day, Sean stuck his head in the door. "Come on kids, I have a surprise for you."

He took them around to the back of the house and there, hanging from the branch of a large oak tree, was a swing.

"Wow!" Patrick exclaimed. "A swing just like my dad used to have."

With a great sadness, Nancy watched her children fight to see who would be first to try the new swing. That swing would be their only Christmas present. She touched Sean's arm. "Thank you. Thank you for everything."

He patted her hand. "I'm glad I could help. And don't try to pay me for it," he said in mock anger. "I won't take as much as a farthing from you."

***

After Sean left, Nancy made a simple Christmas Eve dinner of bacon and eggs and pan bread for the kids. After dinner, they assembled around the pathetic Christmas tree, which was hardly more than a large branch that Nancy had found out back. She'd strung together pine cones and red berries and now the kids draped the string around the tree.

Nancy knew Donal believed in Santa, but she wasn't sure about the other three. At eleven, Maureen must at least suspect that there was no Santa. Maybe the others did as well, but none of them had raised any suspicious questions. Nancy was content to continue the fiction if they were. She was just sorry that she would have no presents to give them.

"How will Santa know where to find us," Donal asked.

"If he doesn't know by now," Patrick said, "it's too bad for us."

"Be quiet, Patrick. I told you, Donal, the Irish Santa is very poor. The few presents he has will go to the poorest of the poor children. So, I'm afraid he won't be coming here this year." Much to her relief, he accepted her explanation without complaint.

"All I want is a ticket to America," Patrick muttered.

"Patrick, what did I tell you—"

There was a knock at the door. Maureen opened it and standing there, weighted down with presents was… "Uncle Neil!" she screamed.

After Neil peeled the children off him, he handed the kids two shopping bags stuffed with gaily wrapped presents. "Here you go, kids. Put these presents from Santa under the tree."

"Is this from the American Santa or the Irish Santa?" Donal asked excitedly.

Neil looked at Nancy, puzzled by the question.

"The American Santa," she said. "Uncle Neil, I was just telling the children that the Irish Santa was very poor and they would not be getting presents from him."

Neil nodded in understanding, but he raised his eyebrows at the sight of the pitiful tree. Tentatively, he kissed Nancy on the cheek. "Merry Christmas, Nancy. That's a truly wretched tree," he whispered.

"I know. Merry Christmas, Neil. What are you doing here?"

"I didn't want to spend Christmas alone. And I knew you were alone, so…"

"I'm glad you came."

And she was, or at least she thought she was. Her mind was a hopeless confusion of emotions. Since arriving in Ireland, she'd had so much to contend with that she'd pushed Neil to the back of her mind. It was hard enough sorting out all the difficulties and problems associated with each country, so for her own sanity, she had to keep them separated. Without realizing it, she'd compartmentalized her mind. The farm and all the trouble it entailed was Ireland. Neil was America. But now, here was Neil, breaking through her carefully laid out categories.

Fiona placed the last present under the tree. "Can we open them now?"

"Sure," Neil said.

"No. You'll wait till Christmas morning."

"Why?"

That was a good question and Nancy didn't have a good answer. The children had gone through so much, why not indulge them a little? "All right. Go ahead."

The kids tore into the packages. Among the many presents, Maureen and Fiona got dresses, Donal got a fire truck, and Patrick unwrapped a baseball, glove, and bat.

Seeing her happy children sitting by the stove, surrounded by presents, gave Nancy a lump in her throat. Two hours ago they were facing the worst Christmas of their young lives, but Neil had changed all that with a suitcase full of presents.

She poured the tea. "You shouldn't have brought all those gifts. You'll spoil them."

"Don't be daft."

From across the table, she studied him and she liked what she saw. "I see you've put on some weight."

Neil patted his flat stomach. "I have. Since I've been home, I've been eating like a bloody horse."

"You look good. The extra pounds have taken away the gauntness." Even his eyes seemed to have reclaimed that old sparkle. Gone was the wariness and sadness that had so shocked her. But she said nothing about that.

"Nancy, have you given any thought to what I asked you back in the States?"

She had and she hadn't. She knew it was pointless postponing a decision. Sooner or later, she would have to confront her concerns about marrying him. Just not now.

Before she could give him an answer, there was another knock at the door. She was grateful for the interruption, but she wondered who it could be. She opened the door to Sean Garrett standing there with a wide grin on his face and weighted down with presents of his own.

"Oh... Sean..."

Sean looked over her shoulder and saw a man seated at the table scowling at him. And his grin faded.

As they did when Neil arrived, the kids mauled Sean. "Are these more presents from the American Santa?" Donal asked.

"No, Donal," Sean said, shooting a pointed look at Neil. These are from the Irish Santa."

"But I thought he had only enough to bring to the very poor kids."

A puzzled Sean looked at Nancy, who shrugged helplessly, sorry she had ever started the whole business about American and Irish Santas.

He got her drift. He tousled Donal's hair. "Well, lucky for you, it turns out he had some left over."

Neil stood up and coughed.

"Oh, Neil," Nancy said, uncomfortably, "this is Sean. Sean, this is Neil."

The two men, around the same height, faced off and shook hands with about as much sincerity as two boxers at the beginning of a grudge fight.

Nancy broke the awkward silence. "Neil, Sean is an old friend who happens to be a building contractor. I've hired him to work on fixing up the farm. You remember, I wrote you what a mess it was. Well, Sean has been doing wonders. He's replaced the roof tiles and as you can see he's put new planking on the ceiling and..." she stopped talking, realizing she was babbling. "Well, then, why don't we all sit down and have a nice cup of tea?"

Neil reached into his suitcase and pulled out a bottle of Irish whiskey. "I've brought something a little stronger. Will you join me?" he asked Sean.

"I will."

Nancy watched nervously as Neil poured the whiskey into two mugs. He held his up. "Here's a merry Christmas to all."

"To all," Sean said, draining his mug.

He put the mug down on the table and Neil immediately refilled it.

"Will you be staying long?" Sean asked.

"I'm leaving the day after Christmas."

"Ah, that's too bad," he said, sounding not at all sorry.

And the rest of the night's conversation went downhill from there.

About an hour after the children went to bed, the bottle was almost empty. Sean stood up, a little unsteady on his feet. "I think I'll be going."

Under normal circumstances, Nancy would have asked him to stay a little longer, but she was relieved that this awkward evening was finally coming to an end.

"Sean, thank you for coming and bringing all those gifts."

"It's nothing." He looked at Neil. "Do you have a place to stay?"

Neil seemed surprised by the question. He hadn't even thought about a place to stay.

"Because if you don't, you can stay with me."

"Oh, no," Nancy said quickly. The last thing she wanted was these two to go off together in their inebriated state. They'd be brawling with each other in no time. She was about to tell Neil to put Patrick in her bed and he would sleep in Patrick's bed, but then she realized they would all be in the same room. That would never do.

Neil solved her delicate dilemma. "I'll sleep here," he said pointing to the chaise lounge.

"That's no place to sleep," Nancy said.

"I've slept on worse."

At the door, Sean delivered his parting shot. "Have a good trip back to the States," he said with a wide grin.

***

With just the five of them and Neil, Christmas day was much more tranquil and stress-free than the night before. Neil spent most of the afternoon playing ball with the kids. He tried to teach them how to hit the baseball, but being Irish he wasn't very good at it himself. He was much better teaching them to kick the soccer ball that Sean had brought for the boys. Shortly after dinner, the kids, exhausted from playing all day, went to bed.

Nancy poured another cup of tea. "Are you back working on the docks?"

"I lasted three days. Then I quit."

"Why?"

"You remember my buddy, Ray Fazio? He went back to his old job at an oil refinery in Bayonne and he's happy as a lark. But it didn't work for me. After three days of driving a forklift, I realized I couldn't settle for that kind of work anymore. Maybe it was the war, or maybe I've matured, but I want to do something more worthwhile with my life."

"So what are you going to do?"

"I'm going to City College in February."

"College? How can you afford that?"

"The government created this great thing called the G.I. Bill. Nancy, the government will actually pay me to go to school," he said in wonder, as though he couldn't quite believe it himself. "Isn't that fantastic?"

Nancy could scarcely grasp the notion that someone like Neil, an immigrant from Ireland, could go to college. "It is fantastic, Neil."

"It's scary in a way. After all, I am thirty-seven. I'm not sure I'll be able to keep up with those eighteen-year-olds. But at the same time, it's exciting." He shook his head in awe. "Not in a million years did I ever think that a dumb Mick like me could go to college. It's a wonder."

"Yes, it is." His startling news set her to thinking about herself. Wasn't America the land of the possible? Maybe someday she could finish high school and maybe someday she, too, could go to college.

"Nancy, you still haven't answered my question. Have you given any thought to what I asked you back in the States?"

His question jarred her out of her pleasant reverie.

"Neil, I'm so tired, I can't even think straight. Let's talk about this tomorrow."

He nodded glumly.

***

The next morning, Nancy and Maureen walked into the village with Neil to wait for the bus that would take him to the airport.

Maureen stood out in the middle of the road, watching for the bus. Soon, she saw it approaching from a distance. "Here it comes," she shouted, running to the side of the road.

The bus pulled off the road and the doors opened.

Maureen kissed his cheek. "Have a good trip home, Uncle Neil. Don't worry, we'll be home soon."

Nancy kissed him. "Have a safe flight."

"I will." He picked up his suitcase. "When will you give me an answer?"

"When I come home, Neil."

"Where is home, Nancy?"

The question shocked her. "Why, the States of course."

"Really? You look awfully content living on the farm. Maybe this is home now."

"No, this is all just temporary. As soon as the court case is over, I'm coming home. To the States."

Neil didn't look convinced.

"If you're coming on board, come on board," the bus driver said. "I have a schedule to maintain."

Neil climbed onto the bus. As it pulled away, he opened a window and leaned out. "Write me about the progress of the court case."

"I will."

Nancy and Maureen stood there until the bus was out of sight. Then she took Maureen's hand. "Let's go home."

Home? Did she use that word out of habit, or was Neil right? Was she beginning to think of the farm as home?

As they walked back up the road to the farm, Maureen said, "Are you going to marry Uncle Neil?"

Oh, God. Her, too? "I don't know."

"Do you love him?"

"I'm not sure."

"Do you love Uncle Sean?"

"For the love," Nancy snapped, "will you stop asking so many questions."

Nancy kept walking, but Maureen stopped in the road and there were tears in her eyes. Nancy turned to look at her daughter. The anger dissolved and she ran to her and hugged her.

"I'm sorry, Maureen. It's just that... everything is so confusing."

***

While his mother and Maureen were in the village seeing Uncle Neil off, Donal, as was wont to do when he wasn't interested in playing games with his sisters and brother, would often go off to explore the countryside by himself. As he got to the top of the loaning, he looked across the fields and saw the Crossan farm in the distance. He'd heard his mother tell Uncle Sean what a nice woman she was and he decided to see for himself.

When he came into the farm yard, he saw Mr. Crossan mucking out the horse stall in the barn. The farmer had a very red face, especially his cheeks, but he was whistling softly and Donal decided that he was a nice man. He stood in the doorway and watched. Finally, Crossan turned around. "Well, and who are you?"

"I'm Donal Cavanaugh. We live over there," he said pointing back toward his farm.

"Ah, so you're one of the wee yanks?"

"What's a yank?"

"Someone from America."

"Then I'm a yank."

Donal stared up wide-eyed at the horse in the stall. Since he'd been in Ireland, he'd seen plenty of horses in fields, but never one up close. He'd petted a donkey his first day in Ireland, but he'd never even touched a horse. The animal was just a tired draft horse used to pull plows and drays, but to Donal it looked like those beautiful horses he'd seen in cowboy movies.

"Can I touch him?"

"Sure. Dolly will do you no harm."

Gingerly, Donal patted the horse's withers. At his touch, Dolly twitched reflexively, as though shooing away a horsefly. Donal quickly pulled his hand back.

Crossan laughed. "Sure it's all right. You didn't hurt her." He studied Donal. "Have you ever ridden a horse?"

Donal shook his head. "No. Never."

"Would you like to?"

"Oh, yes."

"You're in luck. I was just about to take Dolly down to the stream for a drink. Would you like to ride her?"

"Is there a saddle?"

Crossan laughed. "No, little yank, this is a working horse, not like one of those dandy beasts the English use to run down poor foxes."

He lifted Donal up and put him on Dolly's back. Donal felt as though he were ten feet in the air and when the horse shifted her weight from one foot to the other, Donal thought he would surely fall off. He clutched Dolly's mane with both hands as Crossan led the horse out of the barn and down to the stream.

Donal was too scared to even talk, especially when Dolly got to the stream and lowered her head to drink. He was terrified he would slide down her long neck and into the stream. But by the time Crossan had led them both back to the barn, Donal was a veteran rider, even using his heels to prod Dolly on, just like he'd see the cowboys do in the movies.

Crossan lifted Donal off the horse. "All right, little yank, you run along now."

"Thank you, Mr. Crossan. Could I do it again sometime?"

"You'll call me John. Mr. Crossan is my father."

Donal looked around for Mr. Crossan's father. "No, little yank. That's just an expression. You come back around this time tomorrow. I always take Dolly down for a drink around this time of day."

Donal flew across the fields, dying to tell his mother the news. He burst into the farmhouse. "Mommy, Mommy," he shouted. "I rode a horse! I rode a horse!"

Nancy was sitting at the table having a cup of tea with Sean. "What are you talking about? Where would you find a horse?"

"Mr. Crossan has a horse and he let me ride it. I rode it all the way down to the stream."

Nancy's brow creased in concern. "You're too young to be riding a big dangerous horse."

Sean patted Nancy's hand. "It's all right," Sean whispered. "I'm sure it's an old nag Crossan uses to pull his plow. It's not likely she would bolt for the mountains with Donal on her back. Besides, I'm sure Crossan led the animal."

"He did. Her name is Dolly." He beamed. "She's a good bugger."

"Donal! Where did you hear that word?"

"From John. He calls Dolly that all the time. "Come on, you bugger. Pick it up, you bugger."

"First of all, who… who is John?" Nancy sputtered.

"Mr. Crossan."

"Well then you will call him Mr. Crossan."

"I did, but he said that was his father and I should call him John."

Nancy put her head in her hands. "This is giving me a headache."

"Sure it's the custom around here, Nancy," Sean said. "The men and women go by their first names, probably because there are so many with the same last names. There's no disrespect intended."

Nancy shook her head. "All right. But you will not use that word again, Donal."

"What word?"

Nancy looked at Sean in exasperation and tried not to laugh. "Bugger," she said softly. "You will not use that word anymore."

"Why?"

"Because… because it's a grownup word and not suitable for a child."

Donal shrugged and ran off to tell his sisters and brother about Dolly.

CHAPTER TWENTY-SIX

It was nearing the end of January and with each passing day Nancy was growing increasingly irritated by the glacial pace of the court case. She'd been back in Ireland for over two months and so far she'd heard nothing from her solicitor. She'd hoped it would have been settled by now and she and the kids would be on their way back to the States.

By the beginning of February, she'd run out of patience. It was time to confront O'Donnell. She put Maureen in charge of the other kids and took the bus into Ballycastle.

Owen O'Donnell's office still smelled of stale pipe smoke and his desk was still cluttered with books and case folders. Nothing seemed to have changed since her last visit and she began to wonder if O'Donnell did anything at all besides fill his pipe, which is what he was doing at the moment.

"Mrs. Cavanaugh, it is good to see you. I trust all is well?"

"No, Mr. O'Donnell, all is not well."

His bushy eyebrows went up. "Oh, are your neighbors in arrears with the field rents?"

"No, they've been paying, reluctantly, to be sure. I'm here about the case. Has there been any progress?"

He puffed his pipe and was immediately enveloped in a cloud of blue smoke. "Well, as I've told you, these things do take time."

"It's been two months."

O'Donnell's patronizing smile was beginning to get on her nerves. "You yanks are always in such a hurry. You must understand, Mrs. Cavanaugh, that the Irish courts are nothing like your courts in America. We don't have dozens of judges presiding over cases in dozens of courtrooms. We have only one district court and one district judge in this county. And you should count yourself fortunate that the court is right here in Ballycastle. Otherwise, we would have to travel a great distance and wouldn't that be inconvenient?"

"I appreciate all that, Mr. O'Donnell, but what have you done so far?"

O'Donnell rummaged through the clutter on his desk and finally found what he was looking for. He opened a folder – presumably Nancy's – and glanced through it. Nancy was distressed to see how thin the file was. From her experience with lawyers like Isaac Kaplan and Bossart, she'd never seen a file less than several inches thick and she'd always wondered – what in the world could be on all those sheets of papers? If that pathetically thin file he was reading represented his work output, he'd done precious little work on her case.

Nancy watched O'Donnell puff on his pipe as if he didn't have a care in the world and time was of no consequence. And it made her blood boil.

"Mrs. Cavanaugh, I've been engaged in an unusually protracted and lengthy correspondence with your sister-in-law's solicitor. All to no avail I'm afraid."

Now she was not only angry, she was bitterly disappointed. She'd hoped they could reach a compromise that would be suitable to both of them and avoid the time and money of a trial. She'd even authorized O'Donnell to propose to Eunice that she and her husband could live on the farm, provided she would stipulate that it belonged to Nancy.

"What about my proposal that she could live on the farm?"

"Rejected out of hand."

"So that means a trial?"

"I'm afraid so. I've exhausted all other means."

"When will we go to trial?"

"Ah, these things take time."

Nancy bristled. There was that annoying, patronizing smile again.

***

One morning toward the end of February, Patrick came running into the house. "Mom, Grandfather is coming up the loaning."

Nancy went out to meet him with rising hope. The day after that terrible, awful night when she'd stopped her mother from hitting Fiona, she had left rather abruptly in an atmosphere poisoned by tension and recrimination. She had no illusions about ever having a close relationship with her mother, but still, she'd hoped they could at least remain cordial and find some way to repair the damage from all the harsh words uttered that night.

"Father, what a surprise." She looked over his shoulder. "Is Mother with you?"

He looked away evasively. "Ach, she couldn't come what with the rheumatism and all."

"Of course, I understand. Come into the house."

Standing in the kitchen, the four children lined up like victims of a firing squad.

"Say hello to your grandfather."

"Hello, Grandfather," they said unison.

He grunted and pulled a paper cone out of his pocket. "I brought you something." He handed the cone to Maureen. "It's sweets for you and your brothers and sister. Don't eat too much, you'll make yourselves sick."

A stunned Maureen took the offering. "Thank you, Grandfather."

For a moment there was an astonished, awkward silence, then Nancy, recovering from the shock of seeing her father give something to her kids, said, "All right, off with you."

The four kids rushed outside to see what was inside the paper cone.

"Sit down, Father, I'll make tea."

"No, I can't stay. I just came to warn you."

"Warn me? About what?"

He looked around the kitchen, clearly impressed. "You've done wonders here."

"It's a work in progress."

The old man took his glasses off and rubbed them with a handkerchief. "Have you wondered why your case has been taking so long?"

"I have. I went to see my solicitor a couple of weeks ago. His answer wasn't exactly satisfactory."

"It's not him, it your sister-in-law. She's been stalling, hoping you'll get tired of waiting and go home."

Nancy slammed her hand down on the table. "Never. I will stay here until hell freezes over if necessary."

He put his glasses back on and blinked rapidly. "You should know she has another motive as well. She's waiting, stalling, because she wants Judge Geary to hear the case."

"Who is Judge Geary?"

"He comes from a long line of farmers around these parts. She thinks he'll be more sympathetic toward a local resident like herself than to a yank such as yourself."

"Why does everybody call me a yank?" Nancy said in frustration. "I was born here, too."

"Because you went out to America. That makes you a yank in their book."

After her father left, Nancy made herself a cup of tea and mulled over what her father had said. She'd thought the delay was because of her incompetent solicitor, but it would seem it was more serious than that. Eunice was working behind the scenes to rig the trial in her favor and there was nothing she could do about it. What else, she wondered, did that woman have up her sleeve?

***

February turned to March and with each passing week and with no word of a trial date, Nancy was growing more and more discouraged. But life went on and, little by little, almost imperceptibly, Nancy and the kids fell into a comfortable routine. When they weren't gallivanting about the countryside – or visiting the Crossan farm to ride Dolly down to the spring for a drink of water – Patrick and Donal were assigned the task of carrying buckets of water from the well. Maureen and Fiona learned how to make pan bread on the old iron stove. At Maureen's insistence, she and her sister planted red and white rose bushes by the front door. The children were growing to love the carefree farm life and Nancy wasn't sure how she felt about that.

Then one day, Patrick and Donal came rushing into the house. "Mom," Patrick said breathlessly, "there's a man coming up the loaning."

Nancy met him at the door. She was hoping that it might be O'Donnell, or one of his assistants, but it was a stranger. "Good day, sir."

He tipped his hat. "Good day, missus. I'm Mr. Dugan, the truant officer. I'm here to inquire as to why your children are not in school."

At those words, Maureen, Fiona, and Patrick stepped back, aghast. Only Donal, who was too young to go to school, looked on unconcerned.

"Well, the thing is, Mr. Dugan, we won't be staying long. I'm in the middle of a legal matter and as soon as its settled, we're going back to the States."

"Well, that's all well and good, Mrs. Cavanaugh, but until you go back, the children must go to school. That's the law."

"I see. Where is the nearest school?"

"St. Colm's. It's right here in Kilgrin.

**

Unpersuaded by their pitiful howls of protest and despair and end-of-world prophesies, the next day Nancy went to St. Colm's and registered them for school. It was not something she was happy about. She enjoyed having the children about her all day, watching them discover and explore things they would never have seen back in the States. She knew she should have registered the children earlier, but she rationalized that they were getting an equally important education experiencing life on a farm.

On the other hand, she was mindful that everything she did – or did not do – would be a reflection on her. Mr. O'Donnell had warned her that when the trial started, the other side would do everything they could to make her look bad. He assured her that they would delve into her every act, her every utterance, and try to turn it into something malicious, nefarious, or irresponsible.

Monday morning arrived and the anxious and distressed children set out for school. Nancy had offered to take them, but Patrick was mortified at the thought that his mother would accompany them. As he pointed out to her, if they could cross Amsterdam Avenue and Broadway to get to their school back home, they could certainly walk a mile on a county road all by themselves.

St. Colm School, adjacent to the church, was a cold, forbidding pile of gray stones. Dozens of raucous children, intent on draining off their excess energy before they would be forced to go inside, noisily raced around the schoolyard playing tag and kicking soccer balls.

Maureen, Fiona, and Patrick stepped into this chaos. Suddenly, as if on command, all play ceased. Everyone froze and they gawked at the three exotic yanks.

Maureen took Patrick's and Fiona's hands. "Come on," she said, resolutely, "pay no attention."

As they headed for the front door, a cluster of students backed away, as though the three yanks might be bearers of some terribly contagious disease. They almost made it to the front door, but then a husky boy about Patrick's age stepped in front of them, blocking their way.

"You yanks dress funny."

"Please let us pass," Maureen said.

"And you talk funny as well."

"You talk funny," Patrick shouted.

The boy was taken aback by Patrick's retort, but only momentarily. Deciding he'd been insulted, he plowed into Patrick and the fight was on. As they rolled around in the dirt, a nun appeared out of nowhere and descended on the boys like some great black vulture. "Stop this at once," she said in an iron tone that froze the boys in mid-roll.

They got up and dusted themselves off.

"Are we to fight in the dirt like animals then?"

"He started it," the boy said.

'I did not," Patrick said in his defense. "He did."

"Right. You will both report to Mother Superior straight away."

***

While his sisters and brothers were learning what it was like to go to school in rural Ireland, Donal set across the fields to John Crossan's farm. He sat down on a rock at the end of a half-plowed field and watched Crossan guide Dolly and a plow toward him. When Crossan got to end of a furrow, he took off his cap and wiped his forehead. "Good morning, Donal."

"Hello, John. What are you doing?"

"Getting the field ready for planting."

"What are you going to plant?"

"Potatoes. Do you want to help?"

Donal jumped up. "Oh, yes, can I?"

Crossan handed Donal the reins. "Here you steer Dolly while I work the plow."

Together, Crossan and Donal guided the horse and plow back down the field. From years of plowing fields, Dolly was fully capable of pulling the plow unattended, but Donal didn't know that and with great concentration he steered the horse through the furrows with great care.

***

"I'm never going back there," Patrick shouted. "I hate that school."

After their calamitous first day, Nancy called a family meeting and allowed them to vent their frustrations. She listened to Patrick rant and watched Maureen and Fiona nod in agreement with his every complaint.

"The girls are all stuck-up," Maureen said.

"It's true," Fiona added. "No one would talk to us."

"And the nuns are all mean." Patrick scrunched up his face in an imitation of a mean nun.

"Children, we won't be here long. As soon as the trial is over we're going home."

"When will that be?" Maureen asked plaintively.

"Soon I hope."

Donal looked up from his fire truck. "I like it here. I helped John plow the field today."

Fiona glared at him. "Oh, shut up."

"Fiona," Nancy said automatically, "don't tell your little brother to shut up."

***

March turned into April and Nancy studied the calendar with growing despair. God, how long will we have to stay here? Just when she thought she couldn't take another month of uncertainty, she got a message that O'Donnell wanted to see her.

Nancy immediately took the bus into Ballycastle. She wouldn't allow herself to feel optimistic, but, on the other hand, she was hoping for some good news.

O'Donnell stuffed his ever-present pipe with tobacco and said, in his annoyingly soothing way, "I was just notified by the other side. Judge Geary will hear the case."

"Why Judge Geary? My father tells me he may be biased against me."

"We have no choice. The district court judges rotate every six months. And its Geary's turn to be here next month."

"Next month! We have to wait another month? Why can't we go before the judge that's here now?"

"He has a full docket. Besides, no judge will take a case if it might extend into his rotation time."

"So there's nothing we can do?"

"Nothing."

Defeated, Nancy stood up. "When will the trial begin?"

O'Donnell puffed on his pipe and looked out the window. "When Judge Geary says so."

***

Patrick was hiding under the covers when Nancy came in to wake them up for school. He was usually the first one up, but this morning, he didn't budge.

"Come on, Patrick. Time to get up."

"I'm not going to school. I hate it," he said in a muffled voice.

For days now Nancy had been expecting a rebellion. Every day, he came home from school in a foul mood, swearing it was his last day and that he would never go back. But Nancy had a plan. She dropped his baseball bat onto his bed.

Patrick peeked from under the covers. "What's this for? Are you going to beat me? I don't care. I'm never going back there again."

"Maybe you could teach the boys at school how to play baseball."

Patrick pulled the covers away, scowling at his mother, but he picked up the bat and fingered it, lost in thought.

***

Patrick went to school that morning carrying his books – and his bat, glove, and ball. Several boys, including the husky kid that Patrick had a fight with, were kicking a soccer ball in the schoolyard. When they saw what he was carrying, they stopped playing.

"What's that?" the husky kid asked.

Patrick tossed the ball in the air and caught it in his glove. "You guys ever play baseball?"

After school, Patrick and a dozen boys assembled in the schoolyard. After a brief lesson on the finer points of baseball, they chose up sides and the game began.

The game got off to a shaky start. Patrick pitched the ball to the husky kid, who took a mighty swing. The bat slipped out of his hands and Patrick had to duck as the bat sailed past his head. On the second pitch, the kid hit a dribbler back to Patrick, who

276

scooped it up and threw it to the boy at first base. The boy dropped the ball, looked at it lying at his feet, and then kicked it like a soccer ball back to Patrick. The second batter hit a fly ball over the head of the outfielders. Delirious with excitement, he dropped the bat and ran at top speed – toward third base.

But none of that mattered. They all had a grand time and they made Patrick promise to bring his baseball, bat and glove the following day.

CHAPTER TWENTY-SEVEN

Finally, Nancy received word from O'Donnell that the trial was scheduled to begin two weeks from Monday. She marked the date on the calendar relieved that the time had finally come, but at the same time dismayed to realize that six months had passed since they'd come to Ireland. Nancy had expected to be home by now, not getting ready for a trial.

***

The Sunday before the trial was to begin, Nancy went to the bus stop in the village to await the arrival of Neil. When she'd written him with news of the trial date, he'd written back that he was coming over. She tried to dissuade him, but he insisted on coming.

She watched the bus approaching with some trepidation. She was glad that he'd come to support her, but at the same time she prayed he wouldn't bring up the question of marriage again. She had enough to worry about. And besides, she didn't know how she would answer his question. She promised herself that as soon as the trial was over and out of the way, she would give the question some serious thought.

The bus door opened and Neil stepped off. He looked different somehow, more confident, more sure of himself. He even dressed differently.

She gave him a kiss. "You shouldn't have come, but I'm glad you did."

"Don't be daft. I'm sure you can use some moral support."

"Oh, I can."

"How's college?"

"It's great. I'm really enjoying myself, especially after I found out that I could hold my own against all those eighteen-year-olds. Quite frankly, I think most of them are too immature to be in college."

"Is the semester over?"

"No, but I made arrangements with my professors to take my exams early."

She took his arm. "Come on. The kids are dying to see you."

"How about you?"

"I'm glad to see you too, Neil," she said with more enthusiasm than she felt.

***

As they came up the loaning, the farmhouse came into view and Neil was stunned by the transformation. When he'd been here at Christmas, it looked so shabby that he wondered how she and the kids could live there. But now he looked at the white-washed walls, the neatly shingled roof, and the profusion of roses growing up along both sides of the freshly painted doors and his heart sank. It looked like a home.

"You've done a lot."

"It's livable."

Neil studied her, wondering what that meant. "Nancy, what will you do with it when you win the case?"

"I don't know..." she blurted out, instantly regretting her words when she saw the look of hurt on his face. "Mr. O'Donnell did say something that was very troubling."

"What's that?"

"He said that if I lose the case, I'll have to vacate the farm immediately and I will have no further claim to it."

"That won't happen. You will win."

"From your mouth to God's ears."

Just then, the kids, led by Maureen, can rushing out of the house. "Uncle Neil! Uncle Neil!" they shouted as they swarmed over him.

***

Neil left shortly after dinner. Nancy had wanted him to stay, but she had to agree with his reasoning. With the trial starting tomorrow, how would it look for a single man to be staying in a widow's home? Besides, he'd already booked a room in a hotel in Ballycastle.

As he waited for the bus at the crossroads, brooding over the farm and her vague response about it, he looked across the road and saw Logan's Pub. Ah, what the hell, he thought, there's always another bus.

The pub air was gray with smoke even though there were only a handful of men at the bar. He ordered a pint and took it to a table in the corner. One pint led to another as he tried to drown his doubts and suspicions in a sea of stout. After an hour, he switched to whiskey. By now he was quite drunk, in fact so drunk that he didn't notice a man with his face pressed to the window, staring at him. The man hurried off.

Five minutes later, that same man came into the pub with a woman and an older, white-haired man. The three sat down at a table next to Neil. After a round of drinks, the white-haired man said, "Excuse me, sir. I wonder if I might buy you a drink?"

Neil looked at the man with bleary eyes. "What the hell. Why not?"

By the next round the three had moved to Neil's table. The white-haired man held up his glass. "To the future."

Neil grunted. "I'm not sure I want to drink to the future, Mr.…?"

"Timothy Reagan. I'm a solicitor and these are my clients, Eunice and Billy Dunne."

Neil slammed his glass down on the table. "I'll have no drink with the likes of you."

"Now, now. Mr. Cullen. There are always two sides to every story."

"I wanted to settle this out of the court, I did," Eunice interjected piously. "But Nancy, my own sister-in-law, wouldn't hear of it."

"That's not what I heard."

"Well, there you have it," Reagan said. "Didn't I tell you there are always two sides to every story." Reagan stared up at the ceiling. "It's the little yanks I feel sorry for."

That got Neil's attention. "Why?"

"Well, I think it's clear. If Mrs. Cavanaugh wins the case. She'll stay here and that's a fact."

"The children should be raised back in their own country," Billy said, thumping his knuckles on the table for emphasis.

Eunice gave him a sharp look. "Shut your gub, Billy."

Neil waved a hand in dismissal. "You're all daft. Nancy won't stay in Ireland. She hates it here."

"Well, that's not what we've been hearing."

Neil saw the three exchange knowing glances. "And what have you been hearing?"

"She's fixed the farm up lovely," Reagan said. "And I hear the children are having a grand time at their school. I don't want to be telling tales out of school, but…"

Neil was hooked. "But what?"

"Mrs. Cavanaugh and Sean Garrett seem to be, how shall I say it, getting along famously."

Neil shoved his glass aside. "You're a liar."

Reagan raised his hands in supplication. "Now don't kill the messenger, Mr. Cullen. I'm only telling you what I've heard. Ach, maybe it isn't true at all."

"It doesn't matter," Neil drained his glass. "There's nothing I can do about it."

"Well, I don't think that's entirely true."

Neil looked at him suspiciously. "What do you mean?"

"You see, Mr. Cullen, the case hinges on Connor Cavanaugh's intent. If he'd left a will stipulating who the farm was to go to, then there would be no reason for this trial. Alas, that's not case and we are contending that Connor wished to leave the farm to his dear, beloved sister."

In his advanced state of inebriation, Neil was having a hard time following the solicitor's line of thought. "So, what's any of this have to do with me?"

"This is, of course, all hypothetical, mind, but suppose, just suppose you were to testify that Connor told you he had no use for the farm and intended to leave it to his sister, Eunice. A judge would be hard pressed to ignore that evidence."

Eunice patted Neil's hand. "Without the farm to keep her here, she'd surely go back to America with you."

"And the kids would be raised as proper yanks they would." Billy added, flinching from Eunice's hard look.

Reagan, deciding the seed was planted, nodded and they all stood up. "Well, you have a good night, Mr. Cullen."

The three left, leaving Neil to brood into his whiskey glass.

***

The next morning, a very tired and hung-over Neil Cullen made his way unsteadily to the small, but imposing courthouse on Pierce Street in Ballycastle. He'd missed the last bus the night before and had to walk the ten miles back to town. The long walk gave him plenty of time to think about what Reagan and the Dunnes had said. But by the time he fell into bed, he still didn't know what he would do – if anything.

Nancy and Owen O'Donnell arrived a few minutes later.

She stared up at the building uneasily. "I've been waiting for this moment for so long, but now that it's here, I'm scared to death."

"Don't worry, Mrs. Cavanaugh," O'Donnell said. "We will prevail."

"When you win, you'll have a big decision to make, won't you?" Neil said.

"I have to win the case first." Nancy thought she detected an accusatory tone in his voice, but he looked so tired she decided he was probably just cranky.

The interior of the courthouse reflected the Victorian era in which it had been built. The courtroom's high arched ceiling, dark paneled walls, and lofty judge's bench were all designed to convey the majesty and power of the law.

Eunice and Billy were standing in the back of the courtroom huddled with Reagan and their barrister.

Owen O'Donnell led Nancy down the aisle to meet her barrister, a tall, imposing man in a white horsehair wig, stiff collar, and banded black gown.

"Mrs. Cavanaugh," O'Donnell said, "may I introduce Mr. Thomas Quinn, your barrister."

"How are you, Mrs. Cavanaugh?"

"Nervous, but fine, thank you."

Nancy was pleased that the barrister exuded a competence and self-assurance that seemed to elude Mr. O'Donnell. She'd been prepared to change solicitors shortly after meeting him, but then Sean Garrett pointed out that O'Donnell would have no part in the actual trial. That was the job of the barrister.

"I know it's been a long wait, Mrs. Cavanaugh," Quinn said. "But I expect the trial will be over before the day is out."

"Only one day?" Neil asked.

"Yes. It's really a simple question. Who has the right to the farm? We have only a handful of witnesses, and there are no wills or land deeds to consider. Judge Geary has a well-deserved reputation for running a quick and efficient court. You can expect precious few sidebars and he will not brook irrelevant questions or dawdling. Are you ready to proceed, Mrs. Cavanaugh?"

Nancy nodded, too nervous to speak.

As everyone took their seats, Nancy was suddenly besieged by doubts and recrimination. In 1941, she'd made a decision to come back to Ireland to fight for the farm. And now, after all these years, it had come down to this one day. But win or lose, was it worth it? The sacrifice, the disruption to the children's lives, the cost—money that might better have been spent on the children's future education. Was she on a fool's errand?

While Nancy was having her crisis of conscience, Neil, standing in the back of the courtroom, looked at Reagan and their eyes locked. The solicitor nodded and smiled. Neil turned away. He slumped into a bench at the back of the court, lost in thought. He was the only spectator in the court. But then the door opened and Sean Garrett came in. The two men glowered at each other and Sean took a seat across the aisle. A moment later, Nancy's father came in and sat down next to Sean.

The court clerk stepped to the front of the courtroom. "All be upstanding," he said in a loud voice. "Hear ye, hear ye, the District Court of Ireland is now in session. All with cause to plead, please draw near, give attention, and you shall be heard by the Honorable Judge Finbar Geary. God save Ireland."

Judge Geary, a short rotund man in his early sixties, took his seat on the bench. He, too, was dressed in a black gown and wearing a small, bobbed white wig. He scowled down at the barristers, setting the tone for the trial. "Are you ready to proceed?"

Both barristers nodded in the affirmative.

"Call the first witness."

The court clerk called out, "Mrs. Eunice Dunne, please stand in the docket."

Eunice stepped into the witness box, making a big show of wiping a tear from her eye with her handkerchief. Her barrister, Colin Ahern, stood up. "Good morning, Mrs. Dunne."

"Good morning, Mr. Ahern."

Judge Geary glared at Ahern. "I think we've established it's a good morning. I don't want to hear any more of that. Mr. Ahern, do you have a pertinent question for Mrs. Dunne?"

"Yes, your honor. Mrs. Dunne, how long has the farm been in your family?"

"For ages. It would be a shame if my ancestral home, as it were, were to leave the family after all these years."

Geary leaned forward. "Mrs. Dunne, could you narrow down 'ages' for the court?"

"The farm's been in the family for at least three generations."

Ahern continued. "Mrs. Dunne, tell the court what you intend to do with the farm if the court rules in your favor."

"Billy and me plan to farm the land, your honor. Not let it go to waste like it is now."

"I have no further questions."

Judge Geary sat back. "Mr. Quinn, your witness."

Nancy's barrister opened a folder and scanned some papers. "Mrs. Dunne, are you aware that the farm was deeply in debt when your father died?"

"I vaguely recall that."

"Vaguely recall? The farm was about to be sold off to satisfy its many creditors. Didn't some of these creditors come to you for payment?"

"I'm sure I don't remember that."

"Are you saying that it didn't happen or it may have happened, but you don't recall."

"I just don't remember. That's all," she snapped.

Quinn smiled, pleased that he'd been able to break through her pious veil of humility so easily. He looked at Judge Geary, but his face was a mask of neutrality.

Billy Dunne was the next witness. Eunice's barrister said, "Mr. Dunne, what do you want to do with the farm if the court should see fit to award to you and your wife?"

"It's like the missus says, we'll farm the place."

"No further questions, you honor."

Quinn stood up, stroking his chin. "Farm the place? Is that what you said, Mr. Dunne?"

"I did."

"Mr. Dunne, what do you do for a living?"

"I drive a bread truck in Ballycastle."

"A bread truck, I see. Have you ever owned a farm or worked on a farm?"

"No, sir, I can't say that I have."

"Yet, you and your wife have testified that you intend to farm the land. Is that correct?"

"It is."

"I must admit, Mr. Dunne, I'm puzzled by your answer. Would you tell the court how you intend to do that if you don't know anything about farming?"

Billy shrugged. "How hard can it be?"

Quinn was pleased to see that that response brought a slight raising of Judge Geary's eyebrows. "No more questions, your honor."

The next witness was Frank O'Malley. "What do you do for a living?" Quinn asked.

"I am the proprietor of O'Malley Feed and Grain store in Kilgrin."

"Did you ever have any dealings with Mr. Dennis Cavanaugh, the father of Mr. Connor Cavanaugh and Mrs. Eunice Dunne?"

"I did. I supplied Denny with feed and grain for many years."

Geary leaned forward. "And 'Denny' would be who?"

"Dennis Cavanaugh, Connor's father."

"And did there come a time when Mr. Cavanaugh failed to pay his debts?" Quinn asked.

O'Malley chuckled. "Just all the time."

"That'll be enough of that," the judge admonished O'Malley.

"I'm sorry, your worship."

"Did he eventually pay?"

"He was always in arrears. Then he up and died, God rest his soul, and stuck me with several hundred pounds of debt."

"What did you do?"

"What could I do? The son was out in America so me and some other merchants went to Eunice Dunne there, to see if she would pay."

Quinn glanced at Geary, but his expression was still neutral. He continued. "Other merchants? How many other merchants?"

"Must have been a half dozen. Denny, God rest his soul, stuck the lot of us."

"And when you and the other merchants went to Mrs. Dunne for payment of her father's debts, what did she say to you?"

"She said it was none of her concern. She told us to get the money from her brother, Connor."

"And did you?"

"We did. Me and the other merchants were going to put a lean on the farm, but we decided to give the son a chance to make things right. After all, he'd gone out to America and he was probably rich. Mrs. Dunne gave us Connor's address and we sent him all the bills."

"To your knowledge, how long had Connor Cavanaugh been away from the farm?"

"Oh, it must be near ten years or more that old Denny turned his son out. Denny could be real mean when he had the drink in him."

"Mr. O'Malley, please tell the court why you thought that after all that time Connor would pay the bills?"

"Old Denny, God rest his soul, had passed away. The farm was Connor's now. After all, he was the eldest son."

Quinn snuck a look at Geary, but it was impossible to see what the cagey old judge was thinking. "Mr. O'Malley, when you sent those bills to Connor Cavanaugh, what did he do?"

"He wrote back saying he'd pay every single shilling, but it would take awhile."

"And did you get your money?"

"Aye. It took awhile, but we all got paid, and it was just like he said, every last shilling."

"Thank you, sir. I have no further questions, your honor."

"Do you have any questions for this witness, Mr. Ahern?"

A glum Ahern said, "No, your honor."

"Your honor," Quinn said, "I am prepared to call several more witnesses who will testify as Mr. O'Malley has that they were owed money by Dennis Cavanaugh and that Connor Cavanaugh paid them in full."

Ahern stood up. "Your honor, we will stipulate that Mr. Cavanaugh paid the farm's bills."

"Very well. There will be no need to call any more merchants. This court will be in recess until one this afternoon."

CHAPTER TWENTY-EIGHT

Nancy, Neil, Sean, O'Donnell, and the barrister went to have lunch in a cozy tearoom on Mara Street, a few blocks from the courthouse. She'd been surprised and pleased when she saw her father come into the courtroom. She'd invited him to join them, but he begged off saying he had to go home and have lunch with his wife. He promised to return to court in the afternoon.

Nancy passed the tray of sandwiches to Mr. Quinn. "How do you think it's going?"

"Splendidly, Mrs. Cavanaugh. We've established several very important points. First, we've proven that the farm was in debt, Eunice knew that and washed her hands of the matter. Secondly, we've proven to the satisfaction of the court that Connor paid off those debts. Thirdly, your sister-in-law and her husband profess to having a desire to farm the land, but neither of them knows anything about farming. I assure you, their clumsy pretense of being farmers was not lost on Judge Geary." He patted her hand. "This afternoon I will put you on the stand."

"I'm very nervous."

"About what?"

"Testifying. The judge is always frowning at me. I don't think he likes me."

"Nonsense. That's just his way. I believe the man was born with a perpetual scowl on his face. I shouldn't worry about him. You're the last witness, Mrs. Cavanaugh. Barring some unforeseen circumstance or surprise witness for the other side, I'm confident that we've won."

Everyone smiled at his assessment except Neil, who was still thinking about what Eunice Dunne had said to him: Without the farm to keep her here, she'd surely go back to America with you.

***

After lunch, as they were going back into the courthouse, Sean pulled Neil aside. "I hear you had a few drinks with Eunice and her solicitor last night."

"That's none of your business."

Neil turned to go, but Sean grabbed his arm. "What did you talk about?"

Neil slapped his hand away. "I said it's none of your business."

For a moment it looked as though the two men might come to blows, but Neil turned and went inside.

Neil was washing his hands in the men's room when Reagan came in. He went to an adjoining sink and began to wash his hands.

"And how are you today, Mr. Cullen?"

Neil stared at himself in the mirror and didn't answer.

Reagan went on. "I'm watching this trial, but it's not going good for our side and that's a fact. That old fool Billy doesn't know the front end of a horse from the rear. And Eunice saying they're going to be farmers. Well, it's a wonder."

Reagan dried his hands. "Still, I guess it's good news for Mrs. Cavanaugh. I don't know about the little yanks, but she'll be happy enough here. Well, Mr. Cullen, you have a safe journey back to America all by yourself."

The door slammed, leaving Neil to study himself in the mirror.

***

Everyone rose when Judge Geary entered the court. He settled in his high-backed leather chair and adjusted his wig. "Mr. Quinn, call your next witness."

"If it pleases the court, I'd like to call Mrs. Connor Cavanaugh
"

Nervously, Nancy rose and made her way to the dock."

"Please state your name for the court," Quinn asked.

Softly, Nancy said, "My name is…" Then she looked at the stern-faced judge and the pinched-faced Eunice glaring at her and her nervousness gave way to steely determination. "My name is Mrs. Nancy Cavanaugh," she said in a loud, clear voice.

"Mrs. Cavanaugh what did your husband do for a living?"

"He was a longshoreman in New York City."

"Was he paid well for that work?"

"He was not."

Quinn waved a handful of bills in the air. "Then where did he get the money to pay off all these bills?"

"He worked a second job."

"Did that job pay well?"

"No, but he put in long hours and worked overtime every chance he got. He even became a sky walker."

"Sky walker? Would you tell the court what a sky walker is?"

"When they're constructing those tall buildings, sky walkers are the men who walk on the steel beams hundreds of feet in the air. It's very dangerous work, but Connor did it because it paid better than being an ordinary laborer."

"I see. And what did he do with the wages he earned from that job?"

"Every penny from that second job went to pay off the farm debts."

"Did he get any financial help from his sister, Eunice Dunne?"

Nancy looked at Eunice, who turned away. "He did not."

"So your husband, Connor Cavanaugh, paid off the entire debt by himself?"

"He did."

"No further questions, your honor."

"Mr. Ahern, your witness."

The barrister flipped through his notes, looked up at Nancy with a kindly smile and said, "Mrs. Cavanaugh, why did your husband abandon the farm and go to America?"

Nancy was caught off guard by the implied accusation. "Abandon? He didn't abandon the farm; his father drove him away."

"Really? Drove him away, you say. That's most odd. Don't you think it would be highly unusual for a father to turn his only male heir, the one destined to inherit the farm, off the land?"

"I have no idea."

"Tell me, Mrs. Cavanaugh, can you think of a reason why Dennis Cavanaugh would do that to his own son?"

"Dennis Cavanaugh was a drinker. Everybody knows that. Perhaps—"

"Sad to say, Mrs. Cavanaugh, a lot of farmers in Ireland are 'drinkers' as you put it, but I've never heard of one throwing his only son off the land. Does it not seem plausible to you that he would only do something that drastic if your husband had done something terribly wrong."

"Like what?"

"Oh, I don't know, perhaps he was cheating his father out of money or—"

Nancy slammed her hand on the railing. "That's a lie—!"

Quinn was on his feet. "Objection, your honor. The question calls for speculation on the witness's part."

"Your honor"—Ahern interjected— "I'm merely trying to establish motive and the state of mind of Dennis Cavanaugh."

Before the judge could speak, Nancy blurted out, "I don't know what happened between Connor and his father, I wasn't there."

Ahern tossed his folder on the table with a satisfied smile. "Exactly, Mrs. Cavanaugh, you were not there, so you don't know why Dennis Cavanaugh asked his son to leave the farm."

During this exchange, Judge Geary was furiously banging his gavel. "Silence. All of you. Mrs. Cavanaugh, you will kindly confine your answers to specific questions asked. As for you, Mr. Ahern, you know better than to proceed with a line of questioning when an objection has been raised. I instruct the clerk to strike all questions, answers and comments beginning with Mr. Ahern's speculation that Connor Cavanaugh was cheating his father. Mr. Quinn, your objection is sustained. Mr. Ahern, you will cease any line of questioning that is speculative in nature. We've wasted enough time, please move on."

Up until now, the proceedings had been quiet and calm, almost boring, Nancy thought. But the unexpected and confusing exchange of questions and speculation had upset and flustered her. And then the shouting back and forth between her barrister, Eunice's barrister and the judge confused and upset her even further. Her heart pounded in her chest and she heard a loud rushing sound in her ears. She didn't quite understand what had just happened, but she was appalled and humiliated that Mr. Ahern would dare suggest in front of everyone in the courtroom that her husband was a cheat and a thief.

She was suddenly aware that Ahern was speaking to her. "...Mrs. Cavanaugh, did you hear the question?"

"What? No, would you repeat it?"

"I asked if you know anything about farming."

"No, no, I don't."

Judge Geary seemed to sit up, interested in this line of questioning.

"Do you know anything about planting crops?"

"No.

"Birthing calves?"

"No..."

Quinn jumped to his feet. "Your honor, my learned colleague is belaboring the point. I think we can stipulate that Mrs. Cavanaugh knows no more about farming than the Dunnes."

Ahern bowed to Quinn with a cordial smile. "I thank my esteemed colleague for pointing out the obvious, namely that Mrs. Cavanaugh is a hopeless novice when it comes to farming." He spun toward Nancy and pointed an accusing finger at her. "Mrs. Cavanaugh, isn't it true that last November you turned loose from a field, cows belonging to Messrs. Tully, Hogan, and Whelan?"

"Yes, but..."

"What could you have been thinking? Did you not realize that those cows could have run onto a road and gotten injured or lost?"

"I did it because—"

"And isn't it true that you tried to set fire to crops in the field?"

Nancy glanced up at a frowning Judge Geary, who was hanging on her every word. "Mr. Tully and the others were using my land and they refused to pay for it—"

"Oh, really? I see. So your answer," Ahern said, his voice rising, "was to turn the animals loose and set fire to the crops with every intention of destroying those farmers' livelihoods."

"No, I never intended that."

Quinn was on his feet. "Objection, your honor. Mr. Ahern is badgering the witness."

"Sustained. Mr. Ahern," the judge said sternly, "you may ask questions, but you may not badger the witness. Proceed."

Ahern abruptly changed direction. "I thank the court for its wise instruction. Mrs. Cavanaugh, what do you intend to do with the farm if you gain possession of it?"

From his seat in the back of the courtroom Neil had been getting angrier and angrier at the brutal and relentless badgering of the barrister. But that last question made him sit up. He was most interested in the answer to that question.

Reeling from the barrage of Ahern's questioning, Nancy blurted out, "I... I don't know."

"You don't know. Surely you'll not farm it," Ahern said, sarcastically.

"I don't know what I'll do with the farm, I haven't made up my mind."

Ahern's voice boomed over the courtroom, "You haven't made up your mind what to do with a valuable farm that should be producing vegetables and meat and eggs and everything else that the soil has to offer?" He looked at Judge Geary and shrugged his shoulders. "I have no further questions, your honor."

Reagan turned to Neil and raised his eyebrows in supplication, as if to say, "Why don't you testify?"

Neil turned away. As he watched a downcast Nancy return to her seat, the voices of Eunice, Billy, and Reagan echoed in his brain.

The case hinges on Connor's intent...

The children should be raised back in their own country...

Mrs. Cavanaugh and Sean Garrett seem to be...getting along...

Without the farm to keep her here, she'd surely go back to the States with you...

Supposing you were to testify... to testify... to testify...

Neil heard the judge say, "Mr. Quinn, Mr. Ahern, if there are no further witnesses…"

"I would like to testify..." Neil heard a voice – his voice – say.

And all hell brook loose in the courtroom.

Judge Geary looked up and cupped a hand to his ear. "What was that? Who spoke?"

Quinn turned around to Nancy and whispered urgently, "Do you know anything about this?"

Nancy shook her head, bewildered.

Sean Garrett rushed down the aisle and grabbed Quinn's sleeve. "Don't let him testify," he whispered. "He was in Logan's Pub with the Dunnes and their solicitor last night. There's some sort of collusion going on here."

"*You there,*" Judge Geary roared, pointing at Sean. "*Who are you?*"

"I'm a friend of Nancy Cavanaugh's."

"Sit down at once or I'll hold you in contempt of court. Bailiff, if there is another outburst or breech of etiquette I want that person removed from my court forthwith."

Quinn looked over his shoulder and saw Ahern and Reagan smiling at each other. And he knew he had a problem. He jumped to his feet. "Your honor, this is highly irregular. We have no notice—"

Ahern was on his feet, shouting over him. "Your honor, I submit that in the interest of justice everyone has a right to be heard in this matter."

Quinn shouted over Ahern. "But he's not a party to the case—"

Judge Geary banged his gavel so hard his wig went askew. "Silence! Sit down the pair of you." He turned to Neil, furious with this man who had upset the good order of his court. "Who are you, sir?"

"Neil Cullen. I was Connor Cavanaugh's best friend."

"And what could you offer that would have any relevance to the case?"

"Connor Cavanaugh told me what he wanted to do with the farm."

Ahern was on his feet. "This witness must be allowed to testify, your honor. His testimony is most relevant to the case. He can attest to Mr. Connor's state of mind regarding the farm."

Quinn started to rise to object, but the judge stopped him with a wave of the hand. "Very well. I will allow it. Step into the docket, Mr. Cullen."

After Neil was sworn in, Geary addressed the barristers. "I will conduct the questioning of this witness. You will both have an opportunity to question the witness when I'm done. Mr. Cullen, state your full name."

"Neil Cullen."

"And where do you currently reside?"

"New York City."

"And were you a friend of Connor Cavanaugh?"

"I was."

"How long had you known him."

"Over twelve years. We worked on the docks together."

"And did there come a time when Mr. Cavanaugh confided in you what his intentions were for the farm?"

Neil looked into Nancy's confused, bewildered eyes. "Yes."

"And what did he say to you?"

"He said…" One by one, Neil looked into the faces of Nancy, Sean, Eunice and Billy. His future – Nancy's future – hinged on what he was about to say. He heard Eunice's voice again: Without the farm to keep her here, she'd surely go back to the States with you…

Neil took a deep breath, realizing that he was about to do the hardest thing he'd ever have to do his life. All the air went out of him and he closed his eyes. "Your honor, Connor said… he said he wanted to come back to Ireland and farm the land. He said—"

Ahern was caught off guard by Neil's answer. That fool Reagan had assured him that if Connor decided to testify, he would wrap up the case for them. He jumped to his feet. "Objection, your honor, this testimony of this witness is irrelevant and—"

"Mr. Ahern, may I remind you that it was you who said everyone has a right to be heard in this matter. Sit down. Proceed Mr. Cullen."

"Connor never got used to living in America. 'I'm used to cows in the road, not bloody automobiles,' he used to say all the time."

"Then is it your testimony that had Mr. Cavanaugh lived he would have come back to farm the land?"

Neil looked at Nancy, who now had tears in her eyes. "Only if Nancy agreed. Connor said that, as much as he loved the farm, he would never force her to do something she didn't want to do."

There was a long silence, then, Judge Geary said, "Mr. Quinn, Mr. Ahern, do you have any questions for this witness?"

Both barristers shook their heads. Quinn in relief, Ahern in despair.

"Very well, Mr. Cullen, you may step down."

***

The next day, Nancy went to the bus stop with Neil. He seemed uncharacteristically morose and distracted, but she attributed that to his long flight to Ireland and his lack of sleep.

"I wish you could stay for the verdict tomorrow, Neil."

"I've got to get back. I want to talk to my professors about something."

"What's that?"

"I'm going to be a lawyer, Nancy."

"A lawyer…?" Nancy was flabbergasted. He might as well have said he was going to be the president of the United States. Being a lawyer was not something that the likes of Irish immigrants such as Neil or her could ever hope to aspire to. "Why?"

"Because seeing how you were taken advantage of after Connor died, and now, watching your case, there's so much I don't understand. It seems to me that too often the law is subverted and corrupted. I want to be in a position to see that that can't happen to innocent people ever again."

Nancy didn't know what to say. His goal was certainly admirable and lofty, but it was so far above her understanding. A wave of profound sadness overcame her. She felt him slipping away from her, moving into another sphere to someplace she could never follow. "I wish you luck," she said softly.

"There's no doubt the judge will find in your favor."

"I'm not so sure. What is Judge Geary to think of my turning the cows out and threatening to set fire to the crops?"

"I think he'll understand why you did it."

Nancy exhaled. "Mr. Quinn thinks so. He said your testimony was the real clincher."

Neil looked away. "I only told the truth."

Nancy studied him. Something strange had happened in that courtroom yesterday, but she couldn't quite put her finger on it. "Sometimes the truth isn't easy to tell," she said.

"No, sometimes it's not." Neil saw the bus coming. He gave her a hug and a tender kiss. "Nancy, I wish you the best."

There was something about the tone of finality in his voice that she didn't like. "Neil, what are you saying?"

"I'm saying it's time I got on with my life, Nancy. I've spent entirely too much time waiting for you."

Nancy's heart thudded in her chest. "I know you have. You've been very patient and understanding, but I've been so confused and..."

"I know that. But I see something that you can't or won't admit. You're not in love with me and that's the long and the short of it."

She wanted to shout that it wasn't true, but she didn't know if it were true or not. "Maybe I just need more time..." That sounded pathetic, even to her.

"No." He looked around at the trees and the fields. "This is your home now, Nancy. And... well, that Sean's not a bad fellow. I think you'll be very happy here."

The bus pulled off to the side of the road and stopped. Neil gave her a kiss on the cheek and ran for it.

"What about the children?" she called out after him.

As he climbed onto the bus he said, "I'll always be their Uncle Neil."

The door closed and the bus pulled away.

Nancy stood there with tears running down her face long after the bus was out of sight.

CHAPTER TWENTY-NINE

The next morning, both sides anxiously took their seats in the courtroom to await the decision of Judge Geary. At exactly nine o'clock, the judge came out of his chambers and ascended to the bench. Wasting no time, he opened a folder and began to read. "In the matter of Dunne vs. Cavanaugh, this court was convened to decide one issue, and that issue was to determine if the farm of the late Connor Cavanaugh should be passed down to his widow, Mrs. Connor Cavanaugh, or to his sister, Mrs. Eunice Dunne. It should be duly noted that the court is appalled by the woeful lack of a legally executed land deed or will in this case, which would have unequivocally established proper ownership. But the court also recognizes that by custom and tradition, a custom and tradition that has been honored for hundreds of years in this country, precedence has been established that a family farm is handed down to the eldest son."

Geary took off his glasses and looked down at the assembled group, allowing himself a slight smile. "If you will permit me an aside, that is how I came to study the law. My father's farm went to my older brother." He put his glasses back on and continued to read. "In consideration of the above and all the facts, documents, and testimony offered before this court, it is the decision of the court that the farm of the deceased Dennis Cavanaugh, absent any legal documents to the contrary, was rightfully and lawfully ceded to his eldest son, one Connor Cavanaugh, and upon his death, the farm was rightfully and lawfully ceded to his widow, one Mrs. Connor Cavanaugh." He banged his gavel once. "This court is adjourned."

For a moment, there was a stunned silence. Everyone was caught off guard by the abruptness and brevity of his decision. Judge Geary was known for running a tight court, but he was also known for his often rambling and over-wordy decisions. Both barristers had warned their clients to expect an exhaustive dissertation on land rights in Ireland. But then as the import of what he said sunk in, Quinn stood up and hugged Nancy. "Congratulations, Mrs. Cavanaugh, you've won. The farm is yours."

Sean and O'Donnell hugged Nancy as a sullen Eunice Dunne and her team quietly filed out of the courtroom.

While Quinn, O'Donnell and Sean shook hands and slapped each other's backs, Nancy sat back down, hardly able to comprehend what had just happened. The joys and sorrows of the past six years flashed before her eyes. She recalled her happy, hopeful life with Connor... their bitter fights over the farm... his sudden death... the war... the children growing up... the voyage to Ireland... the dark days in her mother's home... the darker days living in a derelict ruin of a farmhouse... then the good days living in a house that had finally become a comfortable home for her and the children.

Suddenly and without warning, the tears came. Since Connor's death, she hadn't permitted herself to mourn properly because there was always something that needed her immediate attention. But now all the battles were over and the grief she'd bottled up inside her for all those years came pouring out. And with the tears and the sorrow came a welcoming catharsis.

***

As the weeks passed, the stress and ordeal of the trial slowly receded from Nancy's memory, bringing her, finally, a sense of peace she had not experienced in a very long time. Before the trial, she'd lived in constant fear that Eunice would win the case and all her sacrifices and Connor's sacrifices would have been for naught. It had taken her awhile, but she'd finally come to accept the fact that she owned the farm and that gave her a real sense of contentment.

Things were going well. The fields were bringing in rent, Sean's repairs had made the house strong and comfortable. She was even seriously considering his idea of building an outhouse in the barn. With the exception of Maureen, Fiona and Patrick were happy in school and seldom talked about the States.

Only a week earlier, she'd been bringing a bucket of water up from the spring when she caught a glimpse of her little white farmhouse nestled in a stand of trees and it took her breath away. My God, it is beautiful. Behind the house she saw her three children taking turns on the swing that Sean had put up for them. Across the fields, she spotted a happy Donal holding Dolly's reins as John Crossan plowed his field. It had just rained and a soothing silence had fallen over the countryside. The serene quiet and the clean, fresh air was in sharp contrast to the fumes and noise of Amsterdam Avenue back home. Maybe Connor was right, she thought. Maybe Ireland was a magical place after all.

Maybe the farm was – home.

It was only when she thought about Neil Cullen that she became sad. She missed him so much more than she thought possible. Even though she knew he was three thousand miles away, she knew she could count on him being there for her and the children in good times and bad. Just the thought that he was there for her when she needed him had always been a comfort. But now he was gone and out of her life. She'd driven him away with her indecisiveness and there wasn't a day went by she didn't regret her actions.

In the past few weeks, she'd been seeing more of Sean, but no romantic relationship had yet developed. She didn't know how he felt, but for the time being she was content to be just friends. He came to dinner at least once a week and they'd even had a date of sorts – he'd taken her and the kids to the picture show in Ballycastle. Nancy wasn't sure if she was in love with Sean or even anything close to it. In a way, she thought ruefully, it was Neil all over again. He was a good, kind man, and the children certainly loved him. But… But…

She recalled her fierce intransigence regarding marriage after Connor's death. Nora had once asked her if she would ever remarry and her response had been an adamant no. She firmly believed that there was only one man destined for her, and that was Connor, and no one could ever replace him. Over the years, she'd thought she'd moved away from that stubborn position, but now she wondered if that belief was still somewhere stuck in her head, preventing her from loving someone like Neil or Sean.

***

Nancy went to town to do her weekly shopping. As she was leaving the general store, she saw a handwritten flyer posted on the wall: Dance at Cashel Hall - Friday night 8 P.M.

When she got back to the farm, Sean was already there repairing a loose hinge on the barn door. "How's it coming?" she asked.

"Good. I'll be done in a few minutes."

"Where's Cashel Hall?"

"That's part of St. Colm's. Why?"

"There's a dance there this Friday night."

"That's lovely." Sean was only half-listening, intent on lining up the hinge with the door.

"Would you take me?"

He looked up and grinned. "To the dance? Aye. That'd be grand—" He suddenly stopped and his whole demeanor changed. "Och, you know on second thought there's no point in going. You wouldn't know a soul there."

"Then it's a good chance for me to meet the neighbors. I'm one of them now."

"You wouldn't have any fun, Nancy. I told you, they're a very clannish crowd."

She would not be deterred. "You used to be such a fine dancer, Sean Garrett. Have you forgotten how to dance?"

He put the screwdriver down. "I haven't forgotten how it was to dance with you."

"Then it's settled. We'll go. I haven't been to a dance in ages."

She walked away smiling. Sean watched her go, lost in thought, and judging by the frown on his face, they weren't happy thoughts.

***

That Friday night, Nancy fed the children early, put Maureen in charge, and she and Sean walked into Kilgrin to attend her first dance in many years.

As they approached Cashel Hall, they could hear the toe-tapping sound of a jig being played on fiddles and accordions.

"Why are you looking so serious, Sean. We're going to a dance not a funeral."

"Are you sure you want to do this?"

"I am." She nudged him playfully. "I want to see if you can still dance."

The hall was not very large, but it was enough to accommodate the thirty or so men and women, some of whom crowded the small dance floor while others stood to the side watching. Up on a raised stage, a band consisting of three fiddles, an accordion and a bodhrán finished a jig and immediately segued into a passable version of Peg 'O My Heart."

As Nancy and Sean came through the doors, all heads turned in their direction. A hush fell over the hall and the whispering and pointing began. As they walked further into the hall, people parted to let them pass. Nancy's happy smile faded in the face of all this hostility and now she knew why Sean had been reluctant to come.

"Let's go," Sean whispered.

"I will not," she said resolutely. "We came to dance and so we will." She held out her hand. "Well, Sean Garrett, aren't you going to ask me to dance?"

Sean cold barely contain his anger. He would have preferred to punch somebody in the nose, but he took her hand and led her to the center of the floor. As they began to dance, Tully and his wife left the floor, followed by the Whelans and the Hogans. And that started a chain-reaction. One by one the other couples left the floor until only Nancy and Sean were left.

"Nancy, can we go now?" he whispered in her ear.

"No."

They continued dancing with everyone sullenly watching from the sidelines.

The song ended and Nancy clapped as though nothing was amiss. "You still know how to dance, Sean."

"So do you."

"All right. I think we can go now."

And on those words, they turned and proudly walked out the door with all eyes glued to them.

As they walked away, Nancy's steely resolve crumbled and she fell into Sean's arms sobbing. "Why, Sean... Why?"

"It's that Kevin Tully. He's the ringleader of this bunch. Sure if he walked off a cliff, they'd all follow him."

"Am I wrong for trying to protect my children? My farm?"

"No, Nancy. You're right. And by God you've got more courage than the lot of them. Come on, I'll walk you home."

***

The next morning, Rose Crossan came to the door with a basket of eggs and butter. Nancy looked at the basket, puzzled. She had been buying staples like milk, butter, and eggs from Rose on a regular basis, but she hadn't ordered anything this week.

"This is a gift from me to you," she said to Nancy.

"Well, thank you, but why—"

"I heard about what happened at the dance last night."

"Oh, that..."

"Pay them no mind, Nancy. They're all Tully's friends. That's why John and I didn't go. We'll have nothing to do with their ilk."

"Why are they that way?"

"They're a class of stupid, thickheaded Irishmen that makes my blood boil. Don't you know you interfered with their nice, cozy arrangement? They were using your land for free and that was just grand. But then a yank – and a woman yank at that –

shows up and tells them what for. They were caught out and they didn't like it one bit. It was not their fault. It was your fault. Can you believe what kind of muddle-headed thinking would come to that conclusion? They're a wonder."

"Is there anything I can do to make things better?"

"Not a thing and I wouldn't even try. I remember reading about your Hatfields and McCoys back in the States and how they feuded for ages. Well, let me tell you, they've got nothing on this bunch. There are people in these parts who haven't spoken to each other for generations and half of them don't even know why."

Nancy wasn't happy with the prospects of being surrounded by hostile neighbors, but at least she had people like John and Rose Crossan to fall back on. And there were more. Most of the women she met in the general store in Kilgrin were nice to her. The butcher in Ballycastle had even apologized for his rude behavior and that of his customers that day. She decided that Tully and friends were in the minority and she could get on with her life very well without them.

The next day, Nancy received a letter from Nora.

Dear Nancy,

Hope this letter finds you and the children well. I have some great news! I got married!!! That's right. I am now Mrs. Nora Guerin!!! Doesn't that sound lovely? I say it out loud all the time. Tommy, that's my husband, is a mounted policeman in Central Park and he looks so magnificent up on his horse in his fine blue uniform and polished brass buttons.

We got married two weeks ago and had our honeymoon in Atlantic City. I won $10, but Tommy lost $50! Oh, well. We had a grand time anyway.

When are you coming home? I miss you so much and there's so much to tell you. I'm no letter writer, so you'll have to come home so I can tell everything in person.

Give my love, hugs and kisses to the kids. I miss them terribly. But who knows, I might have one of my own one of these days.

Well, I have to close. Please come home ASAP!!!!

Love,

Nora Guerin

P.S. I ran into Neil the other day. He looks grand. I still can't believe he's a COLLEGE MAN!!! He said to send you and the children his love.

Nancy put the letter down and there were tears in her eyes. She was so very happy for Nora, but any reminder of the States made her sad. The question of whether to go back to America or stay in Ireland had made her life a bewildering emotional roller coaster ride. One day she was convinced she wanted to stay in Ireland, then something – a letter from the States for example – and she was sure she wanted to return to America.

She blinked the tears away and read Nora's postscript again. He said to send you and the children his love. What, she wondered, did that mean? She folded the letter, determined not to read anything into it. No doubt he was just being polite. It's what anyone would say to a dear friend who was far away.

"Oh, God," she said aloud, "What should I do?"

CHAPTER THIRTY

Three weeks after that dreadful incident at Cashel Hall, Nancy was sitting on her chaise lounge sewing. Patrick and Fiona were doing homework by the light of a dim kerosene lamp. Maureen was heating up a kettle of water for a bath. Donal was sitting on the dirt floor playing with his fire engine. Nancy looked up from her sewing, observed her children at play and work, and smiled at the warm and comfortable domesticity of the scene. Then, she frowned. Something was wrong with this scene, but she couldn't quite put her finger on it. Then, she realized what it was.

"Where are your shoes, Fiona?"

"In the bedroom."

"And why aren't they on your feet?"

"What for?"

"Because that's where they belong."

"It's a lot more comfortable without them," Maureen said.

And Donal added, "No one wears shoes, Mommy."

"Are you a bunch of farmers then…?"

And suddenly the scales fell from her eyes. My God, they had become farmers. She looked around the room again, more carefully this time, as if seeing the farmhouse for the first time. Her children were doing homework by kerosene lamp! Maureen was making hot water in a kettle on a coal-burning stove! And Donal was playing on a dirt floor! Life on the farm it suddenly – or was it finally? – occurred to her, was primitive. She had taken her children away from everything that America had to offer – from electricity to indoor plumbing to… For this?

It was suddenly crystal clear what she had to do. Calmly and with great deliberation, she put her sewing aside. After so many months of vacillation, false arguments, and – now, finally, she could admit it – lying to herself, she realized what must be done.

"We're going home," she said quietly.

Maureen continued to pour the hot water into a tub. "Where?"

"America."

"I don't want to go back to America," Patrick said.

"What are you talking about? You told me you hated it here."

"No, I don't."

"That's because he's the captain of the baseball team," Fiona said.

"Is not, liar."

Nancy was too stunned by Patrick's response to admonish him for calling his sister a liar. "Maureen, don't you want to go back?"

"No. I like it here."

"But you don't even like school," Nancy sputtered.

"Well, that's true, but I have lots of friends here."

"Fiona?"

"I don't want to go back. I have a lot of friends, too."

Her youngest son was her last chance. "Donal?"

"I like riding Dolly and petting the cows."

Nancy muttered, "Mother of God, what have I done?"

***

After the children had gone to bed, Nancy went for a walk to clear her head and assess the situation. She'd been shaken by her children's totally unexpected response to going back to the States. Of course she knew that they liked it here, but she'd assumed that they would be happy to go back to the States if that's what she wanted to do.

It was a spectacularly beautiful August night, cool, as it always was in Ireland, nothing like a typically hot, stifling August night in New York City. The mass of stars overhead was so bright Nancy could have read one of Nora's letters by its light. In the distance, she could just make out the dark mass of the Carragh Mountains looming in front of the horizon. She walked, lost in thought, trying to sort out in her mind a jumble of emotions. She did love it here that was true. Ireland, especially her farm in Kilgrin, was a beautiful, serene place. But after her earlier epiphany, she was convinced it wasn't a place to raise her kids.

She stopped, suddenly aware that she was standing in front of the stump of the tree where Connor's swing used to be. Tears welled up in her eyes. Here was yet another place where she felt his presence. "Connor, I'm sorry..." she said aloud. "I can't stay here. I can't live your dream."

She sat down on the tree stump and the tears flowed. "I convinced myself that this was a magical place because I felt your presence here and I wanted to be with you." She wiped a tear from her cheek. "But you're dead, Connor—" She stopped when she heard the sharp note of recrimination in her tone and repeated it in a gentler tone, "But, you're dead, Connor and I have to get on with my life and the children's lives. I have hopes and dreams for our children, and those hopes and dreams can't be realized living here on this farm. Your spirit will be with me no matter where I live. And I will always honor and treasure your memory. But it's time to go home."

Now that she'd said it out loud, a soothing and overwhelming sense of serenity came over her. She remained seated there for some time, quietly taking in the night, hearing the sound of crickets, the occasional whippoorwill, and, nearby, the scurrying of small nocturnal creatures. She smiled to herself, remembering that first night when she'd been scared to death by a wandering cow. When they'd first moved here, the strange noises of the countryside frightened them. But now they had become used to hearing lowing cows and screeching barn owls at night without fearing that banshees had come to spirit them away. Once she got over her trepidation, she would often take walks at night to clear her head or just enjoy the quiet tranquility of the countryside.

Nancy breathed in the fresh damp air that was scented with newly mown hay. Finally, after all this time, all her doubts were washed away. She was at peace with herself. Connor's death has been a crucible through which she has emerged a stronger and more independent woman.

She looked up at the night sky and a shooting star – blinding in its intensity for just a fleeting moment – flashed across the sky. She took it as a sign from Connor. "Thank you," she said.

She patted the tree stump, got up and went back to the farmhouse.

***

The next night, Sean came to dinner. Nancy waited until the children went to bed to tell him of her decision.

Sean shook his head stoically. "So what'll you do with the farm?"

"Sell it." She studied his expression. "You don't seem surprised."

"I think I've always known you'd go back to America. Neil's a good man."

"That's what he said about you."

"Will you marry him then?"

"No. I waited too long. He's moved on with his life."

"Have you told the children?"

"Yes, but they don't want to go home. They're like their father; they think Ireland is a magic land."

"What'll you do?"

Nancy smiled. "I have a plan."

***

The next morning, Nancy pulled the covers away from Maureen's face. "If you go back to America," she whispered, "you'll skip a grade in school."

"I will?"

Nancy pulled the covers from Fiona's face. "And I'll take you to the Paramount and you can see Frank Sinatra in person."

"I can?"

Nancy sat on Patrick's bed. "And you will be able to see Joe DiMaggio in Yankee Stadium."

"Wow!"

Nancy went to her bed where Donal, who was now wide awake, anxiously awaited his enticement."

"And you, young man, will get your American Santa back."

"Yippee! When do we go home?"

Nancy looked at her kids. "Is it agreed? Do we go back to the States?"

The children looked at each other, then they turned to Nancy and nodded in the affirmative. Nancy flopped down on her bed, exhausted, relieved, and very happy.

***

Her first order of business was to go see her solicitor.

"Sell the farm?" O'Donnell's bushy eyebrows shot up in surprise and he stopped stuffing his pipe with tobacco. "You went through all that just to sell the farm?"

"I only made up my mind the other night."

"Well, how can I be of service to you, Mrs. Cavanaugh?"

She shrugged. "How do I sell a farm?"

"The customary way is to sell it to a ready buyer. Absent that, I would recommend an auction, which will allow you to sell off your furniture and incidentals as well."

"I have precious little in the way of furniture and incidentals, but that sounds like a good idea. Do you know someone who could do it?"

"Aye, I do. When do you want to go forward with this?"

"The sooner the better."

He shook his head. "You yanks are always in such a hurry."

***

O'Donnell moved forward with uncharacteristic speed. He lined up an auctioneer and placed ads about the auction in the local newspapers. Within a week, everything was done.

The morning of the auction, the rain came down hard, but by nine o'clock, it tapered off, giving way to heavy grey clouds. In groups of twos and threes, farmers from near and far made their way up the loaning.

To Nancy's immense surprise, one of the men was her father and she welcomed him at the door.

"Father, you didn't have to come."

"Ach, I wanted to," he said, looking decidedly uncomfortable. "Is it all right?"

"Yes, of course it is. Come in. Come in."

Nancy made tea for her father, Sean, and Liam Woods, a gnome-like auctioneer in his late sixties. Woods pulled the curtains aside and looked out the window at the assembled group with a practiced eye. There were about two dozen men gathered in front of the barn, including Tully, Hogan, and Whelan. "It's a small crowd and that's too bad."

"Why?" a nervous Nancy asked.

"A big crowd is better. Makes the bidding go up quicker." He squinted out the window. "Not many buyers there I'm afraid. Mostly gawkers."

"How do you know that?" Father asked.

"When you've been an auctioneer as long as I have, you get a nose for that sort of thing."

"How much do you think I'll get?" Nancy asked.

Woods poured milk into his mug and frowned. "It's a small farm, not the best land, no tools, no livestock. It should fetch four, maybe even six hundred pounds if we're lucky."

"That's not much," Sean said.

Nancy clutched her tea mug. "It'll have to do."

***

At ten o'clock, Liam Woods, followed by Nancy, her father, and Sean went outside. Woods climbed up onto the back of his wagon and stood behind a makeshift podium. "Good morning to you all, gentlemen." He looked up at the sky. "It's been a soft morning, but it's going to clear and isn't it a fine day for an auction?" He spit into his hands and rubbed them together. "All right now," he said, banging a gavel on the podium, "let's get down to business. I'll start the bidding at three hundred pounds. Who'll give me three hundred?"

There was long moment of silence, then Tully, standing in front, said, "I'll bid a hundred pounds."

Hogan and Whelan stood behind him, grinning.

The old auctioneer squinted down at Tully. "A hundred! Man, that's no bid. Who'll give me three hundred?"

More silence. Then…

"One hundred pounds," Tully repeated, more loudly this time.

"The farm's worth more than that, Kevin Tully, and you know it," Sean said.

"I know it's worth what someone will pay."

Nancy watches the events unfolding with growing rage and helplessness. If there was anyone in the crowd interested in buying the farm, she was sure that Tully and friends had intimidated them into silence. She knew what they were doing, but there was nothing she could do to stop it.

Woods pointed to Hogan. "Cass Hogan, you have the next farm over. This is perfect for you. It'll expand your farming land. Give me a bid, man."

Hogan spit in the dirt. "I'll bid a hundred…" He looked at Tully and chuckled, "and one pounds."

Woods' face was purple with exasperation. He'd never in all his life conducted an auction the likes of this. "Barry Whelan, your property joins the north side. It'll be convenient for your cows."

Whelan pretended to look around him, as though seeing the farm for the first time. "I'll tell you what, Mr. Woods, "I'll bid a hundred…" He grinned at his two friends. "and two pounds."

The three men were enjoying themselves immensely.

"You're in collusion, the lot of you," Nancy's father shouted.

Nancy was taken aback by the vehemence in her father's tone. She couldn't ever remember hearing him raise his voice.

Tully ignored the old man. "Get on with it, Woods. Mrs. Cavanaugh wants to sell the property and I'm willing to buy it."

"But not for such a piddling sum, man."

Tully turned to look at the crowd and grinned, knowing he was master of the situation. "All right, Woods, you drive a hard bargain. One hundred – and three pounds. And that's my final offer. She can take it or leave it."

Nancy stepped forward. "I'll leave it."

Tully sneered at her. He knew she was bluffing. Didn't he have her over a barrel? She wanted to go back to America and there was no one else who would buy the farm. He'd made sure of that. "What are you saying, missus? You're not going to sell the farm? It's a damn long way from here to America."

"Oh, I'm going to sell it, just not to you."

Tully's eyes narrowed, suddenly suspicious of this wily woman. "How will you do that? There's no one will buy it except me."

"Mr. Woods, I'm withdrawing the farm for auction. I want you to take out an advertisement in the London Times—"

"Good God..." Hogan sputtered, "you'd sell to a... a... bloody Englishman?"

"His money is as good as yours."

"But a foreigner has never owned land around here," a flustered Whelan whined.

"There's a first time for everything."

As Tully, Whelan, and Hogan, huddled, Nancy turned and started back toward the house.

"Wait. Two hundred pounds." Tully shook his fist at her. "And not a shilling more."

"Not good enough."

"All right. Two-fifty." A tone of desperation had slipped into his voice.

"Mr. Woods, take out another advertisement," she said. "This one in the New York Times. Maybe a rich Texan will want to buy my farm."

Hogan was scandalized by the very thought. "A Texan... Mother of Jasus! Those men graze giant cows with massive horns."

"Three hundred," Tully shouted hoarsely. "And that's my final offer."

Nancy shook her head. "Still not good enough, Mr. Tully."
Again, she turned to go back into the house.

"In the name of God, woman, what will you take?"

"Six hundred pounds."

"Six—? You're barking mad, you are."

"It's a fair price. Isn't that so, Mr. Woods?"

"Aye," Woods said, glaring at Tully. "And well he knows."

Tully was a defeated man, but he didn't know how it had
happened. He and the others were desperate for the farm, but they
thought they could steal it from the uppity yank for a pittance. Old
Woods was right. The fields were convenient to their farms.
They'd planned it so carefully. After forcefully "discouraging" the
few farmers who expressed interest in buying the farm, they met in
Logan's Pub over a few pints to discuss their tactics. They agreed
they would buy the farm on the cheap and split it among
themselves. Their master plan seemed foolproof. So what had
gone wrong? Why in the name of God wasn't she selling?

He shot a sideward glance at a defiant Nancy. Maybe she was
bluffing. But what if she wasn't? Would an Englishman buy it for
a holiday retreat? Not likely, but he couldn't abide the possibility
that a horde of Englishmen might muck about his fields chasing
after some poor bedraggled fox. And as for a Texan buying the
farm, that was even worse than an Englishman. Hogan was right.
Those Texans did raise giant cows with massive horns. Hadn't he
seen them with his own two eyes in those western picture shows in
Ballycastle? If those beasts were let loose in the fields, he'd have to
keep his helpless cows locked up in the barn. It was all too much
for Tully's weak brain to comprehend. Overwhelmed by it all, he
turned to his co-conspirators for support. "Well, just don't stand
there like a couple of eejits," he hissed. "What should we do?"

"I couldn't abide a Texan here," Hogan offered tentatively,
"but maybe an Englishman wouldn't be so bad."

"Oh, shut your gub, you damn fool. What do you think,
Barry?"

Barry Whelan, completely befuddled by this startling turn of
events, scratched the stubble on his chin. Their master plan had
been quite simple: Mrs. Cavanaugh would accept their low-ball

offer. But that plan had fallen to pieces when the damn woman said no. "I don't see we have a choice," he said.

Tully turned away from his comrades in complete disgust. They were hopeless. It would be up to him to salvage their master plan. "All right, you win, Mrs. Cavanaugh. Four-fifty it is."

Nancy didn't even blink. "The price is six hundred pounds, Mr. Tully." She tried not to smile. "And I'll throw in all the furniture and incidentals."

Tully ran his hand across his face in frustration. "Jasus, Mary, and Joseph... All right. Six hundred it is."

Woods slammed his gavel down. "Done and done. The farm is sold for six hundred pounds. Praise be to God."

Nancy went into the house blinking away tears of joy. Sean followed her with a big grin on his face. Nancy's father watched her go with an expression of awe and admiration.

CHAPTER THIRTY-ONE

A keyed up Nancy made tea for everyone. As she poured it, her hand shook so badly she had to put the pot down. "Look at me. I'm shaking like a leaf."

Her father picked up the pot and poured the tea.

"You were magnificent," Sean said.

"That you were, Nancy," her father said. "You were magnificent."

Nancy looked at him in astonishment. For as long as she could remember, he had never complimented her about anything.

Woods shook his head in wonder. "Never in all my years as an auctioneer, Mrs. Cavanaugh, have I witnessed anything such as that." He shook his head, still trying to digest what he'd just witnessed. "Missus, if you ever want a job as an auctioneer, you have one with me."

"Oh, no," Nancy laughed. "I never want to go through that again."

"Were you bluffing about the ads in the newspapers?" Sean asked.

"Of course I was. What Texan in his right mind would want this bit of dirt?"

***

The next few weeks were a whirlwind of activity. Now that the farm was sold, there were dozens of things that had to be done quickly, including packing clothes and booking airfares to New York.

Once Tully got a look at her "furniture and incidentals" he told her in utter disgust he'd have none of her junk. To placate the still angry and frustrated man, she agreed to have everything out of the house before she left. She made arrangements with a church in Ballycastle to take everything, certain the families who would be the recipients of her "junk" would be happy to have it as she had been.

Sean came out to help her pack. As he was loading dishes into a box, he said, "Do you know where you're going to live?"

"Yes, thank God. The day the farm was sold, I wrote Nora and told her I was coming home and would be needing an apartment. Bless her, she found one in our old neighborhood. That means the kids will be able to go back to their old school and see their old friends again. As you can imagine, they're very happy about that."

Sean was silent for awhile, then he said, "Have you told Neil you're coming?"

"No."

"Why not?"

"It's too late, Sean. I've lost him. Besides, he's probably courting some bright young college girl."

Sean stacked the box on top of another. "Nancy, what you've lost is your mind. What you should lose is that stubborn streak of pride you have. In the name of God, woman, tell the man you're coming home."

The truth was she had been thinking about writing him to let him know that they were coming home. What would be the harm in that? After all, he said himself, he would always be the children's Uncle Neil. Shouldn't he know that his "nieces and nephews" were coming home? Ah, but what if he didn't respond? Nancy couldn't bear the thought that he might ignore her letter. She wouldn't blame him if he did, but she was still too emotionally fragile to find out.

***

The next day, she went into Ballycastle to settle her business with Owen O'Donnell. Since that first day she'd walked into his office, nothing had changed and Nancy realized that nothing ever would. Owen O'Donnell was the last of a dying breed – an old-school solicitor who saw his role as being more a conciliator than antagonist, one who should strive to solve a problem with talk rather than litigation. That's why, she realized belatedly, this case had been so stressful for him. She finally understood that for as long as he would continue to practice the law, his office would always be cluttered with old law tomes, case folders, and the persistent aroma of maple tobacco. And there was something about that stability that Nancy found comforting.

"Ah, Mrs. Cavanaugh," he said, coming around his desk, "it is good to see you."

"And it's good to see you, Mr. O'Donnell."

"I have all the necessary documents for you." He opened a folder. "Here is the lawfully executed deed of sale for the farm." He smiled. "That will make Judge Geary very happy. And here is receipt for the wire transfer of your funds from the sale of the farm to your bank in New York. And finally, here is reckoning of my services, which, as you requested, I subtracted from the farm proceeds. I believe that concludes our business here."

Nancy took the documents from him with a nagging feeling of shame. She had badly misjudged the old solicitor. From the start, she'd been impatient with his tardiness and irritated by his seeming nonchalance about matters that were so very important to her. She knew nothing about the Irish court system or what a solicitor really did. But after the trial, she'd learned that it was O'Donnell who, in his role of solicitor, had gathered all the information and located witnesses that her barrister used so effectively.

"Mr. O'Donnell, I owe you an apology."

"Whatever for?"

"I know there were times when I've been impatient with you. And well, I just want to say I truly appreciated everything that you've done for me and my family."

"Think nothing of it, Mrs. Cavanaugh. It was my pleasure. I know that compared to the sharpie lawyers back in the States, we Irish solicitors must seem like so many country bumpkins. But I would remind you of Aesop's Fables and the story of the *Tortoise and the Hare*. Hares, that's us. Slow and steady."

He kissed Nancy's cheek. "You and your children have a good, safe journey back to the States. It's been a pleasure serving you."

Nancy had become very fond of the man. She nodded, too choked up to speak.

***

On her way down Hillcrest Street to catch the bus back to Kilgrin, she passed a telegraph office and Sean's words of admonishment flashed in her mind: ...lose is that stubborn streak of pride you have... tell the man you're coming.

She stopped, took a deep breath and, throwing all caution to the wind, went into the office. She wrote out the telegram and handed it to the woman behind the desk.

The clerk picked up a pencil. "Let's see what we have here... To Mr. Neil Cullen... arriving LaGuardia Friday 3 P.M. Stop. Flight four-nine-five. Stop. Nancy Cavanaugh. Is that all, miss?"

"Yes."

As Nancy started to leave, she stopped and came back to the counter. "No. I'd like to add something else."

The clerk picked up her pencil again. "Yes?"

"Add... I love you."

***

The day finally arrived. After ten months in Ireland, they were finally going back to the States – to home. While the kids ran outside to take their last ride on the swing, Nancy stayed behind to make sure they didn't forget anything.

Alone in the kitchen, she had a moment to reflect on all that had happened in that short period of time – the untimely move to the farm... the weeks of repairs when it seemed that nothing would ever get done... the battle with the neighbors over the fields... the wandering cow that had scared the life out of them...

the rejection at the dance… the auction that almost turned into a fiasco… Ten months. It seemed more like ten years.

She looked around the silent, empty kitchen and a sadness came over her. It was a far cry from the broken down wreck they'd moved into almost ten months earlier. There was a new ceiling now and after a long epic struggle, she'd managed to restore the old rusty, coal-burning stove to its former glory. Even though she was anxious to go home, she had to admit there had been some good times here, especially for the children. They'd been able to run free. They enjoyed school, with the exception of Maureen, of course, and they'd all made friends that they promised to write. And what child in New York City could boast of helping to plow a field or ride a horse bareback to get a drink of water from a spring? Donal would have his own stories to tell.

She heard a car coming up the loaning. That would be Sean and her father to take them to the airport. She took one last look around. The curtains by the kitchen table had been pushed back. She closed them and smoothed them with her palms.

It was over. It was time to go.

Sean and her father loaded the car and they started back down the loaning. She looked across the way and saw Tully herding cows in her field—his field. She waved, but he turned away.

***

Two hours later, they pulled up to the entrance to the airport's departure terminal. "All right," Sean said, "everyone out. I'll get the bags checked and meet you at the gate."

The terminal gate had large floor to ceiling windows and the four kids pressed their faces to the glass, mesmerized by the great big roaring airplanes taxing to and from the gates.

"Mommy, which one is our airplane?" Maureen asked.

Nancy pointed at a four-engine plane standing on the tarmac with the boarding steps in place. "I think that's it."

"I'm getting a window seat," Patrick said.

Fiona stamped her foot. "No, I'm getting the window seat."

Nancy smiled. All was well if those two were fighting.

"I should get the window seat," Donal said with reasonable logic for someone who was approaching six. "I'm the littlest."

Not to be outdone, Maureen said, "Well, I'm the oldest and I should get the window seat."

Nancy watched her father standing by the window, his hands behind his back, studying the airplanes and lost in thought. He'd been silent throughout the drive to the airport, but that was nothing new. For as long as she could remember, he'd been a man of few words, always deferring to his wife. Nancy had wished it hadn't been that way. How many nights had she cried herself to sleep after being punished by her mother, praying that he would have done something to save her? His unwillingness to interfere on her behalf had been almost as painful as the punishment meted out by her mother. Watching him standing by the window, apart from them, aloof, she wondered why he'd even bothered to come.

He turned away from the window abruptly and looked at the children over his wire rimmed glasses. "You children be good for your mother," he said sternly. The four children involuntarily snapped to attention and nodded.

"Patrick, come here."

Warily, Patrick approached. His grandfather took his whittling knife out of his pocket and handed it to him. "This is for you. Be careful with it, boy. Show Donal how to use it when he's older."

Patrick stared at the knife dumbfounded. "Thank you, Grandfather."

Then Father took a paper cone out of his pocket and handed it to Fiona. "Some sweets for you and Maureen. Don't eat it all at once or you'll get a stomach ache."

"Thank you, Grandfather."

Donal's lower lip quivered and his eyes filled with tears. He'd been left out. He wasn't going to get anything. Grandfather bent down and gently squeezed Donal's cheek. "And you, young man, when you get home I'm going to mail you one of my John McCormack records."

"Thank you, Grandfather. Thank you." Donal rushed to his grandfather and hugged him. Grandfather, looking decidedly uncomfortable, gingerly patted Donal's head.

An astonished Nancy could scarcely believe what she'd just seen. In all her life, she could not recall him ever giving her anything. Her father took her by the arm and led her away from the children. "You have a safe journey, Nancy."

"I will."

There was an awkward silence. Then he said, "Your mother... she couldn't come..."

"I know. The arthritis."

"Och, no. It's not the arthritis." He glanced out the window pretending to watch a taxiing airplane. "I don't know why she's the way she is."

Nancy was too stunned to speak. This was a side of her father she'd never seen before.

"When you went out to America, I never thought I'd see you again."

"Neither did I."

"I see how you are with your little ones..." He took off his glasses and rubbed them furiously with his handkerchief. "I wasn't a very good father."

"You did your best."

"Aye. I did my best." But he didn't believe that for a minute. "You stood up to everyone, Nancy. You're... a strong woman... and I'm... I'm..."

Nancy put her arms around him. It felt so strange to hold him and with a pain in her heart she suddenly realized why. In all her life she'd never hugged her father. He stiffened, not knowing what to do with his hands. Then he tentatively patted her back, struggling mightily to retain his composure. Finally, unable to control himself, he dissolved in a sob and hugged his daughter, holding her tight, for the first time in his life. "I'm so proud of you," he said, his voice cracking.

"I know you are... I know..."

They hugged each other in silence, then a voice over the loudspeaker announced, "Flight four-nine-five for New York now boarding..."

Nancy smoothed the front of her father's jacket. "Dad, I want you to visit us in America."

"I will." There was something in his tone that said he meant it.

"I'll write to you."

"I would like that."

Nancy wiped her eyes and took a deep breath. "All right. Come on, kids. Time to go." She looked around. "Oh, my God. Where's Sean?"

"Last call boarding flight four-nine-five..."

With a final wave to her father, Nancy herded her four children through the gate. As they were walking across the tarmac toward the plane, Sean came running up.

"Mother of God, I almost missed saying goodbye. That stupid clod of a clerk took forever to check the bags. Here's your baggage claim tickets."

He hugged the kids and shooed them up the boarding stairs. Then he turned to Nancy and smiled at her. "What can I say?"

"Sean, thank you for everything. You've been a good friend."

"Och, it was nothing. So, enough of that. What will you do when you get back?"

Nancy shrugged. "Get a job. Get on with my life."

He hugged her. "That's a good plan. You have a good life, Nancy."

"And you have a good life, Sean Garrett."

Nancy turned and rushed up the boarding stairs.

***

The who-gets-the-window-seat brouhaha was already resolved by the time Nancy came into the cabin. A smiling flight attendant told her, "The plane's half-empty, so I gave them all window seats. After we're in the air, they can take their assigned seats."

"Oh, thank you," a grateful Nancy said. She wasn't looking forward to a long flight listening to them argue over window seats.

The flight attendant checked Donal's seat belt. "All buckled up, young man?"

"Yes, miss."

"Good. And where are you going?"

"We're going home. Right, Mommy?"

"Yes, Donal. We're going home."

CHAPTER THIRTY-TWO

Thirteen hours later, after a brief refueling stop at Gander Airport in Newfoundland, the plane touched down at LaGuardia airport in Queens, New York.

All the while they were clearing customs and retrieving their luggage, Nancy kept looking over her shoulder, wondering if Neil would show up. But, not unexpectedly, there was no sign of him. Why should there be? she chided herself. She'd treated him shabbily, and that was inexcusable, considering all he'd done for them. Obviously, he made another life for himself and that's the way it should be.

She would miss him terribly, she knew, but life had to go on and, as a single mother of four, she fully realized what a daunting task that would be. Nevertheless, she was confident she was up to it. She was no longer that timid, 27-year-old housewife expecting a baby. She'd gone through a lot in the past six years – juggling a wartime job and raising her children, living on a primitive farm, fighting for her rights and the rights of her kids. She would be fine. They would be fine.

As the redcap loaded the last of the luggage on his cart, Nancy said, "Come on, kids. Let's go home."

As they headed for the taxi stand out front, Maureen kept looking around. "Is Uncle Neil going to meet us?"

"No, I don't think so, Maureen. He's probably attending classes at his college."

***

Nancy and the children stepped out of the doors of the terminal and their senses were immediately assaulted by a terrifying and bewildering cacophony of horn-blowing taxis and rush of people. After just ten months in quiet, rural Ireland, the onslaught of New York commerce was a shock to their system. It was as though they'd come from the darkest rainforests of the Amazon. Everything was big, noisy, and frantic.

"Look at the size of those cars," Patrick exclaimed, used to the small cars of Ireland. "They're huge!"

Maureen pulled close to her mother as scores of people brushed by them. "Mommy, where are all these people going? Is there something wrong?"

"No, honey. We're back in New York and there's an awful lot of people here."

The redcap loaded their luggage into the trunk of a taxi. As they're about to get into the cab, Maureen spotted Neil.

"Mommy... It's Uncle Neil!"

Nancy whirled and caught a glimpse of Neil running along the opposite sidewalk, dodging pedestrians. He saw them and waved. Suddenly, Nancy's smile dissolved in horror. He was running blindly toward the street where taxis and buses were whizzing by.

"Neil, look where you're going..." she whispered.

He was just about to run into the street, but he stopped and waited for the traffic to pass. Nancy exhaled in relief.

As Neil approached, the excited children rushed up to him.

"Uncle Neil, look at the knife Grandfather gave me..." Patrick shouted.

"And the pilot gave me wings..." Donal proudly pointed to the wings pinned to his jacket.

Neil hugged them. "And what did I promise you when you came home?"

"Chiclets!" they yelled in unison, as he handed each of them a packet of Chiclets.

He broke away from the kids and slowly came toward Nancy. "Are you home then?"

She nodded, not able to read his expression. "I'm home." Suddenly she heard Sean's voice, *Lose that stubborn streak of pride...*

She started to blurt out, "Neil, do you…" but she stopped herself. I can't do it. He didn't come here to see me. He came to see the kids. I will not humiliate myself like that. I just won't.

Lose that stubborn streak of pride...

Oh, damn it! She took a deep breath to summon up her courage. "Neil, do you have something to ask me?" she asked bleakly.

Neil looked at her perplexed.

Maureen tugged at his sleeve. "Uncle Neil, don't you want to marry Mommy?" she whispered solemnly.

Neil's eyes lit up. "Oh..." He took Nancy's hands in his and the children crowded around. "Nancy, will you marry me?"

Her answer was drowned out by the whoops and shouts of the children.

The End

ABOUT THE AUTHOR

Michael Grant lived in Ireland for two years as a child. He currently lives in Knoxville Tennessee with his wife Elizabeth and Beau, their Golden Retriever.

Mr. Grant can be contacted at mggrant08@gmail.com

Made in the USA
Middletown, DE
17 March 2017